THE PLUNGE

Hazel and Wetzon stood inside the entrance listening to the wind, watching pedestrians battling the vicious gusts swathed in coats, hats, and mufflers, bent with the effort. It was not a day for strolling. Even the steps of the Metropolitan Museum, usually thick with people sitting and talking, were deserted.

Edward, clutching his cap, was dancing on the sidewalk outside trying to flag down a taxi. Trash, bits and pieces of newspapers, twigs from trees and shrubbery spun helplessly in the wind. A large, dark object hurtled past the doors, seemingly windblown from way above. Edward stopped and jerked around. His hand shot out, snapped back, covering his eyes. For a moment, he seemed frozen, then he whirled and rushed toward them. A blast of cold air hit them as he threw the door open.

"Jesus, Mary," he screamed, "It's Missus Cunningham!" He pushed past, his face ashen. "Jesus, Mary." Panting, he grabbed up the receiver and punched three numbers. "Come at once, come at once to 999 Fifth Avenue. One of my tenants just jumped."

Bantam Crime Line Books offer the finest in classic and
modern American mysteries.
Ask your bookseller for the books you have missed.

Tender Death

ANNETTE MEYERS

BANTAM BOOKS
New York • Toronto • London • Sydney • Auckland

TENDER DEATH

A Bantam Book

CRIME LINE and the portrayal of a boxed "cl" are trademarks
of Bantam Books, a division of Bantam Doubleday Dell
Publishing Group, Inc.

Bantam hardcover edition / June 1990
Bantam paperback edition / March 1991

ISBN 0-553-28719-2

Published simultaneously in the United States and Canada

---

*Bantam Books are published by Bantam Books, a division of Bantam
Doubleday Dell Publishing Group, Inc. Its trademark, consisting of the
words "Bantam Books" and the portrayal of a rooster, is Registered in
U.S. Patent and Trademark Office and in other countries. Marca Regis-
trada. Bantam Books, 666 Fifth Avenue, New York, New York 10103.*

PRINTED IN THE UNITED STATES OF AMERICA

RAD   0 9 8 7 6 5 4 3 2 1

FOR
DOLORES BULLARD
AND
IN MEMORY OF
HAZEL OSBORN

The author wishes to thank Mary Bryant, Kevin Jennings, Marcia Lesser, Linda Ray, Chris Tomasino, Howard Weiss, and especially Marty, tried and true. For the one and only Kate Miciak and her nurturing, professional Bantam team, the author is eternally grateful.

Buy everything, buy America . . .

Ivan Boesky to one of his traders
(apocryphal)

Where else can so many honest people
make so much money legitimately?

Leslie Wetzon, partner,
Smith and Wetzon
Executive Search Specialists

1

THE MAN ON THE SOFA was bleeding. Thick gouts of blood bubbled from his nostrils and rolled down his gray mustache.

In the first shocking moment, nobody moved. Not even the victim.

"My God!" The harried young woman at the reception desk dropped the phone and jumped to her feet. "Mr. Mitosky! Sir!" She ran out of the room, crying, unnecessarily, "Wait there, I'll be right back," and ran down a museumlike corridor leaving an impression of a too smart suit with a too short skirt.

Wetzon, who had been standing at the reception desk waiting for the envelope Bobby Kohn had left for her, yanked a packet of Kleenex from her handbag and began to pull tissues from it. "Here, please, let me help you."

"Izz notting, notting, please, don't vorry, please. Happens all the time." The man spoke with a Russian-sounding accent as dark red blood continued to gush from his nose, over the crooked mustache, down his chin, onto his white shirt and the lapels of his brown tweed suit. He took the proffered tissues and pressed them to his nose, making an attempt to rise. His eyes were blurs behind dense glasses. A brown fedora with a jaunty feather in its band lay on the sofa beside him; a cane leaned against the arm.

"Please, Mr. . . . er . . . Mr. Mitosky. It's better that you put your head back."

The receptionist returned with a mass of wet paper towels and a plastic bag full of ice cubes, but by this time the torrents of blood had lessened considerably as soon as the man had tilted his head back.

It was then that Wetzon noticed his makeup stopped at his chin, leaving his neck several shades lighter than the unhealthy gray of his face. She stopped in midthought. Makeup?

"Would you like me to call a doctor?" The receptionist offered him the wet paper towels, her face registering real concern.

"Oh no. No, please." His fine hands trembled slightly as he began to blot himself dry with the wet towels.

Two clean-cut young men in dark pin-striped suits, looking as if they had just stepped out of a Paul Stuart ad, came toward them from the wide, subtly lit corridor.

"So I told him, you don't like how I'm handling your effing account? You think you'll get better service from this bimbo at Bache? Well, do me a favor, transfer. You shoulda heard him scream, beg me to keep him . . . I told him, shove it—"

"Ungrateful putz. They're all the same. You make them money, you lose them money, and suddenly they don't remember you made them money. Did you see the financials on Eastern Norfolk?"

"Yeah, looks like management is up to something—"

"Jerry has a buddy who knows someone whose sister is making it with someone at Wasserella. They're supposed to be taking a look."

They passed the scene in the reception area without curiosity or comment and went through the double glass doors to the elevator bank.

Wetzon walked across the plush pale blue carpet dotted with cream fleurs de lis to the large windows that looked out over the New York harbor. To her right was the peace and serene beauty of the Statue of Liberty on her pedestal; to her left was the jumble and frenzy of Wall Street, the financial hub of the world.

Why was the man wearing makeup to make himself look older—because that's exactly what the gray blend did. She remembered that well enough from her chorus dancing days in the theater. Now everyone was so obsessed with looking younger. Mitosky's hands were those of a much younger man, and he was wearing a phony mustache.

The phone system buzzed and the receptionist picked it up. "Yes?" She listened for a moment and replaced the phone. "Mr. Mitosky, sir, the cashier is ready for you now. Do you need any help? It's the first desk on the left."

Mr. Mitosky clamped his fedora on his head, and reaching for his cane, stood. He seemed none the worse for the nosebleed as he limped stiffly down the hall.

On the sofa where he'd been sitting was a crumpled envelope. Wetzon picked it up and smoothed it. It was torn open and empty. The return address was Bradley, Elsworth Securities, in whose reception area she was standing. The envelope was addressed to Dr. Maxwell Mitosky, 601 East Seventy-second Street, New York, New York 10021. Wetzon put it on the reception desk, and the receptionist, who was on the phone, nodded.

A girl in a green suede shirtwaist dress came clicking down the hall in high heels, carrying a manila clasp envelope. "Ms. Watson? Mr. Kohn said to call him after you've read the report and he'll fill you in on the numbers."

Wetzon smiled and took the envelope. Bobby Kohn was giving her the directory of the brokers in his office. "Thank you very much." She placed the manila envelope into her briefcase. "Tell him I'll read it quickly and get back to him." He had promised her he would make notes next to each name in the directory, bless him.

She squeezed on to the elevator with the lunch crowd and came out in the black marble lobby. Most of the clerical workers and a goodly number of the VPs took the escalator down to the underground level where a cafeteria served everything from salads and burgers and pizza to top-quality delicatessen and fresh fish. Something for everyone.

Only the traders and many of the salesmen and -women ate at their desks. Since trading had gone global, lunch hours had virtually disappeared. Most firms had even gone so far as to have a gourmet luncheon catered free of charge to their traders to keep them at their desks and on the phones. One lost window of opportunity could mean millions made or lost for the firm. The trader-feeding program is what it was called; it made Wetzon think of animals in zoos getting fed by their keepers.

She paused at the news counter to read the headline in the *Post*: BUSH BOOSTS TAXES. So much for campaign promises. She took the revolving door out to the gray marble steps that led down to Water Street.

"Hello, Donna Rhodes," she said, recognizing the woman who had been about to enter the revolving door she had just come from.

"Wetzon! Hi." Donna's masculine features softened into a smile.

Donna Rhodes worked for a small regional firm with a specialty in muni bonds, though presently, thanks to the new tax laws, brokers couldn't get enough tax frees to fill the orders from eager clients wanting to lock in tax-free dividends. Not even at Merrill and Shearson, whose bond inventories were legend.

"How are you? How's business?" Wetzon stepped aside, out of the pedestrian traffic, as did Donna.

"Oh, okay, I guess." Her pale-yellow-tinted glasses in rimless frames turned her ordinarily sallow skin golden in the fall sunlight, but the corners of her mouth drifted downward. She wore her thick brown hair short and flipped back behind her ears and in each lobe Paloma Picasso silver "Scribbles."

"Come on, what's the matter?"

"Oh nothing, I guess. Burned out. Bored. The market's not going anywhere. There's nothing to sell. I've been sort of thinking of getting out of sales, maybe being a portfolio manager, or something like that . . . at a bank. . . ."

Wetzon touched the soft, buttery leather of Donna's black coat. "Let's go get a cup of coffee and talk about it. I can't believe I'm hearing this from someone who told me after the crash that she loved the business and would be around forever."

"Oh, Wetzon, I can't now. I've got a meeting with a pension client, but I'll call you."

"I want you to promise me you won't do anything rash until you talk to me."

Donna smiled and nodded. "I promise." She waved at Wetzon and was about to enter the revolving door when the door spun violently, and a man in a brown tweed suit burst through, plunged jubilantly down the steps two at a time, and hit the sidewalk at a run.

Donna smiled and shrugged and waved to Wetzon again. Wetzon waved back and then slowly followed the man to the street, watching as he dodged around people like a quarterback. He had an umbrella tucked under his arm, which he suddenly thrust into a garbage can on the corner of Water and Wall Streets.

Only it wasn't an umbrella, it was a cane.

2

WETZON SLAMMED DOWN THE TELEPHONE. "Oh no, he couldn't do that to me."

"Do what?" Smith asked absently. She had spread a mass of financial reports on her desk and was studying them.

"Greg Castalde—he's left Merrill," Wetzon said, flushed, distressed. "I'm really upset about this. He promised me he wouldn't move this time without me."

Smith looked up. "I told you never to believe what brokers say. They're all scum. Where did he go?"

Wetzon had picked up the phone again and was viciously punching out the numbers. "Greg Castalde, please," she said, making her voice pleasant. "Shsh—" she cautioned Smith. "Oh yes," she said in her best Patsy Preppie imitation into the telephone, "I'm looking for Greg. I've just learned he's no longer with you. No." She smiled, knowing the smile would carry through the telephone, "I'm not a client . . . just an old college friend . . ." she quickly checked the suspect sheet, "from Northwestern. I'm only in town for the day, on a buying trip . . . and there's no answer at home . . . oh, how nice of you . . . thank you so much." She replaced the receiver, pleased. Though why she should have been pleased when the bum had moved without her, she couldn't say. Small victories. And she did love to extract information from the unwary.

"Well, where is he?" Smith demanded.

"Smith Barney, can you believe it?" She was already dialing the number the sales assistant at Merrill had given her.

"Greg Castalde." Great, he'd answered his own phone.

"Hi, Greg, it's Wetzon."

There was a blank silence, then the sound of explosive laughter. "I don't believe this. You tracked me down again. Wetzon, how do you do it?"

"Vibrations," she said.

"Okay, okay, now look, I'm really sorry I moved without you—"

"Greg, I'm happy for you." Behind her, she heard Smith emit a soft, derisive snort. "I hope you cut yourself a good deal . . . or did you work with another headhunter, you rat?"

"What, me? Wetzon, would I do that to you?"

"You, Greg? Never. After all the years we've known each other . . ."

He groaned. "Aw, don't do that to me. Come on, give me a

"And you're trying to change the subject. I've told you hundreds of times, brokers have no sense of loyalty."

"Can't win them all," Wetzon said philosophically. "With the list of brokers from his old office, we might strike gold."

"Humpf," Smith said. "What were his numbers?"

"About half a mil. Don't torture me, Smith." She tucked a loose strand of her ash-blonde hair back into the dancer's knot on top of her head. "I'm well aware that would have been a forty-thousand-dollar fee."

Smith turned back to the papers on her desk. "You are such a Pollyanna, Wetzon. I don't know how you do it, after all this time in the business . . . Well, I must say, this is really wonderful."

"What's really wonderful?" Now Wetzon stood, wriggling her toes in her boots, reaching upward with both hands and then down to the floor, straight-legged, palms flat on the floor. She was still in fairly good shape, but not quite as good as when she took classes regularly and danced eight shows a week. Headhunting was a sedentary job, so much of the work was done on the telephone.

She was glad that Smith was onto something else and the subject of Greg Castalde and her naïveté was forgotten. She held her stomach muscles tight and came up slowly, vertebra by vertebra.

Smith turned around in her chair and grinned. "I heard all of that creaking and cracking. Sounds like you're getting old."

"Well, I'm not getting younger. Neither of us is." Wetzon rolled her head from side to side. "Sitting all day with my phone crooked in my shoulder is not exactly conducive to relaxed neck and back muscles. I've just got to make time to take a class. . . . What's so wonderful?" She came over to Smith, who had turned back to her papers, and stood, hand resting lightly on Smith's shoulder, looking down at piles of accounting statements.

"This company I invested in last year. Can you imagine, it's in the black already, after only one year. It's absolutely amazing."

"Very impressive," Wetzon said politely, but not particularly interested. "What kind of business is it?"

"It's a referral service, for the decrepit and infirm. Exactly the right business at the right time. Everyone we know seems to have aging parents or grandparents or uncles and aunts."

"Except us." Wetzon's parents had died long ago—the year she had come to New York to be a dancer. A drunk driver had run a stoplight at high speed and had hit their car head-on. "Don't sound so sad," Smith said. She rarely talked about her parents or her childhood, except for once in a while when she let something slip. "Aging parents are a tremendous emotional and financial drain on people like us who are just starting to make it. We should consider ourselves lucky."

"Then I wouldn't mind being unlucky, Smith, in this case."

Smith ignored her. "Anyway," she said, "the Grossmans run a counseling service for the aging. They have a staff of professionals who take histories and do in-depth interviews with clients, decide on their needs, and then recommend therapists, exercise teachers, beauticians, nurses, housekeepers, all of whom make house calls. They take a percentage of each fee from the professional and they also charge a nominal fee for the first visit to the client to cover the cost of computers and paperwork."

"Very impressive," Wetzon said.

"Actually," Smith said, "I think they do what we do. They match clients to a particular professional in a particular service."

"This is a Leon Ostrow special, I take it?" Leon Ostrow was their attorney.

"Of course," Smith said. "You know how smart Leon is about these things. He handled their incorporation, and as soon as he heard what the idea was, he knew it would take off. He's offered to handle your investments, Wetzon. You should let him—"

"I'll stick to the stock market, thank you very much. I feel more comfortable there. I like the action."

"Oh, Wetzon, everyone knows you can't get rich in the stock market, not unless you already have millions. It's just too controlled by the institutions. The small investor doesn't have a shot."

"I guess I'm still a gypsy, Smith. If I buy stock in good companies, I'll do all right. I like choosing the companies myself. I like the risk taking and the ride."

Smith slipped the material she'd been reading into a large manila envelope. "And I suppose you've made money in the market," she said, needling. "What good tips have the brokers given you lately?"

"Oh come on, Smith," Wetzon said to Smith's back. Her stomach clenched and anger flared like a lump of hot coal. Smith was always so superior about her business knowledge. "You know I don't listen to those tips . . . anymore."

"Anymore."

Wetzon, smarting, was about to retort when there was a rap on their door. Harold Alpert poked his head in.

"Excuse me, I'm sending B.B. out for lunch. Do you want him to get anything for you?"

Smith and Wetzon looked at each other. Ever since they had hired Bailey Balaban, known as B.B., to be the cold caller and promoted Harold to junior associate, Harold had been playing office manager and big shot. He had become so overbearing and officious he was beginning to drive both of them crazy.

"Your turn to talk to him," Wetzon mouthed.

"I know," Smith responded.

"I'm sorry, I didn't hear you, Smith," Harold said.

Smith put the manila envelope into the file drawer next to her desk. "I'll have meat loaf on a roll and a linzer cookie," she said. "I'm starved. Please don't order tuna again, Wetzon."

"Nothing for me today," Wetzon said. "I'm having lunch uptown with Hazel Osborn."

Harold backed out of the room. They heard him say, "Now here is the lunch order, B.B. Try to get it right this time, if you don't mind." The door closed.

"See what I mean?"

Smith frowned at Wetzon as if she had interrupted an important thought. "I can't, for the life of me, understand what you and that nosy old biddy have in common," Smith said with just the edge of jealousy in her voice. Her eyes glittered. "She's not even rich enough to leave you anything in her will."

"Smith, you're impossible. Everything with you hinges on

money. Hazel is a very special person, and I really care about her. She's my friend."

"Humpf. She can't do *anything* for you. She has no money, no contacts. Friends," Smith declaimed, not for the first time, "friends have to be useful."

"I'm certainly glad you thought I was useful, Smith," Wetzon replied crossly. "What a relief. I was starting to worry about it." She put her pens and pencils back into the pressed glass spooner, studied her daily list of calls to be made. Most had been checked off. "I may or may not be back later." She looked again at her datebook. No appointments. "I can make any calls I have to make from home." She packed her notes and current suspect sheets which contained profiles of the brokers she was working with in her briefcase. "Okay, I'm off."

Smith was watching her, disappointment on her face. "What are you going to do this afternoon?"

"I don't know . . . shop . . . take a class maybe."

"Call me. I'll meet you at Bloomie's. We can wander around."

"What about your party?"

"Oh, everything's taken care of. All I have to do is appear. Besides, that's tomorrow night." She smiled and stood, tall and lean in her gray wool jersey dress and three-inch heels. She towered over Wetzon. "I found this wonderful chef-caterer . . . As a matter of fact . . ."

"Don't tell me," Wetzon said. "I know. You've invested in the company."

"Wetzon, you're really very cruel."

"Am I right? Tell the truth."

"Okay, okay, you're right." Smith walked to the washroom. "Tell me, who are you bringing to my party? Silvestri?" She turned, her hand resting on the doorknob.

"I don't know. Maybe." Wetzon still felt vaguely uncomfortable about Silvestri and Smith because when they had first met, Silvestri had seemed more interested in Smith than in Wetzon. And Smith, who was so sharp about picking up on vulnerability, had promptly sensed this and played on it. Smith was watching her closely now, and Wetzon turned away. Time to change the subject. "Do something about Harold, will you? He's become obnoxious. We've created a monster."

Smith grimaced. "I know, and it's my fault. I felt he needed a better self-image, so I encouraged him. Now I'll have to tone him down a little—"

"A lot," Wetzon said firmly. "I can't stand being around him, and I'm sure it's not an asset when he talks to brokers. Yesterday I heard him tell someone that he and only he could get him an appointment with Bear, Stearns, that Jimmy Cayne calls him for advice all the time."

"He didn't!" Smith was shocked and furious. "That little bastard. Now he's gone too far."

"I told him in no uncertain terms that he could not say that, and he was never to do anything like that again," Wetzon said, "but I think you're going to have to talk to him, too." The truth was, Harold always seemed more anxious to be in Smith's good graces than in Wetzon's.

"My God, if Jimmy heard that, we'd never work for the Bear again," Smith's eyes were black with anger.

Wetzon started to open the door to the front room.

"After everything I've—we've—done for him," Smith raged. She was giving off high-danger sparks.

Wetzon closed the door behind her, smiling.

3

IT WAS BITTERLY COLD. Wetzon pulled the collar of her black alpaca coat up high around her neck and wrapped the leopard-patterned scarf tighter. The big lavender beret slipped down her forehead, almost covering her eyes. She pushed it up and inhaled a deep dancer's breath from the diaphragm and expelled the air through her mouth, making a stream of white winter smoke.

It always reminded her of a short story she had read in high school, of the explorers in the North Pole whose breaths came out shaped in the words they were saying. There was something to be said for the joy of silence, she thought, imagining what it would be like if everything everyone said formed words in the air other. He was expending a lot of energy pitching himself to the freezing passersby, who ignored him. Unthinking, Wetzon made eye contact with him and mentally kicked herself. You just didn't do that with the crazies in New York, if you were smart.

"Please," the young man said, stepping forward with his cup outstretched, "give me money for food." He made it into a dramatic performance, complete with charm and pathos.

Now if he could put all that energy to work at a job . . . or maybe he had been a stockbroker who'd lost his license for unauthorized trading. She smiled at the thought.

"Pretty please," he said with a lilt as she passed him.

He spoke well—too well to be begging on street corners.

"With sugar on it," he said, wheedling, shaking the few coins in his cup. There was something a little too calculated about him.

Get a job, you freeloader, she thought, and kept walking.

"Rich bitch!" he screamed after her. "Rich bitch, rich bitch!" As if he could read her mind.

Damn, she thought, embarrassed, as heads turned to look at her. It was like that short story again. She thought something, and it could be heard out loud.

When she had been a Broadway dancer, she had once worked with a director who had accused her of editorializing. "It's written all over your face," Morton Hornberg had screamed at her. During rehearsals she had stood at the side of the stage after her number, watching him direct a scene with the principal actors. Hornberg was fascinating to watch. The director had a romantic vision and a certain eccentricity, and the combination was either beautiful and sensitive or atrocious. His problem was that he didn't know the difference. Wetzon did, and others did too, but everyone was afraid to tell him.

His attack had embarrassed her, humiliated her. She stopped coming in early and hanging around afterward, just attending to her own rehearsals. A few days later, Hornberg had sent her flowers and asked her to come and sit with him when she wasn't rehearsing her numbers. Remembering, she smiled. It had been years ago, and these days Morty was a star director. She wondered who was sitting with him now. *Oh, you're bad, Wetzon,* she thought, shaking her head.

She got on a number 4 bus and took one of the empty seats in the back. It was twelve-fifteen.

She sat quietly for a few minutes, letting her mind drift, then pulled her half-read *New York Times* from her carryall, unfolded it, and skimmed rapidly through the news articles. On the "Obituaries" page she saw a small notice that Jimmy Bronson, a stage manager she had known from the old days, had died of a heart attack in California. Age, sixty-four. He had left the theater years earlier and opened a successful home maintenance business for the owners of weekend and summer houses in the Hamptons. The article said he was about to take out a touring company of *Fiddler on the Roof.* Well, the very thought of doing that would have been enough to kill him. It was sad. She wondered what had made him decide to try to go back. Maybe he was feeling old and alone and wanted to try to recapture the camaraderie of— God, why was she having such morbid thoughts?

As she was shoving the paper back into her bag, she caught a glimpse of another obituary just above Jimmy's. The lead said:

Maxwell Mitosky, 78,
Retired Economist

The name caught her eye. Mitosky . . . Mitosky. An odd name, but she was certain she had seen or heard it before. She closed her eyes and heard, "Mr. Mitosky, sir, the cashier is ready for you now."

She opened her eyes. Weeks ago. The man at Bradley, Elsworth . . . the one who'd had the awful nosebleed . . . the one who was wearing makeup.

She pulled the newspaper from her bag and read the obituary. Mitosky had been born in London, graduated from Oxford, more degrees from the London School of Economics. Retired professor . . . New York University. Had been living in New York for the last thirty years at 601 East Seventy-second Street. No survivors.

It couldn't be the same man because this man—if he had any accent at all— No, there was no way he could have collected a thick Russian accent. How exceedingly strange.

She returned the paper to her carryall and leaned back in her seat, remembering how the Russian Maxwell Mitosky had raced from the building like no seventy-eight-year-old man and dumped his cane in a trash basket.

4

WHEN THEY MET, HAZEL OSBORN had been doing volunteer work at the Museum of American Folk Art. Wetzon was still a dancer then, supplementing her income by making pillows out of scraps of old fabrics and quilt pieces for the museum shop. One day when Wetzon stopped by to drop off a new batch, Hazel was covering the shop. They had started talking, and they had never stopped. Hazel was like a surrogate mother who understood, loved, and accepted you as you were, without any of the usual mother-daughter psychological interplay.

"I'm a professional volunteer," she had characterized herself. She spent one day a week at the museum shop, three mornings as an assistant teacher in a Spanish Harlem elementary school, and one day with an organization that brought children and music together.

She was a retired social worker, a Ph.D. who had specialized in child psychology and who had studied in Chicago with Dr. Bruno Bettelheim. "My mentor," she called him reverently. She had come to New York to teach at Columbia and had spent the years before her retirement with one of the big settlement houses, working with underprivileged children.

Shortly before their meeting at the Museum of American Folk Art, Hazel had been slowed down briefly by a mastectomy, but it hadn't stopped her for long. She was nearing seventy now, and Wetzon loved her spirit and commitment. And her curiosity.

"It keeps me young," Hazel maintained. "And so does Woody Allen. And so do you," she had said the last time Wetzon had seen her. "Always have young friends, Leslie. They keep you from taking yourself too seriously."

Wetzon got off the bus at Seventy-seventh Street and crossed over to Sant Ambroeus. She and Hazel both loved the café even though it was ridiculously expensive. It was an indulgence but everything was so exquisite, it made them feel special.

She sped up when she saw Hazel's silhouette in her old seal coat through the fogged windows of the café. Wetzon squinted— surely there was something . . . odd. She pushed open the door, and Hazel turned. Involuntarily, Wetzon gasped. Hazel's face was ghostly white and pinched beneath the burgundy felt hat with its racy feather. Seeing Wetzon, she smiled a shadow of her old smile and edged forward. Then Wetzon saw the cane.

"Hey, what's this?" Wetzon stooped to hug Hazel, who suddenly seemed so fragile, even small. An old woman. How could someone change so much in such a short time? Silently, Wetzon chastised herself for not staying in closer touch. "I hope you haven't been waiting long," she said, keeping her arm around Hazel's narrow shoulders.

"No, just got here a minute ago, and this," she said, waving a gloved hand casually toward the cane, "this is just a touch of arthritis. You look wonderful, as usual, Leslie dear, and I am ravenous."

She walked with strained steps, leaning heavily on the cane. Wetzon followed, brooding. Surely Hazel had never said anything about arthritis in all the time they had known each other.

They ordered the cheese risotto and tremezzini: prosciutto, mozzarella, and tomato sandwiches on little Italian breads, and shared everything. Wetzon sipped the hot Italian-roast coffee and set the cup down. "All right, let's hear it. What's going on?"

"Nothing, nothing at all," Hazel said, "except I've made such progress with little Emilio. He's starting to read by himself now. But tell me what's happening with you. You lead a much more exciting life. Catch me up." Her eyes said, *I'll tell you when I'm ready, and not a minute sooner.*

"You are the most stubborn—"

"Don't say old lady because—"

"Okay, you win. Your way." Wetzon broke off a piece of the crisp breadstick and buttered it. "I'm starved, too. This weather—"

"How's Carlos?" Hazel interrupted, just as their food arrived. She loved Wetzon's best friend Carlos. The last time Wetzon had seen Hazel, they'd had dinner in Carlos's loft in the West Village. He had made a bouillabaisse and a wonderful Mississippi mud cake, and they had polished off three bottles of wine. Carlos had regaled them with the current theater gossip, Wetzon had told her latest broker stories, and Hazel had retold the Peepsie stories, which made no sense whatever, but were so funny that the three of them had collapsed in giggles, helpless with laughter.

"He's been busy on the new musical. We talk on the phone, but I haven't seen him in a couple of weeks."

They ate in uncharacteristic silence and ordered chocolate soufflés for dessert.

"I'm worried about Peepsie Cunningham, Leslie," Hazel said abruptly, without preamble.

As a girl, Hazel had gotten it into her head that she would come East from Cleveland to go to college, and at the age of sixteen she had been accepted by Connecticut College for Women. The Peepsies were the girls she had roomed with, six of them, counting her. How they had gotten to be Peepsies was a confusing story, and Hazel laughed so much in the telling, she was never able to finish it. Hazel, to the other Peepsies, was Peepsie Osborn. Anyway, at the last telling, there were four Peepsies left: Peepsie Cunningham, a wealthy widow who lived on upper Fifth Avenue; Peepsie Webber, who lived with her husband in a retirement community in Hartford; Peepsie Kennedy, who still ran her own public relations firm in D.C.; and Peepsie Osborn, our Hazel, who kept everyone informed about everyone else.

"Why?" Wetzon asked, a forkful of soufflé in her mouth, basking in the joy of the chocolate. She much preferred dark chocolate for the look of it was half of the taste, and there was something strange about what tasted like rich, dark bittersweet chocolate but was off-white and speckled like the shell of a bird's egg.

The espresso machine gave a wild asthmatic screech. A girl and a young man in a military school uniform took the table next to them and started bickering with an undertone of nastiness.

"She's gotten so vague," Hazel said. Her clear blue eyes were sharp with concern. "She doesn't remember where she put things. She didn't even know who I was when I was there yesterday. Well, not quite. She was very frightened. I think she knew me, but she didn't know me. Oh dear." She patted the burgundy hat nervously. "I'm afraid I'm not making any sense."

"Does she have Alzheimer's?" Wetzon asked gently.

"Yes, I think so, but it seems to be getting so much worse." Hazel's fingers tapped the table restlessly. "They never had children, you know. She has a niece, a nice girl . . . I haven't seen her in years . . . living in Europe somewhere . . . married a diplomat, I think. It's been years . . ." Hazel was upset and distracted. It was so unlike her.

"Is Peepsie Cunningham living by herself?"

"Yes—no—not really. There's a woman, a decent sort, I think, who comes in every day, bathes her, dresses her, cooks her meals. You know." She put her fork down and wiped her lips with the linen napkin. "We used to go out for lunch and a movie . . . with our senior citizen discount cards. We really liked that. I remember when we saw *Tootsie*. We had so much fun." She broke off. The espresso machine took a long deep breath and whoozed out a hoarse shriek. "We had to stop doing that. She would forget where we were. Once she wouldn't let the waiter take her empty plate away. She made an awful scene." Tears filled Hazel's eyes, and she fumbled in her bag for a handkerchief.

"Oh, Hazel, I'm so sorry," Wetzon said. If you have young friends, Hazel always said, you never have to see them wither and die. She shivered.

"Leslie, do me a favor, please." Hazel paused and for a fleeting moment an expression of guilt crossed her face. She began creasing the napkin between her fingers. "Never mind. I hate to involve anyone . . ."

"No, please, Hazel," Wetzon said, "ask me. How can I help? I want to help. I'm your friend."

Hazel studied her and breathed a soft sigh. "All right. Could you come over to Peepsie's with me now? It's a little hard for me—" She gestured at the cane leaning against the wall behind her chair.

They divided up the bill and, bundled against the cold, came out on the sidewalk into the arctic wind.

Wetzon peered up at the dark-edged, angry clouds scudding across the sky and sniffed. "It's going to snow, I'll bet."

"Please don't say that, Leslie."

Hazel seemed so worried, so sad. Where had her spunky young friend Hazel gone? Right now, Wetzon slowed her pace to match Hazel's awkward gait, the shuffle of an elderly woman.

"What's Peepsie Cunningham's address?" Wetzon asked brightly, locking her arm through Hazel's free one.

5

PEEPSIE CUNNINGHAM LIVED IN AN elegant old Fifth Avenue building across from the Metropolitan Museum.

A stout middle-aged doorman in a gray wool uniform, who had been standing inside away from the draft, came forward when he saw them approach and swung open the ornate glass and carved iron outside door for them.

"Good afternoon, Ms. Osborn," he said courteously, touching his hand to his hat. "I'll let Mrs. Cunningham know you're on your way up."

"Thank you, Edward." Hazel was leaning heavily on Wetzon's

arm, exhausted by their short walk. "This is my friend, Ms. Wetzon."

Edward nodded at Wetzon, went to a vertical switchboard, put a plug into a numbered outlet, picked up a phone, and waited.

"Yes. Ms. Osborn and Ms. Whitman coming up."

Hazel and Wetzon looked at each other and exchanged a smile. No one ever seemed to hear Wetzon's name correctly the first time.

"Elevator bank to your right," Edward said automatically, and then had the grace to look embarrassed when Hazel softly thanked him.

Together, slowly, Hazel and Wetzon moved through the beautiful old lobby: marble floors, deco-patterned, a wide expanse of window looking out on a garden laid out geometrically, somewhat similar to that at the Frick Museum farther down on Fifth Avenue. Several huge arrangements of fresh flowers stood on brass and wood side tables near upholstered armchairs and sofas. It all spoke of another time, of grace and dignity and a quiet, understated grandeur.

Wetzon pressed the button for the elevator while Hazel sank awkwardly down on the quilted brown leather bench opposite.

The elevator door opened and an elderly couple suitably encased in furs and heavy winterwear exited. A lanky young man in the gray staff uniform grinned at them from the mahogany-paneled elevator. "How you doing today, Ms. Osborn? Cold enough for you?" The question, as these weather questions usually were, appeared to be rhetorical, for he stepped aside to let them enter without waiting for a response. He pressed "20" and the door closed behind them.

The little lobby on the twentieth floor also had a patterned, marble floor. Bright red paisley paper decorated the walls. An antique light of etched glass in a leaded shade hung on a brass chain from the ceiling. There were two doors, one to the right and one to the left.

Hazel rang the bell to the one on the right, and as the echo of the chime faded, they heard a small stifled cry. There was a faint click behind them. Wetzon turned, but the other door stayed shut. Perhaps someone was watching them through the peephole. Not so odd in a paranoid city like New York, Wetzon reflected, where even the wealthy elderly were afraid.

The door swept open and an apparition said, "Hello, hello, my dollink. See," she continued to someone over her shoulder, "see, your friend is here. I told you she vould come, my dollink. And you must be Ms. Veetman. So happy to meet you." She grasped Wetzon's hand and pumped her arm vigorously. "Come, I take your coats, it is so cold, is it not, and the vind, such a vind, tch, tch, tch." All this was said at breakneck speed in a thick Russian accent. The speaker was a small, pigeon-breasted woman in a white uniform. A mass of bleached platinum-blonde curls was piled haphazardly on top of her head. She had dense false eyelashes on eyes outlined thickly in black and smudged with gray-blue gold-flecked eye shadow, brightly rouged cheeks, and shiny red-glazed lips. Heavy gold earrings dangled from stretched earlobes.

She hung their coats in the hall closet, still talking. "I make us some nice hot Russian tea," she announced, and swayed off on spike-heeled backless shoes.

"Leslie, you can close your mouth now," Hazel murmured wickedly, more like the old Hazel. "That's Ida."

"God, Hazel, what a piece of work."

"She's the home care person who looks after Peepsie. Let's go inside."

Wetzon, trailing after Hazel, was overwhelmed by the opulence, the gold Chinese wallpaper, the antique oil paintings in heavily carved frames, the fine old English furniture, and Chinese porcelains. A muted old runner ran down the beautiful parquet floor. Two huge urns stood on either side of the spacious archway.

Peepsie Cunningham was a very wealthy widow.

When Wetzon passed under the high, wide archway, she found herself in an enormous square room with more of the same: old English side tables, a rug in the palest blues and beige and rose, an important chinoiserie secretary, more porcelain, a

silver tray holding the tea service, cups and saucers, a plate of tea cakes, linen napkins, and silver spoons which rattled noisily.

"Vell, my dollinks, vhat nice things are girls talking about today?" Ida spoke with a vulgar familiarity, placing the tray on the round tea table near the sofa. "How you like tea, Ms. Veetman?"

"Straight," Wetzon said.

"And you're one sugar and lemon," Ida said to Hazel without looking at her. "And ve know you like with milk and honey, don't ve, my little dollink," Ida said to Peepsie Cunningham, who smiled slyly up at her. Ida handed them their cups, then poured one for herself, adding generous dollops of honey and milk, and settled into one of the club chairs. With a loud sigh she shook off her shoes and tucked her feet up under her.

Hazel's dark left eyebrow rose almost up to the brim of her burgundy felt hat, which Wetzon suddenly realized she hadn't removed. Every wisp of Hazel's snowy-white hair was tucked up under the hat. All at once she was afraid. It wasn't arthritis that was sapping Hazel's strength. The cancer had come back.

Wetzon's reverie was shattered by a clattering noise. Peepsie Cunningham's arm was still extended in the air. She had flung her spoon across the room. Hazel's face registered shock.

"Oh my, vhat naughty girl you are," Ida scolded, shaking her finger at Peepsie. She rose grudgingly and slipped her feet back into her shoes. "I bring another. Tch, tch, tch."

Fascinated, they stared at Ida's rolling walk in the spike-heeled shoes, her protruding rear end broad in the tight white uniform.

"So clever, so clever," Peepsie Cunningham said nastily. She took a big swallow of her tea and turned to Hazel, pleading, "I can't find them. I brought them home, and I can't find them. Please, Peepsie, help me."

Hazel leaned toward her. "Can't find what, dear?"

"You know," Peepsie Cunningham said. "Tell Marion." She turned and gaped at Wetzon. Her voice rose in terror. "Who are you? What are you doing in my home?"

Hazel looked apologetically at Wetzon. Peepsie Cunningham giggled and thrust her teacup at Hazel.

"Want to sleep now, Peepsie, Peepsie, Peepsie," she intoned, yawning widely. She seemed to be having trouble keeping her eyes open.

"Time for nap now, my dollink," Ida said, returning.

"I guess we should go." Reluctance threaded Hazel's words.

She and Wetzon both rose, watching uncomfortably as Ida gathered Peepsie Cunningham up in her arms and carried her out of the room.

Like a bag of laundry, Wetzon thought.

"You let yourselves out, no?" Ida said without looking back.

Silently, they bundled themselves up again for the cold. In the little red lobby Hazel said, "You see why I'm so worried."

"Yes. Is being so panicked a symptom of Alzheimer's?"

"I don't know. But she is terribly frightened, isn't she?"

"No question. Can't her niece come back and take care of her?"

"Peepsie doesn't seem to know where she put Marion's last letter. And I can't remember her married name."

"I'm so sorry, Hazel. My God, all that wealth and all that sadness."

The elevator took them back to the main lobby.

"Cab, ladies?" Edward asked.

"Yes, please," Hazel said. She looked at Wetzon, who shook her head.

"I'll walk up to Eighty-sixth Street and take the crosstown bus."

They stood inside the entrance listening to the wind, watching pedestrians battling the vicious gusts swathed in coats, hats, and mufflers, bent with the effort. It was not a day for strolling. Even the steps of the Metropolitan Museum, usually thick with people sitting and talking, were deserted.

Edward, clutching his cap, was dancing on the sidewalk outside trying to flag down a taxi. Trash, bits and pieces of newspapers, twigs from trees and shrubbery spun helplessly in the wind. A large, dark object hurtled past the doors, seemingly windblown from way above. Edward stopped and jerked around. His hand shot out, snapped back, covering his eyes. For a moment, he seemed frozen, then he whirled and rushed toward them. A blast of cold air hit them as he threw the door open.

"Jesus, Mary," he screamed, "it's Missus Cunningham!" He pushed past, his face ashen. "Jesus, Mary." Panting, he grabbed up the receiver and punched three numbers. "Come at once, come at once to 999 Fifth Avenue. One of my tenants just jumped."

6

"HAZEL WAS DISTRAUGHT," WETZON SAID. "Hell, *I* was distraught." She was lying on her bed fully clothed except for her boots, which she'd pulled off the minute she walked into her apartment.

Smith clucked sympathetically on the other end of the phone line. "That poor woman. What did the body look like?"

"Smith, you are a ghoul, you know that?"

"No, come on, Wetzon, you'll feel a lot better if you tell me," Smith said. "You know how these things fester if you don't get them out."

"There isn't that much to tell. By the time we left the building they had taken her away—"

She shuddered at the memory. She and Edward had pulled Hazel away from the door. "This is a mistake," Hazel kept saying. "A mistake." Somehow they managed to get her to one of the lobby sofas. Wetzon shrugged out of her coat and tucked it around Hazel's shoulders. Edward disappeared and returned with what looked like a painter's drop cloth. Wetzon knew he had gone out to cover what was left of Peepsie Cunningham's mortal remains. Then the police had arrived . . .

"They came fast," Smith said, interrupting.

"I guess it helps if you live on Fifth Avenue."

"Oh ho, she was one of the superprivileged, then."

"You might say that. I've never seen such an incredible apart-ment. It was like a museum—"

"Tell me—"

"Not now. It's been an awful afternoon." Wetzon closed her eyes and saw the shoe again. The small dark blue Gucci with the gold stirrups.

"What did you do with Hazel?" Smith's voice was distorted by something she was eating. "I wish you would open up, sweetie. You know it's going to give you nightmares if you don't talk about it."

"I just can't," Wetzon said. "At least not yet, not now." *And maybe not to you*, she added silently. Why did Smith always want her to share her every thought and feeling? "I called Hazel's doc-tor and brought her over to Lenox Hill. He wanted her admitted for observation."

"Oh my, she must have been in bad shape." The munching sound continued.

"Smith, she was in shock. Peepsie Cunningham was one of her oldest friends—whatever are you eating?"

"Potato chips. Peepsie, what kind of name is that? A turn-of-the-century version of Muffie?"

"Smith, you're so callous. They could be us in thirty or forty years." She pulled the afghan up around her, chilled.

"Oh hardly, Wetzon. I'm not about to take a walk out of my window, especially not on a cold night. And neither are you." Wetzon heard the crackle of crumpled cellophane.

"But what if we were ill and alone, and we didn't know what we were doing?" A funny little pulse fluttered her eyelid. She was depressed by what had happened to Peepsie.

"Wetzon," Smith said impatiently, "you just got finished tell-ing me there was a woman with her, looking after her."

"Right. Ida. A very peculiar Russian lady, who acted as if she were a member of the family. She actually took off her shoes and had tea with us." Wetzon had forgotten all about Ida. Wherever had Ida been when Peepsie Cunningham jumped? "I don't know where she was, and in the confusion I didn't see her again."

"Didn't you talk to the police?"

"No one talked to us, and Hazel was in such bad shape. A lot of the tenants came downstairs and were standing around trying to see what was going on. The lobby got very crowded. So after I talked to Hazel's doctor, I called a cab service and we left."

"Just like that?"

"Just like that."

Except for one thing, Wetzon thought. As she helped Hazel into the cab, she had seen the small dark blue Gucci walking shoe with the gold stirrups in the gutter. Without thinking, she had bent down and dropped it into her big Mark Cross leather carryall, a combination of purse and briefcase. What had possessed her to do so, she couldn't imagine. It had been instinctive. And in her concern for Hazel, she had quite forgotten about it until just now.

"I can't get over that no one stopped you," Smith was saying.

"I think people could see that Hazel was sick—" She choked. "Oh, Smith, it's more than that. Hazel's cancer has come back. She's having chemotherapy, and she can hardly walk."

"I'm really sorry, Wetzon," Smith said. "I know how you feel about her. But she *is* old—"

"Forget it, Smith. Don't say another word."

"Really, Wetzon, what did I say now?" Smith sounded wounded. "You are getting so sensitive."

Wetzon didn't know why she bothered. She and Smith would never see eye to eye about most things. "It's all right, Smith, I guess I'm just upset about what happened. I'm going to lie here and try to catch up."

"Wait, before you hang up, you had some calls—"

Wetzon looked at her watch. It was five o'clock. She groaned. "Okay, let's hear."

"Evan Cornell."

"He's looking for something in management. He calls every couple of months. It can wait till tomorrow."

"Mary Ann Marusi. I hope she's not in trouble again. Kidder hasn't even paid us yet."

"I don't think so. She said she would call me for a drink or lunch after she got settled."

"I hope so, but considering her record . . ."

"What record, Smith? Really, I don't know why you have it in for Mary Ann. She hasn't done anything wrong."

"No, just dummied up her runs from Sontheimer and Company."

"That's not true. You're taking Don Schwartzman's word for that, and you know damned well Don's a liar. He's lied about the end-of-year production of everyone we've placed there. He cheated us. That, if you remember, is why we're not working with Sontheimer anymore."

"How could it slip my mind. I must be losing my grip." Smith laughed lightly.

"Any more calls?"

"Yes. Peter Tormenkov, confirming breakfast tomorrow at seven-thirty at the American Festival Cafe."

"Oh shit. I'd forgotten all about that."

"Who's Peter Tormenkov?"

"Someone Howie Minton referred."

"Jesus, Howie Minton, the great mover," Smith said sarcastically, tweaking Wetzon for always believing Howie Minton when he called her and swore that *this* time he was *really* ready to change firms. Wetzon would set up interviews for him with various firms, they would all make him offers, and then he'd stay on with L. L. Rosenkind.

"Well, you're right there. I admit it." Wetzon laughed. "Anyway, this Tormenkov person works for L. L. Rosenkind and he's unhappy—"

"Just like Howie, I suppose."

"Maybe not. Howie says he really wants to leave and that he has a nice book for a rookie."

"A rookie? God, I hate to work with rookies. You spend as much time with them, more, than with a big producer where we can really earn a fee," Smith complained. "Couldn't you have gotten him to come to the office? It's a waste of time and money buying a rookie breakfast."

"He was so paranoid about confidentiality, I thought what the hell." Wetzon didn't look forward to a seven-thirty breakfast either. She had never gotten used to the Wall Street clock, where the day often started at the crack of dawn and brokers were sitting at their desks at seven o'clock. The day officially began at nine-thirty when the Market opened, but a lot of brokers were on the phone with clients considerably earlier. And those who prospected for new clients knew that the corporate honchos were usually at their desks by seven, without a secretary around to run interference. But Wetzon, who spent all those years in the theater, still felt as if her heart didn't even start beating until ten o'clock. "Anything else?"

"Yes, one more. Kevin De Haven. No message. Just a phone number. Looks like a Merrill number."

"De Haven? Does that name sound familiar to you?"

"No. Don't you know him?"

"No." Her curiosity was piqued, despite her fatigue. "I wonder if it's too late. Let me try him and I'll call you back."

She hung up the phone and dialed the number Kevin De Haven had left.

"De Haven."

"Hi, this is Leslie Wetzon. You called me this afternoon."

"Oh yeah. I was returning your call."

"I didn't call you."

"But I found your name and phone number on my desk this morning when I got back from vacation."

"Well, I didn't call you, Kevin," Wetzon said, baffled. "What do you do?"

"I'm a stockbroker."

"You are?" She suppressed a chortle. "What a coincidence. I'm a headhunter."

"Hey, pal, what field do you headhunt in?" De Haven asked, warming up. Brokers loved to talk. Salespeople loved to talk. So long as you kept the conversation going, you still had a shot at closing the sale.

"Your field. Stockbrokers. Maybe we should talk."

"Maybe we should. I may be interested in using your services."

"What kind of business do you do in numbers?" Wetzon asked casually.

"Oh, three quarters of a mil or so."

"No kidding. You're not a stockbroker. You're a gorilla. When can we sit down and talk?" With the average stockbroker doing somewhere between two hundred and fifty and three hundred thousand in gross production, De Haven was indeed a gorilla.

"How about tomorrow? After the close."

"Great. Where are you located? My office is on Forty-ninth, off Second."

"Well, I'm at 200 Park. Maybe I'll come to see you. Why don't you call me tomorrow at four?"

"Great, Kevin, I'll do that." She hung up the phone and shouted, "Wowee! Gold!" She dialed the office, and when Smith answered, she said, "Guess who lives right?"

"What? Tell me. Who is he?"

"Oh, just a little old three-quarters-of-a-million-dollars producer."

"Holy shit, how did we get so lucky?"

"I don't know, but I'm sure going to find out. He says I called him and left my name and number, but I know I didn't. Someone is watching out for me."

"I'll let you know after I check the cards tonight," Smith said, referring to her tarot reading. "When are you meeting him?"

"Tomorrow, after the close. Maybe at the office sometime after four o'clock."

"Damn it, Wetzon, my party is tomorrow night. You know I have to leave early."

"You don't have to meet him, Smith."

"But I want to. It's not right." Smith was petulant.

"Would you rather I put him off and lose him?" Smith sometimes could get so ridiculous. Even though she was older than Wetzon, Wetzon frequently felt older, or less childish anyway.

Smith's response was an emphatic, "Humpf!"

"Look, Smith, I'm beat. I'll see you tomorrow."

"Oh, Wetzon, wait a minute. I forgot to ask you. Did she own her apartment?"

"What? What apartment?"

"The one that belongs to the woman who killed herself, of course, who did you think? I want you to ask Hazel about it for me. Maybe I can get it at a good price. If Leon and I should get married . . . we're going to need a bigger place."

7

WETZON WAS FORAGING in the pantry closet. There wasn't much. Since Carlos had become a choreographer, his visits were erratic, and she fended for herself with groceries. Years ago, when Carlos's dance career had begun to fade, he had started a housekeeping business. It became so successful that he soon had an army of out-of-work dancers working for him, cleaning and cooking in houses and apartments all over the city.

She closed the door and then reopened it and took out a can of water-packed tuna fish, setting it on the counter.

"When in doubt, bagel it," she said aloud, and cut a sesame bagel in half.

She went into the dining room and put her answering machine on.

"Hello there, joy of my life, this is the boy choreographer, calling to let you know all is well on the firing line, and I'll be there tomorrow sometime. Tried you at the office and got the barracuda, so I'm sure she didn't relay the message."

Carlos. And he was right. The barracuda, commonly known as Smith, hadn't told her. Smith and Carlos hated each other.

"Hi, buddy," Wetzon said to the answering machine. "Talk to you later."

The machine beeped. The next call was a hang-up. Another

beep. Then the strains of Ethel Merman belting out, "There's no business like show business," with full orchestra on the answering tape. A Carlos special. He always did that when he cleaned her tape of old messages, something she never bothered to do.

The apartment was cold. She trailed into the bedroom, shivering, and changed into sweats and heavy socks. The heat was slow in coming up tonight because the thermostat had not caught up with the sudden temperature drop that morning. Outside, the north wind whapped against her windows.

Through the wooden blinds she could see the small trees around the penthouse of the building behind hers, bobbing and bending. As she watched, the stem of a giant sunflower broke off and slammed into her window. She jumped back. The dead sunflower clutched at the glass with tiny dried tendrils, as if it were human, trying to hold on, and failing, finally got whipped away.

Something danced and clutched similarly in the back of Wetzon's mind, teasing her. Peepsie Cunningham in her dark blue silk dress, tossed like a rag doll in the lashing wind amid assorted debris that the wind had churned up.

The tiny dark blue Gucci walking shoe with the gold stirrups. It was still in her carryall, which was leaning against her bed. She took it out and stared at it. It was a real Gucci, monogram and all, not an imitation, and it was hardly worn. There were only a few scratches on the sole. She held it up and matched the sole to the black suede boots she had removed earlier.

"You've got big feet, kid," she said, imitating Silvestri, imitating Bogart.

Silvestri. Thinking of him, she smiled. She had met him last year when she had gotten involved in Barry Stark's murder. He had substance, and it was a real relationship. As real as two people could have with two careers and totally different working hours.

She put Peepsie Cunningham's shoe down on the rug next to her boots, sat up, and called Silvestri at the Seventeenth Precinct.

"Metzger."

"Hi, Artie. Is he there, by any chance?"

"No, he's downtown." Silvestri's partner's voice was raw with fatigue. "Something just came up, and we're in for a long night, I think." She could picture Metzger, with that long, hang-dog face and the pouches under his eyes, slumped at his cluttered desk in the tiny office he shared with Silvestri.

"Okay, I hear you," she said. She hadn't seen Silvestri in three days, hadn't talked with him in two. She missed him. "Just say I called."

"Want me to tell him anything in particular?" Metzger asked half-heartedly.

"No, Artie, thanks." She paused and frowned. "Yes. Not to call me tonight. I have a seven-thirty breakfast and I'm going to bed early. I'll talk with him tomorrow."

The Peepsie Cunningham story could wait. Mrs. Cunningham was, after all, a suicide, not a murder.

Wetzon lay down on her bed again and unfolded the red, white, and blue afghan she and Carlos had crocheted as a backstage project in honor of the bicentennial when they danced for Bob Fosse in *Chicago* in 1976. They had agreed to share it, each taking it for a year, and this was her year—at least until July Fourth. She thought about the choreographers she and Carlos had worked with who were gone. Gower Champion first. And then Michael Bennett and Bob Fosse had both died in 1987. It made her sad and nostalgic.

Drawing the afghan up around her ears, she thought about Silvestri.

The truth was, she was crazy about him, but she didn't find it easy to admit. Not to herself. And certainly not to him. If she admitted it, wouldn't she begin to depend on him more and more and less on herself? She had been by herself for a long time, and except for a few short—very short—affairs there had been no one since Bud Silverberg, whom she had met in college. He had been with the Air Force in exotic Morocco. He had just stopped writing, and she had found out not long afterward from a mutual friend that he had fallen in love with and married a Moroccan girl.

"I can't believe he didn't tell you," the friend had said.

Neither can I, she had thought. Well, this was one relationship she intended to handle very carefully.

She wriggled under the afghan. Silvestri. Smith had no inkling, at least Wetzon devoutly hoped she didn't. Only Carlos guessed, and that was because he knew her so well. "He's good for you," Carlos said. They had been doing basic barre exercises. "And you know I wouldn't just say that. I don't like cops."

"He's a detective," she corrected automatically, bending her leg slightly and straightening it, raising it slowly to the barre.

"Shit, he's a cop," Carlos said, his back to her, doing the same movement. "But I like him anyway, and I like how he treats you." He came back into first position. "And look at you—you've got this glow on all the time now. Come on, let me show you." He turned her reluctant body to the mirror, his handsome face for once very serious. "Look. All the points are softening. It's a by-product of good sex," he added with a lascivious grin.

She had felt herself flush, but it was true. When she was with Silvestri, she could feel all her spikes, as Carlos called them, softening. Chin, nose, elbows, knees. She could feel herself turning to mush, and only half of her liked it. She didn't like not having complete control.

"Damn you, Carlos," she had said, whacking him with her towel. "Get out of my head."

"Listen, dear heart," he said, tenderly, ducking too late. "I'm your best friend, and I love you like a mother, like a brother. And I know you love me. But it's safe to love me, because you know I'm never going to do anything but love you."

She turned her back on him, hunching over the barre, and Carlos came up behind her, placing his hand on her hunched shoulders. She stared at him in the mirror.

"Take a chance," he said softly. "For your sake. I don't want you to be alone." Her image looked at his image in the mirror, stricken. It was the time of the Plague and too many people they knew had died and were dying, would die of AIDS. "No, I'm all right, but I mean I'm not going to be around forever," he said sadly. "None of us can think long term anymore." She had turned away from their images and they had held each other and cried.

So she was trying, but she was frightened by all the emotion of her feelings about Silvestri.

She threw off the afghan and sat up and dialed information for Lenox Hill Hospital, then called to see how Hazel was doing.

"We're not putting calls through to Ms. Osborn tonight," the operator said, "but she is in satisfactory condition."

"All right, then, please tell her that Ms. Wetzon called and will talk to her tomorrow."

"Ms. Weston."

"Wetzon. W-e-t-z-o-n."

"Weston."

Wetzon laughed as she put down the phone. She picked up the dark blue Gucci walking shoe and turned on the television, parking the shoe on top of the set.

The picture came on clear and sharp, and suddenly she was looking at her friend, Teddy Lanzman, solemn-faced, doing a promo for a special coming up on the plight of the elderly in the city. He had come a long way from his days as the token black at Channel 8. It had been ages since she'd last seen him. She remembered he'd been dating someone, a production secretary, or something like that, in David Merrick's office when Wetzon was in *42nd Street*. He had risen from community relations to feature writer and producer. She stood staring down at the screen, her mind elsewhere, then she turned off the news in bright living color and went back to the kitchen.

The kettle was filled, the Zabar's ground decaf measured into the Melitta filter, the tuna fish drained and mixed with Marie's garlic Italian dressing. She put the bagel halves in the toaster oven and sat at the counter in her kitchen.

She loved her little kitchen with the blue-and-white French country tiles on the wall and the white counters. She turned on the tiny television and listened to the business news at six-thirty while she sliced a tomato. Nose to the plate, she inhaled the wonderful smell of a summer-ripe hydroponic tomato, almost as good as the Jersey beefs she had grown up on.

Damn, someone else had been arrested for trading on insider

information. Would they never learn? Did no one remember Ivan Boesky? It was really disturbing because almost every one of these men was young, younger than she, graduates of the best schools, and they were already making big dollars. It was another kind of plague. One didn't die from it, but it was corrupting the entire financial community. She listened to the stock quotes and then switched to the national news.

When the coffee had stopped dripping, she threw the paper filter with the grounds away and poured herself a mug of coffee. She piled tuna fish and slices of tomato on each half of the bagel and ate them one at a time as she read her notes on Peter Tormenkov.

The hunger was still with her, but it wasn't real. She needed a chocolate fix. The chunks of dark chocolate from Li-Lac on Christopher Street that Silvestri had brought her last week. They were in the pantry closet. She took a small chunk and put the rest back on the shelf.

Teddy Lanzman came on the TV screen again with another promo for his special report on the elderly, starting next week. ". . . which help and which defraud," Teddy said. "Please join me and tell your friends. You may not be part of the aged population in this city now, but you will be. And right now, we all know people who are."

"Are and were," Wetzon said, thinking about Peepsie Cunningham and her friend Hazel Osborn.

The rich bittersweet chocolate melted in her mouth and wrapped her in a warm cloak of well-being. She was safe, she thought guiltily. She was healthy. She was young.

8

"I'M JUST GOING OUT FOR A SHORT WALK," Hazel said, opening a dark blue ruffled parasol, and she brushed aside the enormous sunflowers and stepped off the parapet of the terrace they were standing on.

"Wait . . . no, you can't," Wetzon shrieked, reaching for her, catching Hazel's beautiful white hair, which came off in her hand. Terrified, holding the white curly wig, she watched Hazel float calmly away like Mary Poppins and disappear beyond the gleaming gold tower of the Chrysler Building.

Wetzon awoke panicked, drenched in sweat, her hand clutching the fuzzy blue mohair throw that she used as an extra blanket. She was trembling. It was still dark. And cold. The little white digital box that was her radio alarm said five-fifteen.

She lay there, eyes closed again, thinking about Hazel, gradually untensing. The radiator in the kitchen coughed. She turned off the alarm and put on the light.

The red cover of *A Perfect Spy*, at the top of a huge stack of books on the painted American country washstand she used as a night table, caught her eye. She was about a third of the way through it, and it was hard work. John le Carré was not Danielle Steel, Smith's current favorite writer. But Wetzon was a snob about literature and preferred the intellectual rewards that came from meeting a good writer halfway.

It was funny about what people read. Silvestri read biographies, autobiographies, war stories—any war—and Westerns. Carlos read show business biographies and autobiographies and mysteries.

She read about ten pages in *A Perfect Spy*, moving with

Magnus and Rick and Mary and Jack, full of respect for how le Carré was peeling away the layers. Then, reluctantly, she marked the page.

Nothing is what it appears, she thought, inhaling the steam of the hot shower, not in le Carré, not in this world.

She towel-dried her long hair, leaving it loose, slipped on her sweats, and checked the time. Six o'clock. She had an hour or maybe a bit more if she could be sure of getting a cab to Rockefeller Center.

After getting the coffee started, she did a simple workout at the barre, running slowly through the positions, and ended feeling tall and lean. Lean was real, but tall was the impossible dream. Smith always laughed at her, but Wetzon's self-image was tall until she got caught in an elevator surrounded by men, who towered over her, stepped on her as if she weren't there.

She unlocked her door and bent to get the morning papers from the doormat. Next to the *Times* and *The Wall Street Journal* was a yellow rose wrapped loosely in cellophane, tied with a yellow ribbon. She picked it up. It was probably just a promotion from the newspaper delivery service, but it made her feel good, so it succeeded in whatever they were trying to do.

The yellow rose went into a bud vase, which Wetzon carried into the bedroom and put on the painted chest of drawers, where she could see it while she dressed in her pin-striped uniform of the day. It was too early to call Hazel. That would have to wait until after her breakfast interview with Tormenkov.

At her kitchen counter, a mug of hot coffee in front of her, she scanned the newspaper headlines. Nothing unusual. The latest insider-trading scandal, the dollar had fallen against the yen and the deutsche mark, the trade protectionists were insisting on more sanctions against the Japanese, Texaco was rumored to have received a buy-out offer, and another Wall Street guru was predicting doom and gloom and advising the purchase of gold. She moved quickly from page to page, scanning.

In the "Obituaries" section of the *Times* she found what she had been looking for.

EVELYN M. CUNNINGHAM, 72,
DIES IN TWENTY-STORY FALL

Evelyn Morton Cunningham, socialite and widow of
the late S. Alden Cunningham, attorney and presidential
adviser, died in a fall Thursday from the terrace of her
twentieth-floor apartment at 999 Fifth Avenue. She was
72 years old and had been in poor health.

Authorities say they believe Mrs. Cunningham's fall
was an accident or suicide. She had been under a doctor's
care for depression and Alzheimer's disease. She was
fully clothed in a dark blue dress and high-heeled bedroom slippers and may have lost her balance while trying
to close the doors to her terrace.

Sgt. E. D. O'Melvany of Manhattan North said that
the French doors leading from Mrs. Cunningham's bedroom to her terrace had been open and the railing of the
parapet was low. He said it was possible that a gust of
wind could have knocked her over the edge.

Investigators are seeking to question a woman named
Ida, described as Russian, about five feet five inches tall,
blonde hair, about 35–40 years old, who was acting as a
nurse or nurse's aide for the deceased. They are also
seeking information about two women who visited Mrs.
Cunningham shortly before her death, a Ms. Osborn and
a Ms. Whitman.

Wetzon put the paper down. Her hands left wet patches on
the paper. She stared at the coffee mug. "High-heeled bedroom
slippers?"

"Hazel," she said out loud, putting the mug down hard. Hot
coffee sloshed over on the counter and her hand. Abstractedly,
she put her hand under cold water and wiped up the spilled coffee from the counter. What to do? It was quarter to seven. She
had to get going.

In the bathroom she rolled her hair up into a dancer's knot on
top of her head and put gray shadow on her eyelids. A touch of

lipstick and her diamond stud earrings. Her movements picked up speed.

After folding the newspaper into her carryall, she wrapped herself in the long black coat and the leopard-patterned scarf, pulled the lavender beret down over her ears, and was set to brave the elements.

Frowning, she stopped at the door, thought for a minute, then turned and went back to her bedroom. She took the small dark blue Gucci walking shoe off the television set and put it in her carryall, slipping it into the fold of her newspaper.

"Morning, Ms. Wetzon." Larry, her doorman, was sitting near the radiator, smoking. Ashes flecked his uniform jacket. "Your ride is waiting."

"Ride? What ride?" Wetzon squinted into the dim morning. Everything outside, in fact, looked deeply gray. Bits of snow floated and flurried in the small gusts of wind.

Silvestri, wearing a red down jacket and a wool watch cap, leaned against his car, which was double-parked in front of her building. He was blowing into his gloved hands.

"What are you doing here at this hour?" she said, staggering toward him as a sudden gust of wind caught her.

"You told me not to call." He was grinning at her boyishly. "But I left you a message anyway."

"I didn't get a message," she said, checking him out. He looked tired and had a dark stubble of beard. But his eyes, which were slate when he was impersonal and on the job, and turquoise when he let his feelings show, were now the deepest of turquoise. "You never write notes, you never call. You just show up."

"Oh stop grumbling," he said, opening the door for her. "What was on your doormat besides the goddam newspapers this morning?"

The yellow rose. Of course.

"You constantly surprise me, Silvestri," she said truthfully.

He put his hands on her shoulders, and she felt the familiar little shock she always felt when he touched her, even through all the masses of clothing she was wearing. She pressed her face against the soft cold of his jacket and hugged him.

"Good morning, Les," he said.

9

"BECAUSE I DIDN'T THINK. I had to get Hazel to Lenox Hill. I saw it. I just picked it up."

Silvestri put his cardboard container of coffee on the narrow ledge of the windshield and dropped the half-eaten jelly doughnut into the cardboard box on the seat between them. He wiped his hands on his jeans, leaving white smudges.

Wetzon opened a small packet, pulled out a folded wet Wash 'n Dri, and handed it to him. "*Semper paratus,*" she said.

"Christalmighty, Les, you're a pistol," Silvestri said, wiping his sticky hands, then taking the dark blue Gucci walking shoe from her. "How do you know it's this woman's—"

"Peepsie Cunningham. I mean, Evelyn Cunningham."

"Whatever her name is. How can you be so certain it was *her* shoe? There are a lot of ladies all over the Upper East Side who wear Gucci shoes."

She didn't answer him, but when he looked back at her, she didn't waver.

"Okay, okay. Don't look at me like that. I know when I'm losing." He leaned across the cardboard box, kissed her lightly, and pulled back, leaving her with the sweet taste of powdered sugar on her lips and her heart playing games in her chest.

They were parked in Rockefeller Plaza behind the skating rink, near the café where she was meeting Peter Tormenkov for breakfast.

"And look at this, Silvestri," she said, determined to stay on the subject of Peepsie Cunningham. She loosened her scarf and pulled off her gloves. From her carryall she took the folded newspaper and held it out to him.

"Aw, Les," Silvestri groaned, turning back in his seat and taking up the container of coffee. "I'm off duty. I haven't been home in two days—"

"It'll only take a minute. Please, Silvestri."

"You are so goddam single-minded," he said, taking the newspaper. He read quickly, rubbing the stubble on his face. "Oh Christ," he said, finishing the article and looking at her, his eyes cold and flat. "How come you always get involved in this crap?"

"What do you mean 'always'?" she said, insulted. "Only once before. And that wasn't my fault either. And you know it, Silvestri."

"I like things simple and uncomplicated when I'm not working," he said, thumping his hand on the steering wheel, "otherwise I can't come down. And you—you are like a complication waiting to happen."

She turned her back on him and stared out the steamed-up car window, seeing nothing, blinking rapidly to keep from crying.

There was a long silence while they both stared out of their separate windows.

"Oh shit, Les," Silvestri said gruffly, at last. "I'm sorry. I'm tired. I'm grungy. I just wanted to see you, touch you."

"I'm sorry, too. I know you're tired. I guess I should have waited. Or handled it myself."

"Oh no, you shouldn't have. You had to tell me and we have to deal with it."

He uncovered the second container in the cardboard box and held it out to her.

"What's this?" He knew she didn't drink Sanka and that was the only kind of decaf coffee the doughnut shops he favored served. She took it from him, their fingers touching. "Oh, fresh orange juice for forgiveness," she said, intentionally paraphrasing Ophelia.

At least they were facing each other again.

"Okay," he said, "let's talk about this."

"What do you think?"

"'Ms. Whitman,' I presume," Silvestri said, looking at her, tapping the article with his fingertip.

"Yup."

"And the Russian lady?"

"Ida something or other. A home care attendant. Hazel might know more about her."

"And Hazel is at Lenox Hill?"

"Yes."

"Sloppy work, not asking questions, not getting a statement from the two of you, not combing the area around the scene," he said, more to himself than Wetzon. "You just walked away from it and no one even stopped you." He shook his head. "Sloppy," he said again, staring out the front windshield.

"Silvestri," she said softly.

"You're not drinking your orange juice," he answered.

She put the container to her lips. It was fresh and pulpy, the way she liked it.

"Oh my," she said, closing her eyes. "Heavenly. Almost as good as—" She felt the flush begin in her neck moving up above the collar of her coat into her cheeks. "As chocolate. I was going to say chocolate." She smiled at him, suddenly shy. "This is bad, Silvestri. I have to do an interview in a few minutes."

His eyes laughed at her.

"I have to go," she said, reluctant to leave him, or the warmth of the car, even for the short walk to the glass elevator that would take her downstairs to the underground plaza and the café.

"What are you going to do about the shoe?" She knotted her scarf and slipped on her gloves.

"Leave it with me. I know Eddie O'Melvany." Silvestri's tone was now detached, professional. "I'll talk to him. You and Hazel will have to make statements. If it's a clean suicide—"

"A clean suicide . . ." What was a clean suicide, for godsakes?

"I'll check it out. Then I'm going to sleep. I'm beat."

"Do you have to go back to work after that?" she asked cautiously. She didn't want him to think she was making plans, but as she spoke, her right arm in the black alpaca coat, moving without a thought, reached across the seat to him.

"Nope, we made an arrest this morning. I have a couple of days." His fingers met hers, moved upward into her sleeve, and rested just above her wrist. They were leaning awkwardly across the cardboard box to touch each other. "What about tonight?" he said.

"Smith is having a party tonight. I have to go." She hesitated. "You could come," she said, hoping he wouldn't want to. His fingers played lightly around her wrist.

"Don't want to," he said, his eyes locked with hers.

"I could leave early," she said, trying to stay cool. The clock on his dashboard said seven-thirty. "I'm going to be late," she whispered. "I'll leave my key with the doorman."

He nodded. They twined fingers briefly, then let go of each other. She stepped out of the car and closed the door, weak in the knees.

10

PETER TORMENKOV WAS LATE, which was no surprise. Brokers were always late. She spent her life waiting for brokers. She had left her name and Tormenkov's with the hostess and asked to be seated at a table near the skating rink.

"Decaf coffee, please," she told the waitress. "Someone else will be coming and we'll order then." The waitress left two menus and returned immediately with a small pot of coffee and a basket of mixed muffins. Wetzon took a sip of the coffee—it was scalding hot—and slipped out of her scarf and coat, carefully removing the beret so as not to mess her topknot. She rubbed the tips of her cold ears to warm them.

The café was nearly empty, but soon it would begin to fill up for the "power breakfast" meetings that went on all over the city. It was her favorite early meeting place in midtown because it was less frenetic than the Rendezvous or the Drake or even the Crystal Fountain in the Grand Hyatt.

A motorized unit like a combination vacuum cleaner and lawn mower was being driven over the ice on the rink, readying it for the early skaters. The tentative flurries from earlier that morning had become the real thing, scattering in the quickening northwest wind.

Smith was going to be irate if the weather ruined her party. She had been planning this party for weeks.

Voices caught her attention as two people were being seated near her. A very attractive, light-skinned black woman, perhaps about Wetzon's age, impeccably dressed in a black Chanel knit suit, a mink-lined coat over her shoulders, and a younger man, bearded, wearing a foreign-looking brown fur hat and a long L.L. Bean coat over a business suit.

"Ms. Wetzon?" a man in a tan raincoat asked, looking around the café at the other tables. He was tall, very thin, with curly brown hair badly in need of cutting, and very young. He had a barely discernible accent. Eastern European, perhaps.

"Peter?" Smiling, Wetzon put out her hand. He had a limp, damp handshake. "You must be cold. How about some coffee right away and then we'll order."

A second pot of coffee and a basket of sweet rolls arrived with speed.

"I really appreciate your seeing me on such short notice, Ms. Wetzon," Tormenkov said nervously. Under the raincoat he was wearing a finely tailored blue pin-striped suit, rather like Wetzon's, and a crisp white cotton shirt.

"Everyone calls me Wetzon, without the Ms.," she said, trying to put him at ease. "Howie tells me you're a winner."

"Howie? Oh yeah, right, Howie Minton." He fiddled with a sugar packet, opened it, refolded it, opened it again, and emptied it into his coffee.

"Let's order so we can talk," she suggested, impatient to move the interview along.

He ordered scrambled eggs and bacon and she ordered her usual, yogurt and fresh fruit. After the waitress left, Wetzon said,

"You didn't tell me very much about yourself on the telephone. How can I help you?"

"You know I'm at L. L. Rosenkind . . ."

She nodded. Two aging, overweight skaters came out on the ice and began a waltz, spinning and twirling effortlessly around the rink.

"We are basically . . . you know . . . a stock and bond house, and I do a good clean business . . ."

They all say that, Wetzon thought. The next thing he would say is that he did a lot of listed business. She waited for him to begin again, but he stared down at his blueberry muffin, mute.

"So you do a mix of both stocks and bonds?" she prompted.

"Oh no, I do a lot of . . . you know . . . listed stock, you know . . . the Dow stocks and . . . you know . . . options. No bonds."

"What did you do before you came to L. L. Rosenkind?" If he said "you know" again, she would go mad.

"I was with a penny stock house. Randall, Patchin. You heard of them?"

"Yes." Randall, Patchin was a disreputable firm that was constantly in trouble with the SEC, always on the verge of being closed down.

"I know," Tormenkov said, reading her face. "I know what you think of Randall, Patchin. I thought so, too, but no one else would give me a job on Wall Street, so I went there and I left as soon as I could get another job."

Wetzon nodded. She had met many brokers who had started their careers in bad houses and had succeeded at the majors, but many brokers from the penny houses could not make the transition. They were unable to sell the quality stock and product. "And where were you before Randall, Patchin?"

"Brooklyn College."

"Major, business administration?" Of course.

"And economics."

The waitress placed their breakfast orders on the table unobtrusively and left.

"How long have you been with Rosenkind, then?"

"About a year. I worked . . . you know . . . as a cold caller at Lehman . . . you know . . . six months before that. . . ." Tormenkov smeared thick gobs of butter on his toast and talked with his mouth full of egg. "I wanted to stay there and be a . . . you know . . . broker, but they said to go . . . you know . . . somewhere else and . . . you know . . . build up a book and come back."

"Why did you choose Rosenkind? You probably could have gone to Merrill or Dean Witter or any of the big houses with a training program."

"Well, you know . . . I didn't finish at Brooklyn. I only did two years. They all want college degrees, so . . . you know . . . my uncle knew some guy at Rosenkind through the union. My uncle is a glazier. Anyway, you know . . . he was going to help me get started."

"And?" It was taking Tormenkov forever to get to the point. If he sold stock that way, he would never make it, she thought.

"He did. But he . . . you know . . . I can't stay there anymore." He wiped up the residue of egg on his plate with the remainder of his toast.

"Why? Can you be more specific? If I'm going to represent you to a client firm, Peter, I have to know everything. Do you have any customer complaints against you? Any compliance problems?"

He shook his head. "No. My U4 is clean."

"Then why do you want to leave? They will ask when you interview elsewhere. What will you say?"

"I don't wanna talk about it," he said, finally lifting his eyes from his plate and looking directly at her for the first time. "I can't stay there."

"What do you want to do, then?" Wetzon's sixth sense told her there was something wrong with him. "Unless you want to diversify your business, you won't be happy at a big firm. If you want to stick to stocks and options, you're better off with Bear, Oppenheimer, or Lehman. What is your trailing twelve in gross?"

He frowned.

"I mean," she said patiently, "what is your gross production for the last twelve months?"

Tormenkov stood abruptly. "Would you excuse me for a minute?"

"Of course," she said, feeling a chill. Every time a broker left her in the middle of a meeting these days, she thought of Barry Stark. She felt, irrationally, that he would never come back, or worse, be as dead as Barry was when she went looking for him. Don't be a fool, she scolded herself, Pete Tormenkov had left his coat. Much difference that made. Barry, after all, had left his attaché case.

Come on, Wetzon, old girl. Get out of this. She focused on the skaters, weaving and dipping to music she couldn't hear. The older couple were still waltzing, stopping here and there to execute self-conscious little turns, aware they were attracting an audience. A young girl did a lovely pirouette.

"David, you have to keep an open mind," she heard someone say in a warm but professional tone. "Talk to them and see for yourself. They are getting top-quality work. S and C is referring work to them."

A murmured response came from David. Wetzon turned her head slightly, trying to find the speaker. There were certain code words, phrases, that headhunters used: "keep an open mind," "see for yourself," "test the waters," "explore the possibilities," and her all-time favorite, "you owe it to yourself."

"Don't let someone else make a judgment for you," the female voice continued, persuasively. "You owe it to yourself—"

Bingo, Wetzon thought.

"Okay," the man said. "I'll check it out. How does it work? I've never done this before."

"I know they're looking for an '85 litigator with your kind of credentials, so I'm going to send your resumé to Larry Simpson, the hiring partner—"

"I'm sorry," Peter Tormenkov said, pulling out his chair and sitting.

Wetzon, almost disappointed he'd returned, shifted in her chair and saw that the people whose conversation she was eavesdropping on were the attractive black woman and her younger companion.

"So, Peter Tormenkov," Wetzon said, giving him her full attention again. "I'd like to let you get back to work. Let's talk about what you want to do."

"Well . . . you know . . . I can't do anything . . . you know . . . right now. I got . . . you know . . . this deal I'm working on. . . ." he said, doing a complete about-face. "I'm not supposed to . . . you know . . . talk about it."

"I thought you couldn't stay there? Now you've decided to stay?"

"Yes." Tormenkov didn't look at her.

"Okay. You have to do what you have to do." Why was she sitting here wasting her time talking to him? She was feeling decidedly ungracious.

He checked out the restaurant elaborately, then he pulled his chair closer to hers. "Can you keep . . . you know . . . this confidential?"

"That's part of my job, Peter," she said, smiling through clenched teeth. "I wouldn't be around very long if I didn't keep confidences." She looked at her watch. Eight forty-five. God, what a bore. Time to cut this short. Tormenkov was clearly in some kind of trouble, so he was sure to be unplaceable. She would not earn a fee on this one. Smith had been right.

Tormenkov cupped his hand to his mouth. "I'm working for the FBI."

She snapped up, eyes wide. This was a new one. "What did you say?"

"It's a scam. I was . . . you know . . . contacted by this group . . . you know . . . they work as nurses' aides for these . . . you know . . . senile old people . . ." He glanced around nervously, as if he thought perhaps the skaters beyond the pane of glass could hear him. "I better not say . . . you know . . . anything more. It's a secret. I just called them and they said . . . you know . . . I can't leave . . . I gotta work for them until it's over . . . I could lose my license . . . if I didn't." He was on his feet again, shrugging into his coat. "I thought maybe . . . you know . . . after . . . you could . . ." His voice trailed off.

"Why don't you call me when your work with the FBI is finished," she said. This was a new bit of craziness. Just the thought of the FBI using this twit as an operative made her dizzy. And she'd thought she'd heard everything. Brokers tended to overdramatize the already theatrical situation of brokering. The whole business was built on the grand story, the pitch, the hyperbole, the exaggeration. You couldn't take any of it too seriously.

"Thanks for breakfast," he said. At least he left without you knowing her one last time.

"Whew. Have some breakfast, Wetzon," she murmured, watching Tormenkov weave gracelessly around the busy tables. She dug a strawberry out of her yogurt and poured the remaining coffee from the little pot into her cup. Outside, a teacher was giving a lesson to a slim man in a heavy hand-knit ski sweater, who stood stiffly erect on his skates. The wind blew powdery snow indiscriminately over the hardy few.

She dreaded going back outside, but procrastinating only made it worse. She put her credit card on the bill and the waitress, who had been watching, came and took everything away.

"Hello, excuse me, I couldn't help recognizing—"

Wetzon looked up and into the dark, lively eyes of the woman from the next table. Her probable comrade-in-arms. The woman smiled and put out her hand. "Diantha Anderson," she said.

"Leslie Wetzon." Wetzon took her hand. "I recognized a few familiar phrases here and there myself."

"Lawyers," Diantha Anderson said, smiling, presenting her card. She wound a long lime-green cashmere scarf around her head and neck.

"Stockbrokers," Wetzon said, rising, presenting her own card.

"Can I drop you?" Diantha Anderson said. "My office is in the Chanin Building on Forty-second and Lex."

"No thanks, wrong direction. My office is at Forty-ninth, off Second."

Diantha Anderson nodded. "Well, nice to meet you, Leslie. Let's have a drink sometime and talk shop."

"I'd like that," Wetzon said. "I'll call you."

They shook gloved hands and parted on Fifth Avenue, where Diantha Anderson got into a cab and Wetzon, brushing off the dry snow from her coat, strode off eastward to her office.

11

WETZON LOVED WALKING IN THE SNOW, especially this soft, white powder that floated down, noncommittally dusting her face and clothing and floating elsewhere whenever she stopped to shake herself off.

The wind had quieted somewhat. Traffic was light, as if people had heard the weather report and thought better about coming into the city. Uptown on Park Avenue, the trees on the islands in the middle were already etched in white. Snowflakes stuck to Wetzon's eyelashes, rested on her lips and cheeks, moisturizing, cleansing.

New York is truly beautiful in its first meeting with snow, almost on best behavior. But, as they get acquainted, the good manners of both wear off, and they become dirty, icy, lumpy, and dangerous. Ugly. *Just like people*, Wetzon thought. And then reprimanded herself. *Hey, hey, why so cynical all of a sudden, kiddo?*

"Hi, Kate, hi, Steve," she said aloud, saluting with her right hand, as she passed Hepburn's house, and then Sondheim's standing next to each other on Forty-ninth Street. The street was inordinately quiet. Snow muffled all sounds, and no one was out except the crazies. "Wow!" she said out loud again, luxuriating in the wonderful feeling of privacy that comes only with walking on a New York City street in the midst of a snowstorm. The stillness was positively lush. Spoken words emerged heavy and thick, not straying far from the speaker.

She looked around behind her. Some distance away was the lone figure of a man in a trench coat, carrying an umbrella. As she watched, he proceeded to fold and unfold it in a vain effort to shake off the accumulated snow.

On Second Avenue, traffic moved downtown at a snail's pace as the blanket of snow thickened. Horns blew like foghorns, more in warning than anger, which was usually why New York drivers pressed horns.

She sighed. It would only get worse as the day progressed.

She stamped the snow from her boots and whirled around, careful not to lose her footing, to remove the rest of the snow before she opened the door to their office.

B.B. looked up, phone to his ear, and smiled. With his cropped hair and his athletic build, he looked more like a marine than a headhunter in training.

"I'd like to hold," he said politely but firmly into the telephone. He put his hand over the mouth of the receiver. "Good morning, Wetzon."

"Good morning, B.B.," she said, hanging her coat in the closet, counting under her breath, "three, four—"

"Good morning, Wetzon!" Harold burst out of the little cubbyhole they had built for him in the reception area when B.B. had been hired.

"Five," Wetzon said, turning to Harold. It had taken him less than five seconds to make points with her. He was so busy competing with B.B., he seemed to have forgotten that B.B. had been hired because Harold so wanted to become a full-time recruiter and take on his own candidates.

"Good morning, Harold," she said. "How is it going? Didn't you have someone interviewing with Bache this morning?"

"We had to cancel because of the weather. There's a backup on the Long Island Expressway."

"No reason for today to be any different." There was always some kind of backup on the Long Island Expressway. "Too bad. Try to get that rescheduled as soon as possible. Anyone else? Are you doing any interviews here today?" She opened the door to the office she and Smith shared.

"No," Harold said glumly, retreating to his cubbyhole. "The weather's really killed me."

"My name is Bailey Balaban," B.B. said, "and I work for Smith and Wetzon . . . we do executive search on Wall Street . . ."

Wetzon closed the door behind her. She loved their office. Everything was black and white and red. Black vinyl tiles on the floor, white walls and shelves, white filing cabinets, and red countertops. Her section of the room was a little more cluttered than Smith's, with mementos from her previous life as a Broadway dancer, antique odds and ends she had been collecting from flea markets over the years, two strange-looking aloe plants with long tentacles, and piles of newspapers and magazines and suspect sheets with interviews of potential candidates.

Smith's area was more pristine. Client files, several pictures of her son, Mark, at different ages, and a celebrity map of Connecticut, where Smith had a weekend "retreat," showing where all the special people lived.

"Oh Lord, there you are at last," Smith cried. "What a day, and it's not even ten o'clock! Everyone is canceling." She stood up to give Wetzon a big hug. Smith looked gorgeous—tall, thin, wearing a Donna Karan outfit, a black wool jersey draped midcalf skirt, crimson turtleneck, and long black jacket, and high black leather boots.

"Stunning, as always," Wetzon said, returning the hug. "How many appointments did we have?" She turned away to look over her messages. Hazel had called.

"Appointments? Not appointments. My *party.*"

"Oh now, Smith, tell me, who has canceled?" She didn't much care about Smith's party. She was thinking about Hazel.

"The Crowleys, that's who, and Gordon Haworth."

"Well, the Crowleys live in Wilton, so that was to be expected, Connecticut will be a disaster. And Gordon Haworth, if I remember right, has been in D.C. all week testifying again about cleaning up the industry. Anyone else?"

"Not yet, but I just know there'll be more."

"Really, Smith, that's not too bad. Yesterday you were worried that you'd invited too many people."

"You're right. I won't worry about it until later. How was the interview?"

"Weird. He wants to leave, but he can't leave . . . because—get this—he's working for the FBI—"

"What? What did you say?" For a brief instant Smith forgot all about her party and gave Wetzon her full attention.

"You heard me. Can you believe it? He didn't strike me as being overly bright, either."

"He's probably lying," Smith said. "You know they all lie. I'm sure he has a problem, the usual, compliance, unauthorized trading, whatever."

"Maybe, maybe not. There's some kind of scam going on at L. L. Rosenkind that some brokers are involved in, or so he hinted. I think he was trying to find out if he could go somewhere after—"

"After what?"

"After the investigation is completed."

"Well, if it should happen to be the truth, which I would seriously doubt, I hope you didn't say anything that could get us into trouble," Smith said grimly. "The tarot warned me—"

"Smith, what *are* you talking about?"

"Because if he is working for the FBI, he was probably wearing a wire." She turned her back on Wetzon, disgusted, to answer her private phone. "Hi, sweetie pie," she cooed into the telephone, "how's my Leonola today?" She was talking to Leon Ostrow, their lawyer, and her "best beau," as she sometimes called him.

Wetzon felt foolish. She tried to remember what she had said to Peter Tormenkov. Innocuous stuff, for sure. Smith was so paranoid, Wetzon had learned to discount a great deal of what she said. But sometimes, just sometimes, Smith was right.

She sat down at her desk and dialed the number Hazel had left.

What would Hazel think if Wetzon said "sweetie pie" or

"Hazola" into the phone when Hazel answered? She smothered a laugh. Good work, Wetzon. Don't let her get to you.

"Hello." Hazel's voice was hollow, but determinedly cheerful.

"Hi there, my friend," Wetzon said brightly.

"Oh, Leslie dear. I'm so glad to hear your voice. I'm so sorry about yesterday . . . involving you . . ."

"I don't want to hear any apologies from you, madam," Wetzon said with mock severity. "I'm glad I was there with you."

"It was terrible, Leslie. Poor Peepsie. I know she was frightened and confused by her illness, but to do something like that—"

"Hazel, remember, she was not herself. But right now I want to know about you. When are they letting you out?"

"It couldn't be too soon, Leslie. I really hate hospitals. Your nice friend Sergeant Silvestri is coming back this afternoon to take me home. That was so dear of you."

"Silvestri? Oh yes, of course." What was Silvestri up to? "When did he call you?"

"He didn't. He came over to see me first thing this morning."

"God, Hazel, you must have thought he was a bum. He looked awful."

"Now, Leslie, after all this time you should know that doesn't faze me. I liked him. And I see why you like him," she added.

Wetzon felt herself blush. "What time is he coming back?" she asked, flustered.

"Around three. Don't worry about me, dear. I'm very sad, but I'm fine. I have to make some arrangements for Peepsie . . . they still haven't been able to locate Marion."

"Oh, Hazel, do you have to? Isn't there anyone else?"

"There's only a lawyer, who really didn't know her. Besides, I want to."

"Okay, I have an interview around four, if it's not canceled. The weather is horrendous, in case you haven't noticed. I'm planning to come up and look in on you before I go home."

Wetzon felt the angry glare of Smith's eyes on her as she hung up the phone.

"Wetzon," Smith said wrathfully, "if you are late for my party because of that old biddy, I'll murder you."

12

"I THINK HE LISTENS at our door," Smith said.

"Oh, Smith, you're always so suspicious," Wetzon said.

"I think he goes through our private business papers when we're not here."

"Well then, if you do, and you're worried, let's put everything under lock and key."

"Fahnley went belly up," Harold said, coming right into their inner sanctum. They had warned him repeatedly that he was to knock first because he had a habit of barging in boisterously and interrupting business calls or private discussions.

They were eating their lunch, leaning back in their chairs. Wetzon had her boots off and her stockinged, and socked, feet were up on her desk, as she alternately flexed and pointed her toes. Her fingers were yellow with egg salad, which she was in the process of licking off.

She had opened the blinds covering the French doors, and the great white expanse of their backyard and garden, clumpy with snow, made a postcard view. The snow fell without letup.

"Fahnley went belly up?" Harold loved to use Wall Street slang. "Are you sure they're not merging with another firm? Weren't they bought by that Canadian firm, Crossman Peck?"

"Well yes . . . but they're closing the office entirely in two weeks. Crossman is bringing in its own people."

"Anyone there worth working on?" Smith asked. She bent to pull off her high boots. "If I remember correctly, the average age of their brokers is a hundred and five."

Wetzon laughed. "Not far from wrong. I sort of recall talking to a sweet old man once. He said he didn't think he was a likely candidate, but I could call him anytime."

"I'll get the list." Harold spun around eagerly and left them.

"I wonder if I should order another case of wine," Smith mused. "People drink much more in this kind of weather. Wetzon, what do you think?"

"I think I should be checking the list of Fahnley brokers." She didn't move her feet from her desk. "Is Hank Brownell still the manager?"

"Oh yes, Hank Brownell," Smith intoned, doing her W. C. Fields imitation. "Fired from Merrill, hired by Hutton, fired by Hutton, hired by Witter, fired by Witter, hired by Fahnley."

"Hot for Xenia Smith," Wetzon added impishly.

"A little man," Smith drawled. "In every sense of the word."

"Smith, you didn't," Wetzon said, feet hitting the floor, shocked.

"Oh come on, Wetzon, grow up. This is the real world. Besides, sweetie pie, you know me better than that."

"Whew. You really had me going for a minute." Wetzon examined the beginning of a run in her hose. "He was such a pig. But since you know him better than I do, don't you think you should call him?"

"Where would we place him? No, it's a waste of time." Smith crumpled up the paper from her roast beef sandwich and threw it away. "Want some of my cookies? They're chocolate chip from Mrs. Fields."

"No thanks. I'll stick to my apple." Wetzon closed her eyes and frowned. "I think his name was Maurice . . . Maurice . . . Sanderson."

"Who?"

"The old broker from Fahnley. Maybe one of our clients would take him." She opened the file drawer next to her desk and rifled through the *S*'s. "Here he is. Maurice Sanderson, age sixty-nine, as of last year." She skimmed her notes. "Well, he does a small but steady business. Writes big tickets."

"Wetzon, I'm telling you, it's a waste of time." Smith finished the last cookie and dusted the crumbs from her hands and lap.

"I'll talk to Maurice and you start calling around."

"Oh, Wetzon, honestly." Smith threw up her hands. "You'll be the death of me."

"Hi, Maurice, this is Wetzon here, remember me, of Smith and Wetzon, your favorite headhunter."

"Well, it's certainly nice to hear from you right now, Ms. Wetzon." Maurice Sanderson's voice was formal and pleasant. He did not reveal concern in his tone, only in his words. "I think I may be in need of your services."

After Wetzon quickly updated Maurice's figures and background information, she passed it on to Smith, who groaned. "Wetzon, this is humiliating. I can't do it. How will it look to our clients? Let the old geezer retire."

"Consider it a good deed that'll get you into heaven," Wetzon said, "and us a small fee. Come on, Smith. Someone like Maurice can't retire. This is his whole life. He loves it, and it's all he knows after forty years in this business."

"Too old to bother with."

"Try."

The reactions came quickly:

". . . *We don't want brokers that old.*"

". . . *How old? Seventy? You've got to be kidding.*"

". . . *Smith, have you lost your senses?*"

". . . *We don't want these old guys. They take up space and cost us money. How much business does he have? Forget it.*"

". . . *I'll see him if you want me to, but I won't hire him.*"

After five phone calls, Smith swung around in her chair and announced, "I'm giving it up. I agree with them."

"Try Curtis Evans. They clear through the Bear. Tell them he writes big tickets. Please, Smith."

"Does he?"

"What?"

"Write big tickets."

"Of course. Would I lie to you?"

"Humpf."

Twenty minutes later Wetzon called Maurice Sanderson with

an appointment for the following day with Bob Curtis of Curtis Evans.

"There now, doesn't that make you feel saintly, Smith?" Wetzon teased, standing, looking out at their snow-blanketed garden.

"No."

"It's still snowing. You can't even see sky up there. It feels as if we're in an igloo." She shivered and closed the blinds.

"I'm going home to get everything ready," Smith said. "Please try to come early. I need you. You know I count on you."

"Come on, Smith, don't do that. Won't Leon be there? And Mark, of course."

"Not good enough." Smith hugged her again. "I need my little friend."

"I have Kevin De Haven to see around four, and I want to look in on Hazel. Then I'll go home and change and come to you."

"You always put other people before me, even strangers come before me," Smith said, sulking. "I am your dear and trusted friend." She sat down to pull on her boots.

Sometimes you are, Wetzon thought, watching her. *You are certainly my most demanding friend.* But she said, "Not fair, Smith. You know when you really need me, I'm there."

"Humpf. And who are you bringing to my table tonight? Silvestri, perhaps?"

"No, he's working," Wetzon lied, not daring to look at Smith.

"Of course, I don't have to tell you that disgusting pervert is not welcome in my house," Smith said.

"Smith." Wetzon's voice held a warning. "I will not let you talk about Carlos like that, and if you continue to, you will not see me at your party either. And by the way, when he calls me, I expect you to give me the message. He's my oldest friend."

"It's just a wee bit like having Typhoid Mary as your friend, don't you think?" Smith stamped out and slammed the door, leaving Wetzon furious and unfulfilled. The war between Smith and Carlos had been initiated by Smith, although Carlos was a willing participant. They—Smith in particular—now lavished guerrilla attacks on each other and Wetzon was always caught in the cross fire.

She sat down at her desk again and wrote Maurice Sanderson's appointment with Curtis Evans in her calendar.

It was dismaying that the firms did not want to hire senior brokers unless they had huge books and a very active business, which was not very likely. As a broker aged he usually stopped increasing his client base; he expended less energy. His client base aged with him. To the firms, it was all a matter of money. Real estate was costly, overhead was an expensive burden, space was at a premium. Management felt it was more efficient to give desks to younger brokers who were in the process of building a client base. By law, Smith and Wetzon were not permitted to ask a candidate's age, but their clients wanted to know, so they did, circuitously. "What college did you go to, Joe? Oh really? What year did you graduate?" It wasn't difficult, given that information, to guess the candidate's age.

The older broker had become a dinosaur. He usually did a clean business, did not hustle his clients, pitched only stocks he was comfortable selling, like the Dow stocks, and generally acted like the family doctor, building close relationships with clients. But more and more, the larger firms gave lip service to service, pressuring younger brokers to build up gross production, sell, sell, sell. The young brokers swiftly saw the emphasis was on selling the firm's product whether it was good for the client or not.

Wetzon had observed the brokerage business change radically over the last three years. The large firms pushed the broker to sell in-house products, and the young brokers generally did because the tickets for these products were bigger. The older brokers stuck to the stock and bond business, taking seriously the old name for stockbroker, "customer's man."

She respected these older brokers. They had dignity and class and longevity. They considered what they did a profession. They were not in it for the big killing.

Odd, how she kept coming back to aging. Hazel, Peepsie Cunningham, Maurice Sanderson, even the scam Peter Tormenkov had alluded to. Teddy Lanzman's TV series on the elderly. Wait a minute. She looked at her watch. Three-thirty. The phones had gotten very quiet. She opened the door to the reception area.

"What's going on?" she asked.

"Everyone's leaving early because of the storm," B.B. said. "Tell you what—"

Harold came out of his cubbyhole and stood in the doorway.

"Tell you what," Wetzon said, "we'll wait till the Market closes at four and shut down ourselves. Just tell me when you're leaving." She went back into her office and closed the door.

In her address book she found Teddy Lanzman's phone number.

The intercom buzzed.

"Howie Minton on 9–0," B.B. said.

She punched the first extension. "Hi, Howie, you should be on your way home. I hear the Island is a mess."

"I'm outa here. Just wanted to know what you thought of Pete Tormenkov."

"Well, Howie . . ." Wetzon paused. These situations were problematic from an ethical point of view. Howie had recommended Peter, but what Peter had told her was confidential. "I don't know what to tell you. He doesn't seem ready to move anywhere."

"Wetzon, my friend, don't tell me he told you that crap—excuse me—about the FBI?"

"What are you saying, Howie?" she asked cautiously.

"You're a good lady, Wetzon, and I think of you as my good friend, so you can level with me. I can tell by what you're not saying that the schmuck told you." Howie had lost his usual unctuousness. "Pete's working with a bunch of lowlifes. There's no FBI, but there could be, and he's got to get out of here before the shit hits the fan, excuse me again."

"Howie, whatever the truth is, he may have a compliance problem—"

"Wetzon, believe me, would I lie to you? Peter's okay. Let me talk to him and straighten him out. Then you can call him on

Monday—and be persuasive—as I know you can. Say you'll do it for me so I can get the hell out of here tonight."

"Okay, Howie, I'll try. Hope the trip home isn't too bad."

"Be well, Wetzon."

She sat there thinking, playing with her pen, doodling geometrics. Howie was probably right. On the other hand, nothing that she had seen happen on Wall Street was too farfetched. Anything could be true.

She picked up the phone and dialed.

"This is Channel Eight, serving the Empire City in the Empire State."

"Ted Lanzman, please."

"Who's calling?"

"Leslie Wetzon."

"Hold on a moment, please."

As she listened to canned Bach, Wetzon checked off the phone calls she had made from her daily list. Those she had not gotten to, she wrote on her list for Monday. After she spoke with Teddy, she'd call Kevin De Haven, who would probably want to cancel his four o'clock appointment, which was fine with her.

"Well, well," Teddy Lanzman said. "This is a real treat, stranger. How are you?"

"Great, Teddy. I know how you are because I see you on the box all the time—"

"Better than that. I'm getting my own half hour, producing and writing features. And you just caught me. I'm on my way to Detroit in a few minutes, if they're still flying out of Kennedy tonight. Picking up an award for feature broadcasting for my series on the kids in welfare hotels."

"That's wonderful, Teddy, congratulations. I saw most of it. It was heartrending."

"You know, Wetzi, although we don't see each other much, I count you as one of my real friends. Did you ever get my message when that broker was murdered?"

"Yes, I did, and I'm sorry I never got back to you. So many crazy things were happening—"

"It's okay. I understand. I just wanted you to know if you needed me, I was there."

"I knew that, Teddy, and I love you for it. But right now I'm calling you about something I've come across that might be of interest to you."

"Oh yeah?" She could hear the change in his voice.

"The series you're doing on the aged . . . I've heard something about a scam against the elderly, using nurses' aides . . . I guess this doesn't make much sense—"

"No, no, I'm hearing you. I want to hear more, but I've got to get out of here now, or I'll miss my plane."

"I don't know much more than that—"

"Have an early dinner with me on Monday," Teddy said. "Six-thirty, seven. You may be able to fill in the blanks on something I came across in my research."

"But—"

"No 'buts.' Pick me up at the studio on Monday. I'll leave your name downstairs with security."

"We're leaving now, Wetzon," Harold said as she put down the phone slowly, brooding.

"Okay, good night. See you Monday. Have a safe ride home."

She dialed Kevin De Haven's number. It rang and rang and rang.

"Kevin De Haven's office," a very familiar male voice said at last.

"Kevin, please."

"He's gone for the day. Wetzon? Is that you?"

Damn. Tom Hasher, a broker she talked to from time to time, was in that office. "Tom? What are you doing still there in this blizzard?"

"I live only about six blocks from here, so it's no problem. How've you been, Wetzon?"

"Great. How about you?" She had never been able to tempt him out of Merrill, but sometimes he called her with a tip about a fellow broker who was unhappy.

"Real well. Listen," he said in a low voice, "you've got a good one with Kevin. He's going to have to move."

"Oh?" That sounded bad.

"Don't worry. No real problems. Just a style of business that doesn't blend well here. He does a lot with hedge funds."

"Thanks for the tip, Tom."

She hung up and walked to the French doors, parting the blinds slightly. The windows were steamy. She cleaned off a spot and peered out. A deep grayness covered the sky and the mounds of snow on the ground reflected grays and pale yellows from the bleary lights in the buildings above.

The window quickly steamed up again, and she drew a big heart and wrote "Wetzon loves Silvestri" with an end of an arrow going in one side and the point coming out the other. A feeling of panic hit her as she realized what she'd done unconsciously, and, embarrassed, she rubbed her fist on the pane, obliterating the words.

13

WHEN SHE CAME OUT on the street, the ceiling of the sky was so low she felt if she stood on tiptoes, she could actually touch it. It didn't seem as cold as it had been. A sulfurous aura hung over everything.

The snow was still falling but it was lighter now. Still, at least a foot had fallen already and, blown by the wind, the drifts were deep. Supers or handymen from the surrounding brownstones had made an attempt to shovel the sidewalks, and she could hear the sounds of metal shovels on cement, but walking was difficult. To get the bus uptown on Third Avenue would be a major expedition.

Dim lights made the turn from First Avenue and crawled along Forty-ninth Street toward her. The car pulled up to the house next door. It was a cab, and Wetzon, joyously, got to the door as the passenger disembarked.

"Thank God," she said to the driver after she'd climbed in. "And thank you." The driver, a heavy black woman, with a Mets cap jammed low on her forehead, nodded. "Where to? I'm not going to Brooklyn, Queens, or the Bronx." She wore red leather gloves with the fingertips cut off.

Wetzon gave her Hazel's address on East Ninety-second Street.

Traffic was bumper to bumper, creeping up Third Avenue. It took over twenty minutes just to make the turn from Forty-ninth Street, normally a three-minute trip. The side streets were choked with snow, in dire need of snowplows.

Outside Hazel's apartment building, Wetzon hesitantly asked the driver if she would wait and take her through the Park to Eighty-sixth Street near Amsterdam. The meter already read almost nine dollars.

"Okay," the woman said pleasantly. "How about I turn off my clock, and we settle on twenty bucks for the works?"

"Terrific." Wetzon opened the door and promptly stepped into a snowdrift.

The driver leaned out. "But make it fast. I don't want to get stuck here for the night." She flicked her flag up, turning off the meter.

Hazel answered her door, wearing a quilted pink robe blooming with pink blossoms and a ruffled pink cap. She was holding a pair of chopsticks.

"Leslie dear, you shouldn't have come. It's a terrible night," Hazel said. Her eyes were bright and two round rosy spots burned on her cheeks. She looked exceedingly pleased with herself.

"Hazel, what are you up to?"

"Your Silvestri bought me shrimp fried rice after we talked with Sergeant O'Melvany, and then he brought me home. He knew just what would make me happy."

"He's not my Silvestri," Wetzon said automatically, thinking that Hazel looked like a turn-of-the-century little girl.

"Well, let's work on it," Hazel said cheerfully. "But right now I want you to go home, and I'm going to get into bed with my shrimp fried rice and Woody Allen."

"Woody Allen?"

"*Sleeper* is on television tonight."

Moments later, satisfied that Hazel was considerably improved, Wetzon was back in the cab, and they were heading for the West Side.

"Is the transverse open?" Wetzon asked, rubbing the vapor from the window, straining to see outside. She remembered the night that Barry Stark was murdered, when she and Silvestri were cut off on the transverse and Silvestri had been shot.

The driver grunted, and the cab turned into the Eighty-sixth Street transverse through Central Park that connected the East Side and the West Side of Manhattan. Here, the winding, sloping road, which in some places became an underpass, could be treacherously slippery. The driver was bent over the steering wheel, wiping moisture off the windshield with her gloved hand. The windshield wipers moved back and forth dully and not too effectively. Twice, when traffic stalled, she got out to clean the wipers.

When they arrived at her apartment building, Wetzon handed the woman a twenty-dollar bill. "Thank you for the safe ride," she said. "You were great."

The woman touched the visor of her Mets cap. The eyes that met Wetzon's for an instant were shrewd. "My name is Judy Blue, and if you ever need a cab for hire, call me." She proffered a blue business card, which Wetzon slipped into her pocket.

"Thank you, Judy Blue."

She was singing, "'The snow is snowing, the wind is blowing . . .'" softly under her breath as she searched for her key, stamping her boots free of snow on her doormat. It didn't take much to make her feel good. Hazel looking much better, Silvestri . . .

Her door swung open just as she was about to put the key in the lock.

"Boy, am I glad to see you, little one," Carlos said, grabbing her and giving her a bear hug.

She dropped her carryall, and they danced around her foyer together in an impromptu Fred and Ginger number, narrowly missing the white bench and a brass footrest. They ended on the floor, tangled in Wetzon's black coat, laughing.

"You are so crazy," she scolded. "What am I going to do with you."

"Stick with me, and I promise you, we'll stay young forever," Carlos said, very seriously.

"You will always be young, my man," Wetzon said. "But I, *au contraire*, am aging rapidly."

She stood and helped him to his feet. He took her coat and hung it in the hall closet.

"What's that I smell?" she asked, leaning against the wall to pull off her boots. She put them on the mat outside her door. "Hot cocoa?"

"'Tis that. Made it for you from scratch. Although you didn't have the grace to return my call."

"Oh yum," she said, licking her lips and following him into the kitchen. "God, how I've missed you, Carlos."

"Well, I can see that," Carlos said sternly. "You ought to be ashamed of yourself—"

She raised an eyebrow at him.

"You are the world's worst housekeeper. Dust everywhere, no food in the fridge except bagels, the cupboards bare except for tuna fish, pasta, and chocolate." He stopped. She was grinning at him. "Well, at least *try* to look ashamed."

She aped ashamed, hanging her head. Then they looked at each other and laughed.

"You are incorrigible," he said, checking the pot of chocolate heating on the stove.

"So are you," she responded. "Let us not forget, you deserted me. I relied on you to be my housekeeper, and then you ran back to the stage—"

"My art was calling me," Carlos intoned dramatically, hand to his brow.

"I'll bet. Art who?"

He stirred the hot chocolate and poured it into two mugs. "As a matter of fact," he said very casually, "Arthur Margolies, Esquire."

"Carlos, you devil. There's a new love in your life. An esquire, no less."

Carlos merely smiled and looked smug. "Come on," she pleaded. "Tell."

"Yes, a lawyer, and with a big law firm. Very handsome. The truth is, 'I'm in love again,'" he sang.

"'I'm in love again,'" Wetzon sang in response, her arm around his slim waist.

"'We're in love again . . . good news,'" they harmonized, and clicked mugs, toasting each other with hot chocolate.

"I think it's only right," she said, smiling at him. She loved Carlos. They were like two peas in a pod, one light, one dark. They had danced together in musicals, on Broadway, in stock, industrials, taken classes together, cried together over men and careers, and had both left the theater about the same time. Or as they viewed it, the theater had left them. It just wasn't the same anymore. It wasn't fun after Gower Champion, their mentor, had died.

"This is great cocoa," she said, licking the mustache of chocolate off her lips. "And I'm so glad to see you." She checked her watch. "I have to change and get to Smith's party."

"You are not going out on a night like this?" Carlos was incredulous. "And to that—"

"I have to. Smith would never forgive me."

"You don't have to—you know that."

"Carlos, don't butt in. Smith has been so nervous about this party. I couldn't do it to her."

"She would do it to you."

"I don't believe that. I can't. She's my partner, and she's my friend. She's just a little eccentric—"

"Ha!" Carlos said. "There's the understatement of the year." He poured the rest of the cocoa into their mugs, and they went into the living room and curled up on her sofa.

"It's going to be hard for you to get back down to the Village," she said. "Do you want to spend the night?" She didn't know if Silvestri would be coming now or not. ". . . um . . . Silvestri might come by later." She was trying to be blasé, but it didn't work on Carlos.

"Well, well, my darling," Carlos said, pleased. "You don't think I'd horn in on *that*."

"But—"

He waved her faltering protestations aside. "Besides, Arthur Margolies, Esquire, lives on West End Avenue and Ninetieth Street." He smiled a very self-satisfied smile.

"How convenient, you little devil," Wetzon said, kicking him playfully with her toes.

"Listen, my darling, I think it's only right that the two of us, good clean celibates, have found companions in our old age." He grinned at her lasciviously.

"To safe sex," she said solemnly, holding her mug out.

"Safe sex," he said, touching her mug with his. They looked at each other for a long moment.

"How's the show?" she asked.

"The show is great. It's like having an annuity," Carlos said almost apologetically. "I go in and take out the improvements—you know how these gypsies are." He chuckled. "They keep trying to make the show better."

"Now how would I know a thing like that?" Wetzon laughed, knowing that not so long ago, she and Carlos had been guilty of doing that very thing.

"And Marshall's reading material, looking for another show for us to do."

"Why Marshall? How about you, solo?"

"Oh, Les, you know I don't have that kind of ambition. Just give me a little love, a little money, good friends, good health, happy days."

"Carlos," she said. "I just love you to pieces." She pounced on him and kissed him.

Then she told him about Hazel and Peepsie Cunningham.

"Poor Hazel," Carlos said. "No—wrong—good, decent, wonderful Hazel. I'll call her tomorrow. Maybe we can get her to tell us the real origin of Peepsie."

"There's just one thing I left out," Wetzon said.

"Uh oh. I knew it was too simple. Let's have it."

"Well, there's this shoe I found—"

"What shoe?"

"I found a small dark blue Gucci walking shoe like the one Peepsie Cunningham was wearing, in the gutter near the building when Hazel and I got into the cab."

"And?"

"And I picked it up and put it in my bag."

Carlos groaned loudly.

"I'm sure it was Peepsie Cunningham's."

"So?"

"So the newspaper said she was wearing bedroom slippers when she jumped . . . or fell."

"Or fell?" Carlos flung himself backward on the sofa. "My girl, you have done it again. I don't believe it. You've walked yourself right into a murder."

14

IT WASN'T EASY GETTING BACK across town again to Smith's apartment, although it seemed to have finally stopped snowing. The sky had risen, like a dome, and here and there, stars sparkled.

Wetzon had put on high rubber riding boots, tucked her shoes into a plastic bag and the bag into one of the deep pockets of her coat. There were no cabs in sight, as Edward, the night doorman, had morosely prophesied when she gave him the envelope with the key for Silvestri.

So when she heard the *whack, whack* of the snow chains and

saw the lights of the crosstown bus coming toward her, she took it to Second Avenue. Although she had a transfer, there were no buses coming down Second Avenue, so she trudged the nine blocks to Smith's apartment on Seventy-seventh Street.

It was a beautiful night. All the same, she would rather have stayed home, spent the evening catching up with Carlos, but she knew that Smith would have felt betrayed if she didn't come to her party. It was murder trying to stay in the middle while Carlos and Smith brutalized each other.

Murder. It was murder. What had happened to Peepsie Cunningham was murder.

She rang the bell to Smith's apartment.

Smith flung open the door. "Well, Wetzon, at long last," she cried. She was very hyper, possibly a little drunk. "Where have you been?"

"There's this little storm outside, Smith," Wetzon began. She bent to pull off her boots, leaving them with all the other storm equipment piled outside of Smith's door. Over Smith's shoulder she could see a glittering array of people, dressed to the nines.

"Don't stand there, sweetie pie, get right in here." Smith literally dragged her through the congestion to her bedroom, where a coatrack had been set up. It was crowded with fur coats.

"Hi, Wetzon," Mark said, helping her off with her coat. He was wearing a smart gray flannel suit, looking very grown-up for thirteen.

Wetzon kissed him on the cheek. They were now the same height. "Hey," she said. "You're catching up with me fast, kiddo." She rubbed the red spot on his cheek from her lipstick.

"How do you like my baby," Smith said proudly, her arm around her son's shoulders. "Isn't he gorgeous?"

Mark looked up at his mother in total adoration. Smith patted him lovingly on the backside. "Go see if anyone needs anything, baby."

Smith was statuesque in a scarlet sequinned sweater with a deep scoop in front and back and black silk pants. She had a matching scarlet sequinned band around her curly dark hair.

"You look positively exotic, Smith," Wetzon said. She slipped on her shoes. "Here am I in my basic black wool jersey . . ."

"Plain and fancy," Smith said, teasing.

"I think I remember that show," Wetzon said.

"What show? What are you talking about, Wetzon?"

"Never mind, Smith. You wouldn't understand," Wetzon said, suddenly weary. She was always forgetting that Smith's interests were in the business of making money, not in the arts. And somewhere, buried in that teasing, "plain and fancy," Carlos would have detected a put-down. She looked up and caught Smith eyeing her as if she could read her thoughts.

"Come on," Smith said, her arm around Wetzon. "I want you to meet everybody. I know you'll love them. And don't be so sensitive." Almost languidly, she pulled herself up even taller than usual. She was wearing very high heels and stood head and shoulders over Wetzon.

"Attention, attention, I want everybody to meet my dearest friend and partner, Leslie Wetzon," Smith announced to the crowded, noisy room. There was an odd hush, everyone turned to look at Smith and Wetzon, then someone applauded, slowly.

"Leon, dearest, get Wetzon a drink," Smith said.

"Beer, Leon," Wetzon said, "and quickly." She felt as if she were on exhibition. What a strange reaction. When she looked back out over the living room, she realized that everyone was quite drunk.

"Isn't she beautiful tonight?" Leon handed her a glass and poured a Heineken into it. He was wearing a black cashmere blazer and a yellow foulard tie and managed to look taller and more awkward than ever. His glasses sat at the tip of his nose, and his gray wooly hair clumped Einstein-like around his ears.

"She's always beautiful, Leon," Wetzon said, watching Smith move happily about the crowded room.

"What do you think, Wetzon," he whispered loudly. "I asked her to marry me. Did she tell you?" He gestured with the half-empty Heineken bottle.

"Yes," Wetzon said. She took the bottle from him.

"Did she say what she's going to do?" he asked eagerly, leaning close to her.

"No, Leon." She backed away from him. He looked so crestfallen that she added, honestly, "But she seemed very pleased."

Uneasily, Wetzon wondered how it would be if their lawyer was the husband of one of them. It didn't seem right. Maybe, if Smith were to marry Leon, they should have an uninvolved lawyer.

"Leon, sweetie, come over here," Smith called, and Leon was off at a lope.

Wetzon sighed. She saw an empty spot on the sofa across the room and headed for it, squeezing through the glamorous people. All the women were dressed in beads and sequins, the men in dark suits. One of these elegant ladies spilled a drink on Smith's carpet and then delicately rubbed it into the nap with the toe of her silver sandal. The not-quite beautiful people, once removed.

"Well, if it isn't Wetzon-Wetzon, girl headhunter." The gruff voice was a challenge; a hand closed over her arm and held her.

She turned and stared up at the suntanned face, the piercing blue eyes of Jake Donahue. "Jake Donahue, in case you don't remember," he said.

"How could I forget Jake Donahue?" she said, shaken, in spite of the fact that it had been some time since she'd seen him, and then under horrible circumstances. She stared down at his hand circling her arm, and back at him. He removed his hand. She still found him somehow repelling and attractive, at the same time. "You look very well, Jake. When did you get out?"

"Tsk, tsk, Wetzon-Wetzon, nastiness doesn't become you."

Jake Donahue had gotten a three-month sentence by dumping on everyone else in the repos scandal that had wrecked his firm. Three months and a light fine of a hundred thousand dollars, and exile from Wall Street for three years. What amounted to a slap on the wrist, just as Wetzon had predicted. He had destroyed a respected old-line brokerage firm, caused at least three murders, swindled thousands of investors, and he'd gotten the kind of punishment that amounted to "There, there, you bad boy. Now don't let us catch you doing it again."

"You were lucky, Jake."

"I had a smart Jewish lawyer." Leon was Jake's lawyer, and Leon was definitely smart, if a little smarmy. "It was a little like being at a spa, actually. Played tennis, swam . . ."

He was laughing at her, the bastard. She felt angry and helpless crammed in with all these people.

"I'd love to stay and talk with you about old times, Wetzon-Wetzon," Jake said, "but I am being paged by another beautiful lady." He nodded and smiled at a large, horsey-looking woman, a wall of black sequins wearing huge diamond earrings. "Barbara Carstairs, Leslie Wetzon."

At least he had stopped referring to her sneeringly as Wetzon-Wetzon.

The two women showed their teeth—one could not call it smiling—and Wetzon squeezed past Jake Donahue, who squeezed back a little too intimately, and headed again for the sofa.

When she broke out of the crowd, there was a woman sitting in the spot she had earmarked.

"Oh, I've taken your spot," the woman said with a warm smile. "Here, I'll slide over. You're so tiny, we can both fit."

Gratefully, Wetzon set her glass and the Heineken bottle she was still carrying on the coffee table and sat down.

"I'm Arleen Grossman," the woman said with a broad smile. "And I know you are Leslie Wetzon, dear Xenia's partner."

Arleen Grossman was a buxom lady, perhaps in her late forties, with sleek, straight black hair rolled back around her face in a thirties' style. Her hair was so black, Wetzon thought, that it was probably dyed, and the severity of her hairdo was modified by tiny spit curls around her forehead and cheeks. Behind the thin black frames of her glasses were friendly, intelligent amber eyes. A small chin floated on a second chin beneath a fluffy face, somewhat reminiscent of Elizabeth Taylor prior to her stay at the Betty Ford Clinic.

Wetzon sensed an almost coconspirator message from her, a

we're-in-this-together kind of thing. She felt herself being drawn in like a big fish on a line. It was a weird feeling. "I'm afraid you're one up on me. How do you know Xenia?"

"Ah well, it's a long story. We met through Leon."

Wetzon took a swallow of beer and looked at her neighbor with curiosity. She was feeling just a trifle light-headed.

A maid in a black dress with white cuffs, a little ruffled apron, and a little ruffle on her hair came by with a large tray of boiled shrimp and a dipping sauce. There were plates on the tray, and Arleen Grossman filled a heaping plate of shrimp and sauce and set it on the coffee table in front of them.

"For both of us," she said.

"What do you do, Arleen?" Wetzon asked, settling back with the shrimp and beer.

"I don't drink," Arleen Grossman said. "That's why I'm sitting here away from the madding crowd." She crossed her legs with difficulty. She was wearing a tight skirt which accentuated her heavy thighs. "I run a small consulting business," she said. "Xenia has been just wonderful about advice and planning. Of course, you know she's also one of my backers."

"Oh," Wetzon said. "You must be the business Xenia is so impressed with, that was in the black in such a short time."

"Yes," Arleen Grossman said modestly. "We are very proud of our record. In fact, we have just received an award from the City—"

"Arleen, I think we ought to be going." A stocky man with very black hair combed straight back on his bullet-shaped head stood on the other side of the coffee table.

"John dear, this is Leslie Wetzon, Xenia's partner," Arleen said. "Wetzon, that's what everyone calls you, no?" She didn't wait for Wetzon to respond. "This is my brother, Johnny."

Wetzon reached over and shook Johnny Grossman's hand.

"Excuse me for a minute, please." Arleen Grossman struggled to her feet, a shapely, if plump, woman in a tight black silk evening suit. She spoke quietly with her brother for a moment while he nodded, then, smiling, she came back to Wetzon. Johnny Grossman was swallowed up by the crowd in the living room. "A buffet dinner is being served in the dining room," the maid said, moving around the room.

"Well, I guess it doesn't pay to sit down again," Arleen said. "Come, Wetzon, let's you and I fill our plates and chat. I feel we're going to be great friends, don't you?"

She held her hand out to Wetzon, who took it and stood up, dizzy. She hadn't realized how hungry she was. Arleen held onto her hand, drawing her forward. As the crowd in the living room began to thin, Wetzon caught a glimpse of the bulky figure of John Grossman, wearing a hat and overcoat, leaving Smith's apartment.

"I want to hear all about you," Arleen persisted. "Xenia is so fond of you, and we're so fond of Xenia. She's been like a daughter to me." She locked arms with Wetzon.

How odd, Wetzon thought, that Smith hadn't mentioned Arleen Grossman to her, but maybe not so odd. Smith was very proprietary about her friends. She didn't like sharing.

"Oh, there you are." Smith bore down on them. "Well, I see you two have met." She eyed their locked arms with a faint air of resentment. "I'd forgotten what a fast worker you are, Wetzon."

"Dear, dear Xenia." Arleen Grossman smiled benevolently up at Smith. "I'm so pleased circumstances have brought us together. I feel it is so right, don't you?" Her voice and her words seemed to have a soothing effect on Smith, who, as Wetzon watched in total amazement, almost began to purr. Smith took Arleen's hand and touched it to her cheek. "Arleen, you are such a love," Smith said, beaming. "I am honored by your friendship."

"Mom," Mark said, breaking the spell. "Don't you want them to put the chicken out too?"

"What?" Smith looked startled. "Oh yes, sweetie, we'll go tell them together."

"Such a wonderful person, a wonderful mother, too," Arleen Grossman said. "I do so admire what she's made of her life."

She turned to Wetzon. At that moment, one of Smith's sloshed guests, a large white-haired gentleman in a dark blue suit, slipped on a spot of spilled drink on the highly polished floor near the entrance to the dining room and, spinning out of control, fell toward Arleen and Wetzon.

"Look out," Wetzon shouted, but she needn't have, because Arleen Grossman sprang with great agility and actually caught the man before he hit the floor and was helping him regain his balance. It all happened in seconds, and no one seemed to think much about it, except for Wetzon, who looked at the motherly woman beside her with a little awe.

"Now then," Arleen Grossman said, brushing her hands together. "Let's fill our plates and *talk*."

15

SHE MIGHT NEVER HAVE gotten home if Arleen Grossman hadn't insisted on driving her in the Grossmans' snow-covered limousine. Arleen had elicited a promise that Wetzon would call her on Monday and schedule a dinner. She hadn't wanted to because of Smith's reaction, but Arleen had persisted.

They had no chauffeur for some reason—perhaps the weather—and it was John Grossman, whose whole demeanor gave off surly overtones, who was driving the limousine. Grunting, it seemed, was his primary means of communication. A very strange man, Wetzon decided. Totally unlike his sister. Something ugly about him. And thugly.

The city was at a standstill. Snow had drifted to boulder level in some spots, just plain high elsewhere. She remembered only one other blizzard since she had lived in New York. Broadway had been whited out. The show had not gone on—transportation had been crippled. Good thing this was a weekend. One could take the time to see the beauty. By Monday, the city would have dug itself out and be back in the business of making money; the beautiful white fairyland landscape would turn into a gray, soot-splattered arena.

On the other hand, this looked like the real thing. A blizzard of blizzards. It was still snowing. Sanitation trucks moved slowly, lights glazing through the screen of white, sanding the roadways. They were apparently not stemming the tide because the snow was piling up in horrific amounts. Here and there was slight evidence of sidewalk shoveling, but fresh snow covered those areas with dispatch.

The outside door to her building was locked, which meant the night doorman had not gotten there. At least the super had made sure it was locked. Some of the tenants always complained because they didn't like to carry the extra keys. And sometimes someone would just leave the door unlocked. She wondered as she fumbled for her key if Silvestri had been able to get in, or if he had just gone home in disgust to his own bed.

She dusted herself off on her doormat, pulled her boots off, and opened her door. There was an envelope on the threshold. She picked it up. Her chandelier was on, dimmed. She heard voices arguing in the bedroom—gunshots. The television. Her skin tingled. She tiptoed into her bedroom. Silvestri was asleep on her bed and the television was blaring.

She hung up her coat on the shower rod and scrubbed her face clean of makeup, brushed out her hair and braided it into one long braid. Methodically, she laid out her clothes in the living room and slipped into a flannel nightgown. Where had she put that envelope? Probably some communication from the co-op board.

They were shooting at each other again in the bedroom. She could tell by the music it was almost over. Her face, flushed and happy, stared back at her from her bathroom mirror. What are you dawdling for, she asked the pink face with the glowing gray eyes.

Turning off the television, she saw his gun and holster on the floor half under the bed. Her father had owned a rifle and a shotgun and she had even used the rifle once. . . .

She went around to the other side of the bed; something

crunched under her bare feet. The envelope. She picked it up and tilted it to the pale light coming through the window. Nothing was written on it. She opened it up and took out an index card. On the card, printed in crooked, childish letters, were the words: KEEP YOUR NOSE OUT OF WHAT DOES NOT CONCERN YOU.

The card slipped from her hand. What was that about? It had to be a crank message from someone in her building. Maybe the woman who swam at the health club next door and dripped water all over the elevator floor when she came back. Wetzon had complained about it. She wouldn't think about it tonight. It was too stupid. Sometimes living in a co-op was a nuisance.

She lay down beside Silvestri. It was cold. She would have to wake him to get under the quilt. The room was imbued with that pale light, a reflection from the whiteness of the snow and the low clouds. She hadn't bothered to close the blinds. The snow continued to fall.

Silvestri looked young and innocent in sleep. She touched his face. He had shaved. She rolled over and hugged him, putting her face into the hollow between his chest and shoulder, breathing him.

He tensed, waking, then relaxed and held her. "Les . . . about time."

"We're having a blizzard. Almost didn't make it home. City will be shut down tomorrow."

"Good," he mumbled, pulling her closer.

"You have to go anywhere tomorrow?" she asked, folding herself against him.

"We're going to talk to O'Melvany, that's all—"

"Mmmm," she murmured into his ear. "Get under the covers, Sergeant, please, sir." She rolled away and slipped under the covers. The sheets were icy cold. He stood and pulled off his sweater and jeans and socks and came back to her as she held the covers open.

She touched the soft hair on his arms and ran her hands over the bulge of his biceps. "Thanks for taking care of Hazel." She loved him. Should she tell him about the note?

"Nice lady." He wrapped his arms around her.

"Silvestri—"

"Les." His voice breathed warm in her ear.

"What?"

"Shut up."

16

EDDIE O'MELVANY WAS a chain-smoker. The long fingers on his right hand were stained yellow. His narrow mustache was also stained an orange-yellow, or was that its natural color? A glass ashtray on his desk was a forest of butts. He was well over six feet tall and lanky, like a basketball player—St. John's as it turned out. Silvestri told her he had played center for the mid-sixties championship team.

He wore a very well cut dark brown suit with an argyle cashmere vest. Standing with one long leg on the seat of his chair, he was complaining to someone on the phone, all the while taking short drags on a cigarette.

"Half, for crissakes. Half didn't show. So who gets the shit? Yeah well, a lot of good it does me—" He hung up. "Goddamn snow," he said, picking at a thread on his trousers before putting his foot back on the floor. "Jeezus." He groaned and rubbed the small of his back.

In the squad room phones rang incessantly, and one lone detective ran from desk to desk, answering them.

The room was a cubicle similar to Silvestri's but even smaller. There was only one desk. The area had been painted recently. Same old standard gray. Someone had neglected to remove the Wet Paint sign from the ledge near Wetzon's chair.

"So what else you got for me, Silvestri?"

"Leslie Wetzon, Eddie O'Melvany." Silvestri was leaning against the doorjamb, hands in his pockets, face impassive.

O'Melvany put two fingers to his brow and saluted her politely. The action made him grimace and he kneaded his back again. "Sorry. Tough day. My back's out." He walked to the door, limping, and leaned past Silvestri. "Kaplan?" There was no response. "Christalmighty," he said, "who's here to take a statement?" Still no response. "Hey, Alvaro, will you help me out here?"

Alvaro, a swarthy woman with the build of a weight lifter compacted in blue denim overalls, yelled, "Can't, Sarge. We have a possible ten-thirty-one at the Guggenheim. There's nobody else, so I'm on it." She grabbed an overcoat and left, bumping a uniformed officer as he entered the squad room and dived for one of the ringing phones.

"Shit," O'Melvany said. He came back to his desk and rolled some paper into his typewriter. "Shit," he said again, trying to straighten the paper.

Wetzon heard a small, strangling noise and looked around in time to catch Silvestri making no effort to hide a smirk.

O'Melvany, using the hunt-and-peck system of typing, took a brief statement from Wetzon. He stopped typing. "That matches up with what Miss Osborn told us." He lit a cigarette while tamping out another. "Don't see any reason to think we have a homicide here."

"Oh, did you find Ida?" Wetzon asked, exasperated. "And what about the Gucci shoe?" She looked around at Silvestri, who was studying the nails on his left hand intently.

"No." O'Melvany yanked the paper out of the typewriter without releasing the rollers. Wetzon winced. "We have not found this Ida—"

"But it's so simple." She looked at Silvestri. He was smirking again, damn him. She turned back to O'Melvany, who had a tortured look on his face. "Just contact the agency she worked for."

"From what the lawyer told us, there was no agency. She was an independent contractor. A check was mailed to her every week—"

"I don't understand." Wetzon was trying hard not to get angry. She looked at Silvestri again. He was studying something on the ceiling. There was nothing on the ceiling. He was going to be no help. "If a check was mailed to her, then there's an address—"

O'Melvany looked daggers at Silvestri. "Let me explain something, Miss Wetzon. We're dealing with Brighton Beach here. You heard of Brighton Beach?" He didn't give her a chance to answer. "It's a nest of Russian immigrants, some legal, some not. Real old-fashioned professionals, murderers, thieves, chiselers, and cons, black marketeers, from Moscow, Kiev, Leningrad, and Odessa live there among the rest of the Russians. It's called Little Odessa. There are thousands of them there. When someone wants to get lost there, they get lost. You get my meaning?"

Wetzon nodded. "But what about the address?"

"Mail drop. Candy store. Tsminsky's Ice Cream Shoppe. Owner does it for a fee for a lot of people. Conveniently can't remember anything helpful. Brick wall. They may be Jews, but they're still Russians. Built-in paranoia. Being Russian Jews, double paranoia."

"What about the shoe?"

"Would be something if there was another one like it in the old lady's closet, but there wasn't."

"But—"

"Come on, Les." Silvestri's hand was on her shoulder.

"Look, Miss Wetzon. We did our job." O'Melvany looked and sounded bored. She felt frustrated and angry. Talk about a brick wall. "We went over the place thoroughly." He leaned across the desk at her. His breath was rank from cigarettes. "Did it myself. If there was another one like it, we would have found it, believe me. The old girl was in bad shape. Her lawyer even says so. She didn't know what she was doing. She probably didn't even know it was winter and went out on the terrace and *bam*."

"I just know it was Peepsie's shoe," Wetzon said, more to herself than anyone else.

Silvestri's beeper went off.

O'Melvany shrugged and stood up, handing her the typed statement. "You know how much junk was on the streets that day because of the wind? Could have come from anywhere. Every woman in this neighborhood wears Gucci shoes. And you ought to see what the sanitation guys pick up on a normal day in this part of town. It would blow your mind."

Silvestri went into the squad room and made a phone call while Wetzon read the statement. It was full of cross-outs and typos, but it was accurate. She signed it.

"Look, Miss Wetzon." O'Melvany rubbed his back gingerly. "Let's wait till autopsy results come in before we make a final assessment. How's that?"

"Okay." She reached into her bag and pulled out her card case. "This is where you can reach me." Under her business card was Sonya Mosholu's card. "Sergeant, maybe this lady can help your back. I use her when my back goes out. She's a psychomotor therapist." O'Melvany was working hard at being polite. She could see that. He did not take the second card, so Wetzon dropped it on his desk.

"Let me tell you, we haven't given up on finding this Ida. I've talked to one of the detectives from the Six-O, they cover Brighton Beach, and he's keeping his eyes open for her."

Silvestri reappeared. She could see he had something on his mind that he wasn't going to share. "We finished? Good." He shook hands with O'Melvany, slapped his shoulder. "You want in on the game, call me."

"Count on it." O'Melvany smiled. He had a nice smile. It changed his face entirely. Lines like spiderwebs framed his eyes.

"I *know* she was murdered," Wetzon declared, kicking a big clump of snow on the street.

"Except for the Russian woman, you've got nothing, Les." The snow, which had stopped before their meeting with O'Melvany, now was drifting down in thick fine powder in such slow motion it seemed to be standing still. Silvestri's red parka was white with snow. Snowflakes stuck to his dark lashes and brows. Metal shovels scraped on sidewalks, hitting concrete or firmly packed snow.

Silvestri was brushing the snow from the windshield of his precious black Toyota. Wetzon picked some snow from a waist-high drift. She formed one ball, and then another and another, cradling them in her arm.

"You coming?" He turned, blinking the snow from his eyes and she pelted him with snowballs. They stared at each other for a second, and she screamed and took off slipping and sliding down the treacherous streets, dodging drifts and snow-covered garbage cans and two little snowmen with sleds. She was laughing so hard at the shock on his face when she hit him with the snowballs that she had to slow her pace.

She had almost made it to the corner of Second Avenue when he tackled her, bringing her down. They rolled into a drift.

"Mock me, will you?" he said, straddling her, washing her face with snow as she struggled.

"Do you need help, young lady?" An elderly man in a tweed overcoat and tan muffler, wearing an Irish knit rain hat, loomed over them. He nudged Silvestri with his cane.

"Oh, sir, how kind—" Wetzon began.

Silvestri labored to his feet and balanced one foot on Wetzon's stomach. He pulled out his badge and I.D. "Sergeant Silvestri," he said. "Seventeenth Precinct. Just apprehending a culprit."

"Dear me." The old man shook his head. "Tsk, tsk, she looks like such a nice girl." He backed away.

"Yes, doesn't she. You can never tell these days," Silvestri said, pressing down as she squirmed.

"Silvestri, you bastard, let me up. Don't believe him, sir."

The old man gave Silvestri an approving nod and toddled on his way.

"Come on up, culprit." Silvestri pulled her to her feet, exploding with laughter.

"I suppose you think you're funny," she said, trying to brush herself off. "It's downright humiliating the way you cops treat innocent people."

"Come on," he said, still laughing. "I have to report in."

"Oh no."

"Oh yes. I'll drop you."

"You just did." Her foot touched ice under snow and she

slipped, clutching at his arm. Her mind was already clicking away in gear. She would call Teddy Lanzman and—

"No more theories, right?" Silvestri interrupted her thoughts as they drove back to her apartment building.

"What?"

"About the Cunningham suicide."

She gave him a brilliant smile. "Oh, that. I've forgotten all about it. I was thinking about calling Carlos for dinner."

He looked at her, suspicion all over his face.

"Silvestri, don't look at me like that. How can you doubt *moi*?" She leaned over and kissed him and got out of the car.

She was wondering if she could get Teddy to go to Brighton Beach with her.

17

PEELING OFF THE PARAPHERNALIA of winter and snow in New York City took forever. The boots, the wool knee socks, the leg warmers, the layers of clothing, coat, beret, heavy scarf, extra bulky sweater, fleece-lined sweats. It was endless. Gradually, the small, lithe body of the dancer emerged. Under all she wore a leotard jumpsuit in her favorite shade, violet.

She shivered. The apartment was cold. She hopped into the dining room, pulling her leg warmers back on. She had co-opted part of her dining room for a workout area when she had first moved into the apartment. She slipped the towel from the barre, rolled it, and hung it around her neck. She'd been looking forward to this. She found it easier to think when she worked out. She could separate her mind in two parts. The intense concentration of her workout, and whatever was troubling her. At the moment, what was troubling her was Peepsie Cunningham's murder.

That poor old woman had *not* committed suicide.

Ida was the key, wasn't she?

She put a Chopin étude into her tape deck. The little light on her answering machine was blinking. Damn. She pressed Playback and waited. The tape spun and spun. Either a long message or several short ones.

Beep. "Where are you? I need to talk to you." It was Smith; her voice was petulant. Wetzon sighed.

Beep. "Guess what, dancing lady? Never got out. Took me five hours to get back to the city last night." Teddy Lanzman's voice was scratchy. "How about dinner tonight instead of tomorrow?" He sneezed. "If I live that long." He left his number.

Beep. "This is Charlotte Killer, Ms. Wetzon. If you have a complaint about me, say it to my face—if you have the guts."

Wetzon, wide-eyed, stepped back from her machine. The tone of the voice was nasty. She stopped the tape and replayed the message. Had she heard right? Charlotte Killer? Was that what the woman had said her name was? She caught the last two digits of Teddy's phone number, then "This is Charlotte Kellner . . ." She played the rest of the message. Killer, indeed. Wetzon, what's with your head? You're getting carried away with this crime stuff.

One of the purposes of the co-op board was to act as a buffer between tenants. If a complaint was made by one tenant about another, it was to be treated confidentially. At least it was supposed to be.

She had almost forgotten the crudely written threat. Obviously from the loony Charlotte Killer in 12C. She laughed. Screw it and screw her.

She waited. There appeared to be at least one more message. She heard a click, then a disconnect. Probably Smith again.

Beep. "Wetzon, this is Arleen Grossman. I hope you don't mind my calling you at home, but I did so enjoy meeting you, and I hope you'll have dinner with me on Monday evening." She left two numbers. Home and office. Strange woman, this Arleen

Grossman. She didn't believe in giving a body a chance to breathe.

There were no more messages. Wetzon reset the machine and turned it off.

She called Hazel.

"No, I don't need anything, Leslie dear. Of course, I'm very upset about Peepsie . . ."

Wetzon hesitated, then reported her interview with O'Melvany. "Leslie, I don't know . . ." Something else seemed to be troubling Hazel.

"What?"

"Her lawyer says she wanted to be cremated." Hazel stopped. "I know this sounds foolish, but Peepsie was the only one of us who *didn't* want to be cremated. She was so afraid of fire."

"She could have changed her mind. When is the funeral?" She began to do slow relevés as she spoke.

"Well, with the snow and all . . . and no one in her family is left except Marion. I'm the only one in New York. D.C. is closed down, Hartford as well. We decided we would have a memorial luncheon after the weather settles down."

"Good idea." She peered outside. It was still snowing. "Call me if you need anything. Otherwise, I'll talk to you tomorrow." Wetzon hung up. Eventually she would have to tell Hazel her suspicions, but for now . . . She moved to the barre and went into first position.

The phone rang. She let it ring as she finished the movement and answered the phone just before the answering machine clicked on.

"Wetzon, you are home and you haven't called me back," Smith accused.

"Smith, I just got in. Honest. I was over at the Nineteenth Precinct making a statement about Peepsie Cunningham—"

"Who?" Smith was piqued. Her voice was half an octave higher than usual. "Oh, that old lady who killed herself?"

"Smith, you sound very upset. Is something wrong?"

"You didn't call me about my party—"

"I left the apartment too early this morning to call you. I didn't want to wake you. But it was a lovely party."

"You know how I count on you," Smith said. "I don't think you care about me half as much as I care about you."

Jesus Christ, Wetzon thought. She stopped doing her relevés. "What's going on, Smith?"

"You know how we always dish after my parties."

"Okay, let's dish," Wetzon said. She shook out her feet and went back to doing relevés. "I was surprised to see Jake Donahue there, looking as if he just got back from a vacation in the Caribbean."

"He did look wonderful, didn't he? He was with Melissa Diamantidou, the widow of the shipping fortune. Did you see that ring . . ."

Wetzon tuned out. She looked at her watch. She was hungry. It was after one o'clock. She had to call Teddy and get dinner confirmed. She wanted, needed, her workout.

". . . liked you very much."

"I'm sorry, who?"

"Wetzon, you're not listening to me."

"I am . . . I am." She twisted to the right, stretching her back.

"I was talking about Arleen Grossman."

"Oh yes. Nice lady." She changed hands on the telephone and twisted to the left. Should she tell Smith about the dinner invitation for Monday? "Weird brother, though."

"John? Oh, I suppose so. I think he's a little retarded, and dear Arleen lets him do things for her."

"Retarded? He hadn't seemed retarded to me."

Smith lowered her voice as if she were not alone. "Wetzon, I'd really appreciate it if you would not get too chummy with Arleen. After all, she's *my* friend."

And I saw her first? "Don't worry," Wetzon said at once. "I really don't think—"

"I'm not worried. What a strange thing to say, Wetzon. Why should I worry?" Smith spoke in a rush of words. "After all, you and Arleen have so little in common."

Christ, she was patronizing. "Smith, I have lunch on the stove. I really have to go—"

"Wait, sweetie pie, don't hang up." Smith's voice slipped back into her old mode. "I wanted to tell you what I read in the cards for you this morning."

Wetzon rolled her hips, doing a grind exercise, without the bump. "Yes?" Smith and those damn cards.

"Are you going out anywhere today, sugar?"

"You're kidding! In this weather?" Wetzon looked out her windows. All one could see was white. "I'd be crazy. And where would I go? Nothing's running, nothing's open."

Smith was severe. "I do not kid where the cards are concerned. You know that. The cards say you will meet a dark man today and he will carry death with him."

18

THE ONLY AREAS THAT WERE manageable on foot were the streets, which had been, and continued to be, snowplowed and sanded by giant white tanks, and this was where she walked now. Wetzon had agreed to meet Teddy Lanzman at Ernie's on Broadway and Seventy-fifth Street, a noisy yuppie restaurant.

Wetzon, wrapped to the nines, a scarf over her trusty beret and another around her neck, felt as if she were Nanook of the North. She carried an umbrella from which she had to shake snow off every few yards. Thankfully, the strong northwest wind seemed to have abated.

Only two people were in line for cash at the Citibank cash machines at Eighty-sixth and Broadway. Usually the line overflowed out into the street. Otherwise, no cars and few pedestrians, only good old crazy Leslie Wetzon.

She and Teddy Lanzman went way back. They had been

mildly attracted to each other at one time, but nothing physical had ever happened between them. She was either a no-man woman or a one-man woman and she didn't want to obfuscate what she had with Silvestri.

The top of her umbrella dipped inward. She swung it around and down, opening and closing it rapidly to shake off the snow. Two skiers gave her muffled greetings as they passed her on the right, cross-country skiing down Broadway. They were so covered it was hard to tell if they were male or female or one of each.

She felt a weird sensation that if she kept walking she'd enter a different time zone. Turn of the century, perhaps. Except for the streetlights and infrequent snowplows, the city was cast in that eerie yellow-gray light. Under the streetlamp near Zabar's she shook out her umbrella again. In the window was a huge hammered copper stockpot, almost a cauldron. A hand-scrawled sign on white cardboard in black ink said, "This pot was custom-made for a celebrity couple, but they split up. Their loss is your gain." She laughed. Now who would that be? The West Side was full of celebrity couples. For that matter, New York was full of celebrity couples in various stages of coupling and uncoupling.

By the time she arrived at Ernie's, it had stopped snowing. Teddy was at the bar talking to three men in their forties wearing *ABC Sports* sweatshirts, as if he knew them well. The bartender, a beefy, brawler type with a Caribbean suntan, was drinking a beer and sharing a laugh with them.

Near the wide front window facing Broadway an elderly couple were intently winding pasta up on spoons. On the other side of the bar four young women were shrieking with laughter while a fifth was telling a story. Except for those few diners and the hostess and two waiters, the cavernous place was empty.

Teddy waved at her as she unwound the scarf from her head and pulled off the beret. His eyes were bright and she could tell he'd had a few drinks. "Here's my girl," he said to the *ABC Sports* men, loud enough for her to hear. He put some bills down on the bar and came toward her. Tall and striking, he was wearing a cream-colored Aran sweater over a blue-checked shirt. The light color of the sweater drew attention to his high cheekbones, large, strong nose with its narrow bridge, square chin, short wavy black hair, and dark brown skin. The combination of Caucasian features and brown tones made his skin look stained like a fine piece of mahogany. In the right costume he could have passed for an Arab prince, which was a laugh because Teddy Lanzman was Jewish.

"You are a sight for sore eyes," he said, "if you'll forgive the cliché." He bent and kissed her lightly on the mouth. "You are indeed." He looked at her as if he could see how she felt about Silvestri and she blushed. "I don't know, must be the weather or the light in here, but you just turned a hot-pink before my eyes."

They were seated at a table near the five women, who turned to stare as Teddy passed. He was a stunner, that was for sure, and now he was a local celebrity. Wetzon had forgotten what it was like to be with him.

"So who's the man?" Teddy asked. He ordered two Heinekens when their waiter put a basket of rolls on the table. "You're still Heineken, aren't you?" he asked after the fact.

She nodded. "How do you know there's a man?"

"Oh come on, it's obvious. I hope he's not a stockbroker."

"He's not." She pulled a salt stick from the basket and broke it in pieces.

"Won't talk, huh?"

She shook her head. "Not yet. Too new."

"Well, I'm with someone, too. And you two have something in common."

"And what would that be?"

"Not telling till you tell."

They ordered pasta with sun-dried tomatoes and fried zucchini, and Wetzon thought, *there's something different about him. What is it?*

He was staring at her. "God, Wetzi, nothing changes. We don't see each other, but the chemistry's still there. We can just pick up where we left off."

"I know. I was thinking that just now." She buttered the salt stick pieces and put one in her mouth. It was crisp and the salt melted on her tongue. "I wanted to ask you about this feature you're doing on the elderly."

"Yeah. It's really something when you get into it. It's an Emmy maker. I'm getting off on it."

"Did you do the research yourself?"

"Most of it. I have an assistant who did some. Why?"

"I know what it is," she said. "You're not smoking."

He laughed and slapped the tablecloth. "What a memory. My lady doesn't like it. Stopped cold turkey two months ago."

"Fantastic," she said. "Smart lady. Sorry for the digression." She told him about Peepsie Cunningham and Ida.

"You don't think it was suicide?" His voice seemed loud. He looked around. A black man in a dark blue parka came into the restaurant and sat at the bar.

She shook her head. Their dinners arrived, steaming. "Peepsie was terrified about something—"

"Listen, I've seen Alzheimer people. I've talked to them. Some of them are docile, some are hostile, and some are scared—really scared—they don't know what's happening to them."

"I think it may have been that, but I'm sure there was more."

"Okay." He spun some fettuccini on his fork and ate it. "Delicious," he said, rolling every syllable.

"She has—*had*—tons of money. Enough to have a home care person, who might not have been too trustworthy. The problem is, she didn't make much sense."

"Not enough to go on. I'd listen to what's-his-face— O'Melvany, what a name. Wait till the autopsy results are in—" She was disappointed and couldn't hide it. "Look, Wetzi, I'm reporting on the best and the worst home care situations. Lately there's been a rash of beatings, robberies, murders, even. These people are helpless. No families, or families that don't give a damn. They're housebound, bedbound." He shook his head. "I never want to get old. Let me die while I still have it all."

"It doesn't seem to matter, does it, whether they have money or not? Helpless is helpless."

"Sometimes." He answered a salute from the three *ABC*

Sports boozers at the bar. They were heaving on their coats. "Actually, the rich, like your Peepsie Cunningham, have other problems. Where is their money? How is it being invested? What about jewelry and other valuables? You're right about that. They can be ripped off, too." He dipped a piece of roll into the tomato sauce. "But money helps. You can't believe the poverty some of these people live in. A lot are in public housing, living on less than five thousand a year. No one wants to know about them. They've outlived friends, family. They smell, they're ugly, they whine, or they cry. Those that can get around are frail, on walkers, some can't hear, can't see well. Jesus, it's depressing. Everyone would like them to disappear."

She told him about Hazel, about her theory about having young friends. "Hazel is definitely not depressing."

"She sounds great. Do you think she'd do an interview?"

"I'll bet she'd love it. I'll introduce you. She's so full of life, she always makes me feel good." But Wetzon frowned. Something teased at her memory.

The waiter cleared the table and rattled off desserts, including a sinfully decadent chocolate cake, which Wetzon ordered, along with brewed decaf. Teddy ordered bread pudding and regular coffee.

Two young men came in, boisterous from the snow, stamping their boots on the floor. The bartender seemed to know them. The black man at the bar moved down a couple of stools. He looked at his watch. He'd been waiting a long time for someone who was delayed or not coming.

"So how's the headhunting business?" Teddy's eyes had followed hers to the bar and then back. The waiter returned with their coffee and desserts and a soup plate heaping with whipped cream.

"Business is good. Fine, in fact. The stock market goes up; the stock market goes down. It doesn't seem to matter. A lot of people are making huge amounts of money. It's ludicrous, isn't it, that most of the people I deal with have trouble living on a hundred thou a year?"

"Ah, the perils of capitalism," he said, grinning, putting sugar

in his coffee. "What about the insider-trading scams? Has that af-
fected your business?"

"Not really. My area is retail sales, brokers who sell stocks
and bonds and products to the individual investor. Less can go
wrong there, but that doesn't mean crooked things don't happen.
Brokers churn accounts, trade a lot for commission dollars. Clients who don't know better think it's okay if the market is bull
and they're making money, but the minute the market turns
down, all those fat commission charges and losses bring lawsuits.
I just had a broker rejected by a firm because he had chalked up
thirty thousand dollars' worth of commissions on a one-hundred-
and-fifty-thousand-dollar account of a retired schoolteacher."

"Jesus!" Teddy spooned whipped cream from the bowl,
dousing his bread pudding. "I just can't see you in that cruddy
business, Wetzi."

"Listen, Teddy." She pulled out of her buried mental files of
useless information what she had been trying to recall. "I interviewed a broker the other day who is in some kind of trouble. He
said there was a scam at his firm, using the elderly."

"Oh yeah? I'd like to hear more about that. What firm?
What's the scam?"

"I can't tell you the firm or the broker's name without breaking confidentiality, Teddy. And he wouldn't tell me the scam."

Teddy groaned. "Christ, Wetzi, don't do that to me. I'm a reporter, and that's a tease."

She was contrite. "It's very involved. He told me he was
working for the FBI and that's as far as it went."

"Can you get him to talk to me?"

"I'll try."

He dug into his shirt pocket for a small piece of paper from
a two-by-three-inch pad. "Why don't you just give me his name
and I'll call him. He won't have to know where it came from."

"I can't do that, Teddy, but I'll call him on Monday and see
if I can get you together." She felt terrible. "Don't be mad at me,
please. I want to ask you for a favor."

"Quid pro quo?" Teddy said, pressing her.

She shook her head. "No commitment right now. First listen to what I want."

"Okay." He put up his hands, surrendering.

"Are you working tomorrow?"

"I have the *Community Affairs Show* at nine-thirty. It's live."

"And after that?"

"I'm all yours. What'll you have?"

"I want you to come to Brighton Beach with me—"

The table shook with his sudden movement. Coffee cups overflowed coffee into their saucers. A fork fell to the floor. The black man at the bar looked up and caught Wetzon's eyes briefly, then looked away.

"Oh, baby, you are crazy. You figure you're going to look for Ida, the vanished home care person. Isn't that like looking for the proverbial needle in the haystack?"

"Maybe. Will you come with me?"

"I don't know." He frowned. She could see his mind working. "Possibly . . . If I can get a company car. I'm not going all the way out there by subway and neither are you. We're in the middle of a blizzard. Trains will be sporadic because they're aboveground out there. The tracks will be a mess."

"Okay, okay, you don't have to say another word. Do you think you can get a car?"

"Of course. I'll pick you up in front of your building at eleven tomorrow, and we'll do Little Odessa. I don't think we'll get anywhere. These Russians stick together." He grinned at her again. "But it'll give me plenty of time to work you over and get that name out of you."

The name, she thought.

The dense chocolate of her cake was cloying, much too sweet. She pushed her plate away, slightly nauseated. The name of the broker was Russian. Tormenkov. Peter Tormenkov.

19

SHE WAS WALKING ON BROADWAY in the strange yellow light as
the snow continued to fall. Her skirts were getting soaked. She
pulled them up to protect them. Her boots were wet through.
Storefronts had totally disappeared. Snow was piled in mountains
on either side of the street. The pungent smell of burning wood
pervaded the air. She was all alone.

Behind her she heard the old familiar snort of horses and saw
a sleigh coming toward her, bearing down fast, bells jangling. The
high drifts allowed her nowhere to run.

She felt sheer cold terror. Her legs wouldn't move.

She heard the driver shout. Was it a warning or was he urging
the horses on?

She ran then, skidding on the narrow, icy path, barely staying
ahead. She could feel the hot breath of the horses. She was losing, losing. She looked back and saw the driver's face. It was John
Grossman, wearing a high fur hat, whipping the horses on.

"Get her, get her!" a woman screamed. Smith's voice. "She's
stealing my friend!"

Wetzon, heart sinking, threw herself into a snowbank just as
the sleigh would have run her down. The snow welcomed her
and she sank into a cocoon of warmth.

"See, my dearest darling person, I told you not to be afraid."
Ida, in a green velvet cloak, ropes of fur around her white-blonde
hair, was tucking Wetzon into the snow bed.

"No, no, you fool!" Arleen Grossman pushed Ida away and
threw back the snow quilt.

Wetzon's feet were so cold. She saw she was wearing her violet bodysuit and blue Gucci shoes over bare feet. She was shivering uncontrollably.

"Here now, what's going on?" Leon said, descending from
the sleigh. "We can't have this. You have to drive more carefully,

my man." He snapped his fingers and Silvestri appeared, dressed like a Keystone Kop. "Arrest this man at once for reckless driving." Leon pointed to John Grossman.

"Silvestri, you look ridiculous," Wetzon said. "What are you dressed up for?"

"Your dream," he said over his shoulder as he dragged John Grossman away in chains.

"I don't know how you keep getting into these messes, Wetzon," Smith called from the sleigh. She was dressed like Anna Karenina, in a fur-trimmed velvet cloak. "Leon, handle this at once."

"Just get this settled," Wetzon shouted angrily, from the snowbank. "I'm freezing."

Leon snapped his fingers again and Teddy Lanzman—no it wasn't Teddy Lanzman, it was the black man in the parka from the bar at Ernie's—threw a huge fur lap robe over Wetzon's head and picked her up in a fireman's carry, throwing her over his shoulder.

She couldn't breathe, she lost a shoe.

Leon said, "Be sure she keeps her nose out of what doesn't concern her."

She was choking. She fought with the fur wrap. She fought with the covers; sleigh bells jangled and jangled.

I'm dreaming, she thought, trying to beat down her panic. *Silvestri was trying to tell me that.* She stopped fighting.

Sleigh bells were ringing.

I will *wake up,* she thought.

The telephone was ringing.

The telephone was ringing. She must have forgotten to reset her answering machine after she'd checked her messages last night. She groped for the phone and said a muffled hello. A dial tone. Whoever it was had hung up.

Her clock said nine. Late for her. What a horrible dream.

It was freezing cold in her apartment. She stretched under the quilt, flexing and pointing her toes. Had it stopped snowing, she wondered. She sat up and put on her terry cloth robe. The bedroom radiator began to sputter. The room had the peculiar smell of radiator heat when it first starts to come up in a cold radiator.

When she opened the blinds, the sun was out. The blizzard was over. The rooftops of the brownstones below were piled high with clean white snow, reflecting sunlight like thousands of diamond specks. A city bus crawled down Columbus Avenue. Snowplows could be heard. Shovels scraped sidewalks. Finally, voices.

Her phone rang.

She left the blinds open and sat on her bed to answer it. "Hello."

"Hi," Silvestri said. "Where'd you spend the night?"

"What do you mean, where'd I spend the night?" She was indignant. "Right here. Where do you think I spent the night? Where did *you* spend the night? Do you want to call me back and start over?"

"Uh oh." He sounded embarrassed. "I guess I deserved that."

"You did. If you hadn't been so impatient and stayed on the phone for another couple of rings, I would have answered it."

"Good morning, Les." Why did she always feel he was making fun of her? Even that nice little moment of jealousy had an ironic undertone.

"Good morning, Silvestri," she said somberly. "Where are you?"

"Manhattan North. Homicide."

"Sexy." She curled her bare toes.

"You think so?"

She heard puzzlement behind his words. "I'm sorry. 'Sexy' means intriguingly complicated in financialese."

"Does a sexy deal take the place of the real thing?"

"I don't know. I never thought of that. Maybe it does." She wondered, can one get an orgasm from a particularly exciting transaction? Well, it was certainly possible. Was Wall Street an orgasmic setting? Oh yes. She cleared her throat. "Well, is it?"

"Is what?"

"Is it an intriguingly complicated case?"

"Yep. Diplomat murdered. It'll be in the papers."

"Oh yeah? State Department, FBI, and stuff?"

"And stuff."

"Mmmm. Then I don't get to see you for a while?"

"How about tonight?"

"What time?"

"Whatsamatter, you have plans?" Was he making fun of her or was he covering up for himself?

"I'm going to spend the afternoon with Teddy Lanzman." She didn't dare tell him where. He'd kill her for getting involved.

"The guy from Channel Eight?"

"The same. He's working on a feature he wants to get my opinion on. What time do you think you'll get here?"

"Don't know. Don't even know for sure I can." She could feel his antennae go out. Damn.

"Well, if I'm not back, you can let yourself in," she said casually.

"Les?"

"What?"

"Is there anything you want to tell me?" He had such a psychic sense. And he was picking something up from her. Could he read her voice as well as her face?

"I'm not a suspect, Silvestri. Don't treat me like one."

"Les—"

"See you later." She hung up, ran into the dining room, and put her answering machine on.

After a steaming shower, she dressed carefully in long silk thermal underwear, then ski pants and two bulky sweaters, one a turtleneck. She made a pot of coffee and skimmed the Sunday *New York Times*, not really looking at anything but the "Arts & Leisure" section.

She called Hazel.

"I'm reading *Lonesome Dove*," Hazel informed her, "so talk fast because I want to get right back to it. Robert Duvall was good, but I keep seeing Dale Robertson as Gus. He's so sexy."

Now that was the right use for sexy, wasn't it, Wetzon thought. "A great book for a snowed-in weekend." Wetzon paused. "Hazel,

I wanted to ask you . . . Do you remember Ida's last name? Did you ever know it?"

"No, I don't think so, Leslie dear. Why?"

"I'm going for a ride to Brighton Beach today with my friend Teddy Lanzman, the reporter on Channel Eight. I thought I might see if I can find her. Oh, and Teddy would like to interview you for his show."

"I'd like that, Leslie," Hazel said, and then quickly cut through to the important matter. "But do you think it's wise for you to get involved with this? The police are looking for Ida."

"They're not having much luck. But it's not important, Hazel. I just thought if you remembered her name . . . Sometimes people like that are afraid of the police."

"Come to think of it," Hazel said slowly, "I believe that detective . . . O'Melvany . . . had her last name. He'd gotten it from Peepsie's lawyer."

"You didn't hear it?"

"I may have, but I don't remember. Leslie, please be careful."

"I'll be with Teddy. I'll be fine. Don't worry."

Wetzon called the Nineteenth Precinct and asked for O'Melvany.

"O'Melvany."

"Hello, this is Leslie Wetzon," she said cheerfully. "How's your back today?" He was silent. She could feel him trying to figure out who she was. "Silvestri," she prompted.

"Oh yes, Miss Wetzon." He swung right into his prepared litany. "No results from the autopsy. Too soon. Back's the same,

20

TEDDY HAD APPROPRIATED an aging, undistinguished red Land Rover with large blotches of rust where dents had chipped paint. Clumsy chains were stretched across the giant tires.

"I'm glad there's no Channel Eight insignia," Wetzon said, grabbing hold of his hand and heaving herself up onto the high seat. He was wearing sunglasses and a dark brown fleece-lined coat.

"Hey, what do you expect? I'm a pro." He gunned the motor and they moved off toward West End Avenue. The Rover's tires bit into the snow with an almost human gusto. "I don't go into enemy territory all decked out in my colors unless I think it can work for me. Check the floor in the back—under the canvas."

She got on her knees and looked down behind her seat. Under the canvas was a white-and-blue polyurethane sign for the roof of the car. Channel 8, Everything Great in the Tri-State. "You're too much."

"Listen, you can't be too careful. We're an undercover operation, at least for now."

She sat back. "Damn, it's cold. Don't you have the heater on?"

"It's on but it's not working great." He made a left on West End Avenue and headed downtown. The street had been freshly plowed, salted, and sanded. Sunlight dazzled from the snow. Wetzon pulled down the sun visor. It didn't do much good. She took her sunglasses from the black leather backpack.

"So what do you think?" Teddy flipped his sun visor down.

"About what, specifically?"

Everywhere people were digging out. By tomorrow the virgin white would be turning gray and gritty. The decaying process usually took two to three days, picking up speed as the city came back to life and its principal goal, the making of money.

"I mean the scam. This broker—what did you say his name was?"

"I didn't, Teddy." She hoped he wasn't going to keep this up.

"Okay, okay. Where do you want to start?" Teddy eased his foot off the gas and moved left to avoid a creeping city bus. He wiped moisture from the windshield with a paper towel from a roll he had lying on the seat between them. "Better fasten your seat belt." He was excited, she could tell, but trying to cover it.

"You mean in Brighton Beach?" She pulled the worn nylon belt across her body and fastened it.

"No, in Miami Beach." He let the Rover roll to a stop for a red light, barely touching the brake, and gave her a dimpled grin, full of sexual charm, managing to look a bit like a black Tom Selleck.

"Ha, ha, very funny." She rubbed her hands together in her lined suede gloves. She was cold. "I think we should start at that candy store I told you about, the one that's a mail drop." She thumbed through her notes, which she had shoved into the backpack. "Let's see, Tsminsky's Ice Cream Shoppe, with a double *p* and an *e*, no less. How American can you get?" She stuffed her notes back. "And I have Ida's last name. Got it from O'Melvany."

Teddy raised his leather-gloved hand to his dark brow. "I always said you have a good nose. Nice going." They were making fairly good time. Few cars and fewer cabs had ventured out this morning. He drove across a wide-open Fourteenth Street onto Hudson. "I'm going to stick with the main roads." A delivery van moving in a crawl slowed them. "What's the name?" Hudson Street was lumpy and treacherous with snow-covered ice lumps and drifts. "I've been doing some nosing around myself. Asking questions of my Wall Street connections."

"Have you come up with anything? An FBI investigation?"

"Not much more than the general insider-trading stuff. There is something going on with one New York firm, though. Don't know what."

"A member firm?"

"What do you mean, member firm?" He was peering out his front window, trying to figure what the delivery van was doing.

"I mean a New York Stock Exchange firm. If they are members of the NYSE, they're called member firms."

"I don't know. My source said the D.A.'s office is cooperating with an investigation. That's all I could get. Could be anything."

Wetzon hesitated. "Teddy, I want you to promise me something."

"What?" He pulled out to pass the delivery van and the Rover skidded an instant and then made traction. "Jesus." He pulled back to the right around and in front of the van.

"I'm going to tell you something that's privileged and off-the-record . . . for the time being."

Teddy winked at her. "The name of the broker?"

"This is off-the-record, Teddy." Her voice was stern. She had to pool her information with him. Right now, she could use a partner. He might be able to help her prove that Peepsie was murdered and she might be able to get him a major news break above and beyond the feature on the elderly in New York that he was working on.

"Okay," he said, taking his eyes from the road and meeting hers. It was like a handshake. "I'm with you."

"Ida's last name is the same as the name of the broker who told me about the scam. Tormenkov."

"Jesus H. Christ, lady!" His eyes opened wide and he pounded the steering wheel gleefully, as he made a left onto Canal Street and pulled over to the corner. He put on the hand brake but didn't turn off the motor. Canal Street, warehouses and wholesalers, on the rim of both Chinatown and Little Italy, was open for business, Sunday or not, blizzard or not. The streets were shoveled, people were out shopping. "This calls for hot coffee and food." There was a deli-sandwich shop across the street. And it was open.

"Sounds good to me." It was after twelve and they hadn't even crossed into Brooklyn. "Decaf, if it's brewed. No Sanka. Ham and Swiss on a bagel with mustard. But if it's an Italian deli, salami and provolone on Italian bread." She was making herself hungrier, just talking about it.

"I'll be right back. Hold the fort." He jumped out and crossed the street to the deli. Chances were good she'd get her Italian combination. She unfastened her seat belt and leaned across the driver's seat, rubbing the condensation from Teddy's window. The name on the deli was Del Soma's.

She settled back in her seat and refastened the belt. The motor chugged reassuringly, the heater was working. She hoped she'd done the right thing by taking Teddy into her confidence. He was a friend, but he was also a reporter. On the other hand, she needed his help in Brighton Beach. He was as nosy as she was. He would ask the right questions.

She fidgeted. It was taking him a long time in the deli. At this rate it would be another two hours' minimum to get to Brighton Beach.

Steam covered all the windows. She rolled her window down about two inches. On her side of the Rover a coffee shop had opened and a fat Chinese shopkeeper in a red wool hat and red-and-white muffler was selling hot coffee and doughnuts through an opening to the street counter. She sniffed the piquant odors of Chinese cooking. Or was it her imagination? She could also smell the sharp clean aroma of wood burning in fireplaces, mixing with Chinese food and the wafts of curry coming from the famous old Canal Street spice market that had been in the area for years.

God, she was so hungry she felt light-headed. She unfastened her seat belt again and slid over to Teddy's window. She looked back across the street to Del Soma's.

She saw Teddy, preoccupied, empty-handed, not even looking toward the Rover, come around the corner and go into the deli.

21

"I WENT AROUND THE CORNER to a Chinese restaurant I know to see if I could get us some egg drop soup," Teddy said in response to her casual question. "Here, take this." He thrust a cardboard box of coffee and sandwiches at her. "But it was closed." He shrugged and dumped a six-pack of Heineken on the backseat. "What else would I be doing?" He showed her such a wide-eyed innocent face that her skin prickled on the back of her neck. She heard, *Don't you trust me?* unsaid. She thought, *Of course, I trust you. Shouldn't I?*

They were driving again, down Canal and right across the East River, which looked dangerous, with chunks of ice and sporadic little black whirlpools. She had read somewhere that the East River had vicious currents and was a fighting river. They drove off the Manhattan Bridge onto Flatbush Avenue. They were in Brooklyn.

"Do you know how to get there?" Wetzon asked, looking down at the box on her lap. Teddy was drinking coffee with one hand as he steered with the other.

"Yeah. Did a story once on the Cafe Baltic. It's quite a place—the hub of the Russian émigré social scene. And the wheeling and dealing that goes on there . . . You might say"— he grinned at her— "it's a Middle European Four Seasons." He laughed out loud.

"Shut up and drive," she grumbled, knowing he was making fun of her fascination with the famous New York restaurant. She unwrapped her sandwich. "Oh, joy, a hoagie."

"You mean a hero," he said, referring to the Italian-style stuffed sandwiches.

"Hoagie in South Jersey." She pulled out the slimy red pimientos and gripped the bread firmly. "Hate red peppers." She took a big bite. The fruity olive oil dribbled on her chin, and she blotted it up with a paper napkin.

"Your friend Carlos has made quite a name for himself."

"Isn't it great? He's such a talent, and besides that, he's a nice guy."

Teddy stared at the roadway, giving her his magnificent profile. "What's the name of the firm, Wetzi?"

She didn't answer him at first. "Let it be, Teddy."

Turning to her, his eyes crackled, then softened. "Sorry."

"Okay. Let's forget it." She tried not to be irritated, but she could feel herself doing a slow burn.

"I'm going to go around Prospect Park and pick up Ocean Parkway. Say a prayer that it's as good driving as Flatbush." They were making better time than she'd hoped. "This is Grand Army Plaza," he said, referring to a circle with massive monuments draped in snow. She could make out horses among the statuary but very little else. "If we kept going through the park, we'd pass the Brooklyn Museum, the Library, and the Botanic Gardens, but . . ." He drove around the Plaza and along the edge of Prospect Park, passing people on skis, groups of children in vivid winterwear, adults with sleds, some going into the park, some leaving.

"It's funny, isn't it, that most Manhattanites never go to Brooklyn, or any of the outer boroughs." The only place in Brooklyn that she'd been in besides the Heights and Atlantic Avenue for the antique stores, was BAM, the Brooklyn Academy of Music, and that was because of the dance companies that appeared there.

"Unless you grew up in one of the boroughs," Teddy said, "or work takes you there, Manhattanites are the biggest snobs around." He looked over at her. "You're not talking much, lady."

"I'm afraid to. You might get information out of me, digger. You should be doing *Sixty Minutes*."

"Ah, that's just it. That's what I'm aiming for."

"Oh, Teddy! Is there a chance?"

"I'm working on it." He turned onto Ocean Parkway, and the Rover skidded, spinning sharply into the wrong lane. Wetzon braced her hand on the dash and felt her body surge against the seat belt. Teddy steered into the skid expertly, taking his foot off the gas, putting it on again lightly once they were righted.

A cab, which had been driving a distance behind them, passed them and then stopped. The driver opened his door and called out to them. Teddy rolled down his window and waved. "It's okay."

Two cars, oncoming, also stopped until Teddy had the Rover back in the right lane.

"Notice how polite and nice everyone is," Teddy said. "I love New Yorkers. We always get such a bad rap." He nodded at the drivers as he passed.

"I'm noticing that the streets are beginning to look a lot less traveled."

"Well, this is Brooklyn. As we said, an outer borough. Our sanitation department doesn't love Brooklyn as much as Manhattan. Too many poor people here." He edged the Rover left again and they entered a wide, majestic thoroughfare with many lanes and a spacious island in the middle. The spacious island might as well have been in the Antarctic because all the vegetation was completely buried in snow.

"Wow!" Wetzon said. "This must be beautiful in the spring. Are we really in Brooklyn?"

"Dis here is Brooklyn all right, bubbie. God, I love this. Give me my sandwich, will ya—I'm getting in the mood." His preoccupation seemed to have vanished. With few other cars on the road, he threw caution to the wind and began to pick up speed. "We're almost there."

On both sides of Ocean Parkway stood ample stone houses, fronted by small snowy lawns. Some of the houses were attached like row houses, but others would have been classified as mansions in Manhattan. The side streets were almost obliterated by snow.

"You're very quiet, Wetzi."

"I'm not sure how we do this, Teddy." She was beginning to worry whether she wasn't taking them on a wild-goose chase. "Do you think we should just go in and ask at Tsminsky's for Ida and say that I have an old aunt who needs care, or something like that?"

"They're very clannish and careful about strangers here. Hard to shake old habits."

"The KGB will get you if you don't watch out?"

"You got it. How about we do that, leave a name and say we're going into the Baltic for a drink and she can find us there? Then they won't feel they're being pressured and we can wait where it's warm. And maybe we can pick up some information from people there." He waved his arm. "We are now passing the famous Kings Highway."

She looked up at the sky. The blue had turned to gray. She shivered and rolled up the window. "I don't think we have a hell of a lot of daylight left."

"How old a guy is your broker Tormenkov?"

"Late twenties." She rubbed her hands and put her gloves on. It was cold. "Why can't you wait until I can give it all to you?"

"Because I'm a reporter, and I smell something really big here."

A blustery wind battered the white-coated trees with wicked force as they drew closer to the Atlantic Ocean. It was almost as if the sharp winds blowing in off the waters blew the snow inland, away from the beaches. There was always much less snow near the ocean, or so it had seemed to her when she was growing up in New Jersey near Seaside Heights.

"Did he and this Ida look alike?"

"Not at all. It's probably just coincidence. Tormenkov may be as common a name in Russia as Smith is here." She said it, but she didn't believe it.

Teddy made a sweeping turn and drove down a broad street with rundown storefronts, clothing stores, cleaning establishments, a furrier, the Restaurant Odessa, which had the marquee of a movie theater, and a boarded-up furniture store. On the other side of the street she could see a windswept boardwalk and farther, the beach and the ocean.

"I'm giving you a quickie tour of Brighton Beach Avenue,"

Teddy said, "then we'll park behind the Baltic. There's a lot there and we won't be so obvious."

They passed a movie theater showing *Conan the Barbarian*.

The people on the street, and there were quite a few bustling along, scarves to faces, hands to hats, looked foreign. The men wore flat caps or berets. Robust women in various versions of the omnipresent quilted polyester storm coat had woolen scarves tied under their chins and carried shapeless plastic grocery bags. Everyone looked middle-aged or older.

"Where are the children? Where are the young people?" she asked out loud.

"They don't hang around." Teddy pointed to the left. "There's your ice cream shoppe." He pronounced the *e* as a second syllable.

"It's open." A small surge of adrenaline raced through her.

He drove another block, the chains clanking on the almost snow-free road. "There's the Baltic." He made a left and another left and pulled into a lot with a small assortment of cars. The Rover was the only one without a blanket of snow on it. The lot itself was windswept and almost clear.

Wetzon gathered up the remains of their sandwiches, paper wrappings, and the empty coffee containers and took them with her when she slid out of the Rover. "It's amazing. There's so much less snow here," she said.

He took the box of garbage from her and dumped it on top of an already-more-than-full garbage can as they walked off the lot.

Wetzon looped the strap of her backpack over her shoulder, making it a shoulder bag, and looked around. The sun had given up for the day and the air was bitter cold. The wind chill probably brought the temperature down into the single digits. She shivered and fished her lavender beret from the backpack and pulled it on over her ears. She folded up her sunglasses and put them away.

They walked right to Brighton Beach Avenue, shoulders braced against the fierce ocean wind. The Cafe Baltic had once been a bowling alley. Someone had strung colored lights around the front of the building but couldn't quite hide the giant kingpin and the ball.

"Here we are," Teddy said, stopping in front of Tsminsky's Ice Cream Shoppe. In the grimy window was a dusty display of cheap plastic ice cream arrangements on white pegboard stands. A sad-looking sundae with pink ice cream, an ice cream soda with a dirty straw, and a banana split with orange bananas. A greasy black sandwich board listed sandwiches and prices. Tuna fish was listed as $1.50. A sign in the window, crudely hand-lettered, with misspellings, listed the specials of the day as home-made borscht, and a stuffed cabbage dinner for $5.00. Alongside was writing in Russian. Cyrillic letters.

"Can't beat these prices," Wetzon said, looking up at Teddy.

"Let's go." As he opened the weather-beaten outside door, a bell rang.

Behind the counter a squat woman, her head a Brillo of dark curls, was pouring water into a coffee machine. She turned at the sound of the bell, put down the large stainless steel pitcher, and wiped her broad hands on her apron. Her small dark eyes were deep set. She looked from Teddy to Wetzon and let her eyes rest on Teddy. She cleared her throat nervously.

A man sat at the far end of the dingy counter, slurping soup noisily from a large spoon. He looked over at them and put the spoon down loudly. His body stiffened.

Wetzon looked at Teddy. Did they think because he was black that he had come to rob them? Or was it something else?

"Vat I can get for you?" the woman asked suspiciously. Under the apron she wore a wine-colored wool sweater with tiny de-signs. It looked hand-knit.

"Are you Mrs. Tsminsky?"

The woman gave a barely perceptible nod and looked over at the man.

"I'd like to get in touch with Ida Tor—"

The woman, agitated, interrupted. "I don't know nossing."

The man came around the counter and stood next to the woman. "Leave us alone," he cried. "Ve don't know nossing. You have no right—ve are in America . . . you go avay—" There was pleading and terror in his voice.

"Mr. Tsminsky . . . Mrs. Tsminsky, please," Wetzon said, growing frightened. "I don't mean you any harm. I'm just trying to get in touch with Ida." She felt Teddy's arm on her shoulders. "My aunt is old. I need someone trustworthy to take care of her—" She saw the woman's eyes flicker, change. She glanced over at her husband, whose hands rested on the cutting board near a few pieces of lettuce and several slices of pale, waxy winter tomatoes.

A shadowy figure stopped in front of the window and appeared to be studying the menu. Tsminsky looked out. "No, no," he mumbled. He looked back at Wetzon and Teddy. "No," Tsminsky said, this time loudly. "You make trouble, go avay and leave us alone!"

"You'll be doing Ida out of a good job," Teddy interjected.

"Right." Wetzon nodded, feeling guilty for frightening them. "We'll wait awhile at the Baltic. If you can get in touch with Ida, maybe she can meet us there."

The woman looked to her husband again, her hands playing obsessively with the hem of her apron, rolling and unrolling it. The movement was hypnotic, lulling.

"Wait! No!" Teddy shouted, backing into her, crushing her off-balance back against the door.

"What—" Wetzon's view was blocked by Teddy's shoulder. Teddy grabbed her forcibly, lifting her off the ground, swung around behind her, and pushed hard. The door gave under the pressure of their bodies.

It was then that she saw the long butcher knife in the man's hand, his wild, fear-filled eyes.

She heard the woman scream.

22

"GODDAM, I WISH I HAD a cigarette."

They stood panting on the sidewalk outside of Tsminsky's Ice Cream Shoppe. Teddy's dark skin had a grayish hue in the pale light. Beads of sweat covered his upper lip and forehead in spite of the extreme cold.

"Please, Teddy—" He was taking great strides and dragging her along with him. It had all happened so fast Wetzon had not had time to be afraid. And she wasn't now. She was curious. Why such a violent reaction? Tsminsky could just have said, no, go away, and left it at that. She remembered what Eddie O'Melvany had said about built-in paranoia.

The Atlantic wind blew needle breaths on her cheeks, numbing them. The drops of sweat on Teddy's face turned to ice. Teddy came to a stop in front of the Cafe Baltic. Almost reluctantly, he released her, first reassuring himself by looking up and down the street that they were safe from attack, that the madman Tsminsky had not followed them out into the street with his knife.

"What did we say that upset him so?" Wetzon was dancing from one foot to the other, trying to keep warm.

"Upset! That's some understatement, Wetzi. He might have killed us."

She shook her head. "I don't think so."

He turned suddenly belligerent. "You yuppies are so into yourselves, you have no sense of danger. You don't know these people. It's a good thing I'm here with you."

Wetzon gave him a cold hard look. "I do not consider myself a yuppie, you shithead. Don't you ever talk to me like that again."

She walked away from him, down the street. Winter twilight was rapidly turning to evening. People were not hanging out on the street tonight. And of the few that passed them, undoubtedly heading home, no one seemed to have noticed the incident at Tsminsky's Ice Cream Shoppe.

"Hey, wait a minute, Wetzi." Teddy came after her and took her arm. "Come on, I'm sorry. I didn't mean it. I know you're not a yuppie." He gave her his big, charming grin and hugged her, but Wetzon was stiff in his embrace, still angry. "Come on, say you forgive me."

"Okay," she said with great misgiving. Funny how you think you know someone well and then you see maybe you don't know him at all. She didn't remember Teddy being so abrasive, but they had been friends a long time ago, and people change. She was certainly not the same person she had been then. "Don't you think it's strange that no one even noticed when we rushed out of the store?"

"Around here," Teddy said, "people make a point of not noticing."

One entered the Cafe Baltic through a revolving door, like a department store. They came into a cold, dimly lit lobby, with a coat check on the right and a lectern decorated in varicolored strips of Christmas lights on the left. Neither spot was occupied.

The tiny slivers of ice on Teddy's hairline and upper lip melted. He pulled a folded handkerchief from his back pocket and wiped his face without unfolding it. "I don't know, Wetzi," he said, shaking his head. "We've stepped into deep shit here."

"I'm still trying to figure out what happened. One minute we were asking nicely and the next minute he went at us with a knife. You really moved, Teddy. You don't really think he would have hurt us?"

"Would you have wanted to give him the benefit of the doubt?" He unzipped his coat. "Did you get a look at that guy in the window? Do you think that's what upset him?"

"Don't know. Could have been just some passerby." She stuffed her gloves, beret, and scarf into the backpack. "But it was just before he went crazy on us—"

"Tuvya!" A tiny man, his gaunt face full of seams and gnarls, came out of a dark passageway beyond the gaudy lectern. He was dark-skinned, like a gypsy, with large moist black eyes, and was wearing a black velvet jacket, black tuxedo pants, a frilly white shirt, and a red silk ascot fastened in place by a large glittery tie-pin that looked suspiciously like a real diamond. "Long time no see," the little man said in a thick Russian accent, and his laugh thundered. "And who, I may ask, is pretty lady?"

"This is Wetzi. Wetzi, say hello to my friend, Misha Rosenglub."

Wetzon held out her hand and Misha Rosenglub bowed deeply and kissed her hand, barely brushing it with his breath. It was an incredibly delicate movement. Wetzon was charmed.

"Vetski? You are Russian?" Delight spread over Misha's face. A gold tooth glinted in his red mouth. Was he wearing lipstick? He was still holding her hand.

"No." Wetzon smiled at him.

"No, she's not Russian, Misha, and that's quite enough of your Continental charm. She's *my* girl and we're hungry."

Damn, Teddy was getting on her nerves. First she was a yuppie, now *my girl*.

"Oh, of course, of course, forgive foolishness. Come in, come in. I take coats."

The revolving door deposited three ladies in moth-eaten fur coats and sequinned and tulle evening gowns and a bearded man in a fur hat and a bulky raincoat, who carried a folded newspaper under his arm. The little lobby had suddenly become crowded.

Misha was energized. "Follow, please, *mesdames et messieurs.*" He winked at Teddy and Wetzon and did a little bob and dance before moving forward. "Coat check, coat check!" he boomed. "Come, come, everyvon."

The poignant strains of an accordion drifted out at them. Wetzon, looking down at her ski pants, bulky turtleneck sweater, and boots, felt conspicuously underdressed. They followed the new arrivals down the short passageway which opened into a large room jammed with white-linen-covered tables, round and rectangular, of which a surprising number were occupied and glutted with food. There was a modest dance floor and a raised platform at the far end of the center of the room for a bandstand. A few empty metal music stands were scattered about and a huge silver grand piano took up half the platform. A lone accordionist in a shabby black tuxedo, a red silk scarf around his neck and over one shoulder, sat on a chair playing a mournful melody. Several women's voices full of sorrow and somewhat off-key accompanied him from the tables out front.

Around the outer edge of the room were semiprivate banquettes covered with red velvet. Very few of these were occupied.

A tall, thin waiter in a black suit, white shirt, and black bow tie took charge of the man and the three women who had come in behind Teddy and Wetzon.

They were in a tacky 1940s-style nightclub. The ceiling held three concentric circles of theatrical lights which danced in opposing directions. A hallucinogenic haze hung like a smoky saucer over the room. Everyone seemed to be smoking except Wetzon and Teddy. Large brass coatracks loaded down with coats stood in various spots around the perimeter of the room, sharing space with a dozen palm trees, real or artificial.

The Baltic was a curious mixture of tacky and old-world Continental. Silverware clattered on heavy white commercial china, tables were candlelit. A grandly proportioned woman, wearing a long black skirt, a glittery sweater, and high-heeled silver sandals, was dancing stiffly to the accordion music with a small bald man, who bulged in a tight brown suit with wide lapels. Every once in a while he would spin his immense partner around into a graceful whirl.

Wetzon closed her eyes and smiled, picturing herself and Carlos when they had done the revival of *She Loves Me!,* dancing in just such a café set. She looked around to see what Teddy was thinking. He was gone. She was standing quite alone. Misha had also disappeared.

She felt invisible, discombobulated, as if she were in the midst of one of her dreams. The room was sweltering . . . Where was Teddy? Tuxedoed waiters rushed by, precariously balancing huge platters of food for the horde of diners in gaudy finery who crowded the room.

"Come, Vetski," Misha said, reappearing at her side. He

touched her elbow lightly, trying to steer her to a banquette. She resisted politely but firmly. "Teddy is coming right back. I think I'll wait for him."

"I take coat, then. So varm here, no?" His dark eyes watched her. She couldn't read them.

"No, thank you." She was sweltering, but what if they had to make a fast getaway? Where the hell was Teddy?

"You are okay, Vetski?" Misha brought his face close to hers. He smelled of cigarettes. Everyone did. "Ah, here is Tuvya now."

About fucking time, Wetzon thought. Teddy, carrying his coat over one shoulder, came out of swinging doors to their left, followed by a tiny, plump woman, her hair in a heavy braid like a tiara on her head. She was swathed in burgundy satin, just short enough to show well-shaped calves and tiny feet in spiky high heels that matched her dress. Large diamonds glittered in her ears and on her surprisingly delicate wrists and fingers.

The woman's high-cheekboned face was flushed crimson from the heat in the kitchen, and she was a little short of breath, but her dramatically black-rimmed eyes were bright and perceptive. Her hair was a dye job somewhere between brown and red, having settled at a pale rust. There was something about the way she held her head and neck that made Wetzon think she might have been a dancer a long time ago.

"Ilena, my dollink, this is Tuvya's friend, Vetski—"

"You are Russian?"

"Give up your coat, my little Russian princess," Teddy said, grinning at her. "Vetski." He looked completely recovered from their flight. "Let's sit down. I could eat a horse." He took her coat and gave both to Misha. "Maybe you can help my friend Vetski here. She has a problem with one of your . . . comrades . . ." He laughed. Misha and Ilena joined in, but to Wetzon's eyes it was wary laughter and their faces showed no emotion. Why was Teddy being such a klutz? She made a small pass with her boot at his foot, which he ignored.

"Come, vee sit down, vee eat, vee talk," Ilena said. She raised her long hand with its narrow wristbone and long elegant fingers high in a sort of flourish, and two waiters shot into the kitchen and came back with trays of food, preceding them to one of the rectangular tables in front of the banquettes. The table was already set with china, silver, and glassware. When they finished laying out the spread of *derma*, stuffed cabbage, baked fish, caviar, and slabs of roasted meat from the giant trays, it was almost impossible to see the tablecloth. Two fifths of Absolut vodka and an enormous bottle of seltzer stood among the platters. As Wetzon watched, another waiter, dwarfed by an oversized tray laden with food, set a bottle of Hennessy cognac on the table.

"So vhat is problem then?" Ilena said as soon as they were seated, Ilena and Misha on the outside, Teddy and Wetzon on the banquette. "Wodka for everybody," she shouted to the hovering waiter, who came over and filled the large shot glasses. "Come, vee drink, dollinks, and vee vish ourselfs good health, long life, and God bless America."

Wetzon laughed. The vodka in her glass had tiny dark specks floating in it. She dipped the tip of her finger in and tasted it. Pepper.

"*L'chaim*." Teddy tipped his head back and downed the entire shot glass.

"*L'chaim*." Misha and Ilena did the same.

"Come on, Vetski," Teddy said, teasing her, knowing she never drank anything but beer.

She made a face at him and took a cautious sip. A cold pool of heat warmed her mouth and burned her tongue. She held the cold-hot liquid, savoring the flavors, then let it run down her throat, where it exploded. "Help, fire," she gasped, taking the glass of seltzer Teddy had ready for her.

"Eat, eat," Ilena urged, pushing a plate of *pelmeni* at her and dousing them with vinegar and sour cream. "Must eat with wodka. Is essential."

"So, Vetski, tell us—" Misha gave her hand a reassuring squeeze.

"It's a long story—" Wetzon skewered a *pelmeni* and placed it in her mouth. The taste was exotic, tart, oddly soothing.

"Ida Tormenkov." Teddy interrupted her with an impatient wave of his hand.

Misha's face turned pale. "Ida—"

Ilena's silent gesture with her head was so small anyone could miss it. Wetzon, however, did not. Darn. Why had Teddy done that? It was not her style to plunge right in and it *was* her story. She had caught that quick exchange between Misha and Ilena and nudged Teddy's knee under the table with less force than she wanted to.

A violinist joined the accordionist and the two began to wander among the crowded tables, playing a spirited melody that everyone seemed to know. Patrons were clapping in time to the music.

"Misha, Ilena, you know everyone here." Teddy just blasted forward like a bull in a china shop. There was a long pause. Wetzon's fingers played with the fog that had formed on her cold glass.

"Is for us strange name," Misha said finally, with a studied blankness.

Ilena rose, unfolding herself like a dancer, and shouted in Russian to a waiter, who came scurrying over with a platter of pumpernickel. When she tilted her head, Wetzon noticed Ilena had a large raised red mole near the corner of her mouth. There was something about her—"Wait, you are Ilena Milanova, aren't you?" Wetzon remembered the dancer with the Kirov—she had actually seen her dance once when the Kirov had toured the United States years and years ago. That Ilena, a sylph of a creature, had been their star. When she had applied with her husband to emigrate because they were Jewish, her career had ended abruptly. It had taken them years to get out of Russia.

"Ah yes, my dollink," Ilena said, beaming, her face softening. Her blue eyes filled with tears. "See vat happens ven vee stop dancing." She patted her heavy bosom, then tapped Wetzon's hand sharply with her index finger. "Must never stop dancing."

"Me? How—"

"Can alvays tell. Hair, head. Is like clothing vee vear. Is in blood. In soul. Mine . . . yours." Her hand fluttered on her breast.

Wetzon was overwhelmed. "I was never like you, Ilena. I

danced on Broadway—in the chorus. I was just a gypsy." She buttered a slice of pumpernickel, which was slightly stale. She took another sip of vodka and ate a big bite of pumpernickel. The last thing she wanted to become was woozy.

"Is all family," Ilena said.

"Vetski finds jobs for stockbrokers now." Teddy tipped his head back and drank another full shot of vodka. Wetzon glared at him. It would be terrible if Teddy got drunk.

The waiter with the small, neat beard, who had brought the pumpernickel and was now refilling their glasses with vodka, stopped and stared intently at Wetzon. Wetzon stared back, then looked away. Nervous, she took a large swallow of vodka, choked, and broke out into a sweat. "Ladies' room," she gasped, staggering to her feet.

Ilena smiled and pointed across the dance floor. "Is healthy sveat. Wodka sveat."

Teddy laughed too loudly. "Can't take you anywhere, Vetski."

Oh shut up, Teddy, she thought.

"Is nothing." Ilena's eyes darted around the room.

"Is piece of work," Wetzon said, fixing Teddy with a tough look because he was howling with laughter. She headed for the ladies' room.

"Vat is piece of work?" she heard Ilena ask.

The music had picked up and diners were jumping to their feet and dancing in circles. The extravagantly dressed women far outnumbered the men. Wetzon wove her way through and around the dancers and into a small dark corridor which ended in two doors. *Mesdames* on one and *Messieurs* on the other.

She entered *Mesdames*. Red-flocked wallpaper, gold moldings. A Formica counter with flecks of gold. She pushed back her sleeves and wet her wrists with cold water. Sweat was coming from every pore. Jesus. Her lips tasted salty. She used the bathroom, came out, and splashed her cheeks with cold water, patting them dry with a paper towel. She rummaged in her backpack for the small tube of Nivea she always carried and rubbed some into her hands and face.

She was furious with Teddy. He was about as subtle as a ten-ton truck. Some reporter. They'd accomplished nothing. She hadn't found Ida. She'd terrified a poor shopkeeper and his wife who probably thought she was KGB . . . but imagine meeting Ilena Milanova in a place like this. She smiled coldly at herself in the mirror and touched up her lipstick.

A pudgy middle-aged woman in a short, pale blue taffeta dress which exposed a lot of fleshy thigh in sheer hose with black floral designs came into the small room. "Excuse, please," she said. She was wearing a light blue picture hat and looked like a hooker playing a Southern belle. Her eyes were heavily outlined, the lids blue-shadowed, and she squeezed by Wetzon, checking out Wetzon's costume with distaste. Wetzon looked at herself in the mirror. Ah yes, she was definitely the misfit in this group.

She smiled at the woman and went back out into the dark hall, slipping the backpack strap over her shoulder. Someone came out behind her, the woman. Wetzon did not look back.

Something—thick and woolen—came across her throat, choking her. Pulling, fighting the arm, she smelled a sharp cigarette odor. She couldn't breathe . . . her throat . . . Her hands tore at a face, a beard. She tried to scream. The world swirled deep, deep blue. She was blacking out. *They're killing me*, she thought. She began the slide on a long sliding pond.

23

IDA WAS WAVING AT HER. "Go avay . . . go avay . . . you make trouble . . ."

"Poor thing," someone said.

Wetzon opened her eyes and saw floating blue and yellow spots. She blinked. Her throat . . . she had a terrible lump in her throat she couldn't seem to swallow away.

"Poor zing." The woman in blue taffeta rustled, bending over her, fanning her with the large blue hat. "You must have faint."

Wetzon was lying on her back on the floor in the dark, narrow hallway to the bathrooms. "No . . . no . . . where is he? Did you see him?" Her voice came out in a croak.

"See who, dollink?" The woman rearranged her spectacular hat on her head and stabbed it in place with a long pointy hatpin. "Vas no vun here but you on floor." She smelled of face powder and Poison.

Wetzon pulled herself upright. God, her throat was raw. The floor was filthy. She brushed cigarette butts off her hands and clothes. Ugh.

"Okay?" the woman asked. "You vant I should bring someone to help?"

"No." Wetzon stood up uneasily. Her backpack was at her feet. This wasn't a robbery. "I'll just go . . ." She pointed to the ladies' room. She shook herself. Her shoulders were tender where he'd gripped her. "Are you sure you didn't see anyone?"

"No vun, belief me." The woman shrugged her fleshy shoulders. She was lying and she knew Wetzon knew it. Her bosom billowed. "I tink, dollink, you vear too much clotink. Body must breathe. No air . . . faint." She smoothed her puffy dress on her broad hips. "You okay now. I see that."

A man, cigarette stuck in one corner of his mouth and a bottle of vodka in his hand, turned into the short dark hallway, and the woman in blue taffeta brushed by him quickly. He made a leering remark in Russian that sounded suggestive to Wetzon's ear, and the woman cackled.

Wetzon picked up her backpack by the strap and went into the ladies' room. She saw with relief as she slammed the door that the man in the hallway was clean shaven.

Her face in the mirror was pale and her eye shadow was smeared gray on her right cheek. Her throat felt awful. Gingerly, she rolled down the high neck of her sweater. Her neck was bruised red. She knew she was in over her depth now, but it was too late to wish she had never come here. Hazel was right. She should have left it to the police.

The woman in blue had lied. Was she part of a mugging team with the man who had attacked her? Or did she just not want to get involved? Maybe the woman had recognized him . . . Oh hell. Her swallow was pain-filled, forcing tears to her eyes. She wet her face lightly and dabbed at her eyes with a Kleenex, wiping away the smeared gray shadow. She redid her makeup as well as she could, thinking only about how long it would take them to get home.

When she came out into the restaurant, the dancers were stamping their feet and clapping. A balalaika had joined the other instruments and someone in a white tuxedo was sitting at the silver grand piano. Around the floor were a multitude of bearded men, short beards, long beards, curly beards, red beards, brown, black. It was bizarre. She had not seen the man's face, so she would never be able to identify him.

"Miss . . . miss . . . vait!" It was the waiter who had stared at her. Instinctively, she shied away from him. He caught her by the arm. "No, vait . . . please." She wanted to scream, but there were so many people around her, she felt foolish being frightened. "You maybe help my brother," he said in a menacing tone.

"What?" She tried to back away.

"He stockbroker."

Wetzon stared at him. He didn't look menacing at all. She stopped a nervous laugh. My God, Wetzon, you're getting as batty as they are. "I'm sorry. What firm is your brother with?" She felt the pain in her throat as she spoke.

"Hoffman, Parker." It was a penny stock firm of poor repute. "No so good place. Maybe you help him?"

"I'll try." She fished in her backpack for her card case and gave him her card. "Tell him to call me."

"Tank you, tank you." He put her card in his pocket and started away.

"Wait"—Wetzon touched his sleeve—"His name?"

"Roman Grodsky."

Smith would laugh, Wetzon thought. She wished she could see and talk to Smith right now. Wherever Wetzon went she always seemed to meet a stockbroker. It was a standing joke with them that if Wetzon were shipwrecked on a desert island, a stockbroker would come out of the jungle and ask her to place him. For godsakes, Wetzon, someone just tried to kill you and a minute later you are politely handing out your business card.

The smoke in the noisy room was stupefying. She could just barely swallow. She wanted to scream, *Someone tried to kill me*, but she was a stranger in a foreign land.

As she made her way back to the table, she saw Teddy was hunched over, talking to Misha. Ilena stood several feet away, shouting and waving a white silk chiffon scarf, directing her waiters. She turned to Teddy and Misha once and said something, shaking her head emphatically. Misha was gesticulating angrily, the ubiquitous cigarette that every Russian seemed to smoke attached to his fingers.

Wetzon slipped onto the banquette next to Teddy and he patted her knee, acknowledging but not looking at her. He was engrossed in his conversation with Misha. She could not hear what they were saying. The din was deafening. But she didn't care about anything right now except her throat. Teddy seemed to be pleading with Misha. ". . . protect my sources," she heard him say at one point.

Misha shook his head, smacked Teddy extraheartily on the back, and stood to look at something in the middle of the restaurant, a traffic problem of some sort that was making Ilena scream with frustration. Ilena stamped her foot. The music and dancing continued at a frenzied pace. Three men were *kazatska*-ing with more enthusiasm than technique while waiters continued to move precisely with trays of grotesquely heaped platters of food. On the periphery a quartet of people were fighting to get their coats. A brass coatrack toppled over, but it held so many coats, and the music was so loud, it made no sound. Misha, frowning, flung himself into the crush to take charge of the dispute.

Wetzon shivered. The room felt cold. The ceiling lights traveled around and around overhead. The music suddenly sounded hollow. Diners were demanding their checks. "What—"

Teddy turned away from the strange scene on the floor of the restaurant and stared at her. "What's with your voice?"

"Someone tried—"

"What?"

She closed her eyes briefly and shook her head. She rolled down the high turtleneck of her sweater. Teddy's head snapped back. "Holy shit! How did that happen? Don't talk. Shit! Let's get out of here." He touched her shoulder and she jumped.

"Jeeze, I'm sorry, Wetzi. Should have been paying attention. You were gone a long time—"

"What did you get out of Misha and Ilena? Do they know Ida?" She pitched her voice from the top of her throat.

"They say no, but they know everybody."

"So what were you and Misha arguing about?"

He was evasive. "I asked him if he knew anything about that stockbroker and a scam."

"Shit, Teddy." She was upset. "That's all confidential stuff—"

The music grew thinner and thinner. Only the accordionist was still playing. Everyone was leaving the restaurant.

Wetzon looked questioningly at Teddy. "Come on," he said, "let's get Misha and find our coats. I want to know what's going on—"

They walked out to the middle of the now empty dance floor. Misha was arguing heatedly in Russian with the accordionist, who was swigging vodka from a bottle next to his chair and packing up his instrument. When Misha threw his hands up in exasperation, Teddy moved in on him, pulling Wetzon along. The accordionist picked up his bottle and the accordion case and left.

Only the waiters, Ilena, and a few stragglers still remained. A drunk lay with his head on one of the small tables, a long arm dangling on the floor, out cold. The kitchen staff were grouped around the swinging doors, whispering among themselves. Finally, a spokesman was designated. A tall man in a chef's hat and a dirty apron stepped forward, his cavernous face and red-rimmed eyes gave him a look of dissipation. He spoke to Ilena, who immediately began shouting and waving her arms.

Misha looked helpless. Volumes of uneaten food were left on the tables.

"What's going on here, Misha?" Teddy said, taking Misha's arm.

Misha shrugged elaborately. "Zere vas accident. People get nervous."

"An accident? Here?"

"Not here. Down za street. Who knows. You leave now, Tuvya."

What kind of accident would clear out a whole restaurant, Wetzon wondered.

Misha smiled a cynical smile as if he knew what she was thinking and went for their coats. Ilena was still arguing with the kitchen staff. Wetzon's eyes teared. She was sorry now she hadn't taken another sip of vodka before they left the table. It might have made her throat feel better.

Misha came back and silently handed over their coats.

"Come on. I'm getting you out of here," Teddy said, looking at her with concern. He helped her on with her coat and shook hands with Misha. Misha near-kissed Wetzon's hand again with great ceremony. She pointed across the floor to Ilena and nodded at Misha.

"I tell her bye-bye, Vetski. Vee see again, soon, no, Tuvya?" He stood on tiptoe to kiss Teddy on each cheek.

On the street the frigid wind stung her face. Down the wide avenue in the direction of Tsminsky's was a tremendous crowd of people and rolling lights in whites and ambers from police cars and emergency vans. A lot of lights and a lot of cars. Perhaps the whole clientele of the Cafe Baltic and Restaurant Odessa in glitzy array now milled on the sidewalk there. In the background was the steady crash of rough surf on the beach just beyond the boardwalk, and sweeping around them, the damp, salty, purifying blast of the ocean.

Teddy looked torn. "Listen, Wetzi, if I were any kind of friend I would get you the hell out of here, but I'm a repor—"

She put her hand on his arm. Nodding, she pointed toward the crowd and the lights. She was just as inquisitive as he was. What did another fifteen minutes matter now?

"Wait here a minute. I have an idea." Teddy went back into the Baltic and returned quickly with a bottle of cognac. He pulled the cover off and took a swig, skimmed the mouth of the bottle with the palm of his hand, and handed it to her. "Sip," he ordered, scanning the crowd, beginning to edge away from her. "Just wet the inside of your mouth and let a little dribble down the back of your throat, if you can. It's a great anesthetic."

She did as he suggested and felt immediate warmth and then fire. Her eyes burned, her throat mercifully began to numb. She handed the bottle back to him. He recorked it and dropped it into a deep pocket inside his coat.

"Come on." He kept his hand in the center of her back, pushing her firmly closer to the milling throng of people. A siren sounded; a police car pulled away from the curb.

"What happened?" he asked a bulky man with a large mustache, wearing a cap with earflaps. The man looked at him suspiciously. "Was there an accident?"

"A shooting, zere vas," a woman next to the man said. "Vas a—"

The man muttered something harsh to the woman and she stopped talking. They moved away from Teddy and Wetzon.

Teddy looked around in the garish light. A CBS truck pulled up on the other side of Brighton Beach Avenue and stopped with a screech of tires. A Channel 8 van followed almost immediately.

"Hot shit," Teddy said, jumping up and down with excitement, running to the van, leaving Wetzon. The pain in her throat was coming back with a vengeance. What was she doing here anyway? Peepsie Cunningham's Fifth Avenue apartment and Hazel seemed so far away. This was another country. She wandered after Teddy.

"Hey, Ted. How'd you get here so fast?" A lantern-jawed woman scrambled out of the van. She didn't seem happy to see him.

"Ear to the ground, Gretchen."

Gretchen glowered, came around to the back of the van, opened the doors, and pulled out a hand-held camera. "Christ, what a cold mother it is out here," she said. She was built like a bantamweight fighter.

"Let me help you," Teddy said, reaching for the camera.

"This is my story, Lanzman," Gretchen said, putting her face in his, "so don't try to muscle in like you always do." She had a mean, tough look on her face.

"I was here first." Teddy gave her back mean.

"Don't mess with me, Lanzman. I have a long memory." She thrust the camera at him. "You can hold the camera while I cover the story." When he didn't take it, she dropped it.

"Fuck you, Gretchen." Teddy grabbed the camera before it hit the ground. His voice was conversational, but there was a fury underneath.

Gretchen locked the back of the van. "Well, let's have it, yes or no? I don't have time for this crap." Her eyes skimmed over Wetzon, who stood behind them, watching.

Teddy shrugged and hoisted the camera on his shoulder. "What went down here?"

"Couple of Russian immigrants offed in their store." Gretchen took out a notepad and pen and began to elbow her way through the crowd.

24

WETZON CLUTCHED TEDDY'S COAT. Their eyes met.

"The Tsminskys?" Teddy called, moving quickly after Gretchen.

"Something like that. Names all sound alike to me," Gretchen said over her shoulder.

"Anyone else coming to cover us?"

"Nah . . . couldn't get anyone. I was doing the storm out at Grand Army Plaza—nature stuff, you know—so Carl told me to get the hell out here."

They were almost to the front of the crowd. Wetzon followed in their wake.

The police had cordoned off the area. Two CBS people—very preppie young men—were having trouble pushing through from the other side of the milling gawkers.

"What's happening, Officer?" Gretchen asked one of the two cops in front of the wooden horses that had been set up around the Tsminskys' shop. Men were moving in and out of the narrow store.

"Was it a robbery?" Teddy demanded, holding the camera and taping. Gretchen threw him a look of pure venom.

The policewoman moved back and forth from one foot to the other, trying to keep warm. "Can't say," she answered Teddy. Her name tag said Reilly and she looked too young to be a cop. "Ask the lieutenant," Reilly said, then she mumbled something to her cohort and they laughed.

Gretchen hissed a warning at Teddy under her breath and made a note in her notepad. "What's your lieutenant's name?" she asked. A police van, lights flashing, stopped with a screech of brakes, spraying snow. Four uniformed men got out and began to force the crowd back.

"Gelbart. That's him." Reilly pointed to a big man, broad as a wrestler, wearing a tan storm coat and a hat, like a fedora, with a brim. He came out of the store and held the door with a gloved hand, talking to someone in the shop, his massive back to the disgruntled onlookers who were shouting at him, demanding information.

"Fantastic! The hulk. He's my man." Teddy took the camera from his shoulder and dumped it on Gretchen, who, surprised, caught it.

"You fucking s.o.b.—" she sputtered, but Teddy was already talking to Gelbart.

Wetzon and Gretchen, with the camera working, moved in to the edge of the wooden barricade. The horizontal lights from the roofs of the police cars spiraled around and around, bleeding into the darkness, mingling with the orange flashes from the top of the ambulance. The crowd fell still.

"Time to go home, folks," a man in a navy windbreaker announced through a bullhorn. "If you have any information you want to give the police, do so now or call us on our special number, 555-1111. We'll keep all information confidential." The crowd began to disperse silently.

Funny, Wetzon thought, for such a noisy, exuberant people, they were terribly subdued. Was it generalized fear or the respect of foreigners for authority?

The front window of the Tsminskys' store was shards of glass. The display was smashed beyond recognition except for a lone orange banana. The killer had not even bothered to open the door. She thought of the shadow figure that had stood and watched them when she and Teddy had been talking to the Tsminskys and she shivered.

Gretchen went beyond the barricade, right up to where Teddy was standing. He was talking to Lieutenant Gelbart, making rapid notes in his small notebook.

". . . Uzi," Gelbart said. "They didn't have a chance. These Russian bastards are brutal." Two detectives came over and took him aside. "Okay," he said, holding his hat against a sudden gust of wind. "Let's get this over with." A man carrying a small black medical bag left the store. "That's it, Ted," Gelbart said. "Stay in touch."

His eyes rolled over Wetzon, who had her lavender beret pulled down over her eyebrows. She had not dispersed with the crowd. She smiled at him. Maybe Silvestri knew him or he knew Silvestri. She had gotten soft on cops, Carlos said. He was probably right.

"Who are you, bright eyes?" Gelbart said.

"Friend of *mine,* Gelbart," Teddy said possessively. He put his arm around Wetzon and turned her so that her back was to Gelbart.

"Leslie Wetzon," she said over her shoulder to Gelbart, the hulk.

Gretchen took a quick spin around the area, getting footage, while two young stragglers watched.

"You shouldn't be so friendly with them." Teddy was annoyed, pushing Wetzon in front of him.

"Them?"

"Cops."

"Why not?"

"They're all lowlifes. There's not much difference between them and the ones they chase."

"I don't believe that, Teddy." She knew Silvestri wasn't like that.

"Trust me, Wetzi. I see it all the time. You live in your own little safe white world." He sounded bitter.

Gretchen was loading the camera into the van when they came up and she was angry. She climbed into the driver's seat. Teddy closed the door for her and leaned against it. "Sorry, Gretch," he said, grinning.

"I'll get you for this, Lanzman." She rolled up her window, started the motor. Her headlights snapped on. She raced the motor and was out of there in seconds.

"Fucking bitch dyke," Teddy said. "She didn't even ask if we needed a ride." He took out the bottle of cognac and they each had a swallow.

"Well, we don't, so forget it."

"Let's get the fuck out of here."

Wetzon's throat was tight, but she was feeling better. In fact, she was feeling really good. She'd enjoyed her little flirt with the hulk, aptly nicknamed. She did a little time step on the wind-swept street. Good God, Wetzon, she said, stopping herself. Two people are dead and you are dancing in the street like some kind of fool. "I'm drunk," she said out loud.

"Come on, Wetzi, make tracks," Teddy yelled at her from halfway down the block.

They turned the corner away from the activity and lights on Brighton Beach Avenue into an almost eerie darkness. The one streetlamp reflected light hazily on the snow in the parking lot behind the Cafe Baltic. The lot was deserted except for the Land Rover, a large friendly tank waiting for them. It was almost as good as being home. Only the large and friendly tank seemed to be listing to one side.

"Fucking shit fuck!" Teddy shouted, and stamped his feet. They walked around the Rover. There were deep gashes in two of the tires. He kicked the closest tire hard and hopped around holding his foot.

Wetzon laughed. He looked pretty silly.

"This is not funny, Wetzi." He ran back to Brighton Beach Avenue, and she followed him, taking giant steps.

"May I? Yes, you may," she said. She wanted another sip of cognac and he had the bottle. The police cars and the ambulance had gone. Brighton Beach was still as death. "Still as death," she said.

"What the fuck are you talking about?" Teddy was walking in circles, stamping his feet and raging. "How the fuck are we going to get back at this time of night?"

"Cognac," Wetzon said, holding out her hand for the bottle.

"And that fucking bitch dyke went off and left us."

"She didn't know—" He gave her a look of total blind fury. "Jesus, Teddy."

He pulled out the bottle of cognac and took a mighty gulp. "Here, keep it."

"We could take a cab," she suggested, and put the bottle to her lips.

"A cab? Oh really? Just like that we're going to get a cab out here at this time of night. There isn't even a fucking pay phone around."

He was right, of course. She took a swallow of cognac and corked the bottle, cramming it into her backpack. She looked up the street and blinked. A mirage was coming toward her. A cab with its center light on.

She poked Teddy and pointed. "Sonofabitch, I don't believe it," he shouted, and ran out into the street like a jumping jack and flagged it down.

Chains clanked on the bare street as the driver came to a slow stop. They ran to the door, opened it, and crawled in.

"Where can I take you folks?" the driver said in a friendly voice, turning to them.

It was Judy Blue.

25

IT WAS A CHARITY AFFAIR for Russian dissidents at the Brooklyn Academy of Music. She was dancing a strange pas de deux with Ilena Milanova, Ilena in diaphanous red chiffon, Wetzon in white. Although her feet seemed to know the steps, the music was unfamiliar. She and Ilena were totally in sync. Bearded dancers in black tights, white shirts, and bow ties were gliding around holding red lacquer trays of herring. Stock certificates were draped on their forearms, like napkins. She was thrilled to be dancing with Ilena.

Suddenly the orchestra stopped. Wetzon looked up. For heaven's sake, Leon was conducting the orchestra. He shook his shaggy gray head as if he were Leonard Bernstein, poked his glasses up his nose, and tapped his baton on the glitzy lectern. The music changed to "I Got Rhythm."

Her feet, in patent leather Mary Jane tap shoes, began the old-time step she had done as a child. She turned to her partner. It was Judy Blue.

"What are you doing here?" Wetzon asked, not missing a step. "I didn't know you could dance."

"You're missing everything, my girl," Judy Blue said. "Keep your eye on the conductor."

Where had Ilena gone?

They finished the number with a shuffle off to Buffalo. Harvey Lichtenstein, whom Wetzon knew because he ran the Brooklyn Academy of Music and was very supportive of dance companies, was standing in the wings in black tie, talking to Smith. He nodded to Wetzon.

"I'm worried about you," Smith said. "You invest your money in stocks. If the market goes down, you won't have anything."

"You have me," Silvestri said, holding out his hand to her.

"Do I?" Wetzon said.

"You have me," Carlos called from the other side of the stage. "At least for now."

"I'll take your bow for you," Smith said, rushing out onto the stage.

Wetzon ran after her, taps clicking. "No, no!" Smith was wearing Wetzon's costume and was bowing as if she had done the number.

A trapdoor opened under Wetzon's feet and she began to fall. "Silvestri," she screamed, reaching for his hand. But he wasn't there. She clutched the stage where the trap had opened, her body swinging in space.

"Where are you going?" Teddy asked, kneeling down.

"Teddy, please help me," she cried.

"Sorry. Got a lead to follow."

The lights went out and someone stepped on her hands. She screamed with pain and, letting go, hurtled into empty space.

A siren pealed.

She awoke thrashing. Her alarm had gone off. Six-thirty. She stopped the alarm and lay there, breathing unevenly. Another dream and such a threatening one, too.

It had been late when she'd come in last night and she had torn off her clothes and fallen into bed in her silk thermal underwear.

Flexing her feet, then pointing, she got out of bed. Her throat was only mildly sore. She checked her neck in the bathroom mirror. It was black-and-blue, but surprisingly not swollen, and her throat was hardly sore at all.

She did a quick stretching workout after her shower, then played back her messages.

Silvestri couldn't get there.

"Wetzon, this is Sonya. You know, your ex-friend, Sonya Mosholu? Pick up. Damn, why aren't you there? Wetzon, this person you referred to me actually came to see me wearing a gun. Hello? . . . Damn it, Wetzon. I'm a sixties person. I hate guns. I hate people who carry guns . . . Oh never mind. I hate the way I sound." She hung up.

Wetzon laughed. O'Melvany to Mosholu. Contact!

The next call was from Carlos.

Then Smith.

Carlos again, sounding upset. He left a strange number.

Smith again, also upset.

Damn! She got the coffee going and called the number Carlos had left. It was only seven o'clock.

A voice she didn't recognize answered.

"This is Leslie Wetzon. I'm sorry to call so early but—"

"Arthur Margolies here." A very nice voice. "Hold on, Leslie Wetzon."

Carlos came on right away. "Les—"

"Carlos, what's wrong?"

"Tommy Lawrence died."

"God no." She sank down on the floor near the telephone. She and Carlos had known Tommy since they'd known each other. He'd been on almost every show with them. He couldn't have been more than thirty-four or -five. "When?"

"Last night. It was so fast . . ."

"Did you know he was sick?" She began to cry. The youngest, the nicest, the most talented . . . the beautiful boys and men she had known.

"Yes, don't get mad. He didn't want anyone to see him. You know how he felt about his looks."

"I know. But at least I could have talked to him on the telephone." Tommy was a beautiful boy when Wetzon had first met him, with a kind of blond virginal purity that belied his sexual appetites.

"He had pneumonia. He was in an oxygen tent. Oh, Les—" Carlos began to sob.

The other voice came back on the line. "I'm sorry about your friend," he said softly.

She wiped her eyes on the sleeve of her sweatshirt. "Arthur?"

"Yes."

"I'm sorry that this is the way we meet."

"I am, too."

"Take care of Carlos."

"I will. He said to tell you there's going to be a memorial service later this week."

"Okay. Just let me know."

She hung up the phone and cried for Tommy Lawrence and all the others. She was afraid for Carlos.

Her phone rang. She hesitated before she answered it, drying her eyes on the bottom of her sweatshirt.

"Wetzon? Wetzon? Hello?" It was Smith's son, Mark. He sounded terrible.

"Mark? What's happened? What's the matter?"

"Wetzon, Mom is really upset. Can you come right away? I don't know what to do. She won't talk to me." His voice trailed off.

"Mark, honey, tell her to pick up the phone for me. Okay?"

He came back a moment later. "She said to leave her alone, that she wants to die."

"Okay, you know she isn't going to die, so why don't you make a pot of tea, and I'll be right over." She sighed. Smith went through moods that were wild swings of smug joy and deep depression. The slightest thing could set her off, from not being able to get a reservation at an *in* restaurant to an imagined, or real, slight by a client. She was hypersensitive and when Wetzon told her not to take these things personally, Smith accused Wetzon of not knowing when people were insulting her. Wetzon couldn't win.

Wetzon focused on getting dressed and over to Smith's. Mark sounded ready to crack. There was too much emotional involvement for a thirteen-year-old. Having grown up without a father, Mark was too attached to Smith, and Smith used his attachment as an emotional crutch. He needed a social life, more friends his own age.

Wetzon dressed for business, because there was business to do today, in a brown tweed suit and a camel hair sweater. She did a bare-bones makeup and packed a set of morning vitamins into her carryall with her papers. The backpack was on the floor near the door, and she emptied it, taking her wallet and notes. The bottle of cognac she put on the kitchen counter.

Wrapped for the North Pole, she ventured out on Eighty-sixth Street. There was no doorman to be seen and her super, Camillo Peresi, was shoveling the sidewalk, whistling as he did so. The sun was so bright and warm it was melting the icicles that hung randomly from the dark brown canopy of her building.

"No one showed up today yet," Camillo explained, giving her his broken-toothed smile. He was wearing a small, black beret and looked like a Basque peasant. He stopped shoveling and leaned on the shovel. Since he lived in the building, when the staff didn't show he was responsible for everything.

"I'm sorry," Wetzon said, looking up and down the street for a cab. She was distracted, not so much about Smith, but by Tommy Lawrence . . . and Carlos. The sidewalks had been shoveled and the gutters were piled high with snow. Camillo had shoveled a neat entrance between the snow piles and the street, which was a white carpet with spots of slush and dark road showing through.

The air felt almost balmy.

A cab stopped in front of her building and a thin, tanned man in a leather coat got out, being careful not to get his fine black leather boots wet. He was carrying a Louis Vuitton traveling bag over his shoulder and a matching Vuitton briefcase. He and Wetzon nodded at each other familiarly, as longtime neighbors would. He was the art director at a big advertising agency, traveling incessantly between New York and Los Angeles.

"Welcome home," Wetzon said. "We've been busy while you were away." She held the cab door for him.

"So I see." He wagged his head of reddish curls.

"How was California?"

"Cold and damp."

"'That's why the lady is a tramp,'" they both said, as Wetzon got into the cab and gave the driver Smith's address.

The City was digging out with obsessive efficiency. The main streets were entirely cleared and the side streets, although narrowed by snow-encrusted cars, were at least passable. She made a mental list of people to call. Kevin De Haven, Peter Tormenkov, Hazel, Teddy . . . Last night—seeing Judy Blue like that—out of the blue . . . Judy Blue. It was too much of a coincidence, but why would it be anything else but? And Teddy had been in a dumb funk the whole way home. He hadn't even offered to help pay for the cab when they'd dropped him on Ninth Avenue.

"Announce me please, Tony," she said to Smith's doorman, and went to the back of the lobby where two small, swarthy women, made round by their outer wrapping, were complaining to each other in Spanish about the subway system. They got on with her and got off at different floors.

Mark was waiting in the doorway, watching for her to get off the elevator. His face was stained with tears. She would have to talk to Smith about him.

"No school today?" She touched his cheek, then stepped back and pulled off her boots.

He shook his head. "We're closed because of the storm." They went into the apartment and Wetzon closed the door behind them.

Too bad, she thought, disengaging herself of her coat, scarf, and hat, handing them to Mark. She could have packed him off to school and dealt with Smith herself. "Where is she?"

"In her bedroom." He was wringing his hands like a worried little old man. "Do you think she's okay?"

"Of course. You know how tough she is. I'm sure something just upset her for the moment." She walked to the closed bedroom door and knocked gently. "Smith?"

"Go away." Smith's voice, clogged with hours of crying, came through the door. "I'm going to kill myself."

Mark howled, "Mom!"

Wetzon turned Mark from the door. "Wait in the kitchen and keep the tea hot." He looked at her plaintively. "Go on." She waited until he was gone. "Smith, stop this nonsense and open the door right now." She rattled the doorknob. It was locked. "Come on, my friend, talk to me. I have so much to tell you about yesterday." No response. "Of course, if you don't want to hear . . ." She heard a small sound from behind the door. A footfall. The key turned in the lock, but the door didn't open.

Wetzon opened the door. The room was a mess. Smith stood unkempt and disheveled in a ragged striped bathrobe. Her hair was wild and uncombed. She looked emaciated, anorectic. She swayed and Wetzon caught her.

"My God, Smith, what happened?" The bed looked like a combat zone. Covers half on the floor. Pillows scattered all over the room. A glass on the night table was tipped over. On the carpet near it, a dark, wet spot. An ashtray was clogged with cigarette butts. Clothing and towels covered the floor. Wetzon had to negotiate over an obstacle course which included magazines and shoes to get Smith to the bed. She tried to straighten the crumpled sheet, gave up, and let Smith sink to the bed. When Wetzon righted the blanket she dislodged a plastic makeup bag and an electric razor. Finally, she covered Smith and sat down on the bed facing her.

Smith moaned.

"Okay, Smith, what the hell is going on?" Wetzon reached over and smoothed Smith's dark curls. Smith was silent, her eyes downcast. "I'm going to leave without telling you anything about what I've been up to . . ." She got to her feet. Smith reached out a bony hand and grabbed Wetzon's shirt. "Okay, then tell me."

"Leon's betrayed us," Smith whispered.

"What? How?"

"He's having an affair with Arleen Grossman."

26

WETZON CALLED THE ANSWERING MACHINE in the office and left a message that they would be late. "How do you know Leon and Arleen Grossman are having an affair?"

Smith had showered and was wearing her crimson-and-black dressing gown. She had miraculously repaired herself and was now glowing with a kind of supernatural radiance. "I know." She sat down at her dressing table, sweeping a medley of lingerie to the floor, and stared at her face in the mirror approvingly; dislodging a lipstick and two tortoiseshell combs which fell on the carpet, she pulled her hair dryer out of the clutter on the table and turned it on.

Mark brought a bamboo tray of tea and fresh orange juice. "I strained the juice just the way you like it, Mom." Wetzon smiled at him and took a glass of orange juice. He waited patiently for Smith to take hers, but when she didn't, he set the tray down on the carpet near her.

"Give Mommy a big kiss, sweetheart," Smith said over the whir of the hair dryer. "Be a good boy and get us a dozen mixed croissants and muffins . . . you know where the money is."

"Okay, Mom." Mark kissed her cheek and the hot air from the dryer blew his dark curls against hers. Their hair was exactly the same deep brown.

"Such a sweet baby," Smith murmured, fluffing her hair. She

turned off the hair dryer and dropped it back on the dressing table.

"I think you're imagining it—or did you read it in the cards?" Wetzon sat on the foot of the bed sipping the juice.

Smith shook her head stubbornly and put on a mauve silk blouse and her plum Donna Karan suit. "Is it cold out?" She picked up the glass of orange juice from the tray on the floor and took a swallow.

"Not like yesterday. Yesterday was a killer." Damn. Wetzon wondered if her everyday language was always so chock-full of those bloody expressions or were they floating around in her subconscious, surfacing when she got involved in a murder.

Smith sat again at the dressing table and dusted her face lightly with powder, using a long sable brush. "So what do you have to tell me? I want to hear."

"First tell me why you're so sure about Leon and Arleen." She watched the tiny grains of the face powder fly up in the air, float briefly, and settle on the plum suit. "He told me Friday night that he had asked you to marry him."

"Humpf." Smith put magenta eye shadow on her narrow eyelids and accented her almond-shaped eyes with a small upward dark line and finished with black mascara in three layers. Her sure hand with makeup always fascinated Wetzon. Her touch was more theatrical than Wetzon's had ever been.

"Seriously, Smith. Why would he be having an affair with Arleen Grossman? She can't hold a candle to you."

"Oh, Wetzon, I love you dearly, but sometimes you are so dim. Don't you see how manipulative she is? And men are such fools." She took the glass of orange juice and went into the living room. "Bring the tray, would you, Wetzon, there's a dear, and put it in the kitchen."

"But I thought you liked Arleen." She never seemed able to keep up with Smith's rapidly changing emotions.

"Well, I did, but I wasn't stupid enough to fall for that line of garbage she was handing out."

Oh weren't you, Wetzon thought, leaving the tray on the

counter in the kitchen and returning to the living room. "Well then, I certainly don't intend to have dinner with her."

Smith was stirring the tarot cards on the table, her palms barely touching them. They seemed to be moving of their own accord. Wetzon shivered. Smith turned and gave Wetzon a piercing look. "What a totally selfish thing for you to say, Wetzon. I'm really surprised at you."

"What?"

"You *have* to have dinner with her to find out for me what is going on between her and Leon." She gathered up the cards and began laying them out in some kind of order.

I give up, Wetzon thought. "Okay, I'll have dinner with her, but only for you. And not tonight. I'm really beat." She sat down on the sofa, watching Smith's sure hands on the cards.

"Didn't she want you to have dinner with her tonight?"

"Yes—but—"

"Wetzon, you really don't care about me at *all,* do you?"

"Smith, you know that's not true. All right, I'll have dinner with her tonight. I have to see if I can meet Kevin De Haven after the close and get that going . . ."

Smith gathered up the cards again and shuffled as if she were shuffling a regular deck of cards. Then she palmed them and held her palms out to Wetzon. "Cut," she ordered, narrowing her eyes, intent on the cards.

Wetzon touched the smooth oversized cards and pulled her hand back in surprise. The cards were hot, as if they had been heated. Smith glared at her until she cut the deck.

I hate this, she thought, watching Smith lay out the cards. *She still makes me feel inadequate, even after all this time.*

"It's that dark man again," Smith muttered. "So much danger." She tapped a crimson fingernail to a card showing a man lying dead, his body pierced by many swords. "It's Silvestri, sweetie pie, it has to be . . . he's your dark man and he's surrounded by death."

In spite of herself, Wetzon felt a chill of fear. She didn't want anything to happen to him. Not Silvestri. "There are other dark men in my life, Smith, besides Silvestri."

"If you mean that fag, he's irrelevant. He doesn't qualify—"

"No, I did not mean Carlos. I meant Teddy Lanzman."

"Teddy Lanzman . . . Teddy Lanzman. Who is that? Is he a broker? His name is so familiar." She tapped the card again. "This is not Silvestri's usual card. Teddy Lanzman . . . wait a minute, not the newsman on Channel Eight? That Teddy Lanzman?" She put the cards down carefully.

"He's pretty dark," Wetzon said, smirking.

"He's black." Smith was scornful.

"So?"

"Black, Wetzon. If you ask me—"

"Don't say it. I'm not asking you."

"Are you going to tell me about it?"

"Not if you don't keep your personal prejudices to yourself."

"I don't know, Wetzon, it's getting harder and harder to have a conversation with you about anything, but I'll accept your reservation."

"Teddy is doing a feature on the life of the elderly in the City—"

"Hi, I'm back." Mark burst through the front door, still wearing his boots.

"Boots! Boots!" Smith called reprovingly.

"Oh gee, I'm sorry, Mom." He backed out of the apartment, still clutching the large paper bag.

"Why don't you set up in the dining room, sweetie pie, while Wetzon and I finish talking." Smith seemed transfixed by the cards on the coffee table. "He's a very dangerous man. I don't like him."

"Smith, honestly, you don't even know him." But Smith's firmness combined with that little seed of doubt Wetzon already felt after her trip to Little Odessa with Teddy. After all, Smith had been right about Rick Pulasky, the doctor Wetzon had gotten involved with last year.

"I don't have to know him. The cards know him. I've seen him on television." Suddenly the cards fell from her hand. Her eyes turned oblique. "Of course, I could be wrong. It could be

Silvestri." She gave Wetzon a radiant smile and stood up, yawning. "I'm really hungry," she said.

"Do you want me to make an omelet for you and Wetzon, Mom?"

"Oh no, sweet baby, this is just perfect." Mark had set up a large platter of assorted muffins and a separate platter of croissants. A fresh pot of tea sat on a Salton warmer. There were three little jelly bowls of jam and a crock of butter. And three place mats with matching napkins were set with glass mugs, silverware.

"What a love you are, Mark," Wetzon said as he poured herb tea into the glass mugs.

"Isn't he though?" Smith reached for a corn muffin. "Oh nice, still warm." She broke it into sections and buttered each section deliberately. "So tell me what happened to you yesterday. You may sit and listen," she said to Mark, "if it's all right with Wetzon, but no interruptions."

"It's okay," Wetzon said. She began with Peepsie Cunningham's death, her disbelief that it was suicide, and Teddy's feature on the elderly. "And how about that this Ida has the same last name as that broker I interviewed?" She ate a portion of a carrot muffin. "This is good."

"Which broker?"

"The one who's working for the FBI."

"The FBI?" Mark said. "Gee."

Smith frowned at Mark. "Spare me, Wetzon, the fantasy life of stockbrokers. Do you want more tea?"

"No." She described the visit to the Tsminskys and the Cafe Baltic, leaving out Teddy's peculiar behavior. "Then when I went to the ladies' room—"

"What time is it?" Smith stood, dusting muffin crumbs from her lap. She looked at her wrist. No watch. She seemed suddenly distracted. "Mark, sweetie pie, clean up for Mom, that's a good boy."

"It's almost nine," Wetzon said. "I think we'd better get going." She was talking to empty space. Smith had rushed out of the room and Mark had taken the teapot into the kitchen.

"Smith, why do I always end up talking to myself when I'm trying to have a conversation with you?" She found Smith in her bedroom touching up her lipstick.

"Oh, was there anything more to your story?" She fumbled under the debris on the dressing table, found her watch and large gold shell earrings, and put them on.

"Damn it, Smith, you didn't give me a chance to finish."

"I hate foreigners." Smith fluffed her hair in the mirror. "They come here, abuse our generosity, and get rich. They hate us and they have no gratitude."

"And you have no logic and no generosity," Wetzon said, getting angry. "The Tsminskys weren't rich. They came from a totalitarian country—" Why did Smith always seem to say outrageous things that aroused Wetzon's ire? Were they supposed to do just that?

"They're Communists." Smith began to coat her lashes with another layer of mascara. "Probably all KGB spies."

"Whatever they were, they're dead now."

"What?" Smith's mascara wand froze in her hand. She stared at Wetzon's reflection in her mirror.

"You heard me."

"Well, why didn't you tell me? God, Wetzon, it takes you so damn long to get a story out. How did it happen? When did it happen?"

"You cut me short, Smith, and you know it." She précis'd the events leading to the murders and ended dramatically, "It happened after I was mugged." She closed her eyes and waited for the explosion. It wasn't long in coming.

"That does it, Wetzon!" Smith slammed the mascara tube on her dressing table. "I'm beginning to think you need a keeper." Wetzon grinned at her in the mirror. Smith turned and glared at her. "You've made this all up to distract me from the truth about Leon and Arleen."

"I have not." Wetzon was indignant. She rolled down her turtleneck and showed the black-and-blue bruises.

Smith jumped to her feet and enveloped Wetzon in a bony

embrace. "This is terrible. Just terrible. I told you that reporter was trouble. What did the police say?"

Wetzon extracted herself from Smith's smothering embrace. "We didn't call them. People were rushing out of the restaurant because they'd heard the Tsminskys were murdered."

"How were they murdered?"

"They were Uzi'd right through their store window. It was horrible."

"Uzi'd! I told you—KGB. I said it before and I'll say it again, louder. Why you would want to get mixed up with those people, I don't know. The old lady was an obvious suicide. You're looking for trouble when you stick your nose into other people's business—"

Wetzon's eyes flicked over Smith. She was wishing Smith hadn't used that turn of phrase when the buzzer from the lobby sounded. Wetzon jumped.

"I'll get it," Smith said, charging past Wetzon and pressing the intercom in the foyer. There was a garbled response. "Thank you, Tony. Send him up."

"Were you expecting someone, Smith? I thought we were going to the office."

Smith's olive skin tones tinged a deep wine. "I have an appointment. I almost forgot," she said. "Maybe you should go ahead." She didn't meet Wetzon's eyes.

The doorbell rang. Mark came out of the kitchen. "Mark, be a sweetie and watch TV in your room till Mother finishes her meeting with Mr. Hodges."

"Okay, that does it. I'm leaving," Wetzon said. "Is my coat in here?" She put her hand on the brass knob of the closet door.

"No! No!" Smith pushed her away from the door. "Mark!"

The doorbell rang again.

Mark came running with Wetzon's things. Smith took her coat, rushing her on with it. Wetzon, her scarf trailing, picked up her leather carryall and opened the outside door.

A tall man in rimless sunglasses, wearing an open tan trench coat, a brown suit, and a brown hat was waiting in the hall. He had just lit a cigarette and Wetzon saw a flash of gold lighter as his gloved hand went into his inside pocket.

Wetzon inhaled smoke and coughed.

"Sorry," he said. His lips were a narrow line, almost not there, followed by a receding chin on a long neck with a pronounced Adam's apple. He stepped back to let her out. Under his arm he carried a large manila envelope. He went into Smith's apartment and closed the door behind him.

"Here's your hat, what's your hurry?" Wetzon grumbled, dropping her bag and leaning down to pull on her boots. Her scarf, wrapped loosely around her neck, pressed painfully against her bruises. She straightened to relieve the pressure. The edge of the scarf was caught in Smith's door. She pulled at the scarf and the door opened a crack. The scarf came free.

"Did you bring it with you?" she heard Smith say.

Hodges had a gruff voice with a distinct Harvey Lacey Queens accent. "Hold your horses," he said.

The door clicked closed.

27

WHY IS IT, SHE THOUGHT, hanging her coat in the office closet, *that whenever I get involved in Smith's personal life or I involve her in mine, I feel as if I've been through a meat grinder?* She poured herself a cup of coffee. *Why do I put up with her at all?*

They had been partners for almost five years, and it had been hard work and a lot of fun in the beginning. And it still was, most of the time. If Wetzon were to dissolve their partnership . . . Smith would be devastated, she would never understand.

Wetzon took a sip of the coffee and missed her mouth, dribbling liquid down her chin. *After all, Smith is my friend. She cares for me—she even loves me in her own way.* She dabbed at her chin with a Kleenex. *What it breaks down to is, I'm comfortable with her. I wouldn't want to work alone, and the idea of starting all over with someone new . . . the explanations to clients and candidates. Oh hell,* she concluded, shrugging, *I'm too old to change.*

Harold's door was closed. B.B. was on the phone and a second button was also lit, indicating Harold was talking to someone. B.B. smiled at her. "I'll have one of my associates give you a call about management opportunities on the Island," he said. He was getting to be a pretty good prospector. "In the meantime, why don't you give me your home address and I'll send you our business card?" He wrote out the address the broker gave him on the suspect sheet. Wetzon looked over B.B.'s shoulder. The home address was Oceanside, and the broker was presently working in Manhattan. That meant he had a long commute, particularly on a day when the immediate world was digging out of a major blizzard.

"Very good, B.B.," she said when he hung up. She patted his shoulder. "I think it's a good idea to stick with the Manhattan brokers today. If they're commuters they might be ready to work closer to home. The Long Island Expressway had to be a disaster this morning, and I'm sure the trains are all running late coming in from Connecticut and Westchester, too."

B.B. handed her the suspect sheet. "You might want to talk to this guy at some point, Wetzon. Aren't we looking for a manager in Melville?"

She studied the profile of the broker and sipped coffee from her *Wall Street Journal* mug. "Ten years with Merrill, so he's vested . . . and Merrill doesn't let brokers transfer to other offices . . ."

"Why not?"

"Perversity. That, and the fact that a manager is paid an override, that is, a percentage of the profits his office makes. They've lost so many good brokers because they won't let them relocate to another office closer to home. It's stupid and shortsighted, and I hope they keep it up because it's good for us." She went into the office she and Smith shared.

"Do you need Smith? Harold's on with her now."

"No." She slipped her carryall under her desk and looked at her schedule for the day. "I just left her." There were no messages propped on the buttons of Wetzon's phone, where they were usually placed. She looked over at Smith's desk. There were at least a dozen pink message slips on Smith's phone. She stood in the doorway. "No messages for me?"

"Sure there are. I left them on your phone." B.B. wrinkled his forehead and got up from his chair. He was wearing a gray wool flannel suit and a light blue lamb's wool sweater over his white oxford cloth button-down shirt and blue-and-red rep tie, preppie all the way. If and when he would be ready to interview brokers, they would have to make him over into the crisp investment banker mode. "Gee, I don't know. Maybe I mixed them up with Smith's . . . although I was sure I separated them." He thumbed through Smith's messages.

"Oh, hi, Wetzon." Harold stood in the doorway, blinking. "I didn't know you were here." He was holding a wad of pink message slips in his right hand.

"Have you seen my messages, Harold?" She eyed the ones in his hand.

"Yeah, I have them." He handed them to her and actually looked embarrassed.

The phone rang. B.B. scooted around Harold, back to his desk. "Smith and Wetzon, good morning."

"I don't understand, Harold," Wetzon said. "Why do you have my messages?"

"Ah . . . um . . . Smith called in while I was sorting them and I guess I forgot I still had yours in my hand."

B.B.'s head jerked around. He stared at Harold before he said, "Kevin De Haven for you, Wetzon."

"Okay." Wetzon took her messages from Harold's grasping little fingers. "If you don't mind, of course," she said, voice dripping irony, which was wasted on him. The little shit had read her messages to Smith. "Go to your room," she said, dismissing him with a wave of her hand. Normally, she didn't mind if Smith knew who was calling her because they worked in the same room, so it was impossible to keep secrets, but this was blatant interference. The big question was why did Smith want to know who had called her?

"Wetzon, pal." De Haven spoke with a Nelson Rockefeller drawl. "Sorry about the other night. Didn't mean to stand you up."

"I didn't mind, believe me. How about today? After the close?" She sorted her messages, crooking the receiver between her shoulder and her ear.

"Looks good. Call me at four."

She hung up.

Hazel . . . Maurice Sanderson . . . the seventy-year-old broker. He'd left a message confirming his appointment with Curtis Evans today at four-fifteen.

"B.B.," she called, "please call Bob Curtis's secretary and confirm Maurice Sanderson for four-fifteen today."

"Okay."

She waited until she heard him talking to Curtis's secretary, then she dialed Sanderson's number.

"This is Maurice Sanderson."

"Hi, Maurice, Wetzon here. Hope you weathered the storm all right."

"A little snow doesn't hurt me, Ms. Wetzon. Is everything still on for today?" He had a slow, deliberate delivery.

B.B. came to the doorway and gave her the high sign.

"Yes. How long do you have to make a decision?"

"Till the end of the week . . ." His voice trailed off.

"Well, let's see how your meeting goes with Curtis Evans. And, oh, Maurice, bring your production runs. Curtis Evans, if you remember, clears through Blander Horowitz. It costs them if their brokers write a lot of small tickets." If Sanderson's ticket size was small, he was dead in the water. She didn't think she could sell him anywhere, not with his age and low production figures. She hung up the phone with a sigh.

"What does 'clear through' mean?" B.B. asked.

"It's the operations side of the business, the exchange of securities for cash on delivery. All of the large- and medium-size

firms do their own clearing, but it's too expensive for most of the
small ones, so the large firms rent their clearing facilities for a fee,
and the small firms get the advantage of the large firms' research
and product. And then there are firms that are just clearing firms,
do nothing else but."

The phone rang. B.B. backed out of the office. "Good morning, Smith and Wetzon. She's not in. May I take a message? I expect her momentarily."

Wetzon closed the door and went back to her messages.
Howie Minton had called. The message said, "To remind you."
Okay, okay, Howie, she would get on Peter Tormenkov. She
looked at Peter Tormenkov's suspect sheet and punched out his
number.

"Mr. Tormenkov's office."

"Is he in?"

"He's meeting with a client and he'll be in later. May I take
a message?"

"No, thank you. I'll call later."

One of her messages was from Arleen Grossman. She might
as well deal with it before Smith got in and put on the pressure.
She dialed the number Arleen had left.

"TC Associates, good morning."

"Arleen Grossman, please. Leslie Wetzon returning her call."
She was put on Hold while Mantovani played in the background.

"Wetzon, dear Wetzon, what perfect timing you have."
Arleen's throaty voice was full of affection. "I was just about to go
out on a consultation for a major *Fortune* 500 corporation." She
paused, to let the importance of it sink in. Wetzon wrinkled her
nose at the telephone. Arleen was obviously not just a name-
dropper, but also an event dropper. A see-how-important-I-am
person. "I do hope you'll be able to join me for dinner tonight."

"I'd be delighted," Wetzon lied. "I'm doing an interview with
a major stockbroker later in the day . . ." She swallowed hard to
keep from laughing. She hadn't been able to resist and Arleen
probably wouldn't even notice. ". . . and I'd like to drop in on a
friend of mine who hasn't been well. . . . But after that, I'm all
yours."

"Lovely." Arleen's warm voice didn't react to Wetzon's mischief. "Shall we say seven-thirty, then? Does that give you enough time? Where does your friend live?"

"On the Upper East Side." The conversation was beginning to irritate her. She wanted it over with. The phone rang.

"My dear, I hear your telephone and I'm keeping you. Shall we say Le Refuge? It's quite nice and the food is—"

"I know it, Arleen." She did, having been there with a client, the principal with a small firm, and a stockbroker the client was trying to recruit. In fact, it had been her friend, Laura Lee Day, who was now a stockbroker at Oppenheimer. Le Refuge was bistro-charming and the food was good, solid but uninspired. It was just barely on the right side of la-di-da, which is what Carlos and she called the self-consciously smug spots, popular with the yuppie crowd, that had blossomed all over their New York.

B.B. knocked at the door, opened it, and mimed a phone call.

"Hold," Wetzon mouthed.

"Good," Arleen said briskly. "Till then."

"Yes, fine. Bye now," Wetzon said.

"Oh, and, Wetzon dear," Arleen said with an oddly melodious laugh. "Don't try to resist me. I intend us to be great friends."

The receiver still nestled in the crook of her neck, Wetzon parked the near-threat in the back of her mind to retrieve and think about later. She looked at her watch and sighed. It was nearly lunchtime. "Who's on my line, B.B.?" She heard the faint sound of conversation from the earpiece in her neck.

"Donna Rhodes."

Wetzon put the phone to her ear and was about to say, "Hello, Donna," when she heard two voices arguing in a foreign language. Russian? A man and a woman. The woman was doing most of the talking and from her tone, she was in a fury. The man's voice was muffled. She hadn't known that Donna was Russian . . . Wetzon looked down at her phone. The Hold light was blinking. Puzzled, she pressed the Hold button. "Donna?"

"Hi, Wetzon, how are you?"

"Great, Donna. Can you hold a couple of seconds more or shall I call you back?"

"It's all right. I'll hold. I've been thinking about what you said a few weeks ago—"

"I'll be right back." Wetzon put Donna back on Hold and pressed the line where she'd heard the argument in Russian. Dial tone. They were gone. She'd probably cut the connection when she switched to Donna. Crossed telephone wires again. It happened frequently in heavy rains and bad weather, as if the fragile digitals broke down under excessive moisture. And they were so close to the UN, it was understandable that sometimes when the wires crossed, the languages were other than English.

Wetzon's thoughts were tripping over each other. On the other hand, had the lines somehow not disconnected after she had completed her conversation with Arleen Grossman? And had she just overheard Arleen speaking Russian? Russian with, what seemed to Wetzon's ear, as much fluency as Ilena and Misha Rosenglub.

28

"DONNA, I'M SORRY." Wetzon pulled out her file drawer and leafed through the *R*'s for Donna Rhodes's suspect sheet.

The outside door slammed, and Smith barreled in. She kicked their office door shut and dropped her new black diamond mink coat carelessly on her chair, making no move to stop it as it slid to the floor.

"Wetzon," Donna said, "I think I'm finally ready to sit down and talk."

"At last!" Wetzon pulled Donna's suspect sheet out and studied it. "I'm so glad you thought through what I said." What a coup it would be to get someone of Donna's caliber out interviewing.

"You've been really professional, and I have no interest in working with anyone else, so I think we should meet."

Smith was waving at Wetzon with wide sweeps of her hands, trying to get Wetzon's attention. Wetzon turned away. Smith should know better than to distract her when she was obviously talking business. "Thank you, Donna. That really makes me feel good. What's your schedule like this week? Except for today, I'm fairly clear . . ."

"How about sushi lunch on Thursday?"

"Thursday it is, sushi, you're on. I'll call you in the morning and we'll pick a place. I'm partial to Takesushi on Vanderbilt. But give me a clue about your thinking, so I can put my mind to work. What's going on?"

"A lot of things, I guess, starting with the new manager. He took me to dinner not long after he got here, and you know me, I listen, and sometimes I hear between the lines. He's old style, from Charleston. He's got three sticks after his name. I said to him, 'Tell me about yourself,' and he starts giving me his family pedigree, would you believe it, starting with George Washington's wife. All I wanted to know was his background in the business. I don't give a shit about his family tree."

"He's not New York. He's going to have trouble here."

"And lately we can't even get the cold callers we used to get—"

Behind her, Wetzon could hear Smith begin banging and thumping things on her desk. "Doesn't he like using the cold-calling system?" Not all managers did. In fact, many managers felt cold calling—that is, calling strangers over the telephone and trying to sell them stocks, or bonds or products—was bad for the brokerage business and was closer to a bucket shop sales approach.

"No, it's not that. He said he's open, and if it works, he's willing to keep it up, but we can't get enough callers because half the ones we had didn't pass their drug tests and they were let go."

"That gives me a start. I'll talk to you Thursday." Wetzon hung up the phone and jotted the time of their meeting on her calendar for Thursday and a reminder to call Thursday morning to fix time and place. "I don't know what this business is coming to, Smith."

"You don't know what?" Smith demanded. She was sitting on her desk, swinging her feet impatiently. Her knee-high designer waterproof boots were near her desk, leaving muddy puddles on the parquet floor.

"Half of the cold callers at Bernard Schultz couldn't pass their drug tests and were fired." Wetzon pulled an old *Business Week* from her wastebasket, rose, opened it, and put it under Smith's muddy boots. She straightened up and grinned at Smith. "Okay, brat, what do you want?"

"You are such a fusspot," Smith said, arms folded.

"Do you want to have to pay to get the floors sanded again?"

"That is so unimportant in the scope of things, Wetzon. You always think so small. I've tried so hard to teach you my way of—"

"Spare me, please, Smith." Her jaw tightened involuntarily.

B.B. knocked at the door and teased it open. "Lunch orders?"

"Chef salad for me," Smith said, "with vinaigrette dressing and an onion roll."

"Rare roast beef on a roll with Dijon and no greens."

"My Lord, what have we here?" Smith said, clapping her hands. "Rare roast beef! To what do we attribute this change in diet?"

To the fact that we'd like to kill you, Wetzon thought. It was weird. Anger always gave her an intense craving for rare beef. Some atavistic memory. "'A foolish consistency is the hobgoblin of little minds,'" Wetzon quoted Emerson. B.B. laughed.

"You really talk such garbage sometimes, Wetzon," Smith said resentfully. "Close the door please, B.B." B.B. got out of the room quickly. "I don't think you should perform for B.B. You are really making him into some kind of a pet. It's unfair of you when he's working for both of us—"

"Oh, shut up, Smith! You have some nerve saying that to me when you had Harold read you my messages. Are you spying on me, or what?"

"Oh, sweetie, no," Smith gushed, a you-have-wounded-me-to-the-quick expression on her face. "I would never do that. I just worry about you. The cards, you know, and that Teddy Lanzman. I thought you might not tell me if you were going to meet him."

"Don't worry," Wetzon said without gratitude. "I'll keep you informed." She already regretted having involved Smith in this. "Do you want to tell me about the detective?" She couldn't resist returning the needle.

"What detective?" Smith slipped off her desk and flipped through her messages. "Oh, look, Jake Donahue called."

"Probably wants to thank you for his coming-out party. That's the fastest in and out of prison I've ever seen, and with no trial."

"Wetzon, you have no forgiveness in you. Leon had Jake plead guilty and cooperate and you have to understand that three months is like thirty years to someone like Jake. He was absolutely devastated by the experience."

"Oh yeah? He didn't look devastated to me."

"You don't understand him as I do."

"I'll bet. I wonder what kind of deal they made."

"Well, of course, I know because Leon told me, but I'm not at liberty to say . . . Leon is so brilliant."

"Is he really?" She was being sarcastic, but it was wasted effort. "What did the detective tell you?"

"Are you having dinner with Arleen Grossman tonight?"

"Yes—after I meet with Kevin De Haven." Smith frowned. "We do have a business to run, you know. And after I see Hazel, which reminds me . . ." She picked up the phone and dialed Hazel.

"I've been waiting for your call. How did it go in Little Odessa yesterday?" Hazel's voice was mildly reproving.

"Very interesting, if nothing else. I'll tell you about it later. How are you feeling?"

"Mentally, just brimming over with energy," Hazel said, "but physically, pooped."

"I'll come up after an end-of-the-day interview, how's that?"

"Oh goody. How about stopping at Patek's and picking me up some pasta salad and chocolate chip muffins and whatever else looks good?"

"What time are you meeting Arleen?" Smith was going through her messages yet one more time, throwing most of them away. She rarely responded to her phone calls. Wetzon compulsively called everyone back, even the people who were trying to sell her something. "Waste of time," Smith said, throwing another slip away. Smith's dictum was that returning phone calls was not an efficient use of time. "If someone really wants to talk, they'll call back."

"Catch me up on what's happening," Smith said.

"We have Maurice Sanderson going to see Bob Curtis this afternoon."

"What an embarrassment. The old fart should just retire gracefully."

"He can't, Smith. It's his whole life. I told you that. He'd die without something to get up for every morning. We've been through this before. So let's just agree to disagree. Do you want to tell me what you want to know from Arleen so I know what I'm doing?"

The phone rang twice. The light stayed on the first button, so Harold was talking.

"I know she's going to try to get information out of you, Wetzon, so don't you dare tell her anything about me." Her voice was sharp.

Wetzon stared at her. There were strain lines around her eyes and around her mouth. She looked worried. "Why would I tell her anything about you?"

"Oh, Wetzon, I love you, but you're such a simpleton. Arleen's very smart. She'll wheedle it out of you and you won't even know it. I want you to promise me you won't tell her anything."

"Okay, I promise, but I still don't know what you want me to get out of her—"

Smith dug into her huge Ferragamo handbag and pulled out

a small box. She crooked her finger at Wetzon. "Come here a minute, sugar."

Wetzon got up, curious. The box contained a Sony minicassette recorder. "I don't believe this," Wetzon groaned.

"Don't say no, please, Wetzon, sweetie pie. It's so important to me. I just need you to do this."

"No."

"Please." Smith looked up at Wetzon, teary-eyed. "You know I would do it for you."

"Oh shit, Smith. How do I always let you get me into these things?" *And it always ends up backfiring on me somehow*, she thought, remembering the key she had found after Barry Stark was murdered and how Smith had gotten her into trouble with Silvestri because of it.

"Thank you, thank you, thank you. I am so grateful to have a loyal friend like you." Smith jumped up and planted a big kiss on Wetzon's cheek. "Now, look." She turned back to the little machine on her desk and pressed a button.

Wetzon's voice repeated, "Oh shit, Smith. How do I always let you get me into these things?"

Smith hit the Stop button and rewound the tape. "Look, all you have to do is put it in your bag and press it on as soon as you sit down with her in the restaurant."

The phone rang. For Harold again, obviously, because he didn't interrupt them.

"But what if she should find out I have it?"

"Wetzon, please don't be foolish. How would she find out?" Smith pressed the minirecorder into Wetzon's reluctant palm. "Just put it in your bag and don't forget to turn it on."

Wetzon looked at the machine in her hand. It was tiny and clever, and if she didn't feel as if she were being used, she might have been more fascinated by its size. It was not much bigger than a pack of cigarettes.

Harold knocked and opened their door. "I didn't know you knew Ted Lanzman," he said to Wetzon, part accusatory, part respectful. "He's so . . ." He looked for the right word. ". . . nice," he finished lamely.

"Well, he is and I do." Wetzon smiled and put the cassette recorder in her carryall. "Why?"

Smith turned in her chair and looked at them, annoyed.

"He's on the phone for you, Wetzon."

She picked up the phone. "Teddy? What's up?" Smith was paying rapt attention.

"Peter Tormenkov, that's what." His voice was low and full of pent-up excitement.

"I haven't been able to reach him. I'm really sorry. They said he was out—"

"Yeah, with me—" He was actually crowing.

"You? Oh no, Teddy. I asked you not to."

"Wetzi, look, I'm sorry. It's a big, big story—you don't know how big—and it's all mine! I've got an exclusive. Shit, and I have you, my old friend, to thank for it."

His old friend. Ha! "Teddy, stop for a minute." He had betrayed her confidence. How could he have done that to her? She slumped dejectedly over her desk.

"Can we meet tonight?" He plowed right through her, her upset, her feelings. "I'll tell you the whole story, Wetzi, honest. Listen, you did the guy a favor. And by the way, I think you were right."

"Right? About what?" She had been wrong about *him*, certainly.

"The old lady."

She snapped to attention. "Peepsie Cunningham?"

"Yeah."

"Tell me—"

"Later. I'm meeting with Tormenkov again tonight. He's getting me proof. I'll have the rest of it. We're making a little exchange." His laugh was a derisive bark. "I'll fill you in on everything later."

"I'm not going to be free till after nine or nine-thirty." She felt torn. She wanted to know more, but she was furious with him.

"Look, that's cool with me. I'll be at the studio writing the voice-over, cutting the tape for the next segment. You can pick me up there."

"It may be as late as ten." She would have liked to tell him what she really thought of him, but she had to know the truth about Peepsie's death. "You're sure you'll be there that late?"

"Yeah. Late night for me. You know the address. Go in the main entrance. I'll leave your name with the security guard and he'll give you a pass. He'll tell you where to find me."

29

AT FOUR-THIRTY WETZON WAS on the street again heading for the Trattoria in the Pan Am Building at Park and Forty-fifth Street, where Kevin De Haven had said he'd be having a drink with his buddies after the close.

The snow had dissolved under the daytime thaw, creating rivers of slush at crossings. Pedestrians bunched up at intersections looking for a safe place to cross. Soon enough the flooded gutters would be frozen over and even more treacherous. At the moment, however, cabs and delivery vans raced unyieldingly over the slick wet streets. Where tires met puddles, indiscriminate tidal waves of melting snow, ice, and mud were cast on the unwary.

Wetzon walked down Second Avenue looking for a place to cross. It was daylight saving time dusk, and what had been an almost balmy day receded quickly into a quiet, deadly cold. Offices had closed early, and travelers were sparser than usual at this hour. The cold was subtle. Her cheeks began to numb as she trudged across Lexington Avenue and up the small hill on Forty-fifth Street toward the Trattoria. She wriggled her fingers in her cashmere-lined gloves to keep them from freezing.

"I'm having some drinks with my pals," De Haven had said.

"How will I know you?" The bar would be jammed at four-thirty. It was the beginning of Happy Hour.

"I'm the tall, dark, handsome one. You can't miss me."

Jesus. "All right. I'm wearing a black coat," she'd said, "and a lavender beret. You can't miss me." It was like talking to the wall. She knew he wasn't listening. What's more, she didn't like this kind of meeting. There would be other people around and it would be difficult to talk privately.

When you got right down to it, she didn't like anything that had happened today. She felt she had lost control not just with Kevin De Haven, but with everything else. She thought back over the events of the day. Smith had railroaded her into having dinner with Arleen Grossman. And she was damned sorry she had mentioned anything about Teddy Lanzman to Smith.

"You can't meet him after you have dinner with Arleen," Smith had asserted when Wetzon finished her conversation with Teddy.

Wetzon, preoccupied with what Teddy had just told her, had looked up. Smith was standing with her hands on her hips, outraged.

"And why not, pray tell?"

"You're going to go flying all over the city at all hours of the night meeting dangerous people."

"Oh, Smith, really. I'm a big girl, you know. I can take care of myself. And besides, Teddy's not dangerous." Was he?

"No, it's not safe. Believe me, I know. You're to call me after you finish with Arleen and I'll go with you."

"Are you kidding?" Wetzon had studied her with narrowed eyes. Smith's face registered only sweetness and concern. So why did Wetzon feel there was more to it than that?

"After all, I have only one partner." Smith's gaze was tender. "Where would I get another like you?"

"True." Wetzon smiled at her. "And where would I get another like you?" She leaned back and put her feet out in front of her, wriggling her toes. "But I think Teddy would be put off if I brought a stranger—"

Smith brushed her off. "Nonsense. He would understand— that is, he would if he's *really* your friend. It's not wise to make yourself a target, alone on the street in that neighborhood late at night."

What the hell was she talking about? "Target?"

"What's so urgent about seeing him anyway? Did he find that awful Russian woman?"

"You mean Ida? No. He's found out something about Peepsie Cunningham that may prove she was murdered." Wetzon prudently edited out any mention of Peter Tormenkov. It wouldn't do to let Smith know any more than she already knew.

"Really? Well, I suppose you just can't wait till tomorrow to hear about it. So I'll have to go with you." She yawned.

Damn. "I don't need you to go with me." *I don't want you to go with me.* Wetzon chose her words carefully. Smith was so sensitive and the last thing she needed now was for Smith to be insulted. Smith's eyes were off in the distance. She had tuned out. "Smith?"

"Wetzon?" Smith came back from wherever she had gone. "You are to call me the moment you leave Arleen. Where are you having dinner, by the way?"

"Le Refuge."

"Humpf. I like that place. She has never taken me there."

What an odd thing to say. Who was Smith really jealous about, Arleen or Leon? "Smith—"

"Yes?" Smith had sat down at her desk again, her back to Wetzon.

"Does Arleen speak Russian?"

"Whatever do you want to know that for?" Smith turned to her impatiently. "I think you have Russians on the brain. Why would she speak Russian? She's an American like us."

B.B. knocked on their door and delivered lunch in little shopping bags from Zaro's.

"The phones are quiet today," Wetzon said, lifting up the upper half of the roll and checking the roast beef. Good, rarer than rare. She squeezed processed yellow mustard out of the little plastic pack and spread it on the underside of the roll. Probably all chemicals. She looked at her messages. "I really have to call some of these people back." She caught Smith's eye. "Don't say

it." She held up the palm of her hand to Smith. "I know, it's a
waste of time."

Smith wrinkled her forehead. "What did Howie Minton call
to remind you about?"

Wetzon took a bite of her sandwich, viciously. "To try to do
something about that broker in his office."

Smith looked blank. "What broker?"

"You know, Peter Tormenkov. The one who's working for the
FBI."

"How could I ever forget." Smith stretched. "I don't feel
much like working today."

"Why don't you give yourself an afternoon off and hit
Bloomie's on the way home?"

Smith pursed her lips. "Maybe I will. But you must promise
me you'll call me after dinner."

"Oh, that's what it's all about. You just want to be sure I tell
you everything I've learned about Arleen and give you the cassette before I go out into the night and get mugged or killed."

"Wetzon—" Smith dropped her plastic fork into her salad.
"That is just terrible of you. You don't know how to accept the
fact that I love you and care about you. Sometimes I think we
have a very one-sided relationship." She looked hurt, and Wetzon
felt a pang of guilt. *It always ends up like this,* she thought ruefully.
And who was right? Probably Smith. Smith was eccentric and
hard to figure out, and Wetzon got tired of all her double talk and
vague put-downs. She kept trying to keep the relationship
mostly business, but Smith wouldn't let her.

The phone rang.

"Okay, okay. I promise I'll call you."

"And we'll go meet Teddy Lanzman together."

B.B. knocked on the door. "Leon for you, Smith."

Thank you, Leon, Wetzon thought, relieved. She got up and
went into the bathroom.

"Hmmm." Smith picked up the phone just as Wetzon was
closing the door. "Maybe Leon should come with us, too. Hello,
sweetie," she breathed into the phone. "Hold on a minute . . .
Wetzon, I think Leon should come with us."

Wetzon slammed the bathroom door.

30

THE FRONT OF THE TRATTORIA, where in spring, summer, and fall there was a lively outdoor café, looked desolate as Wetzon approached. The vast area, denuded of gay tables and chairs, had been shoveled clean of snow, but was freezing slick underfoot and dank. Beyond it were the bright lights of the restaurant.

Wetzon went into the Trattoria through the Pan Am Building. Men and women, mostly young, were standing and sitting around the bar, two and three deep. The crowd was boisterous, rowdy even.

Without taking off her coat and beret, she strolled around the U-shaped bar, eyeing the drinkers, trying to keep her face bland but friendly. She wasn't feeling friendly. She was annoyed with herself and De Haven for the nebulous quality of what should be a professional meeting.

A man with graying sideburns, drinking something bourbon-colored, caught her eye and gave her a studied wink. She nodded at him noncommittally and moved on. He was too old for De Haven, but one had to be wary. People often described themselves quite differently from how they looked when she met them.

Two men and three women in their twenties were whooping it up as Wetzon came around the right side of the U slowly. She looked them over as she passed. One young man was tall, dark, and attractive, if you liked the type. Very smooth, well-dressed in a dark blue pinstripe, crisp white shirt, and yellow power tie. A stud. The other young man looked like a fighter, tall and barrel-chested, florid, with small pale blue eyes, tightly curled blond hair, a turnip-shaped face with high cheekbones narrowing to a small chin. His pinstripe was light gray, and his wide tie was blue with white polka dots. A hair too Broadway. The three young women were sitting on barstools, laughing loudly at whatever the handsome young man was saying, while devouring runny red Italian-style hors d'oeuvres from a plate they were passing back and forth.

Wetzon made a mental bet with herself that the stud was Kevin De Haven, but took another turn around the bar.

To her left, the dining area was less than active, but the linen-covered tables were set and ready for the dinner crowd, which usually consisted of a mix of tourists and locals from the corporations in the area. There were at least five brokerage firms with branch offices in the Pan Am Building. And Grand Central Station, which was attached to the Pan Am Building, was the biggest intersection for commuters in New York, handling New York State and Connecticut.

She traveled along the U again, noticing the middle-aged man had been joined by another, short, stout, balding. They both eyed her as she did her tour, turning obviously on their stools. *Fuck off*, she thought, unbuttoning her coat. It was warm.

When she came alongside the two men and three women this time, she paused in front of the attractive young man. The girls stopped laughing. One flipped her long dark hair back over her shoulder with a slender, scarlet-tipped finger.

"Kevin," Wetzon said.

"I told you you wouldn't have any trouble finding me." He had the easy smile and slick way of a man who was equally successful in sales and with women. "Come on, sit down. What're you drinking?" He had a half-finished beer in his hand.

"Heineken. How about taking a table?" She pointed to the small tables to the right of the bar. The women were watching her, ranking her competitively.

"Nah. It's okay here. A Heineken here, and another for me," Kevin told the bartender. He motioned to the young women. "Take off, girls. We're going to talk serious business now." The women picked up their drinks, slid off their stools, and stood around the florid young man.

"This is my buddy, Joey," De Haven said. He gestured at Joey. "Come on over here and meet Wetzon."

The barrel-chested young man came forward and shook Wetzon's hand. "Joey Mancuso, Wetzon. We've talked."

She remembered her brief conversation with him. It had been about two months ago. He was a braggart, full of how important he was, how much money he made. "I remember. We should talk again soon."

"I'm not ready to do anything yet, but call me." He was friendly. She heard little of the bombast she'd gotten over the phone. But she knew that didn't mean anything. She had discovered early on that brokers usually revealed themselves to her as if she were a shrink, either on the phone, which was their couch, or on a one-to-one meeting. They knew they could trust her.

Joey Mancuso took the girls a little way off and De Haven sat down next to Wetzon. The bartender poured beer into her glass from the green Heineken bottle and set the bottle down in front of her. He gave De Haven something on draft.

"Stay on top of Joey, Wetzon. He's my buddy and he's a good man."

Wetzon remembered how the broker who had originally referred Joey had described him: "A time bomb waiting to go off."

"Let's talk about you, Kevin. How'd you start in this business?" The bar was noisy and overcrowded, and she'd have to concentrate on his answers because she didn't want to make notes in the open.

"Well, let's see, while I was at Seton Hall, I got a job as an assistant trader at Jersey Coast Securities. It's a small institutional house in Jersey City. Then after I graduated I came on board as a trader." He let his eyes rove over a tall blonde with Farrah Fawcett hair and a red fox coat down to her ankles. She returned his sensual stare with one of her own and moved on.

Wetzon waited, fixing her face with its most pleasant smile. It was not unusual for brokers to treat her like Mom, a sexless accepter of who they were, who would love them regardless. "And how did you get to Merrill?" she asked, studying the package he was and wondering why she did not find him at all sexy.

He turned back to Wetzon without embarrassment. "I met my manager, Jim Black, on the Path train. He's one hell of a guy, by the way. He's been like a father to me. He got me over here."

"What kinds of clients do you have? What kind of business are you doing?" The beer was giving her a small glow.

"Hey, they're hedge funds, you know, they're institutional. I write big syndicate tickets."

"So you need a big wire house firm. Okay. Next, the million-dollar question is, why do you want to leave?"

"Now, don't get me wrong, Wetzon. I don't want to leave. They've been real good to me, and I love this guy, Jim Black. I'd do anything for him. But they want to reduce my payout on my institutional accounts, and that's just not right. They made me promises when I came here and now they're breaking them." He was talking with sincerity raised to the nth degree, looking straight at her.

She didn't believe him. Something smelled wrong. "I'm surprised they're letting you keep institutional clients at all—"

"Yeah, well, if they mess with me I'm out the door." He grinned at her, a big charming lopsided grin. "So, Wetzon, pal, what can you do for me?"

She'd have to think through very carefully how she could present him. "Whom have you talked to?"

"Smith Barney. They love me. Have a nice up-front cash offer. I'll probably take it."

Oh yeah? She knew that Smith Barney didn't make nice up-front cash offers. At least not since it had been bought by Sandy Weill, the brilliant and respected Wall Street strategist, who had built Shearson into a megafirm and then sold it to American Express. But then, they could always change their minds for a gorilla. And Kevin De Haven was definitely a gorilla. "You should see Prudential-Bache before you make a final decision, and Shearson. Shearson is probably the strongest syndicate firm right now."

"Set 'em up right away, okay, Wetzon? Tomorrow if possible. And listen, Wetzon, don't talk to Joey until I'm set."

"Okay."

The bartender sidled over near them. "Anything I can get for you folks?"

"And I'm not saying I'm leaving Merrill either," De Haven said, ignoring the bartender, giving her a movie star smile. "This guy Jim Black is a prince, a real prince. And he's been darn good to me."

"Check, please," Wetzon said, and reached for her wallet, but De Haven stopped her arm.

"No way," he said. "No lady ever pays a check for me."

"Well, if you put it that way . . ." She smiled. She would dine out on that for a long time because brokers never pick up checks. But for that matter, why should they? Who invited whom for a drink?

They exchanged business cards, and she hopped off the barstool.

"I'll call you tomorrow with some appointments. Don't rush and accept something without thinking it through. You've got to see other firms for a basis of comparison." She shook hands with De Haven, waved at Joey Mancuso, and went out in the cold to Vanderbilt Avenue where she caught a cab up to Patek's on Madison and Eighty-ninth to get Hazel's dinner.

Wetzon left Patek's balancing a heavy shopping bag and her carryall. The sidewalks were spread with sand and salt, but walking was difficult because of the slick spots. Snow lay in dirty frozen mounds in gutters.

The mercury streetlights threw eerie shadows on the icy landscape of Carnegie Hill, as this area of Manhattan was called, because the beautiful Carnegie Mansion on Fifth Avenue had presided over the neighborhood since the early part of the century when this was all open farmland. Now the Carnegie Mansion was the Cooper-Hewitt Museum and Carnegie Hill was a mix of giant stone-and-glass buildings, low storefronts, elegant town houses, brownstones, and old brick pre–World War II apartment houses. Hazel lived in one of the latter.

When Wetzon turned east on Ninety-second Street, she felt rather than saw a car make the turn as well. The streetlights were out and the street was dark. About halfway down the block she stopped briefly to switch hands, shifting carryall and shopping bag. The car that had made the turn was a shadow, its lights off. It stopped behind her in front of a brownstone. Wetzon kept on to Hazel's small apartment building just off Park Avenue. The only light on the street came from the windows of apartments.

The sound of a motor behind her made her aware of the car again. It crept along behind her almost as if watching her progress. The hairs on the back of her neck prickled. Wetzon walked up the two steps to Hazel's building, opened the door, and went in, closing it quickly. She placed her bags on the marble floor and turned. It was hard to see anything on the street because of the darkness, but she thought she saw the car, not moving, waiting in front of the building.

Without thinking, she stepped outside. Another car made the turn and, lights glaring, came down the block, its driver leaning on the horn. The lights suddenly came on in the waiting car, blinding Wetzon. The waiting car gunned its motor and with tires shrieking, sped away, turning right onto Park Avenue and disappearing. The second car followed at top speed, and as it went out of view, Wetzon saw the second car had been a cab.

31

IT WAS HARD NOT TO connect this incident with Judy Blue, the peripatetic cabdriver who had kept appearing in her life, always under strange circumstances. Had Judy Blue been driving the cab? Who was she? Wetzon knew coincidence played a peculiar part in life in New York City. She always seemed to meet people who knew people she knew. Her life was made up of giant links in a great chain of connections.

But Judy Blue? Was Judy Blue following her, and here was the real puzzle. Could it be connected in some way to Peepsie Cunningham? *Come on, old girl,* she thought, *it was only a cab, and there are thousands of cabs in New York City.*

"Five, Ms. Wilson." Hazel's elevator man—there was no doorman—broke the spell. Most elevator buildings in Manhattan in good neighborhoods had either doormen or elevator men, depending on which a majority of tenants preferred. The best buildings had both. Hazel's elevator man took the heavy shopping bag and carried it down the hall to Hazel's door as Wetzon followed.

An insistent buzzing sounded from the open elevator. The elevator man set the bag down on Hazel's brown sisal doormat and headed back to the elevator.

"Thank you." Wetzon rang Hazel's doorbell as the elevator doors closed.

Hazel, in the same pink-and-white robe and pink-ruffled cap, leaning on the cane, opened the door and gathered her in. Wetzon loved Hazel's openness, her warmth, her joy in life. It was supporting, contagious. The joy is in the journey, Hazel always said.

"I can't stay long. I'm due at Le Refuge at seven-thirty." Wetzon hung her coat and beret on the Victorian oak coatrack in the foyer and pulled off her boots. It was already six-thirty. She picked up the bulging shopping bag and her carryall and followed Hazel's slow progress into the kitchen, placing the shopping bag on one of Hazel's carved oak kitchen chairs. She plopped herself in another chair and watched Hazel unpack the goodies.

"You look pretty perky," she said, smiling at Hazel.

Hazel's blue eyes sparkled as she peeked into a small paper bag. "Oh yum, brownies. I do love brownies."

"I thought the shrimp and pasta salad looked luscious, so I brought you some."

"Lovely." Hazel opened the old-fashioned glass doors of her kitchen cabinets and took down china plates, placing one in front of Wetzon. "For tasting only," she hastened to say as Wetzon started to protest, at which point the tea kettle began to whistle. "Tea?"

"Oh yes, but not old rope." They laughed. It was their joke.

Wetzon could never remember the name of the tea that Hazel had given her to taste long ago when they'd first met, but Wetzon had told her it tasted like oily old rope and it had stuck. Hazel loved old rope. She had first sampled it in India and had found it again in specialty stores here when she got back.

"Irish Breakfast?"

"That's more like it." Wetzon flexed and pointed her feet. She was just starting to warm up.

Hazel measured leaves from two tins into two covered individual teaspoon strainers, placing one in each teacup. Then she poured boiling water into each cup and set one cup in front of Wetzon. Wetzon took a deep breath, inhaling the steam.

"Oh, how I'd love to be having dinner here with you tonight instead of—" She stopped. She was embarrassed that she'd let Smith manipulate her into eating with Arleen and didn't want to tell Hazel.

"You work too hard, Leslie dear." Hazel opened the rest of the containers with little exclamations of pleasure. "Oh! Um! Ah!" Her face was blotchy, scaly in spots, red and pink and white.

"How are you feeling?"

Hazel ignored her and put a single shrimp and four green fusilli on Wetzon's plate.

"Taste this. It's wonderful."

"Okay," Wetzon said. "I get it. Well, kindly let me know when you're ready."

Hazel gave her a flinty look and Wetzon laughed.

"They think they've located Marion, through the State Department. Isn't that wonderful? I'll tell you, Leslie, it's such a relief." She dipped her fork into the chicken curry and lifted it to her mouth, closing her eyes, smiling, chewing slowly. "Um. This is quite my favorite." She put her fork down and swirled the strainer in her teacup. "You see, Peepsie named me as one of her executors, and I'll tell you truthfully, once Marion gets here I intend to resign and let Marion and the lawyer handle it. She left a sizable estate, mostly to Marion and a great deal to her favorite causes. The Metropolitan Museum, Connecticut College, of course. I had no idea there was so much money . . ." Her voice drifted off sadly.

"I'm sorry, Hazel."

"Oh dear. Life goes by so quickly."

"'The joy is in the journey,' as you've always said."

"Of course." She smiled. "We had so much fun always, all of the Peepsies." She sighed and picked up her fork again. "Why don't you tell me about Little Odessa? I want to hear everything."

Wetzon spun out the story, dramatically, picking at the spread of food on the table as she did so. Hazel interjected light comments until Wetzon came to the attack outside the ladies' room, and Hazel's pale blotchy face turned white under the frilly cap.

"Oh my, this is terrible. Leslie dear, I feel responsible for your getting involved in this. I'm worried about you. I will never forgive myself if . . . Have you told your nice young man?"

"No, I haven't told my nice young man." Wetzon smiled, gently mocking Hazel's words. "He's on a big case and I haven't seen him, but really, there's nothing to worry about. It was an attempted mugging and that could happen anywhere. And he didn't get anything and I'm not hurt. See?" She did not roll down the neck of her sweater. In spite of Wetzon's reassurances, Hazel was becoming more and more agitated. "Hazel, come on, please, I promise I'll tell him, but it's not related." She then described what happened to the Tsminskys.

"Dreadful. Those poor people. They come all this way, from such a terrible place, and then this." Hazel clucked and shook her head.

"It sounds like a Mafia hit and Teddy says it may have been Russian Mafia. Smith thinks it's KGB." She grinned at Hazel. "Smith sees Russian spies under her bed. I suppose it's because her ex-husband was with the CIA."

"Now, Leslie dear, tell me the truth, you didn't find Ida, and there is nothing to make you believe Peepsie was murdered. Or is there something you're not telling me?"

"Hazel." Wetzon paused. She looked at her hands and then at Hazel. "Yes, there is something I'm not telling you." She told

Hazel about the blue Gucci shoe she had found on the street.

Hazel looked stunned. "But they found Peepsie's slippers. They were on the street near her . . . oh dear . . . I see what you mean, what if they were thrown out after . . ."

"Exactly. The question is, where is the other shoe? It wasn't anywhere in the apartment or on the street. O'Melvany told me they looked everywhere."

"But why would anyone have done such a thing? Peepsie couldn't hurt anyone . . . she couldn't even remember who I was sometimes. She was so helpless and frightened . . ."

"She was very frightened. Don't you remember? She started to tell us something when Ida came back into the room—"

"Yes. She thought you were Marion. She started to say something about—" Hazel closed her eyes, thinking, opened them, and shook her head.

"I know. I've been trying to remember." Wetzon ran her fingers around the smooth lip of her flowered teacup. "I'm going to meet Teddy later tonight," she said, "at the studio. He thinks Peepsie may have been murdered also." She stopped, considering. "When we first got together, the night after the blizzard, Teddy told me about some of the scams against the seniors— whoops—" She looked at Hazel and grinned. "I know you hate that word. I'm sorry."

Hazel's eyes twinkled suddenly. "We who are in our twilight years forgive you for the moment—but don't let it happen again." She shook her finger at Wetzon.

Wetzon blew her a kiss across the table. "You are younger than anyone I know—and that's the truth." She finished her tea and looked at the large oak school clock on the pale yellow wall. "I have to get going."

Hazel pulled a change purse out of the pocket of her robe and gave Wetzon a ten-dollar bill.

"No," Wetzon said, waving her hand. "This is on me. You do next time."

"That's a deal." Hazel folded the bill back into the change purse and slid the change purse into the pocket of her robe. "You haven't told me why Teddy thinks Peepsie was murdered."

"I don't know. That's what I'm going to find out. He wasn't able to talk. He said he'd have all the pieces tonight." She pushed back her chair and stood up. "It's very complicated, Hazel. Ida has the same last name of a stockbroker I'm working with. Let's wait until we hear what Teddy has."

She went into the foyer and got her coat and beret and came back into the kitchen. Hazel hadn't moved from the table. She had that look on her face. "I'll call you tomorrow, okay?"

"Leslie, do you think you should go there alone late at night? Isn't the television studio in the West Fifties where that gang called the Westies are?"

"Smith will not allow me to go alone, or so she says. I'm supposed to call her after I finish dinner." She kissed Hazel's cheek. "Be good."

"How could I be anything else?" Hazel's voice sounded rueful. Wetzon could feel her eyes on her as she left the room. Actually, she hadn't made up her mind about Smith, and at the moment she was inclined to meet Teddy alone.

32

LE REFUGE IS AN UPSCALE East Side Manhattan version of a Normandy inn, deep in the heart of yuppie country.

Wetzon had opted to walk the ten blocks from Hazel's apartment because she wanted time to think. Her breath came in little smoky puffs as she walked briskly on the glazed sidewalks, framed by frozen snowbanks. Her thoughts danced around in her head like the little Ping-Pong balls with the lottery numbers on them: #1 Peepsie, #2 Teddy, #3 Ida, #4 Peter Tormenkov, #5 the Tsminskys, #6 Misha and Ilena, #7 Hazel, #8 Arleen Grossman . . . all bounced around her.

Kevin De Haven popped uninvited into her mind. Was it a

waste of time to work with him? Probably. But she always played each situation out with the realization that she worked just as hard to place a low-end producer, maybe harder, as she did a high-end producer. Something about Kevin told her he might be trouble. He was too sharp, too glib, too good to be true.

True . . . blue . . . free-associated her right back to Judy Blue. Wetzon had not seen any slow-moving, unlit cars—or cabs—en route to Le Refuge, but somehow she had the feeling that she'd not seen the last of Judy Blue.

"Dum, da, dum, dum," she hummed ominously as she opened the door of the restaurant, with its blue-checked bistro curtains, and entered a long, narrow room with tables to the right and a high walnut bar to the left. It was not a bar for drinkers or even leaners; it was really just a sideboard from which the waiters poured wine or drinks were mixed. A woman in a red silk dress, a black cashmere sweater draped over her shoulders, large tortoiseshell combs in her medium-length curly brown hair, came around from behind the bar.

Wetzon shrugged out of her coat and deposited it and her scarf on the woman's waiting arm. "Thank you. My name is Leslie Wetzon. I'm meeting Arleen Grossman."

"Oh yes, Ms. Wesson. If you'll wait just a moment, I'll hang up your coat and come right back."

Wetzon smiled as the woman went past the bar and down the flight of stairs to the coatroom. Whitman, Wilson. Now she was salad oil.

The woman returned and handed her a plastic tag with a number on it. "Ms. Grossman called a short time ago to say she was delayed."

Blast. This was really annoying. "Did she say how long she'll be?"

"No, I'm sorry. Why don't I show you to your table? Perhaps you would like to have a drink while you're waiting."

"Yes, please." All she really wanted to do was to go home, shower, and put her feet up before she had to meet Teddy. This was such a waste of time and energy. Damn Smith.

The woman led her past a large French country hutch which

displayed bright jars of jams and preserves, mustards and vinegars, in pretty bottles and jars. On every flat surface there were vases and crocks filled with fresh flowers, lilies and wildflowers. They walked through a small almost private room of little character and into a larger, square setting with exposed brick walls and an enormous old stone fireplace.

The wood tabletops had an aged look created by stain, usage, and varnish, and each table had its own folksy pot filled with fresh flowers. Large blue-and-white homespun dish towels were folded as napkins at each place setting beside long-stemmed wine glasses and water goblets. Simple fluted-glass shades covered light bulbs which gave off muted light. There was something festive and cheery about the setting. And otherworldly. Cultured voices rose and fell in a discreet hum.

She was shown to a table in the rear of the room, near the fireplace. The four country-style wood chairs had cushioned seats, and Wetzon chose the chair facing the entrance to the room and looked around while a waiter cleared the table for two diners.

To her left were an older couple and a younger couple. The women looked like mother and daughter, same beaky nose, same receding chin. The two men were in business suits and were probably lawyers since they were discussing the acrimonious dissolution of yet another of the major national law firms.

At the table in front of her was a young couple who were holding hands across the wood top. They broke their hold, it seemed reluctantly, only when their first course was served.

Silvestri materialized in her mind's eye. It would be nice to be meeting him, not Arleen. He raised his eyebrow at her. On the other hand, if she were here with him, he wouldn't let her go off half-cocked, he would say, getting involved in something that was none of her business. She made him disappear.

She ordered a Perrier with lime. Arleen was already fifteen minutes late. She reached into her carryall to get her Filofax to look at tomorrow's schedule and her fingers touched the minicassette recorder. Damn. She had forgotten all about it. Smith would kill her. She pulled the bag to her lap and arranged the little machine so that she could press the button easily. When she looked up she saw Arleen Grossman in the doorway, bearing down on her. She felt herself flush, as if she'd gotten caught doing something unprincipled. Which she was. Damn that Smith. She pressed the button, unobtrusively she hoped, and put the bag on the floor at her feet.

Arleen swept into the room, more imposing than Wetzon had remembered, in a full-length silver fox coat with a wide shawl collar, which she obviously had no intention of consigning to the checkroom. She was wearing high-heeled boots, and tiny bits of fur floated in the air around her. Her jet-black hair was in the same tight coronet with the little spit curls, and her amber eyes behind the large round tinted lenses were enormous. Everyone in the room turned to stare.

"Wetzon dear." Arleen dropped her coat on one of the extra chairs. She was literally poured into a black metallic outfit, a tight-fitting, long-sleeved sweater showing every bulge where her bra cut into thick flesh and a long tight skirt emphasizing the great expanse of hip and thigh. In her large earlobes were gigantic teardrop diamonds; on her bosom floated a glittering necklace of diamonds in the shape of a soaring bird.

Wetzon pressed her back against the chair slats, instinctively trying to put more space between herself and Arleen Grossman. *A predator,* she thought. *What the hell was Arleen all dolled up for? And what an exhibition.*

Arleen settled into a chair with a small flounce and fluttered her bejeweled fingers at their waiter. "A Bellini, please," she said in her incongruous baby doll voice.

The waiter, a slim and muscular young man, wearing a small white apron over black pants and white shirt, looked startled and caught Wetzon's eye accidentally. She smiled. He nodded. He was a dancer. It was a sixth sense dancers had: they recognized each other. She knew it. He knew it. Maybe they'd even worked together once. He was about her age, perhaps a little older.

He handed them the menus and a small slate on which the specials were chalked. Wetzon ordered the warm chicory salad and the grilled trout. *Let's get this goddam show on the road*, she thought impatiently.

Arleen ordered the sorrel soup and a steak with *pommes frites, naturellement*. Fat for fat. *My, you are bitchy, Wetzon*, she thought.

"Wine, dear?"

"Not for me. I'll have another Perrier, though."

The waiter placed a narrow wooden board of sliced French bread and a small pottery crock of butter in the center of the table. At once Arleen reached fleshy fingers for the bread and butter. She was wearing a gargantuan ring made up of baguettes of diamonds and what looked like emeralds arranged in a circle, coming to a raised peak in the center where a diamond rested. On her left wrist she wore a wide gold-banded watch whose face was framed with small diamonds.

"Now then." Arleen patted her hair and favored Wetzon with a toothy smile, her face not changing one iota except around her enormous pink mouth. Where had Wetzon read that a real smile produced laugh lines around the eyes? "Isn't this just lovely?"

Wetzon knew she was sinking in her chair, trying to hide under the table. Quickly she switched her mental motor to computer automatic as she did when she interviewed a broker who was outrageous in appearance or more likely, attitude.

"I feel such a warmth about you," Arleen was saying, "that I know I can tell you absolutely anything and you will be my friend."

"Thank you, Arleen," Wetzon said politely, but she wanted to shriek and run from the table. Why did she have such good manners?

"Dear Xenia told me you are an orphan, and I just want to tell you I understand. I am an orphan, too."

"What?" Wetzon was incredulous. She felt a fire begin to smolder in her breast. How dare Smith tell anyone anything personal about her? "Really, Arleen, I tend to think of children as being orphans, not adults. I was no longer living at home when my parents died." And it's none of your goddamn business, she longed to add.

Arleen's eyes filled with tears, and suddenly Wetzon felt ashamed. Oh dear, maybe she had gone too far.

"That's all right, dear." Arleen patted her hand. "I do understand how you feel. It's easier not to talk about it. You see, I never do. But I feel so close to you, that you are so empathetic, I can tell you that my mother was murdered."

"My God!" Wetzon's exclamation was involuntary.

"Yes, it's painfully true. And by my father, I might add." Arleen's full face was almost obscenely solemn. "I was delivered shortly thereafter, in a caul. It was what saved me, of course. No one knows the extent of the trauma on the child of that kind of birth." She smiled modestly. "I have made it my cause in life. I received my undergraduate degree in psychology from Duke, on scholarship. Actually, I finished in three years, and my Ph.D. from Boston University two years later. For years I have treated people, children especially, who were deprived of mother love at an early age."

Wetzon was flummoxed. She already knew more about Arleen Grossman than she ever wanted to know.

The waiter delivered Arleen's soup and Wetzon's salad, which was studded with small lardons of bacon. Wetzon used the food to break the spell Arleen had created. "This is delicious," she said.

"So is this. Would you like a taste?"

"No, thank you. I know it's very good. I've had it before."

"Of course, your thought must be," Arleen said, continuing her intimate monologue as if there had been no break, "why did my father murder my mother?"

Wetzon stared at her. She seemed to be waiting for an answer. "Was your father arrested for the murder?" she asked finally.

"Oh no. They could never prove he did it, but I knew. That's why he left me with a black wet nurse and took my sister, who was six at the time, and came to New York, where he and my mother were from originally."

"Left you where?"

"In Baltimore."

"How awful."

"I was given a lot of love and care by this wonderful black lady until my father came back and tore me from her arms and took me to New York and placed me in an orphanage."

"Where was your sister?"

"She was living with him and my stepmother."

"He married again?"

"Oh yes, very quickly."

"And left you in an orphanage? How horribly cruel." Somehow cruelty by a parent was overwhelming. But this parent had been a murderer. Or was he?

"Yes, until I was seven. My dear sister used to visit me and bring me little presents she bought for me with the few pennies they allowed her to keep from her labor. They made her go to work, you see, to help support them."

"Finished?" The waiter cleared their plates from the table.

"They removed me from the orphanage and took me home to Washington Heights. I was so thrilled. I thought everything would be all right from then on. But my stepmother had had a child with my father. She was sexually abusive with my half brother. You have met my brother. You see the damage that was done to him. She made my sister and me do all the work around the house and fed us from scraps from the garbage."

"How awful, Arleen. What about your father?"

Tears sprang into Arleen's already damp eyes. "He was a weak man. He did nothing. Turned his back. He was an evil man, manipulative." Her mouth twisted and her eyes hardened. "I do not forgive him. I forgive no one for evil toward me."

Suddenly the restaurant seemed cold and drafty. "But look what you've made of your life, Arleen. You're a respected psychologist. You own your own successful business. You have accomplished so much."

"Yes, this is true." Arleen nodded, preening. "That is absolutely true, my dear Wetzon."

"I always wondered how children can grow up in poverty and despair and how some can rise above it and others are crushed by it. Is it in the genes?"

"You are so intuitive, my dear, that is why I like you so much.

I wrote a paper on just this subject for *Psychology Today* a few years ago, and of course I have lectured extensively on the subject. Perhaps you saw me interviewed by Phil Donahue?"

"Ms. Wesson?" The woman in the red silk dress looked inquiringly at Wetzon.

"Yes?"

"There's a telephone call for you."

"For me?" Only Hazel and Smith knew she was here. "Excuse me, Arleen. Where can I take it?"

"Follow me, please." The woman in the red dress led her back through the restaurant, past a hanging wooden wine rack filled with wine bottles, to the staircase beyond the bar. "There's an extension in the coatroom."

Wetzon went down the short flight of stairs. Straight ahead were the bathrooms; to her right was the coatroom and the phone, off the hook. She picked up the phone. "Hello?"

"Did she say anything yet?" It was Smith, sounding frantic.

"Smith, for godsakes, no she hasn't."

"Did you remember to put on the tape?" Her breath came in short pants.

"Yes, but really, Smith, this is ridiculous. Arleen's a nutcase. She just told me this off-the-wall-story—"

"I can't talk to you now, Wetzon. Just call me when you're ready to leave. Don't forget, I'm going with you." There was a click, leaving Wetzon with the dead receiver in her hand, nonplussed. She was convinced Smith was having a nervous breakdown.

But the real question in Wetzon's mind was, what does Arleen want of me?

When Wetzon returned to the table, the waiter was serving their dinners.

"Nothing terrible, I hope." Arleen scrutinized her face with a discomforting thoroughness.

"No. Just business. I'd left the restaurant phone number with my office, just in case."

Wetzon tasted the trout. It was heavenly.

"I do believe I am a good judge of character," Arleen said, demolishing her fillet of beef. She broke a chunk of the crisp French bread into pieces and began sopping up the red juices on her plate. Wetzon watched, fascinated by her thoroughness.

"Well then," Arleen continued, "I want to tell you that I do feel I can trust you, our having shared so many similar events in our lives. I know you share my deepest feelings." She gave Wetzon a mesmerizing look as her hands and mouth worked the blood-laden bread. "I have only your best interests at heart. You do believe me, don't you?"

"Well, of course I do." What the hell was all this leading up to?

"Then you will understand that what I'm going to say to you is for your own good and you will treat it confidentially."

"Yes." Get on with it, dammit.

The waiter came with dessert menus and they ordered coffee and the Paris-Brest.

"I want your promise that what I am about to tell you will be kept in confidence."

Wetzon crossed two fingers on her left hand, which lay in her lap. "I promise." *You're bad*, she thought. *Don't you trust anyone? No*, she responded silently.

Arleen drew breath in and released it slowly. Her face swelled visibly. "Your partner is your enemy."

Wetzon held up her hand. "Wait. Stop."

Arleen continued, a faint smile around her lips. "You must not trust Xenia. She has difficulty with the truth. She says terrible things about you to others."

Wetzon put her hands to her ears, but not before she heard Arleen's final words. "She is jealous of you and she will try to destroy you."

It was the most amazing thing. She wanted to scream at Arleen, "Stay out of my life, get away from me," but she'd been brought up too well. One just didn't make scenes in restaurants. But one should.

Her thoughts came rapidly, one on top of the other: Smith was right, Arleen Grossman was not to be trusted. Wetzon put her hands on the edge of the table, pushing her chair back. She didn't notice the woman in the red silk dress until she stood at Arleen's left.

"Ms. Grossman, your driver asked us to let you know immediately that the call you've been waiting for has come through."

Arleen smiled benignly, her first chin disappearing into the roll of the second. "Wetzon dear, I do hope you won't mind if I cut our lovely evening short." She spoke as if nothing had happened, as if she had not been saying those terrible things. "I have been waiting for this call from my English subsidiary. I may have to take an extensive leave—" She picked up the check, glanced at it, and took two crisp one-hundred-dollar bills from the bulky black leather envelope she carried. Handing them with the check to the woman in the red dress, she stood and leaned toward Wetzon, obviously meaning to plant a kiss. Wetzon, seeing it coming, ducked.

Arleen looked amused. She smoothed her lacquered spit curls with dimpled fingers. "You'll see I'm the best friend you have and someday you'll thank me." She slipped her silver fox coat around her massive shoulders and sailed away, a swollen perambulating bird.

Wetzon shook her head to clear her mind. It was weird. Arleen and Smith were strangely similar. Smith always said things like that. "You'll see I'm right," and "One day you'll thank me," and "I'm the best friend you'll ever have." Wetzon sat at the table for a minute oblivious to the activity in the restaurant, then looked at her watch. Nine-thirty. She had to move quickly. First, call Smith and talk her out of coming along to meet Teddy.

She walked to the front of the restaurant dodging waiters with trays, heading for the pay phone in the basement. She paused near the picture window with its horizontal homespun half curtain and looked out into the night. The streetlamp lit up the front of Le Refuge, spotlighting a large black stretch limousine. The discharge from its running engine against the cold air gave it a surreal appearance as if it were floating in a swirl of whitish smoke. The car moved slowly forward. A lean man in a tight cloth overcoat, collar turned up against the wind, and a Russian-style fur hat pulled down over his ears, walked to the limousine.

The limousine paused. Its rear door opened. The man took a quick look around, his glasses glinting in the street light. Wetzon let out a sharp breath.

The couple at the table nearest the window stopped eating, looked at her, curious—as only New Yorkers are curious—momentarily—and then went back to the important matter on their plates.

The tall man got into the limousine beside Arleen Grossman. The door closed and the limousine pulled away.

There was no question in Wetzon's mind as to the identity of the tall man. Smith's instincts were on target again. It was Leon Ostrow.

33

WITH A CERTAIN AMOUNT OF trepidation Wetzon put the quarter in the pay phone and dialed Smith's number. It rang and rang. No response. Strange. Perhaps she had dialed the wrong number. She hung up and tried again. Again, no response. She disconnected and stood thinking. Where was Smith? What could have gotten her—and Mark, as well—out on a bitter night like this? Especially as she had been waiting for Wetzon's call. Smith was so unpredictable. Well, no matter, at least Wetzon was off the hook.

She sighed, not looking forward to telling Smith about Arleen and Leon. That damn minicassette recorder. Somehow she would have to edit out what Arleen had said about Smith. She sighed again. The coat check woman gave her an inquiring look. "It's all right, just thinking out loud," Wetzon told her. Clearly, Arleen was trying to drive a wedge between Wetzon and Smith, but for what purpose?

She rummaged in her carryall looking for the recorder. She

would erase the tape and let Smith think the machine had goofed. Smith would be incensed, would rail at her that she was an incompetent, that any dummy could work one of those. Well, fine. She wouldn't mind anything Smith said at this point. She would try to protect Smith and be as supportive as she could. Poor Smith.

Where the hell was it? Her bag was such a clutter. She really should clean it out. Wetzon gave up and went into the ladies' room. Piece by piece, she unloaded her carryall on the ledge over the sink. There was no minicassette recorder in her bag.

Arleen had removed it. Who else could have? Who else would have cared to? When Smith's call had come in, Wetzon had left the table, left her bag on her chair. *What a dunce you are, Wetzon,* she thought.

It was time to meet Teddy. At the coatroom Wetzon presented the plastic disk to the coat checker and was wrapped and capped and out on the street minutes later.

A cab stopped in front of Le Refuge, and Wetzon waited with thinly veiled impatience while a man in a gray overcoat and gray fedora paid the driver and entered the restaurant with a thin woman in mink, a gray silk scarf loosely wrapped around her dark hair. People were eating later and later in New York, it seemed. Almost as if it were a European city. The major difference was they still got up at the crack of dawn, to exercise and rush off to the Street and make money.

It was dark and quiet when the cab dropped her at Channel 8. This far west on Fifty-seventh Street was mostly commercial: factories, warehouses. The television station was the only twenty-four-hour business in the area, except for its substantial competitor, CBS, two blocks east.

A tiny flutter of excitement stirred her. Teddy now believed that Peepsie had been murdered, and he didn't—or hadn't—known much about the case. So what information did he have that would lead him to think this?

Channel 8's main entrance was up about ten low steps to a large, flat stone building twelve stories high. The lobby was widely exposed to the street because of the glass doors and plate glass that surrounded the doors. A husky blue-uniformed guard with a comic Mexican mustache sat behind a curved high faux marble counter, reading a newspaper.

Wetzon, mounting the steps which had been shoveled clean and scattered with that new salt equivalent like little white BBs, sensed the guard sizing her up. She pulled the brass handle of the glass door. It was locked. The guard watched her but didn't move. You'd think he'd get up to investigate, she growled to herself. She motioned to him and pointed to her watch, smiling politely.

He stared at her and looked down at a large appointment book on the counter in front of him. Then, grudgingly, he folded his newspaper and got to his feet, ambling to the door. His height was a surprise. He wasn't much taller than she, but he was built like a tank. Muscles bulged under his uniform. He had an emblem on his sleeve that said C-8 Security, and a white clip-on ID with his picture that said Torres. He picked up a key chain hanging from his belt and squatted, taking his slow, sweet time about unlocking the door at its base and opening it a crack. "Yeah?"

Wetzon was freezing. She hopped from one foot to the other, trying to keep warm. "I have an appointment with Ted Lanzman. My name is Leslie Wetzon."

The guard looked at her without changing expression and grunted, then finally opened the door just wide enough for her to squeeze through. He surveyed the dark, empty street suspiciously and pulled the door shut. There was a solid click when the lock took.

Torres sauntered back to the counter and picked up a plastic ID from under his *Wall Street Journal*. "He's expecting you. He's in room 24B in the annex. He said you're to meet him there." Despite his Mexican *bandito* looks, Torres spoke perfect, unaccented American English. Probably an actor with a night job. Torres handed her the plastic card with the clip. Her name was handprinted on it: Ms. L. Watson. She clipped it to the lapel of her coat. *If she was Watson, where was Holmes?*

"How do I get there?" She unbuttoned her coat and tucked the ends of her belt into each pocket.

"Night elevator to five. Turn right, walk straight through. You'll see where the buildings connect. The doors aren't locked. They're up there. You'll hear them before you see them." He didn't crack a smile.

Was that supposed to be a joke?

The night elevator was obviously more for service than for looks. It stood waiting, a big metal affair with its doors open. There were at least a dozen cigarette butts of various lengths on the scuffed metal floor, and the battered steel enclosure reeked of stale tobacco.

She pressed 5 and the machine hummed into action, doors slid closed, with a creak. The floors blinked above the doors: 2, 3, 4, 5. The doors grumbled open and Wetzon stepped into a long empty corridor. Fluorescent lights blazed overhead. She turned right. Heavy cameras and equipment lined the walls, some covered by canvas, each with the imprimatur of the channel. The floors were carpeted in industrial beige, and her boots made a sluffing sound as she walked. She passed doors with glass windows and above each door was the word *Studio* and a number; some had a letter as well. The studios were dark.

The corridor ended with two large metal doors, also with windows. She pushed on the doors, and they opened easily, letting her into what she assumed was the annex, because the floor dipped a fraction lower although the carpet was the same. It was a different building. The walls here were plaster rather than the stone or marble of the main building.

And now she could hear the voices. They were muffled, but the contentiousness was audible.

The light was on in room 24B. Through the glass window she saw a production room. Twelve high-tech TV monitors lined one side of the room, beneath which were a cluster of knobs and switches, heavy-duty professional equipment, much more complicated than the light boards from her theater days. Four people were sitting at a control board, watching one of the monitors, waving their arms, all shouting at once. A woman and three men. The woman and one of the men, short, with a scruffy beard, were about Wetzon's age, perhaps younger. The other two men looked older. One was sitting with his feet up on the control board table. Kinky sprouts of red hair framed a wide bald path on his head. The fourth, who wore jeans and a red sweatshirt that had RUTGERS in black letters, was pushing and turning dials on the control board.

Wetzon knocked on the door. No one paid attention, no one even looked up. She opened the door.

"Cut that fucking part," Kinky Sprouts said. "It's too fucking long as it is—"

The woman, dirty blonde strings of hair hanging in her eyes, took a pencil from behind her ear and stabbed it toward Kinky Sprouts. "No one's cutting—"

"Excuse me," Wetzon said.

They looked at her and looked away.

"It's fucking not up to you, Joan."

"Well okay, so where the fuck is Teddy? Let him decide."

"Excuse me—"

"Yeah? Looking for someone?" Joan stuck her pencil back behind her ear and stared at the monitor.

"Teddy Lanzman. He's expecting me."

All four exchanged knowing looks.

"He went up to his office for a minute—hey, guys, what the fuck is keeping Teddy—"

"You know him, man, a minute, a half hour. He's probably on the phone—"

"Listen, you can wait here, or you can catch him upstairs," Joan said.

"Upstairs?"

"Yeah, his office—seventh floor—main building. River side." Joan didn't look up from the monitor.

"Thank you." No one turned around to look at her.

"I don't see why we can't get thirty seconds off here."

"No way. That's a fucking great shot of that old woman taking out her teeth."

"It's shit, Joan! *Shit!* But I'll give it back to you under the credits."

"No fucking deal," Joan screamed.

Wetzon headed back to the elevators. The hallway yawned empty in front of her and she quickened her pace. The dark-windowed studio doors seemed to be staring at her. When she pushed through the metal doors to the main building, the hooded equipment eyed her with menace. She was an intruder here. She shivered. Thank heavens the elevator bank was straight ahead.

She was thinking how stupid she was being when the ceiling lights flickered and went out, leaving her in utter blackness. "Shit!" she heard someone say and realized it was she. God, she was spooked.

The lights flickered again twice and came back on. Relief flooded her. What the hell was she so nervous about? She rushed to the night elevator and pressed the Up button. No motor sound, no hum. Nothing. The light on the elevator button did not go on. She pressed Down urgently. Nothing. Damn. She hit both the Up and Down buttons frantically. The lights went out, this time without the flicker. Unreasonable fear washed over her.

But wait, she wasn't in complete darkness. There was some kind of light coming from the corridor in front of her. She moved toward it, her right hand lightly skimming the wall. It was the stairwell. Dim light was coming from the stairwell. They must be on a different current, maybe DC current or on a different line. Probably then, the elevator was out. She would take the stairs to Teddy's office. Only two flights up and if his office was on the river side, it would be the first office, right or left, by the stairwell.

She pushed open the windowed metal door by its metal bar and stepped into a wide stairwell. The door slammed behind her with a loud echoing thump. Then it was absolutely still. She gathered up the front of her long coat and began climbing the stairs.

On the sixth floor she peered out into a dark corridor. No lights, no people. A door opened somewhere above her and she heard heavy footsteps coming down in her direction. She stopped and waited. If she got caught on the stairs, she'd have nowhere to run—wait—what was she doing to herself? Caught?

What was she worried about? It was probably Teddy or someone who worked here. Caution, caution, for crissakes, Wetzon. Cool and calm.

The steps came closer. "Motherfucking shit," a woman's voice said. A short dumpy woman came into view. She was lugging a hand-held camera. It was Gretchen from the other day in Little Odessa. She didn't seem surprised to see Wetzon.

"Hi," Wetzon said, relieved. "Are the lights out on the seventh floor, too?"

"Fucking lights are fucking out in the whole fucking building, except for the stairs. And who knows how long they'll last in this fucking place." She stopped next to Wetzon and shifted the camera to her other shoulder. She was wearing khakis and a red flannel shirt hanging out from under a navy down vest. Gretchen brushed past her and continued down the stairs. Taking a deep breath, Wetzon began the climb to the seventh floor.

A moment later the lights in the stairwell went out, came on, went out, and stayed out. Black hell. Desolation.

"Fucking shit!" Gretchen's voice echoed up from below.

Wetzon clutched the stair rail. Feeling for each stair with the toe of her boot, she kept moving. She could hear Gretchen cursing and held the sound in her head gratefully to keep her balance. It seemed to take forever to get up one flight.

Her hand touched the metal bar of the stairwell door, and she knew she had reached the seventh floor. Perhaps she should just wait here till the lights came on. No. That could be the rest of the night. She would find Teddy and at least they would wait it out together. The darkness pressed in on her. She felt a momentary panic, shook it away, and pushed on the metal bar to open the stairwell door. No magic. The lights did not come on. If anything, it seemed blacker than the stairwell, and here there was no Gretchen cursing for her to anchor on to. Just oppressive silence.

She stood, trying to determine which office was Teddy's, when she heard what sounded like a door opening near her. There was a faint flare of light and two funny flat noises, one right after the other, as if someone were swatting flies with a flyswatter. She pressed her body back against the wall near the stairwell door, not moving, concentrating, all senses aroused. The faint light disappeared.

She was not alone. Someone was in the corridor with her. "Teddy?" Her voice stuck in her throat. "Teddy? Is that you?"

There was no answer, but she could feel a presence coming closer. Fear, like a bright red light, burned through her body. She knew she had to get away from the stairwell. In her mind's eye she saw herself thrown, falling down the stairs, landing in a broken, crumpled heap. She edged along the wall in the direction of the elevator bank.

Whoever was in the hallway with her was not Teddy. Teddy would have identified himself when she called out to him. Her fingers touched the metal doors of the elevator. At that moment she heard the stairwell door crack open; footsteps sounded on the stairs momentarily before the door swung closed. She was alone. Or was she? She heard the sound of breathing, heart thumping, a funny rustling sound. Foolish, Wetzon. Her own breathing, her own thumping heart.

She inched back to the stairwell, got her bearings, and found the door to the office on the right. It was closed, locked. She edged across the hall. There was that funny rustling sound she'd thought she'd heard before. She stopped and listened.

Something, someone, grazed her, throwing her against the cold stone wall. The stairwell door opened and closed, and for the second time she heard running footsteps. She set her bag down. She was shaking all over. She had come to meet Teddy, get information, and go home. It had been a long day and now it was an even longer night. Maybe she would just sit right down here on the floor till the lights came on or until Teddy found her. If he had gone back to the editing room, maybe they would tell him she had been looking for him. At that thought, she almost laughed. That single-minded group wouldn't even think to tell him.

Oh what the hell. She steadied herself and felt for the edge of the door to the office opposite the locked one. Maybe this was Teddy's office. "Teddy?" She held on to the doorframe. The door was partly open. "Teddy?" She stepped forward again, inching her way into the room, sideswiping a file cabinet, bumping another hard metal obstruction. "Shit!" She turned away and tripped over something round and hard on the floor and fell forward against a chair. She sat down hard.

Okay, thank you very much, she would just sit here and wait for the lights to come on. There was something wet and sticky on the arm of the chair. She wiped her hand on her coat. Spilled soda or beer, probably. It was warm here and she was tired. What the hell was it that she'd tripped over? She reached down toward the floor and ran her hand around. It was wet here too. Her hand touched a narrow, round object and she picked it up. It was long and heavy. And hot. She dropped it, frowning, puzzled.

Suddenly, the lights came on with blinding red intensity.

It was an optical illusion. She was sitting in a room that had just been painted with wet red paint.

Red paint had spilled all over the desk in front of her. Red paint mixed with other stuff. She wondered what kind of mess Teddy had left his office in, but she could ask him because he was there, looking for something under his desk.

"Teddy . . ." She stood up. She could see his shoulders in his parka. One hand lay clutching some red papers on the top of his desk amid the red mass of bone and brains and hair that had been his head.

34

"YOU LOSE A BUTTON, MISS?" A sonorous voice pierced the fog that held her close and warm. A man's voice.

"Please go away," Wetzon mumbled, raising her head from her arms but not opening her eyes.

"Hey!" A woman's voice this time. Someone shook her shoulder, not too gently.

"Come on, Ms. Watson, snap out of it." The man's voice again.

She was reluctant to open her eyes. She might see it again. Teddy's headless body. Teddy—her friend Teddy Lanzman—She opened her eyes. Now she remembered where she was. The precinct.

Irma Ignacio—Detective Ignacio—set a white Styrofoam cup in front of her. "Drink some of this. You'll feel better."

Wetzon reached for the cup with both hands and held it to her lips. Hot coffee. Inhaling deeply, she breathed steam from the hot liquid up into her sinuses, clearing her head of clumps of cotton wool, or at least that's what it felt like. Her hands were cold and she warmed them on the cup before she swallowed what she was certain was pure caffeine.

A quilted down coat, not her coat, rested on her shoulders. She struggled to focus on her surroundings, setting the cup down on the scarred wooden desk and looking for the first time at the man who had spoken to her. He was sitting on the corner of the desk, one foot on the floor, the other swinging back and forth, smoking, watching her.

"Who are you?" She remembered seeing him with the other detectives, but she hadn't spoken to him. Irma Ignacio had interviewed her. Interviewed? *Really, Wetzon,* she thought, *you have to get your act together here.* Question, or interrogate, were the operative words here.

"Morgan Bernstein, Detective Sergeant."

"Where's my coat?" she asked, pushing her hair away from her face with the back of her hand. Her voice sounded whiny. They had taken her fingerprints and then someone had painted her hand with thin wax; the paraffin test was standard procedure in cases like this, they'd told her. It would eliminate her immediately as a suspect. She had been able to wash her hands afterward, but she still felt creepy, as if she still had Teddy's blood on them. Maybe she should have protested about taking the tests, maybe she should have demanded an attorney, but she was exhausted, and, anyway, they said it was routine in gunshot cases. Everybody had to have the test and be fingerprinted. And she had discovered the body.

Bernstein didn't respond to her question. He had brittle blue eyes buried under bushy eyebrows which traveled like ivy in a continuous thick curly line between his eyes. He was wearing a black knitted yarmulke on his curly hair, pinned in place by a brown bobby pin. He stubbed his cigarette out in a cheap plastic ashtray and emptied the ashtray in the metal wastebasket next to his desk, banging it against the wastebasket longer and with more force than necessary.

They cased each other like two adversaries, warily. He was broad-shouldered and solid as a rock, the only signs of age being a paunch that pushed past his striped shirt and stopped well over his brown leather belt and the gray threads in his brown hair.

Having taken his measure, Wetzon asked again, more firmly, "Where's my coat?" She moved her attention to Irma Ignacio, who was small, lean, and tough in a gray polyester pantsuit and a black turtleneck sweater. She, too, was smoking. The coat behind her on the chair was a woman's gray storm coat, smelling of cigarettes. She vaguely remembered Detective Ignacio taking it off and putting it on Wetzon's shoulders.

"We're holding it," Ignacio said.

"In protective custody?" *Oh, Wetzon,* she kicked herself mentally. *Don't be such a smart ass.*

"Sure." Bernstein wasn't amused. "What about this button?" He shoved a shiny brass button at her, practically under her nose.

She pushed his hand away, angry. "Don't do that! If you want me to look at the button, hand it to me like a person. You are not the gestapo."

He dropped the button in the ashtray and with a sarcastic flourish, presented it to her. She picked it out of the ashtray, brushed the ashes off, and looked at it. It was the kind that was put on blazers. "It's not mine." She looked down at her brown tweed suit. Plain and simple brown bone buttons.

"Have you ever seen it before?"

"Well, I don't know if I've seen this one, but I've seen a lot that look like it." Bernstein was waiting, swinging his foot back and forth, back and forth. Black socks, brown shoes, crepe soles. "It's a blazer button. I think it's fairly common."

Bernstein put the button in a small Glycine bag and the bag in his desk drawer. "Let's get a statement," he said to Ignacio.

"Can I go home after I give you a statement?" Wetzon asked. Bernstein got off the desk and walked to the glass wall that looked out into the squad room. He didn't answer her. Wetzon directed her next question to Ignacio. "Can I call someone and let him know where I am?"

Bernstein turned, his manner threatening, his voice loud. "You think you need a lawyer, Ms. Watson?" He walked back to his desk.

"I didn't say I was going to call a lawyer." Wetzon felt a little uneasy, as if she was missing something. Why was he yelling at her? "Should I have a lawyer? Are you holding me here for some other reason? And my name isn't Watson, it's Wetzon." He shot an inquiring look at the plastic card she saw he had on the desk in front of him. The ID she had been given when she got to Channel 8. Wetzon reached down for her carryall. It wasn't there next to her chair. "My bag—where's my bag?"

Bernstein pulled out her carryall from somewhere behind his desk. He handed it to her without comment. His phone rang. He leaned across the desk and picked it up. "Yeah?" He listened. "Okay." He hung up and returned his attention to Wetzon, who was digging in her bag, looking for her wallet.

"You must already know what my name is. Don't tell me you

didn't go through my bag." She watched him for a reaction. There was none. Just like Silvestri. She produced her wallet. Her driver's license was in the slot where her American Express Card usually was and vice versa.

"We'd like to get a statement now while it's still fresh," Ignacio said, lighting up from a stub, her gold hoop earrings swinging.

Still fresh. Teddy was dead. "Oh God, Teddy is dead," Wetzon said.

"If you were such good friends, why did he give security the wrong name?" Bernstein demanded.

"Maybe he didn't. Maybe he asked someone else to do it for him. People always hear my name wrong."

"That's your story?"

"May I make that call now?" She already knew she wasn't going to call Leon. She felt sad about that relationship. It would probably never be the same again. It was bad judgment to mix business with—what? Sex? It complicated everything.

"Who do you want to call?" Bernstein coughed, a dry hacking cough, and put out his cigarette in the battered ashtray.

"Silvestri. Seventeenth Precinct." *Take that, you mean bastard*.

Now she got a reaction from Bernstein. Surprise, quickly replaced by suspicion. "Silvestri? You know him?"

What does one say, she wondered. We're an item . . . he's my boyfriend . . . we're lovers . . . shit. "Yes," she answered, staring Bernstein down. She felt her cheeks getting hot.

Bernstein looked at Ignacio, who shrugged, then picked up the phone and dialed out, then waited. "Silvestri there?" He ran a stubby finger under his yarmulke and scratched his head. "Yeah, well, have him call Bernstein at Midtown North. Tell him we're holding a friend of his over here." He gave the word *friend* a nasty twist. "That's it." He replaced the phone, stretched, and walked to the door, again looking out in the squad room. "Let's get a statement here. Ignacio? Anyone around to do it?"

"Jesus Christ, Bernstein." Ignacio stood up, brushed around him, and went out into the squad room. She returned a second or two later. "You know God damn well no one's around now. We want to get a statement, we put it on tape. Don't do a number on me, man."

Bernstein coughed and sat down at the desk, facing Wetzon.

Wetzon looked at Ignacio sympathetically. Whatever profession women pushed their way into, they were still having to face that secretary or assistant image that men had of them. It was the same in finance as it was in the police department, Wetzon thought dismally. Ignacio had been the first detective to talk to her after they'd gone over the murder scene at Channel 8. And she'd been thorough and professional. She had given Wetzon her coat when they'd taken the bloodstained mess of her own away. Teddy's blood. She had sat in the dark in Teddy's blood without knowing he was lying there with . . . not three feet from where she sat.

Involuntarily, Wetzon flung her hand out in front of her to wipe away the hideous memory, knocking over the Styrofoam cup, spilling its contents, thick and brown with coffee grounds like coagulating blood, onto the desk. "Oh shit, I'm sorry." She gnawed on her bottom lip and looked at Bernstein, who began wiping up the spilled coffee with a wad of Kleenex from a box Ignacio held out to him.

What had Bernstein said on the phone? He'd used the word *holding*. ". . . we're holding a friend of his . . ." "What do you mean 'holding'?" she asked sharply.

"Just what I said." Bernstein's face and manner were unnecessarily nasty.

"Cool it, Bernstein." Ignacio sat down at the other desk. She took a stack of paper forms from an inside drawer and rolled a sheet into her typewriter. "Okay, Ms. Wetzon, we already have your vitals. So why don't you tell us how long you've known Ted Lanzman."

"I think maybe I'll just wait until Silvestri gets here." She sat back and watched anger roll across Bernstein's face like a movie wipe. She reached into her carryall and pulled out the paperback *Dancing on My Grave*, Gelsey Kirkland's autobiography. She had met Gelsey at Carola Trier's studio, where injured dancers came for physical therapy. She opened the book to the bookmark and tried to read.

Time inched along. Bernstein stewed. He stood, noisily shoving his chair against his desk. "We'll wait, but he's not around. It could take all night."

"Let it. I don't care." She did not look up from the book, but she saw through her lashes Ignacio's restless movement.

Ignacio clicked her nails across the keys of the typewriter, sighed, opened and closed her desk drawer. Finally, she gave Bernstein the eye. "I'll get some more coffee."

"Why don't you tell us the truth, Ms. Wetzon? It'll go easier for you in the long run."

Wetzon had been reading one line over and over, thinking about what to do. She let her eyes meet Bernstein's. "Are you threatening me?" She replaced the bookmark and closed the book. "Why did you take my fingerprints and give me that test?"

"It's automatic with anyone at the scene of a crime."

"I'll bet." She loathed Bernstein. He was treating her as if she were Teddy's murderer. He had no right.

Ignacio brought three cups of coffee, holding the cups bunched together. She kicked the door closed behind her. Wetzon took a big swallow of coffee, burning her mouth and throat. She needed the caffeine to revive her. Bernstein had a right, if he thought she was the murderer, to see what he could get out of her before she asked for a lawyer. She had to have a lawyer; that was clear now. She would have to give in and call Leon. "Am I being charged with something? Because if I am, that's it, and if I'm not, I'll be happy to help you out with what I know."

Ignacio looked at Bernstein, who shrugged. "I suggest you cooperate with us, one way or the other," Ignacio said.

"Very well then, I'd like to call my lawyer," Wetzon said.

"Be my guest." Bernstein gave his phone a rough shove at her across the desk.

"Dial nine for outside," Ignacio said.

She picked up the phone and dialed 9, then paused. She would call Carlos's friend, Arthur. He was a lawyer. What the hell was Arthur's last name? She closed her eyes . . . Arthur . . . Arthur . . . Margolies floated right across her closed eyes like a banner flying in the wind. West End Avenue. She called information and got Arthur Margolies's phone number.

"How long have you and Lanzman been lovers?" Bernstein moved in on her suddenly. Ignacio watched her benignly.

"We were never lovers. It wasn't that kind of friendship." She hung up the phone and promptly forgot Arthur's number. Damn.

"Then what did you fight about?" Bernstein leaned over at her, crowding her.

"Back off, Bernstein," Ignacio said, giving him a warning look. "Let the lady be."

"Well, Ms. Wetzon?" Bernstein growled.

Good cop, bad cop, Wetzon thought. *Were they thinking to trap her?* She started to get up.

"No, sit down, sit down." Bernstein motioned angrily with his hand. "All we want is your story. Just the facts." Jesus, he thought he was in *Dragnet*.

She sat and picked up the phone again, going through the same process, this time dialing Arthur's number.

"Start where you think it begins," Ignacio said.

"It begins in Sergeant O'Melvany's precinct," Wetzon said abruptly, getting mild pleasure from the startled looks on both Ignacio's and Bernstein's faces. She sat back and listened to the steady ringing in her ear of Arthur Margolies's unanswered phone. It was the middle of the night. Her watch said two o'clock. They had either turned off the phone or didn't hear it. She was so tired.

There was a small click. "Please leave a message and I will get back to you."

"Arthur, this is Leslie Wetzon. I am being held by the police at Midtown North, Detective Bernstein. Please call me here as soon as possible." She replaced the phone. "He wasn't there. I'll have to try again."

"What does O'Melvany have to do with this?" Ignacio asked.

"Peepsie Cunningham either committed suicide or was murdered in his precinct."

"Peepsie?"

"I'm sorry. That's a nickname. I don't remember . . ." Her brain was going. Why couldn't she remember Peepsie's real name? "Teddy was doing a series on the problems of the elderly . . ." She felt very much alone suddenly. Isolated from her friends. She thought about the evening in Little Odessa. "Gretchen!" She had threatened Teddy and was coming down the stairs just before the murder.

"Who is Gretchen?" Bernstein and Ignacio exchanged glances.

Maybe she was talking too much. She would just tell them about Gretchen and then shut up and wait.

Bernstein's phone rang. He picked it up. "Yeah? Okay." The receiver came down again, hard.

"What about this Gretchen?" Ignacio asked, looking a question at Bernstein.

"Gretchen—Teddy had a fight with her in Brooklyn. He took a story away from her and she was furious. She told him she'd get him—Then I met her coming down the stairs carrying that camera . . . when I was going up to Teddy's office."

Ignacio picked up the phone, dialed one number. "Baker, see if you can get a last name for a female reporter on Eight—Gretchen something or other—and get her in here." She hung up.

"What were you doing at Channel Eight tonight?" Ignacio said.

"I told you." She played with the bookmark. Stop talking now, Wetzon, she told herself.

"Tell us again."

"I'd rather wait until I can get someone to protect my rights."

"No one's interfering with your rights, lady. You just remember that." Bernstein leaned toward her and shook his finger at her. He looked up, over her head, and nodded, but it wasn't at her. A door opened and closed behind her. Silvestri. She felt him there before she turned and saw him. Ignacio rose.

"Silvestri." Bernstein's tone was a touch defensive. "Long time no see."

Silvestri put his arm around her waist, lifting her, pressing her against the silky cold of his jacket. "Les? What's going on here? Bernstein? Jesus Christ! Someone want to tell me why you're rousting my girl?"

"Guy was killed tonight. She found the body—"

Silvestri's arms tightened around her. She buried her face deeper into his jacket. The stiff bristles of his beard scraped her forehead. "Look at me, Les." He relaxed his hold.

"She had his blood all over her," Ignacio said.

Wetzon raised her head and looked at Silvestri. Dark circles ringed deep turquoise eyes. He wore a couple of days' beard. "I didn't kill Teddy," she said. She could feel his hands warm on her back through the jacket of her suit.

"Her prints are on the gun," Bernstein said.

35

SHE WAS DOING *GRANDS JETÉS* in a white tutu up and down the aisles of the trading floor at Whitebread Sallman, which was teeming with activity. The corps de ballet, dressed as shirt-sleeved traders, followed her, clutching stock certificates in their hands. She spun around the frenzy with total assurance, confident that her technique was perfect. How wonderful that Jerome Robbins had done a ballet for her, connecting both of her worlds.

Having completed her solo, she came to a glowing rest near the maestro, whose back was to her for a moment. "How was I, Maestro?" she asked breathlessly.

"Wonderful, wonderful, Wetzon." Leon turned to her. He was wearing a plastic name tag that said Maestro on the lapel of his black cashmere blazer.

"Leon! what are you doing here?"

He opened his mouth to answer her.

"FBI! FBI!" someone shouted.

"It's a raid," a voice near Wetzon cried. "Take this, and snap to it." She took what was thrust at her and raised it to her eyes. It was a red, enameled figure of a Russian peasant woman similar to those she had seen at the UN gift shop, the kind whose head comes off and there's another doll inside whose head comes off and there's another doll inside. She did just that, discarding the pieces until she came to the last tiny enameled figure, which was that of a man whose head did not unscrew. She tucked the figure under her leotard into her bra. It was pulsating weirdly.

The corps de ballet *comme* traders surged around her madly, rocking back and forth, making her dizzy.

"Here, hold this," Gretchen said, handing her a camera and disappearing into the melee.

Wetzon looked at the camera, but it was not a camera; it was a metal wastebasket filled to overflowing with ornately designed stock certificates, which must have been collected from the corps de ballet.

"Tanks for holding, dollink," Ida said, reaching for the wastebasket. She was wearing Peepsie Cunningham's mink coat, which was ludicrously too small for her.

"No!" Wetzon tried to pull away.

"Let me help you," Arleen Grossman said. "Tell her how helpful I can be, Xenia."

Smith, looking like a movie star in a white strapless evening dress, diamonds in her ears and on her throat, smiled at Wetzon. "Really, Wetzon, Arleen and I know what is best for you. You must do as we tell you. Look at you. You're nothing but a dancer trying to succeed in the business world. You could never have made it without me." She pushed Wetzon hard and pulled at the wastebasket.

"No! No!" Wetzon lost her balance, falling. She would be trampled under the stampeding horde.

"Gotcha!" Bernstein, wearing the full costume of a Hasidic Jew—bearded, side-curled, long shiny black coat, beaver hat— took the metal wastebasket from her.

"Caught her with the goods," Ignacio said.

"Fingerprints all over the evidence."

"You did it. Admit it." Someone shook her.

"Book her."

"Book her."

They were shaking her back and forth between them.

"No, I didn't do it. I didn't do it. Stop shaking me."

"Les! Wake up!"

She opened her eyes and snapped up like a jack-in-the-box. "Silvestri! My God. What a horrible dream. They were all in on it together."

"In on what?" He brushed her hair away from her face. He was sitting on her bed, facing her with those wonderful turquoise eyes that made her dizzy when she looked into them.

She sank back against her pillows and pulled the quilt up around her bare shoulders. "It was like a conspiracy . . . I don't know . . ." Her hair was loose, all over the place. "What time is it?"

"Nine."

She sat up again and tried to get out of bed, but he was sitting solidly on the quilt, pinning her down. "Jesus, Silvestri, I've got to get to the office."

"Not just yet." He had that steely look on his face, and she knew she was going to get a lecture on interfering in police business.

She leaned back and closed her eyes. "All right. Let me have it."

"You are really the fucking nosiest buttinsky. You were told to stay out of it. O'Melvany told you. I told you. You almost got yourself killed last night. I still can't figure out why the killer didn't—"

"You know I didn't kill Teddy."

"I know."

"How could they think I did?"

"They can think anything, Les. They don't know you. They were doing their job. The paraffin turns out to make it unlikely that you fired the gun, but there was a slight residue on your hand and your prints are all over the silencer."

"But I explained that. I tripped over something on the floor in Teddy's office and picked it up. I didn't know what it was. I only held it for a second because the lights came back on and I dropped it when I saw Teddy. I didn't even know what it was until they told me."

"Les, you're a material witness. They can't make a case on you, but they sure as hell think you know more than you're telling."

"Oh, Silvestri—"

"Listen, kiddo, I know you damn well by now, and I think you're holding out."

"I'm not," she protested weakly.

"None of that who-me crap, please, Les."

"Okay. Can I get up now?" She stretched under the quilt. Her muscles were stiff. She could do with some barre work.

"Only if you promise me you'll let the department handle this."

"Oh, Silvestri." When he looked at her like that she felt herself dissolving inside out.

"No, I mean it."

The downstairs bell buzzed.

"Jesus, who is that?" *Saved by the bell.*

"That lawyer, Margolies. He called this morning. You left a message for him to call you at Manhattan North. When he called here, I told him to come over at nine-thirty." The buzzer sounded again. Silvestri stood up. "I think you're okay. Bernstein can get rough, but I don't think they can prove a case. Otherwise they would have had someone from the D.A.'s office there."

As soon as he left the room, Wetzon got up and scooted to the bathroom, hair flying.

"Hey, what are you up to?"

"Shower, Silvestri. Be right out." She closed the door on him firmly. One minute more and she would have promised him anything. She turned on the shower and stood under the hot water, letting it gush like a waterfall over her. She was missing something. Something that connected Peepsie, Ida, Teddy, and Peter Tormenkov. Maybe she could get Peter to tell her whatever it was he told Teddy. Shit, maybe that's what had gotten Teddy killed.

She rinsed the soap out of her hair and then turned off the hot water, giving herself a final jolting icy rinse.

She felt clean and renewed with her hair pulled back in a ponytail, wrapped in her white terry robe. Now she could face whatever she had to face.

"Birdie, I swear." Carlos was carrying a big, fragrant pot of coffee into the living room as she came down the hall. "You always manage to be right on the cutting edge of things." She followed him as he put the coffeepot on a trivet on the glass top of the antique rope bed she used as a coffee table. The mugs were already there. He turned to her; his beautiful dark eyes with their long lashes had a trace of sadness. "Give us a hug. Are you okay? Can't have anything happen to you." They held each other for a moment and then let go.

Silvestri was leaning against her built-in wall of books, hands in his pockets, watching.

"I'm okay," she said through a big lump in her throat.

"Well, good! That's what I want to hear." Carlos took her shoulders and turned her around. "This is Arthur."

He steered her to the sofa and sat her down next to a thin, well-dressed man of about fifty with thick wiry iron-gray hair, mustache, and beard. The subtle glen plaid of his dark gray suit matched where his sleeves fit into his shoulders and across the breast pocket, so that it looked like one continuous pattern. A very expensive, hand-tailored job. He looked at Wetzon with serious but kind brown eyes behind horn-rimmed glasses. Arthur Margolies had dignity and class—and she liked him.

"Well, Birdie?" Carlos was reading her mind again.

She grinned at him. "Flying colors."

"Well, now that that's settled, we can get the show on the road." He poured coffee into each mug and handed them around.

Arthur Margolies stroked his beard and took a gold Cross pen out of his inside pocket and a yellow legal pad from his soft leather briefcase, which lay on the sofa between him and Wetzon. "As your lawyer, I must advise you that I don't think Sergeant Silvestri should be present when we talk. What you tell me is protected by the attorney-client relationship. But what Sergeant Silvestri hears, he is honor-bound to disclose if he feels the law has been broken."

Dismayed, Wetzon looked at Silvestri, who remained impassive. "I understand what you're saying, but I did not break any laws, and I want him here." Besides, wasn't she his girl? He had said she was, and in that moment, it was what she wanted him to say, needed him to say. But she was nobody's girl. She was her own person, and there was a part of her that resented Silvestri's proprietary statement and part of her that was drawn to it.

"All right then, suppose you tell me everything from the beginning." Arthur had a nice calm voice with a trace of New York City accent.

"Okay." She looked over at Silvestri. He stared back at her over the mug of coffee he held to his lips. She took a deep breath. He was going to kill her when he heard the whole story.

Arthur cleared his throat politely. Carlos made a conductor movement with his hands as if he held a baton. She was keeping everybody waiting while she tried to solve the enigma of modern man and modern woman.

She started with Peepsie Cunningham, mentioned Ida, and paused when she came to Peter Tormenkov, looking thoughtfully into her coffee.

"Everything, Les, and while you're at it, kindly include an explanation of those marks on your neck." Silvestri left the bookcase and sat down on the big ladder-back chair facing her. She saw his gun in his holster when he adjusted his jacket. Dismayed, her hand flew to her throat as if to hide the evidence. "No editing."

Carlos, sitting cross-legged on the floor, took in the drama through narrowed eyes and chortled.

"Oh shit!" Wetzon looked from Silvestri to Carlos, back to Silvestri. "You guys act as if I purposely leave things out."

"Why don't you surprise us."

She shot Silvestri an outraged look, but it was wasted. She sighed and skipped mention of Peter Tormenkov. She could always tell them later.

"I called Teddy Lanzman, who was an old friend—" Her

voice cracked. "I still can't believe it—I can't—" She swallowed hard. "We met for a drink. He was doing a feature for Channel Eight on the elderly. I thought he might have a clue about some scam . . . something that would help me prove Peepsie was murdered. Anyway, he agreed to go to Brooklyn with me to help me find Ida—"

Silvestri made a noise like a growl. She flushed and put her hands to her face, keeping her eyes on Arthur, who was making copious notes.

She'd done everything wrong. When she flipped lightly over the attempted assault at the Cafe Baltic, Silvestri put his mug down on the glass top of the coffee table a little too hard. He got to his feet. Carlos wagged a finger at her. "Naughty, naughty," he mouthed.

Silvestri was furious. She could tell by the set of his shoulders, by his eyes. He began prowling around her living room, bristling with anger.

Arthur stopped writing. "Anything wrong here?" He looked at Silvestri.

Wetzon studied her palms. "Silvestri warned me to stay out of it—"

"But you didn't, did you, Les?"

"I couldn't—"

"Enough." Arthur held up his hand. "You can argue about it later. I just want to know what I'm dealing with here."

"You're dealing with a hardhead," Silvestri said.

Carlos clapped his hands. "Amen. But do go on."

She sped over the Tsminskys' deaths and Teddy's confrontation with Gretchen. Finally, she described the phone conversation with Teddy, again leaving out Peter Tormenkov. "When I got to the studio—"

Her phone rang.

"Sit still. Your machine is on," Silvestri ordered. "Finish this."

They all listened automatically to the *click, click* of her answering machine as it took the call. A woman's voice said, "Leslie Wetzon, this is Diantha Anderson. We met the other day at the American Festival Cafe. I would like to talk to you about something very important. Please call me as soon as possible." The machine clicked off.

"Diantha Anderson . . . Diantha Anderson . . ." She frowned. The legal recruiter. "I wonder what she wants and what could be that important. I met her only that once . . ."

Silvestri shrugged.

"Then if it's not urgent, I'd like to go on," Arthur said, taking a clean page and folding the used ones back. His writing was very neat and cursive.

Wetzon recounted the funny popping noise she'd heard on the seventh floor.

"Silencer," Carlos commented.

"Maybe," Silvestri said, hands in pockets again, pacing.

"And I know someone was in the hallway with me." She looked at Silvestri. "Two someones."

"Forgive me," Arthur interrupted, "but if that person was the murderer, why didn't he try to kill you?"

Silvestri muttered something unintelligible under his breath.

"I don't know," Wetzon said. "It was dark. He couldn't have seen anything more than I could. And I know that after I heard the first person on the stairs, there was still someone in the hall-way with me. Then I heard the stairwell door open and close a second time and another set of footsteps on the stairs." She concluded with her fall over the round object that had turned out to be a gun with a silencer.

"That may explain why you weren't shot. The murderer dropped, or left, the gun after he shot Lanzman," Arthur said. He flipped through his pages of notes on the yellow legal pad. "Is there anything else? Anything you may have forgotten to mention?"

"Not our Birdie. She has a mind like a steel trap." Carlos arched an expressive eyebrow at her.

"Shut up, Carlos." She was starting to get testy about being on the hot seat with them. "Yes, Arthur. There was a button. The police found a gold blazer button. They asked me about it. It wasn't mine."

Arthur took a final sip of coffee. "I'll get the police report, but

I think you're all right for now, Leslie. If your prints were only on the silencer and not on the gun, it's unlikely they can make a case—"

"What about the paraffin test? Won't that prove I didn't fire the gun?"

"You touched the silencer," Silvestri said.

"Damn it all, he was my friend," Wetzon cried, anguished. "And I think maybe something he was checking on for me got him killed. What could he have found out that made someone kill him?" She had to get to the office and try to find Peter Tormenkov.

"I wouldn't jump to any conclusions. He was an investigative reporter." Arthur put his notes in his briefcase and took her hand. "It may not have had anything to do with Mrs. Cunningham's death, but I think you ought to have some protection." He looked over at Silvestri. "What do you think, Silvestri?"

"I don't need—" Wetzon began.

"Agreed." Silvestri cut her off. His girl again? Does his girl have any say in it? She smoldered on the sofa, sure if she stood up she'd leave a round smoking hole in the upholstery.

"Good, that's a relief." Carlos jumped up and went to the hall closet, handing Arthur a conservative Harris tweed and slipping on his own full-length white-and-fawn lynx.

Wetzon sat on the sofa and watched Silvestri huddle with Margolies in her foyer. "You are all acting as if I can't take care of myself."

"You can't." Carlos came around the coffee table and sat down next to her. "This is serious, Birdie. You listen, just this once." He gave her a furry hug.

"I like Arthur, Carlos."

"That's good. I told him you had to."

"You did? You're terrible!" She felt depressed suddenly. "I think he thinks I'm an idiot."

"You are." Carlos kissed her forehead. "But Carlos loves you anyway. And I hate to say it, but I think maybe Silvestri does, too."

"Yeah? Well, he doesn't show it."

"Carlos. I'm on my way downtown," Arthur called from the door. He wrapped a black-and-gray houndstooth scarf around his neck and shook hands with Silvestri.

"Wait, I'll go with you." Carlos went to the door, pulling Wetzon along with him. "The memorial service is next Tuesday, at five-thirty, Birdie, at Sardi's, in the Belasco Room."

"I'll be there." She shook Arthur's hand. "Thank you."

"I'll be in touch," Arthur said. "Keep a low profile."

When she closed her door, she saw Silvestri was talking on her phone, back to her. She looked at the *Times* and the *Journal* on the floor near her umbrella stand. Carlos must have carried them in. Teddy's picture was on the front page of the *Times*. He would have liked that coverage. She sighed. She'd have to catch up on the rest of the news later.

Get dressed and go to work, she told herself as she propelled her body into the bedroom. Black wool crepe suit today, violet-and-cream silk blouse. She could hear the low rumble of Silvestri's voice from the dining room as she dressed. Peter Tormenkov, Peter Tormenkov, she hummed to a tango beat in her head.

She had just finished putting her hair into the usual knot and was standing in front of her makeup mirror in the bathroom with the mascara wand in her hand when Silvestri came charging down the hall, cursing to the sound of crumpling newspapers.

She gave him her best smile when he came into view. He looked like a thundercloud.

"Do you know anything about this?" He waved a folded newspaper in her face.

"What is it with you, Silvestri?" She'd been wrong. He'd been right to be angry with her, but this was too much.

"A stockbroker's been murdered." He pointed at something in the newspaper, hitting the paper with his finger.

"Oh come on." She looked in the mirror and mascara'd her lashes. "Do you think I'm involved in every murder in the industry?" She put the mascara wand back into its container.

"Yeah well—"

"Okay, let's see. It's possible I knew the guy. After all, I know thousands of brokers—" She took the paper from him and looked at it.

Stockbroker Dies Gangland Style in Car in Brooklyn

A stockbroker with the Wall Street firm, L. L. Rosenkind, was shot to death gangland style late yesterday in a car in the Brighton Beach section of Brooklyn, the police said. The stockbroker, Peter Tormenkov, 31 years old, was shot four times in the upper body. The police found him face-down on the front seat of the car.

36

SILVESTRI GOT BACK ON THE PHONE after Wetzon told him everything she knew about Peter Tormenkov. This time she'd made a point of telling him that Tormenkov was also the missing Ida's last name.

If there had been a rift between them before, there was a major gulf now. She felt him withdrawing into a professional mode, away from her. She smoothed the white-on-white bottom sheet of the bed and pulled the matching top sheet straight, covering it with the quilt. She was trying not to cry. Why couldn't he understand that telling him everything from the beginning would have meant she relinquished control of things in her life? She wasn't ready to do that. Maybe she would never be. Moreover, he had been such a grouch about Peepsie and the blue Gucci shoe when she had first told him about it. She plumped up the pillows with more energy than necessary.

She had work to do in the office. Kevin De Haven to set up

for interviews. She wanted to check on Hazel . . . She had to get on with her life.

And what about Teddy Lanzman, a little voice whispered.

"I don't know," she answered, sitting on the edge of her bed, her boots in her hand.

"What don't you know?" Silvestri said in a detached voice. He was leaning against the doorframe, looking at her legs in their sheer black hose as she pulled on her boots.

"Teddy." She stood up, heart thumping, bending slightly to straighten the boots, feeling that damned magnetic attraction between them that she was sure he felt too.

"If you're going to your office, I'll drop you. I'm on my way downtown."

"Okay." She wanted to ask him, *Where are you going? Why? Does it have anything to do with what I just told you?* But she didn't. She brushed past him, trying to stay as detached as he seemed to be.

Methodically, she checked that the gas jets were off in the kitchen, put the mugs and the coffeepot into the dishwasher. Silvestri, in his red down jacket, watched her as she folded both newspapers into her carryall and opened her closet door.

"My coat—" The room swayed, and she held tight to the doorknob. The police had taken her beautiful black alpaca coat . . . soaked with Teddy's blood and . . .

"You'd better not wait for it. Just get a new one." Silvestri's voice was gruff and impersonal.

Get a new one, she thought. Just like that.

She took her new Burberry with the wool plaid lining out of the closet and put it on. She wrapped the long cashmere scarf that matched the lining around the collar and plunked the lavender beret over her topknot, pulling it down over her ears. A quick once-over in the mirror on the inside door of the closet told her she would do, despite a dark pouch under each eye.

They said nothing to each other until Silvestri double-parked his car in front of her office. He turned to her, his arm on the back of the seat. Close, but not touching. "I want your word this time that you won't do anything about Teddy Lanzman's murder, that you'll let us handle it." He spoke with an odd formality.

She looked into his cold slate eyes and wished she hadn't. "I promise." She could hardly hear her own voice. "But what if—"

"No 'what ifs,' Les." Silvestri thumped the back of the seat with the flat of his hand. "Anything comes up that sounds even a touch suspicious, you call me or Metzger, you hear? That's not a request either, that's an order."

"Okay." She opened the door and cold air gusted into the car.

"Where you going to be later?" It was not a personal question.

"In the office all day, then—gee, I don't know, Silvestri." She hated the way he made her feel. "I should be home by nine. Why?"

Silvestri didn't respond. She sighed and slipped out of the car, slamming the door. By the time she'd negotiated her way over the grubby pile of snow between the street and the sidewalk, Silvestri had gone.

Was it better to be alone, she wondered, not to have any relationship, than to have to deal with the demanding problems of two strong-minded people trying to find a way to be together?

She nodded and smiled at B.B., who was prospecting enthusiastically for the cold-calling program at Lehman. He was doing very well with his first real assignment.

She hung her coat in the closet next to Smith's luxuriant black diamond mink. Giving the mink an envious little pat, she closed that door and opened the one to the office she and Smith shared. Smith looked up, phone hugged between her ear and shoulder. Her hands were busy putting a coat of scarlet polish on her long oval nails. She didn't react to Wetzon's bright "Hi."

The *Times* was spread on the floor around Smith's desk. "I don't feel I have to think about this, Larry," Smith said. "After all, he was with you eight months. We are under no obligation to return a fee if a broker leaves after that length of time." Her eyes met Wetzon's. "You have to take into account the reasons for his leaving." She paused. "No, I'm not blaming you . . . but . . ." She left it hanging. "Very well, I promise you I will think about it." She hung up the phone and turned in her chair, watching Wetzon look at her schedule in the calendar on her desk.

"Who left?"

"Carl Mattollo."

"Really? Where'd he go?"

"Hambrecht and Quist."

"Well, they're a nice firm. You're not going to give Larry any money back on him, are you?"

"Are you crazy? Not a penny! No way." She laughed.

"Good!"

"You never called me last night and now you're involved in another murder." There was an accusatory tone in her voice.

"I did call—twice. There was no answer. And what do you mean, another murder?"

"I was probably in the shower. You should have tried again. And by another murder I simply mean that last year it was Barry Stark and now this. Sweetie pie, you just don't know how to take care of yourself."

"Don't say that, please." Smith always made her feel as if her judgment was bad, that she couldn't make decisions. "Where was Mark?"

"I arranged for him to spend the night with a friend because I was going to Channel Eight with you. None of this would have happened if I'd been with you." Smith was the old sure-of-herself Smith again.

"Really?" Wetzon smiled, shaking her head. "What makes you think so, partner mine?"

"I don't think, I *know*." She closed the bottle of nail polish with the palm of her hand, fingers spread, and blew on her nails.

"Smith, about the cassette of Arleen—" Wetzon picked up the pink message slips. Not too many; that was good.

"Oh, forget it." Smith flipped her hand. "It's not important. I really shouldn't let you get me so crazy—"

Laura Lee Day had called, Howie Minton, Kevin De Haven. Kevin—that was top priority. She stopped. What the hell had Smith just said? "I really shouldn't let *you* get me so crazy"?

Wetzon put the messages down on her desk. "I'm sorry, Smith? What did you say?"

"I said, you got me all worked up about Leon and Arleen and none of it was true." Smith smiled a sweet, forgiving smile.

"I *what?*"

"It's all those years in the theater, poor dear. You tend to over-dramatize everything."

"I can't believe what I'm hearing, Smith." What was this, everybody-take-a-poke-at-Wetzon day?

"Sweetie, you look absolutely wrung out," Smith clucked. "And I hate to complain when you seem to have so much on your mind, but you must consider our business. It's really terrible publicity for us when you get involved with people who get murdered."

"Smith, my friend Teddy—read my lips—my friend was murdered horribly last night. I'm upset and you bet I'm wrung out. You would be too."

"Please, dear, don't get so worked up. I love you and I worry about you." She came over and took Wetzon's hand. "Maybe you should take some time off. I think Silvestri is a very bad influence on you."

The phone rang and seconds later B.B. poked his head in. "Howie Minton, Wetzon."

"Wait," Smith ordered imperiously. "Did you see the item about the broker with L. L. Rosenkind who got himself murdered? Isn't that the same one you met the other day? The crazy one I told you to stay away from?"

"Yes." Wetzon picked up the phone. "Howie? What's going on down there?" She turned her back on Smith and sat down at her desk.

"Wetzon." Howie's voice was shaky. "The FBI just came in and arrested Blake Robards. We were having a sales meeting. They pushed their way in and took him away in handcuffs, right in front of everybody."

"Blake Robards? Your manager? Are you kidding?"

"Yeah. He's a partner, for crissakes. What do you hear?"

"Nothing. Why should I know anything about it?"

"You met Pete, you talked to him . . . did you read about him in the paper today?"

"Yes, but—"

"They came in and went through his desk—"

"Who is they?"

"The FBI. Jesus—Wetzon—"

"What were they looking for?"

"Who the hell knows?" He gave a snorting laugh. "Someone had cleaned it out even before they got there."

"Howie, what do you know about Peter? Why did you really want me to take him out of the firm?"

"Believe me, I was just being a nice guy. He wasn't doing so well, and he wasn't getting along with the right people. And I thought I could do you a favor. You've been my friend." Howie was dancing. He knew more than he was saying.

"That's really nice of you, Howie."

"You know, all of a sudden it got so Blake had it in for him. I thought he was going to get fired."

"Was he doing something illegal?"

"Now, Wetzon," Minton drawled, "I'm your friend. You're my friend. I wouldn't say anything like that. What did he tell you?"

"Nothing, Howie, absolutely nothing, except that he was working for the FBI on some kind of scam that was going on in your office. You and I talked about it, don't you remember?"

"Shshsh. Don't say that, Wetzon. You never know who's listening. Peter was a crazy guy, pathological liar and all that. I told you he made it all up. Isn't that right? I never said anything about a scam. Isn't that right?"

"That's right."

"So don't get into it any deeper, Wetzon, or we'll both get in trouble." The warning was cold and clear. She wondered if someone was listening to their conversation. "I know you understand." The line disconnected. And as she held the phone, she heard a second click, as if someone had hung up after Howie.

"Now what?" Smith asked.

"I don't know. The FBI just took Blake Robards out of

L. L. Rosenkind in handcuffs in the middle of a sales meeting, in front of all the brokers."

"I love it!" Smith's face was gleeful. She clapped her hands together. "He's one of the worst human beings I've ever met."

"Oh, you're just prejudiced because he never wanted to work with us."

"You are so right. He wanted us, if you remember, to kick back part of our fee to him. And, he told Leon that we would never make it in this business."

"Yes, I remember." They smiled at each other, sharing the memory. They had been outraged. "What goes around, comes around."

They got out of their chairs simultaneously and clasped hands in the center of the room.

"We've come a long way, baby," Smith said.

"Haven't we just."

Harold opened the door a crack. "Ah, Smith . . ."

"Yes? Either come in or close the door. Don't sneak around."

He came in. "I just got a referral in Pittsburgh. Can you open Shearson for us there?"

"Humpf. What are the specs? Did you do the interview?"

Harold handed her the eight-by-eleven suspect sheet with the interview of the broker. She shared it with Wetzon. "What do you think? He's only doing two hundred and twenty-five thousand after twelve years in the business."

Wetzon shook her head. "Not worth it. If we're going to open a region, we have to present a real gem as a first candidate. Right, Smith?"

"Right, Wetzon."

"But, Smith, he's really good, and he wants to leave Dean Witter," Harold whined. "I know if I called the manager at Shearson—"

"I'm *sure* I didn't hear right, Harold." Smith voice was frigid. "Did you say you want to call the manager *yourself* and introduce this broker?"

"Ah . . . yes . . . no . . . well, maybe." He faltered, stammering.

"No one—repeat—*no one* talks to managers except *me*. Do you understand?"

"Yes, Smith. I understand. I just thought—" He began backing out of the office.

"Just do the job, Harold. Don't be creative."

Harold closed the door.

"Jesus, Smith, don't you think you were a little rough on him?"

"Nonsense. He needs it. The minute we weaken, he'll be all over us, Wetzon. Believe me. I know." She dismissed him. "What did you think about Kevin De Haven?"

"He's good, but he does a ton of syndicate with retail and institutional clients. It's tricky. Merrill wants to cut his payout down to regular institutional—say eleven to eighteen percent. He's been getting about thirty-five."

"He'll have the same problem somewhere else. The big firms don't want to pay retail commissions on institutional business anymore."

"He's already got an offer from Smith Barney."

"They don't do that much syndicate. Where are you going to send him?" She moved back to her desk.

"I told him that. I think maybe Shearson, Bache. Any other suggestions?"

"Um . . . no." Smith tested her nail polish with the tip of her finger and looked pleased. "You want to talk about the murder? I saw an indication in the cards, remember? That's why I wanted to go with you. I'd like to hear what happened. Have you talked to Leon?"

"No. Actually, I tried to get Leon at the time and couldn't, so I called a lawyer I met through a friend. And truthfully, I'd rather not talk about it now. Do you mind, Smith? Give me a day to recover. I'll talk to you about it tomorrow, okay?"

Smith nodded. "I really think you should talk to Leon. He called me first thing this morning. He tried you at home and got your machine."

"I'll touch base with him." She had no intention of doing anything of the kind, but this would keep Smith happy for the moment.

"I'd better go and straighten it out with Harold," Smith said, tossing her dark curls.

As soon as Wetzon was alone she set up appointments for De Haven that afternoon at five o'clock with Shearson and eight-thirty tomorrow with Pru-Bache. Then she notified De Haven.

"Did you tell them what I need? That I need syndicate?"

"I did. Just go and talk. You have to make an educated decision, and you don't have to commit to anything."

B.B. knocked, opened the door, and handed her a small shopping bag with a big red ribbon bow on the side. "This just came by messenger for you, Wetzon. And there's a Diantha Anderson holding."

"Oh, how exciting! A present." Wetzon took the bag from B.B. and set it on top of her desk. "Oh, tell Diantha Anderson I'm in a meeting and I'll call back. Get a number."

"There's a card on top." He closed the door.

The card said, "In your present situation, you can never have too many. Love, Laura Lee." Laura Lee Day, the stockbroker she had placed at Oppenheimer almost two years ago, who had become her friend.

Wetzon opened the small box, tore away the tissue paper, and took out a marble peach. It was a duplicate of the peach Laura Lee had given her previously, the one that Wetzon had shattered last year defending herself after she'd gotten involved in Barry Stark's murder.

"Gee, that's terrific. It looks real," B.B. said, touching it.

Wetzon put it in his hands and called Laura Lee.

"After reading the papers this mornin', Wetzon darlin', I just figured you might need ammunition to stop another murderer."

Wetzon laughed. "I hope not. I'd like to keep this one." She took the peach back from B.B. and put it on her desk. "I was going to call you anyway. Can we have a drink?" She wanted to try an idea out on Laura Lee. There was something from that dream she'd had . . . something nagging at her. Well, if she was right, she'd be a good girl and tell Silvestri.

"Can it wait? I'm off to Acapulco this afternoon—they're rewarding me with a freebie for being such an outstanding producer. I'll be back in the office next Tuesday. How's five o'clock at you-know-where?"

Wetzon smiled. You-know-where was the Four Seasons. "Would love to, but can't. I have a memorial service at five-thirty—theater friend died—how about earlier?"

"You can meet me at my furrier at four."

"Your furrier?"

"Yes. I'm pickin' up my new coat—Three-fifty Seventh Avenue. Fillis Furs. Okay? Got to go, darlin'."

The day disappeared into a maze of calls, candidates, prospects, referrals, clients. Curtis Evans had said no to Maurice Sanderson. "Not doing enough business" was also code for "too old." Damn. She had only one last shot to try for him. "Don't worry," she reassured him. "I have one more idea which may work out."

She tried to reach Hazel intermittently but got a busy signal, then no answer.

She called the midtown office of McKinley, Samson and talked with Gary Greggs about Maurice Sanderson. "He's got some hefty clients, all in fixed income. You won't have to pay him anything to come in. Sit him with a younger producer. Maurice will eventually retire and leave you his book."

"I don't know, Wetzon. I still have to pay you." Greggs wasn't too enthusiastic.

"Just see him, Gary."

"Okay, okay. Get him here tomorrow. Four-fifteen."

She arranged it with Maurice and tried Hazel again. Still no answer.

At five she collected her papers and made up a schedule for the next day. She still had five or six calls to return, including the one from Diantha Anderson. They would all have to wait because she was going home to bed.

"Who did you make an appointment with?" Smith asked, ending her telephone conversation.

"Laura Lee . . . next week."

"Laura Lee Day darlin', that phony Southern belle."

"Smith, I don't know why you have it in for Laura Lee. We placed her, she sends us referrals. She's my friend."

"You know how I feel about making them your friends."

"Them. You make it sound as if brokers are our enemies."

"They are. They are not to be trusted."

"Look, you know I don't choose my friends because of what they do—"

"More's the pity." Smith picked up the phone to dial out. "Oh, by the way. Arleen likes you very much and you're not being very nice to her. It's really embarrassing to me. All you ever think about is your brokers. I wish you would be more sensitive to my needs, Wetzon."

37

WETZON WAS IN A FOUL MOOD as she paced back and forth on the pearl-gray velvet carpet in the showroom of Fillis Furs, paying no attention whatsoever to the gray raccoon coat that covered her like a blanket from her neck to her ankles. Everyone around her was getting murdered, and over the last week Smith had gotten chummy again with Arleen, Hazel seemed to be avoiding her, she had not succeeded in finding a spot for Maurice Sanderson, and Kevin De Haven had not made up his mind about where he wanted to move. And worst of all, petty as it seemed, she had not heard from Silvestri.

Esther Fillis clapped her hands together, gold bracelets jangling. "Stunning! Absolutely stunning." The tiny lady in the dark brown gabardine slacks and beige silk shirt nodded her honey-blonde head vigorously.

"Now if you would only remove that unpleasant frown from your normally sweet brow, darlin' Wetzon," Laura Lee said, giving Wetzon a probing look, "all will be well."

"I can't afford a coat like this, Laura Lee," Wetzon protested halfheartedly.

"Of course you can, Wetzon. Don't tell me you want to wait until some fool man comes along and presents one to you."

"I didn't mean that."

"Well, didn't you tell me just last week that business was wonderful? And look at yourself in the mirror. Look what it does for your eyes." Hands on Wetzon's back, Laura Lee pushed her closer to the three-way full-length mirrors. Wetzon's clear gray eyes had taken over her face, highlighted by the silver gray of the coat.

"Oh dear," Wetzon murmured, stroking the soft fur, captivated by her image in the mirror.

A plump dark-haired woman came into the room carrying a caramel-brown fur coat on a hanger.

"Oooh, goodie, here's my treat." Letting Esther hold the coat, Laura Lee slipped her arms into the sleeves and drew the wide shawl collar up around her ears, wriggling in ecstasy. The sharp peaks of her blonde-streaked brown hair dipped and blended with the fur of the collar. "Mr. Stone Marten, darlin', I do love you."

"It's divine," Esther Fillis said, fussing with the hemline, straightening the shoulders. Laura Lee's coat had a glamorous quality to it, rich shades of brown, but Wetzon, looking at herself again in the mirror, much preferred her puffy-sleeved raccoon. *Hold on there*, she thought, *it's not yours. Take it off at once.*

Laura Lee spun around. "What do you think, Wetzon? Look at the back. Isn't it marvelous?"

"It's beautiful, Laura Lee."

"Okay, Esther, I'll trade you. You can reline minkie here and send her to me." She picked up her black mink coat from a chair and gave it to Esther, who put it on the hanger she was still holding.

"What about the raccoon, Miss Wetzon?" Esther asked.

"I don't think—"

"She'll take it, Esther. As a matter of fact, she'll wear it. Didn't you just finish telling me, Wetzon, that you had to buy a new coat?" Laura Lee pointed to Wetzon's Burberry on another chair. "And put that boring old thing in a box and mail it to her."

"But Laura Lee—"

"Treat yourself, y'hear, Wetzon!" Laura Lee studied herself with satisfaction in the mirror. "Don't we look grand? Admit it."

"Okay, yes, we do, but—"

"Where do you keep your money, darlin'? I've been meaning to talk to you about this anyway . . . in a savings account, right? Collectin' five percent interest, right?"

"Well, yes."

"We've got to sit down and talk about financial planning for you." Laura Lee shook a finger at her. "I'm going to call you the minute I get back from Mobile next week and you will come and talk to me."

"Do you think it needs to be shortened?" Wetzon squared her shoulders and turned to the mirror. Laura Lee was right. She could afford to treat herself and she would. She deserved this coat.

"Not on your life. Just pick it up when you step over doggy-do, darlin'."

Wetzon was positive everyone was staring at them when she and Laura Lee stepped out of the building on Seventh Avenue and Twenty-eighth Street. Self-conscious, she adjusted the sleeves of the coat and drew her beret down over her ears. The day had ended with the abrupt finality of a winter day in New York. A magic wand passed over the city and it was suddenly night. Fur and garment workers were streaming out of the buildings, pouring onto the street, heading for the subways, the IRT on Seventh Avenue, the Independent line on Eighth, and the BMT on Broadway, and the PATH trains to New Jersey.

"Did you say you're goin' to Sardi's?" Laura Lee waved her arm and one cab pulled over to the curb while another screeched to a stop in front of it, cutting off the first.

"Amazing," Wetzon said. "Must be the coats." It was usually impossible to get a cab during rush hour and now they had two.

"When you got it, flaunt it," Laura Lee said.

Wetzon opened the door of the first cab and started to get in.

A hand shot out from the depths of the cab and grasped her wrist. "What—" She felt herself being pulled into the cab. "Wait. No!" She grabbed the side of the cab with her free hand.

"Get her!"

"Hold it!"

"No, no!" She heard Laura Lee scream.

Someone grabbed Wetzon around the waist and tugged her the other way, toward the street, pulling her free, back to the sidewalk. The cab went into gear and drove away, back door swinging until it was closed from inside.

"Well, I swear!" Laura Lee panted, still holding her around the waist. "If that wasn't the damnedest thing. What did he think he was going to do, steal your coat right off your back even before your check cleared?"

Wetzon was shaken. "God, do you think it was that?"

"Are you ladies okay?" The driver of the second cab shouted. He was on the street next to his cab, his short coat open, his hand inside the coat.

Wetzon, taking it all in like a camera, knew he was a cop. Silvestri was having her watched, damn him. Bless him, she reversed herself.

"Someone tried to get her into the cab to steal her coat," Laura Lee sputtered. "What the hell kind of world are we livin' in?"

"Close call." The driver was young, with dark shaggy hair, deceptively bohemian. But his body language said *alert*. "Where can I take you?" He got back into his yellow cab, which had a dented right fender.

"Come on, Wetzon darlin'." Holding the front of her coat as if it were an evening gown, Laura Lee got into the cab. Wetzon picked up her beret, which had fallen off in the tussle, and followed her. "He didn't get your coat and to hell with it. Driver, we're goin' to Sardi's on Forty-fourth Street and then you-all can drop me on Fiftieth and Sixth."

Wetzon's heart was still hammering as she checked the driver's identification card on the dashboard. "Michael Stewart." She had once known a Michael Stewart, a playwright of unusual talent and wit, who had written *Hello, Dolly!* among other hits. Dead now.

"Wetzon, are you all right?" Laura Lee stared at her sympathetically. "Come on, you want to tell me about this new murder you're in the middle of, or would you prefer to tell me nice things about this new man in your life?"

"What new man?" She looked at Laura Lee, surprised, and caught the eye of the driver, Michael Stewart, watching them in his rearview mirror. He was listening, too.

"Oh come on now, it's all over your face. And that face is turning bright red."

Wetzon touched her fingers to her hot cheeks. "Not right now, Laura Lee. And about Teddy Lanzman, let's just leave it that he was an investigative reporter who may have made somebody mad and I walked in on it." She ran her hands down the silvery fur. It was a lovely present to herself. "Tell me something. If I came to you with stock certificates—say, five thousand shares of IBM that I inherited from my rich Aunt Jane, what would you do?"

"Whose name are they registered in?"

"Oh. Okay. My Aunt Jane's name."

"You would have to get me a copy of the will and probate and it would have to be legally transferred. There are forms to be signed."

"Would a brokerage firm cut corners and do it without getting legal proof?"

"Darlin'." Laura Lee batted her eyes at Wetzon. "What are you-all asking?"

"You heard me."

"Okay. Serious stuff here. The answer is, no way. This is all very thoroughly covered by the Exchange. And I might add, the SEC."

"What about an individual broker? Could he do it and bypass regulations?"

"Impossible. Compliance would pick it up immediately. What are you up to, darlin'?" Laura Lee looked stern. Her Southern drawl had all but disappeared. "Not considering stock fraud to pay for your new coat?"

"Pish tush, Laura Lee. Help me out here." She caught their driver's eye again. He'd stopped for the light at Times Square and Forty-second Street. "I'm trying to figure out what Teddy might have stumbled onto—" She closed her eyes. Horns honked. Rush hour traffic leaving the City clogged every cross-section.

"Seriously, only your Aunt Jane could cash in those stock certificates, Wetzon, and she's dead."

"How do you know?"

"Know what? That she can cash in the stock certificate or that she's dead?"

"That she's dead."

"Well, darlin', you just told me."

"Okay, what if she were alive?"

"Then she can cash in the stock certificate herself."

A faint buzz went off in Wetzon's head, like the beginning of her alarm in the morning. She flashed back to the man with the nosebleed . . . Mitosky . . . the one with the thick accent, who pretended to need a cane. He'd been waiting to see the cashier at Bradley, Elsworth. "Even if you didn't know her?"

"No. Of course, she would have to bring proof of who she is. You know, birth certificate or passport, driver's license. Usual stuff."

"Really? That's it?"

"Sure."

"Then what?"

"She signs the back of the certificate and we issue her a check for the amount at market price."

"What if she was not really Aunt Jane? What if Aunt Jane really had died and I was pretending to be Aunt Jane?" The obituary for Mitosky had said he had been born in England and—

"Why, Wetzon. *Age*, darlin'. It wouldn't fit. You're not the same age as the birth certificate. I don't believe you would do any such thing, anyway. Besides, we would eventually discover she had died."

The buzz in Wetzon's head became a loud alarm.

"Laura Lee, listen carefully. What if poor old Aunt Jane was not dead, but was not well and perhaps a little forgetful? What if I, or someone closer to the right age, took her stock certificates and all the necessary proof material and pretended to be Aunt Jane—and walked into a brokerage firm—?"

"Wetzon, my God, that is the most terrible thing I have heard." Laura Lee's kohl-rimmed eyes went round with disgust.

"Could it happen, Laura Lee? Just tell me, yes or no," Wetzon pressed her urgently. "Could it happen?"

Laura Lee pursed her glossy crimson lips. She stared at Wetzon for what seemed like a long time. "Yes," she said.

38

"THIS JOINT IS JUMPIN' . . . This joint is jumpin' . . ." The cast album of *Ain't Misbehavin'* could be heard faintly over the din of voices spilling over from the second floor of Sardi's. The coatrack near the door was loaded with coats, and Wetzon wasn't going to give up her new coat anyway, so she squeezed into the crowded room wearing her raccoon.

Dancers—young and old gypsy friends, actors, men and women—leaned against the bar, the walls, the two columns in the center and back of the large room, and each other. Many were smoking, all were drinking, and obviously had been for some time by the look of the bleary eyes, by the slurred voices.

She pushed her way to the bar—wine only. "White, please," she said. She could really use a beer.

"Wetzon! Hey, where've you been keeping yourself?" She took the glass and, turning, saw Phil Rinaldi, a press agent she knew from several of the shows she'd been in.

"Philip! Gee, it's been years. Are you still working with Mary

Bryant?" Mary had been Hal Prince's press agent on almost all of his musicals.

"No. I did *Phantom* for Fred Nathan, and now I'm out on my own."

"That's great. I bet it's keeping you hopping."

"It's okay." Wetzon remembered Philip had once wanted to be a playwright. "Mary's over there talking to Mort Hornberg."

"Mort Hornberg? No kidding? Quite a response Tommy's getting." She looked around. "Have you seen Carlos?"

"Yeah, he's here somewhere. Everybody is."

Everybody was. Hal Prince gave her a moist peck on the cheek. Bob Avian, who had worked so closely with Michael Bennett, hugged her. Fred Ebb waved and smiled. Margie and Sheldon Harnick greeted her like a long-lost friend.

"Remember me?" she asked Mort Hornberg.

"How could I forget?" He had lost most of his hair and had fat bags under his eyes, partially hidden by his California tan.

She stopped to congratulate Joel Grey on Jennifer's success. "It's really wonderful, isn't it, Wetzon?" he said, holding her hand briefly before someone pulled him away.

Mary Bryant looked good, but tired; Ruthie Mitchell seemed to have shrunk with the years. She had been so formidable when she stage-managed the Prince shows. If a dancer or actor was a moment late on a cue, he took a real risk that Ruthie would run him over with a piece of scenery.

"Flossie, chic as ever." Wetzon bent to place a kiss on costume designer Florence Klotz's beautifully lined face.

"Wetzon, you look marvelous! What are you doing now?" Flossie took her hand, bracelets clinking.

"I'm a recruiter, a headhunter, on Wall Street."

Liz McCann, the producer, overhearing, said, "Wetzon, you really left the theater at the right time. It's just not fun anymore."

She felt that. She had been part of the glory days and they were over, at least her glory days in the theater had come and gone.

"Atención, atención!" Carlos cried, jumping on a chair. "Now that we are sufficiently sloshed." He swayed and Marshall Bart

steadied him, hand on his back. "So kind, darling." Carlos surveyed the eccentrically dressed crowd of theater people, fluttering his fingers in answer to Wetzon's fluttering fingers.

"'Sing out, Louise,'" someone called, quoting from *Gypsy.*

"Thank you, thank you."

Someone wedged himself into a narrow space next to Wetzon, bumping her. She looked up into the gaunt, haunted face of Steve Sondheim. "Hi, Steve."

"Wetzon." Sondheim nodded to her. She was surprised he remembered her. He looked cadaverous under his scruffy beard. She'd heard he had fully recovered from his heart attack a few years ago.

"We are gathered here today," Carlos said from his chair platform, "to honor our friend, Tommy Lawrence. No pompous words."

"Here, here."

"How about a few."

"All right," Carlos said. "A few pompous words. *Au revoir,* old friend. Tommy would have loved this turnout—"

"He had a great one!"

"Okay, okay—" Carlos said. "Do you realize that if someone were to throw a bomb into this room right now, he would wipe out what's left of the whole creative thrust of the theater?"

"Amen!"

"Let's hoist one for Tommy." Carlos raised his hand holding a glass of wine. A hush fell over the room. "It's your bow, Tommy." Someone near Wetzon sniffled.

"Tommy." Glasses were raised around the room. "Tommy."

Then slowly, almost reluctantly, they began to take their leave.

"I'm a little drunk, Birdie," Carlos said, giving her an immense hug. "What do you think? Was it all right? Was it enough?"

"Yes. Tommy would have loved it." She kept her arm around Carlos. He was wearing a red velvet jacket over a black silk turtleneck. "You look very elegant tonight."

"Mmmm, so do you. That's some coat. A gift from a client?"

"A client? Are you crazy? Only two clients have ever even *thanked* me since we opened our firm."

"Then surely a thank-you from a grateful broker."

"A contradiction in terms. It says here that her face broke up with hysterical laughter."

"Ah, of course, a loving cop? Is that a contradiction in terms."

Wetzon curled her lip at him. "You wanna lose your dearest friend? No, this coat is my treat to me. Anyway, my black alpaca had an unfortunate accident." She felt depressed as she spoke. She felt surrounded by sudden, unexpected death.

"What are you doing for dinner, dear heart?"

"I was about to ask you."

"Let's grab a cab and go to David K's for Peking Chicken."

"And lots of beer."

When they were standing on the sidewalk, Wetzon looked up and down the street.

"There's a cab." Carlos waved at an unoccupied taxi.

"No, wait." Wetzon saw what she'd been looking for—Michael Stewart's cab with its dented right fender. "Here's the one I want."

Carlos gave her his this-lady-has-lost-her-marbles look, but he followed her into the cab. "My Birdie has turned mystical," he commented, settling back.

"David K's on Sixty-fifth and Third, please, Michael." She sank back against Carlos and propped up her head on his lynx shoulder.

"Me oh my, we have a personal chauffeur and a raccoon coat." Carlos kissed the top of her beret. "Business must be booming."

"Oh shut up, Carlos. Michael is my bodyguard, aren't you, Michael?" She paused, then added mischievously, "Arranged by agreement between my lover and your lover." She raised her eyes in time to catch the startled reaction in Michael Stewart's, reflected in the rearview mirror.

It was too early for the normal East Side dinner crowd, so they were seated without delay.

"You are such a Little Iodine," Carlos said fondly as he

speared a dumpling with one chopstick. "This is the best sesame sauce I've ever had."

"Silvestri's mad at me," Wetzon said, trying to pick up a dumpling with both chopsticks.

"I don't wonder."

"Says I hold back information. Butt in where I don't belong."

"Which you never do."

"Oh, Carlos."

"Oh, Birdie."

They ordered two more Heinekens and attacked the Peking Chicken.

"Listen, let me try something out on you." Wetzon bit into the envelope of chicken meat, crispy skin, and hoisin sauce, and rolled her eyes. "Enchanting."

"Shoot."

She shivered. "Don't say that."

"Sorry. Tell me already." Carlos spooned rice from a bowl and sopped up the sesame sauce, scooping the mixture expertly into his mouth with his chopsticks.

"There are all these elderly people who are incapacitated for one reason or another. They have home care attendants taking care of them. Most of them can afford to pay for their own care. Are you with me?"

"Always, luv."

"Say the elderly person owns stocks and has the stock certificates. Couldn't the home care attendant have fairly easy access to all of this, plus identification and stuff?" She broke a wing apart and ate through the crisp skin to the tender white meat. "What if the attendant took the certificates to a brokerage firm and pretended to be the elderly person and cashed in the stock?" She brandished the wing bone for emphasis.

"But, Birdie, brokerage firms aren't that stupid. And don't you think the home care person would be taking a major risk of getting caught?"

"Yeah." She plunked the bone down on the plate in disgust. "You're right, of course. There must be more to it than that."

"Unless of course it wasn't just the home care attendant involved." Carlos dipped a big piece of white meat into the crock of hoisin sauce, tipped his head back, and dropped it in his mouth.

Wetzon knocked over the bottle of Heineken with her right hand, spilling the small amount of beer left in it on the table-cloth. "Holy shit, Carlos, that may be it. Why not a stockbroker? Why not a manager? Why not a *whole* brokerage firm working on the scam with a *group* of home care attendants? Maybe that's what Peter Tormenkov told Teddy that got them both murdered."

39

WETZON CALLED HAZEL from David K's, and she and Carlos stopped at Greenberg's on Madison Avenue and bought half a dozen rich, buttery brownies, then chased over to the Food Emporium and picked up a pint of Häagen-Dazs vanilla while Michael Stewart waited patiently in the cab.

The night was black and cold with a kind of cutting damp-ness typical of New York City in winter. It sliced through cloth, but not fur apparently, for Wetzon felt the intensity only on her face.

She touched Carlos's nose as they waited for Hazel to open her door. "You have a cold nose," she said.

"At least mine's not red."

"Well, who could tell on you, anyway." She nudged him with her hip.

When Hazel opened her door, she found them jostling each other like two little kids. They stopped and stared at her for a long second and burst out laughing. "I think we rang the wrong chimes," Carlos said.

Hazel was dressed in bright red sweatpants and a matching

sweatshirt that Wetzon had given her last year for Christmas. On her head she wore a startling red Afro wig. Her face was chalky white, but she was smiling. "Come on in, kids." She stood back, holding onto the door with one hand, leaning on her cane with the other. "You both look beautiful as always. My, my, look at your coats." She patted Wetzon's raccoon, admired Carlos's lynx.

"Yes, don't we look just ever so smart and successful?" Carlos said, hanging his and Wetzon's coats on the coatrack.

Wetzon took the box of brownies and the ice cream from Carlos and headed for the kitchen. "You guys just sit and have a gossip." She wrinkled her nose. A sweet, familiar odor floated in the air.

Carlos stood at the steps to the living room and flared his nostrils. "Ah yes. I do believe an old friend has been here."

Hazel looked embarrassed and giggled.

Wetzon inhaled deeply. There it was. Pot. Once recognized, its essence reminded Wetzon in one fell swoop of road tours and summer stock, cramped living quarters, tired muscles. She felt no nostalgia for those days.

"Oh me, oh my," Carlos said. He danced down the two steps into Hazel's living room.

"I might have known you'd pick it up," Hazel said. She seated herself in the rocking chair. She was wearing white socks and Reeboks. "It's for medicinal purposes—and I'm not sharing."

Carlos laughed and kicked his shoes off, settling down on her gold damask sofa.

"Selfish. No matter. I've sworn off. I'll just sit here and breathe it in. I can get a room high."

Wetzon served the brownies, each with a scoop of ice cream, and sat down on the sofa next to Carlos. She had read an article about how smoking marijuana helped combat the side effects of chemotherapy. Hazel's face was drawn under the comical red wig, but she did look a lot better than when Wetzon had last seen her. A metal walker stood unobtrusively next to the rocking chair.

"What have you been up to all week?" Wetzon asked. "For some reason I get this feeling you've been avoiding me."

"Leslie dear, that was your friend who was killed, wasn't it?"

Hazel rested the plate in her lap, giving Wetzon her total attention.

"Yes. It was awful." She closed her eyes and saw the scene again, the blood . . . She shuddered and almost dropped the plate. She opened her eyes and the image disappeared.

"Oh, my dear, I'm so sorry."

Wetzon sighed. The ice cream on her plate began to melt into the brownie. "Did he ever call you, Hazel? To interview you?"

"Someone from his office did call—to get my schedule—and said he'd be calling to make an appointment. But of course, that was before—" Hazel placed a large forkful of brownie and ice cream in her mouth, clearly relishing the taste.

Wetzon eyed her enviously and set her own plate down on Hazel's walnut coffee table, next to the large book on women artists. She felt sick. "I think Teddy's murder may have had something to do with Peepsie's," she said.

Hazel's hand holding the dessert shook and she steadied the plate with her other hand. "Then you are convinced Peepsie was murdered? Please explain. Why do you think they are connected?"

Wetzon quickly ran through the events of the previous week.

"Well, of course," Hazel said thoughtfully, "Peepsie did have a lot of stock. Alden was on the board of directors of so many different corporations . . . I'm sure it's all been accounted for . . . she did have a lawyer . . . I'm so glad Marion will be here soon . . . early next week, I should think . . ." She rocked back and forth slowly in the chair, eating the brownie with an absent expression on her face.

"I smell wood burning," Carlos said, poking Wetzon and pointing at Hazel.

"What are you thinking, Hazel?" Wetzon demanded, standing. That sharp mind was cooking away on something. And she had managed to evade Wetzon's question about whether Hazel had been avoiding her.

Hazel's clear blue eyes focused, and she smiled reassuringly at Wetzon and Carlos. "I'm sorry, my dears, it was nothing. I guess I was just thinking how peculiar life is. Somehow it seems a relief to me that Peepsie was a murder victim rather than a suicide. Isn't that ironic?"

"Not so ironic." Carlos put his empty plate on the table and began on Wetzon's untouched portion. "At least you know that your friend had not done something totally unlike herself, even though she was sick."

Hazel's eyes turned vague again. Then, as if she suddenly remembered them, she said, "Oh dear, I was just thinking about something I want to do tomorrow. My, my." She looked pained. "I'm getting as bad as Peepsie was." She finished her brownie and ice cream and set her plate on the floor beside her. "So forgetful." There was a smile behind her eyes.

"You're not forgetful at all, Hazel, and you know it," Wetzon said, picking up the plate, frowning.

"Oho!" Carlos cried, watching the interplay. "We have another keeper of secrets here. A plotter." He put his shoes on. "I hate to break this moment up, but we girls have to get our beauty sleep or we look oh so haggard in the morning." He collected the plates and disappeared into the kitchen. Hazel and Wetzon could hear the water running in the sink.

"You're not going to tell me what you're up to, I take it?"

"Not just yet, dear. I want to work it out for myself. But I promise you I will tell you as soon as I do."

That was all Wetzon could get out of her before they left.

"I'm worried," she told Carlos when they were back in Michael Stewart's cab. "I think something I said clicked when I told her my theory about the home care service and the stock certificate scam."

"Well, not to be. Hazel is a lot smarter than you are about mucking in where she could get hurt."

"Oh yeah?" *I wouldn't count on it,* she thought, but she kept her thoughts to herself because she could tell by the tenseness of Michael Stewart's shoulders that he was extremely interested in what they were saying.

Traffic was backed up on the transverse between the East Side and the West Side on Eighty-sixth Street, and they were stuck in the middle of the Park for fifteen minutes before the traffic started moving again. When they got to Central Park West, they saw there had been an accident. A cab had skidded on the icy street, into the crosstown bus near the exit to the transverse. A uniformed policeman was directing traffic around the accident scene. It did not look, in spite of all the lights and police cars, as if anyone had been hurt, but a lot of broken glass lay on the street amid the ice.

There was a parking place in front of Wetzon's building and Michael Stewart pulled into it and turned off his lights and his motor.

"Oh joy," Carlos gushed. "You mean I get to walk home all by my lonesome on this cold night?"

"Gee, Michael, can't you just take Carlos . . . Carlos, are you going to Arthur's?"

"Where else?"

"Can't you just take him over to West End and—?"

"Ninetieth Street."

Michael Stewart didn't answer. He took a peaked cap from the seat beside him and put it on his head.

"I guess not, Carlos."

"Ah well."

They climbed over a mound of frozen snow onto the cleared sidewalk strewn with white ice-melting beads and stood under Wetzon's awning. Carlos put his arms around her. "Good night, Birdie. I love you."

"I love you, too." She kissed him between the eyes and he shivered delicately.

"I have four words for you." His voice was a sexy whisper in her ear.

"What are they?"

"Buy low, sell high," he said.

"You're terrible." She pushed him away and watched him trudge off with a brief wave.

Javier opened the inside door for her. "There was lady here looking for you little while ago," he said.

"There was? Did she leave her name?"

"She said . . ." He shrugged. "I forget."

"What did she look like?"

"Tall, black lady. Very nice. She wait awhile, then go."

"Damn." Could it be that Diantha Anderson again? She was the only tall black lady Wetzon knew. "Was her name Ms. Anderson?"

"Yes, that's it."

What the hell could that woman want of her? She had been calling her all week. Now she was invading her home. "If she comes back, tell her I'm not home, please." She would deal with Diantha Anderson tomorrow, from the office. What could be so urgent that she was tracking Wetzon down at home?

She decided to ignore the little blinking light that announced she had messages on her answering machine—just this once—but found herself back in the dining room after her shower, staring at the exasperating thing. Finally, she sat down at the table and pushed the button to rewind the tape and once that was done, the other button to play back her messages.

Smith.

Bernstein. He left two numbers. Screw him. She was glad she hadn't been home and she didn't intend to call him back until she talked to Arthur.

Smith again, sounded annoyed.

Diantha Anderson. There was a pleading tone in her voice that disconcerted Wetzon. "Oh dear, I'd really better call her," she murmured.

There were two hang-ups.

Silvestri hadn't called.

She was about to turn the machine off when Hazel's voice came on. "Leslie dear, I hoped you'd be home because I'm very tired and I'm about to turn my phone off and go to bed. I don't want you to worry, but I have something in mind that may help us find out what really happened to Peepsie. I'm going to sleep on it and I will let you know more as soon as I have it worked out. In the meantime, you are not to take personally anything I do or say."

40

SHE WAS THE FIRST ONE in the office the next morning, having spent a restless night, her thoughts sprawling from Peepsie and Teddy to the Tormenkovs, Kevin De Haven, endlessly, and back to Hazel.

Now, with the coffee dripping automatically, Wetzon sat down at her desk and scanned the front page of the *Journal*. Nothing about anything.

The New York Times had a follow-up in the Metro section on Teddy's murder. No new information, but the police were tracing down leads. Channel 8 had offered a twenty-five-thousand-dollar reward for information leading to the arrest of his murderer. Pictures of Teddy at work, in black tie getting an award, disconcerted her. She couldn't forget how he had looked when she'd last seen him. She folded the *Times* and put it under her desk, turning back to the business news of the *Journal*.

"Good morning," Harold said in the doorway, surprise in his voice. "You're here early." He took off his old man's brown rain hat with the brim and hung his down coat in the closet. B.B. arrived soon afterward.

Wetzon looked at her watch and picked up the phone and called Hazel.

"You caught me at an awkward time, Leslie dear." There was a tremor of excitement in her voice. "Let me call you back later."

"Hazel, what's going on? What are you up to?"

"I have someone with me right now. I'll talk to you later, dear. Don't worry." She hung up.

Wetzon's fist punched her desk. She felt frustrated. She looked at the receiver in her other hand and hung it up. On her desk in front of her was Kevin De Haven's suspect sheet. She picked up the phone again.

"De Haven."

"Hi, it's Wetzon. Can you talk?"

"Sure, Wetzon, old pal," De Haven drawled.

"How did it go with Shearson?"

"I really liked that guy Magundy, Wetzon. Seems like a straight shooter."

"He is. What did he say about syndicate? Can he cover you?"

"Says he may have too much demand in his office. Wants me to meet the regional guy . . . ?"

"Rogers? Matt Rogers?"

"Yeah, that's the guy. I said okay but don't take too long. I got an offer I'm sitting on from Smith Barney."

"You told him that?" Brokers talked too much. About themselves. About their clients. About their firms. And about each other.

"Yeah, why fool around? I want everything on the table so we can deal. And that's the other thing, they don't make deals. I won't go anywhere without a deal. I told you that."

"I know, Kevin. But I hate to make a judgment without giving them a shot at you. Let me get you some feedback. Remember, you have Loeb Dawkins at five o'clock this afternoon, at 440 Lexington, ninth floor. Jay Campo."

"Later, Wetzon."

She confirmed the appointment with Jay Campo, then dialed Dick Magundy at Shearson.

"He's good, Wetzon, but I don't know if I want to handle him. He's going to take a lot of work and he's a burnout candidate. I've got a lot of people here to share syndicate with. He won't get enough in my office. I'll fix it for him to meet Matt Rogers and maybe Matt will find another office for him, if Matt wants him."

"That's fair."

"The other thing is, he's looking for a deal, and we don't buy brokers. You know that."

"I know. I was hoping you guys would fall in love with each other."

"He's got to look at it as a career move. We're the best firm on the Street now—"

She hung up the phone. Firms that didn't make deals used expressions like "it's a career move," and "we don't want anyone looking for a deal," and "we don't buy brokers." And every goddam firm she represented thought it was the best on the Street right now. She was probably wearing too many hats. It was something to talk to Smith about.

She dialed Gary Greggs to find out what he thought of Maurice Sanderson. "Forget it, Wetzon. That guy is an antique. Send me the living, if you don't mind." What was she going to do with Maurice?

She took out her client book and flipped through the pages. Under *Misc. Firms* she saw she'd written First Westchester Securities, 120 Broadway, and the phone number. Frank Willkie, a broker she knew, had become manager there recently. He was looking for brokers. Maybe he would take Maurice.

She got Frank Willkie on the line. "Listen," she said after they had taken care of amenities, "I have a broker I'm working with I think you should see."

"Okay."

"Frank, he does steady business, but his gross is in the neighborhood of a hundred thousand."

Frank groaned.

"And he's seventy years old."

"Jesus, Wetzon."

"You'd be doing a good deed and it wouldn't cost you anything. You can make money on him."

"What do you mean?"

"You could just give him a higher payout—say, fifty percent for six months—"

"Ha! That's all I'd be willing to do, but I'd still have to pay you."

"Okay." She was ready for that. "How about if you give me three percent on his trailing twelve and five percent on his future twelve?"

"No way. Let's face it. I lose money on the deal. Come at me again."

"Jesus, Frank." She thought for a minute. Smith would kill

her. "Okay, how about three thousand down and five percent if he does over a hundred and fifty in a year?"

"How about two thousand down and five percent if he does over two hundred?"

"That's it?"

"That's the best I'll do."

"Okay. When can you see him?"

"Right away. After the close, today, tomorrow. Don't wait too long or I'll change my mind. Have him call me and I'll set it up with him directly."

She called Sanderson and gave him Frank Willkie's number. "I really would like to go to a big name firm, Wetzon, like Shearson or Bache," Sanderson said, without gratitude.

"They won't take you, Maurice. I'm telling you the truth. You're just not doing enough production. Two hundred is their cutoff, and you've been in the business too long from their point of view to be doing just two hundred." She felt squeamish about telling him the truth, but he had to know what the climate was so he could make the right decision. She got him to commit himself to calling Frank Willkie and hung up thinking she worked harder on the small producers than the big ones. And if Maurice Sanderson should be hired by First Westchester, she and Smith would probably never see more than the two-thousand-dollar down payment. There was no way he would do two hundred thousand in gross commissions in the year ahead. Even if he lived. Damn, why was she being so negative?

She called Silvestri at the Seventeenth Precinct. Even if he was mad at her and never wanted to see her again, she'd better fill him in on the stock certificate scam theory, if Michael Stewart hadn't done it already. Silvestri wasn't there and neither was Metzger. She left word that she'd called. Good. She'd done what she'd promised.

Her next call had to be to Diantha Anderson. She located the earlier message among her message slips and was about to call her when Smith came breezing in carrying Wetzon's raccoon coat on its hanger.

"You bought a fur coat? You sneak. Without me. Here, put it on so I can see it."

Wetzon laughed, taking it from Smith. "It was an accident, Smith. Honest. I had to meet Laura Lee, and she was going to her furrier—"

"I've always told you if you wanted a coat, you should use my furrier. You don't know anything about dried-out skins . . . It's so easy to get cheated."

"Oh, Smith—look—do you think I got cheated?" She modeled the coat for Smith.

Smith studied her grudgingly. "Well, it does suit you. Although mink is so much richer . . ."

"Yes, for older ladies, not for me." She didn't look at Smith as she took off her coat and hung it next to Smith's mink and came back to the office.

Smith was standing, waiting, arms folded. "Humpf. I suppose you meant that to be funny."

"Oh come on, Smith, laugh. It was a joke."

"Close the door," Smith ordered. "I have to talk to you privately."

Uh oh, now what? Wetzon closed the door. "I got home too late to call you last night."

"You never return calls anymore. I don't know, Wetzon . . ." She sat down on the edge of her desk and eyed her fingernails.

"What do you want to talk about?"

"Leon thinks we should buy Arleen's business."

"We? You and Leon?"

"No, you and me, of course. Wetzon, really. Why would Leon and I buy her business? Leon is not my partner."

"What would we do with her business, Smith? It makes no sense to me."

"Run it. Of course it makes sense. It makes very good sense. She has an extremely profitable business."

"We have enough to do running our own business. I don't want to buy another business. We're making nice money. I don't want to risk our capital. And if her business is so profitable, why does she want to sell it?"

"Wetzon, sweetie pie, you always think too small. It's your background in the arts. I want you to think about it and we'll talk it over with Leon."

"Just tell me this, why does Arleen want to sell her business all of a sudden?"

"Well, I'm not saying she does. What would you say if I were to buy it myself?"

"It's entirely up to you, of course, but who would run it?"

"She would continue to run it. I would own it. That's the way Leon would set it up." Smith seemed tense and jumpy; her words came in jagged phrases. "But, sweetie, I'm not going to take no for an answer. Really, I want you to promise me you'll think about it. The financials are wonderful—"

"No more about it now," Wetzon insisted, turning away sharply and tearing a gigantic hole in her hose on her desk drawer. "Damn!" A new pair, too. She took the spare she always kept in the drawer and went into the bathroom to change, ignoring Smith.

When she came out, Smith was on the phone. Good. Wetzon opened the door to the front office. "B.B." B.B. was making notes on a suspect sheet. "Any good prospects you want to go over with me?"

"I have two more people on my list to call," B.B. said. "Here's the mail." He handed her a rubberbanded bundle and she took it back to her desk to sort. Then she dialed Diantha Anderson.

"Anderson Associates," a cool female voice answered.

"Diantha Anderson, please."

"She's not here right now. May I take a message?"

"Yes, this is Leslie Wetzon. Just tell her I returned her call."

"Oh, Ms. Wetzon. She asked me to arrange a meeting as soon as possible . . . today. At your convenience, but she said to tell you there is some urgency. She'll be calling in for her messages."

"It's really not convenient." Wetzon thought for a moment. "But I know she's been trying to reach me. Ask her if she can meet me in the street lobby of the Hyatt on Forty-second and Lexington at five-thirty this afternoon."

"I'm sure that will be fine."

"Call me, please, if it's not. I'll be here all afternoon." She left her phone number and hung up.

She took a call from Arthur Margolies assuring her that she was not a suspect, but that she was a material witness and, therefore, could not leave town.

"I have no intention of leaving town, Arthur. Should I return Bernstein's call?"

"I'll do that for you. If I feel you should talk to him, I'll call you back."

That was a relief. She felt she was in good hands with Arthur.

"Let's go to Bloomie's tonight," Smith cut in. "I feel the urge to spend money. And we can have dinner at Yellowfinger's."

"Can't. Have to go over prospects with B.B. after lunch and I have a meeting at five-thirty. How about later in the week?"

"You're on, sugar. Who are you working on?"

"I may have found a place for Maurice Sanderson."

"Oh, please, I thought we were rid of that old fart."

Wetzon reported her conversation with Frank Willkie. "We won't make much, but—"

"But we'll go to heaven," Smith finished. "Okay, okay. God gave me Pollyanna as a partner."

"De Haven saw Shearson this morning. It went well. Dick wants him to meet Matt Rogers."

"Matt'll love him."

"But will Matt love him enough to give him an up-front deal?"

"I doubt it. You know how Matt is about money."

"Yes. He'll try to cheat us out of our fee."

"Nice, Wetzon."

"True, Smith."

"Where else are you sending him?"

"He sees Jay Campo at Loeb Dawkins this afternoon. Keep *les fingairs* crossed. Would be a lovely fee."

"Wouldn't it just."

•   •   •   •

The phones heated up in the afternoon and, intermittently, Wetzon went over the interviews B.B. had done.

"Here, for example, we need more biographical information," she told him. "Degree, when he graduated, is he married, children." And, "Get home address and phone number whenever possible. You can sometimes get a relationship going by relating to where he lives. Also, you can sell him on working closer to home."

Silvestri called just before four. "What's up?"

She caught Smith's teasing look. "Would love to but can't right now."

"When?" His voice sounded dead.

"Later?" She hesitated. "Maybe after seven?"

"Right." He hung up without saying whether he would call or come by.

It hurt. She had let him get to her, she had gotten involved, felt vulnerable. She stared down at her appointment book with blind eyes.

"Anything wrong, sweetie?" Smith asked. Did she sound hopeful?

"Not really. We're just having scheduling problems. He's been working nights."

"So he says."

"Oh, Smith."

The next call was for Smith, and she was still talking when Wetzon put on her coat and beret and said good night. It was almost five, and she was running a little late.

It was a relief to be out on the street and away from Smith. Too close quarters. The office had begun to make her feel claustrophobic.

"Need a ride, lady?" A cab stopped for her. "Hey, don't I know you?"

It was Judy Blue. "Judy Blue. Why do you keep turning up all the time?" Oh, but of course, Judy Blue must work for the Department, too, just like Michael Stewart. "How's Silvestri?"

"Who? What? Who's Silvestri?" Judy Blue was doing a good job of pretending to look puzzled.

"Okay, Judy Blue." Wetzon got into the cab. "You can take me to Dollar Bill's on Forty-second and Grand Central."

Judy Blue spoke into what looked like an intercom. "Fare to Grand Central."

After Judy Blue dropped her at Dollar Bill's, Wetzon went upstairs and bought a half dozen pairs of sheer black hose, put the package into her carryall, and walked the half block to the lobby of the Hyatt.

No sign of Diantha Anderson. She'd give her twenty minutes and that was it.

A gray-haired man in a corduroy car coat was berating a meek little woman, probably his wife, about the shopping bags and bundles she was carrying. "We always end up like immigrants with packages." The woman looked humiliated. Wetzon felt sorry for her.

Leaning against the marble wall on the left was a tall, athletic-looking man in a tan trench coat reading *The New York Times*. He looked up momentarily and then went back to his paper. The door to the street opened and another tall, well-built man in a tan raincoat came into the small lobby and walked toward her as if he were going to ask directions. Beyond him, Wetzon caught a glimpse of Diantha Anderson approaching the glass entrance door.

The man reading the *Times* folded it, set it on a nearby marble ashtray, and strolled toward Wetzon. "Leslie Wetzon," he said, taking her left elbow. The other man in the trench coat stood on her right. Wetzon looked from one to the other. What was going on? She saw Diantha's alarmed face. Saw her pause several feet away, near the crowd of conventioneers who had just disembarked from a chartered bus with masses of luggage. "Who are you? What do you want?"

"We'd like you to come with us, please," the first man said. "Without making a disturbance."

"Who are you?" she demanded.

"Federal Bureau of Investigation," the second man said.

41

"STOP! THIEF!" A woman screamed.

A group of luggage-laden foreign tourists who had obviously just gotten off one of the airport buses pushed forward, disconcerted by the woman's scream, responding, perhaps, to all the terrible stories they'd been told about life in New York. On the verge of panic they pressed against Wetzon and her two companions in the small lobby, jabbering and shoving. The men in the trench coats resisted, vainly trying to hold back the surge.

"Look out!" someone cried. "He's got a gun!"

"Where is he?" Mounting hysteria filled the area. Voices rose in fear and anger.

An arm came at Wetzon from the right, locked onto hers, and jerked her, stumbling, sideward. A clear voice enunciated in her ear, "Come with me quickly, no questions." The voice had the sound of iron in it, and Wetzon was not about to argue.

She put herself into Diantha Anderson's care as they burrowed into the confused and milling crowd of arms, legs, cameras, bodies, and luggage. Then Diantha pushed through a glass door to the right of the lobby and they were free and racing down a corridor with stores on both sides. They plunged into Grand Central Station along with the hordes of rush hour commuters streaming like lemmings to trains and subways.

"Okay, wait!" Wetzon shouted over the cacophony of people and trains. She stopped to catch her breath at a stand that advertised baked potatoes to go. "We're free—"

"No, we're not—look"—Diantha pointed back down the corridor from the direction they'd come and Wetzon saw a tall man in a trench coat enter from the Hyatt side door, just as they had.

"Let's get out of here, get a cab."

"No." Diantha grabbed her hand. "It's easier to get lost down here at this hour, if we just keep moving."

They changed their route then, going farther underground, into a sloping tunnel that led to the West Side Shuttle trains, which ran every few minutes, carrying passengers from the East Side to the West Side. The tunnel, its walls advertising the glamour of New York, Broadway shows, restaurants, and films, was a virtual dormitory for the down-and-out. The homeless with their belongings in shopping bags, dirt-encrusted beggars, drifters sat on flattened cardboard boxes or stood along the tunnel, asking for money. Others slept, buried in newspapers or old carpet or towels; some even had blankets. The area had a putrid odor. Commuters poured without pause through the tunnel in both directions, eyes averted, unseeing.

Diantha came to a halt in a hollow where a passageway led off to Grand Central proper. "We've got to talk, but not here and not now." Her eyes burned into Wetzon's.

A man, his shoulders hunched, his hair matted in dreadlocks, edged toward them, his filthy hat outstretched. "Could you spare some change?" the drifter wheedled. He thrust his hat at them. Diantha pulled some coins from the pocket of her fur-lined storm coat and dropped them into the hat. "Thank you, sister, thank you."

"I am not your sister," Diantha hissed, turning furious eyes on him. The man scrambled back into the main tunnel.

Wetzon was losing her patience. She was tired of running from something she didn't understand, tired of being so nice and cooperative. "Would you mind just giving me a clue?"

Diantha ignored Wetzon's question and came back with one of her own, peering nervously back and forth in the tunnel, eyeing the crowds of people rushing home. "Who were those men? Cops?"

"They said they were FBI." Wetzon spoke the words but she found them impossible to believe.

Diantha's face clouded. Perspiration glinted on her upper lip. "Look, we can't take any chances here. Before anything, we've got to lose them."

"We have."

"I wouldn't count on it. They'll be all over us, whoever they are." Her mouth twisted. "We've got to split up. I'm too tall. They've seen me with you, they'll look for me. I stand out. And they'll be looking for the two of us." She rested her hand on Wetzon's shoulder, squeezing it thoughtlessly.

Wetzon stepped away, as if to go, and Diantha let her hand fall to her side. "I think it's time you told me what's going on."

"There they are! Dammit!" Diantha's eyes were wild. She reached into her pocket. For a panicked moment Wetzon thought Diantha was going to pull out a gun, but she had a hand-kerchief in her hand, and she used it to blot her face.

"Where?"

"Please! I'm begging you. It's a matter of life and death." Diantha dipped into her handbag, a brown leather clutch almost as large as a briefcase, and removed a key from a red leather change purse. "We don't have time for explanations now, but I promise you, you'll see and understand why I'm doing this, why I have to do it this way." She pressed the key into Wetzon's palm and closed her fingers over it. "Six nineteen East Sixteenth Street. It's a brownstone. Ring my bell. Two short rings and one long. Count ten and do it again. Then go in." She gave Wetzon a small push forward. "I'm going to double back and take the Lexington train. I'll meet you there as soon as I can."

"But what does this have to do with me?" Wetzon was truly confused. At that instant she saw a tall man in a trench coat who stood out from the regular subway travelers. He was looking for someone, searching the faces in the crowd. This time when Diantha tugged her, she went willingly. They began weaving themselves in among the stream of people rushing to the Shut-tle.

"Please," Diantha said. "Don't be frightened by anything you see there—" She sped up, pulling Wetzon with her. "When we get to the crush around the turnstiles, just join the crowd and go down and take the Shuttle to the BMT, then take the BMT to Fourteenth. I'm going back."

Wetzon nodded. Her hands were cold. She took her gloves from her pocket and put them on, holding the key in the palm of her right hand, inside the glove.

Here it was wall-to-wall people, shoving and pushing to get through the turnstiles from both sides, coming from the Shuttle and going to the Shuttle. It seemed so stupid to Wetzon that there weren't enough doors to let out the masses coming from the Shuttle, because the Transit Authority saw fit to keep half the doors chained closed so as to prevent people from sneaking in. She turned her head once to look for Diantha, spotted her taking off the fur turban, and then she was swallowed up in moments, tall as she was.

Wetzon hesitated at the turnstile. She didn't have a token.

Someone pushed her hard. "Get out of the way, lady, move it," a man in an expensive tweed overcoat snarled.

Damn. She backed away from the turnstile and saw the man in a trench coat waiting near the foot of the staircase leading to the Shuttle. She tore the lavender beret from her head and shoved it into her carryall, and let herself be carried along with the rush hour crowd back down the tunnel from which she'd come, the tunnel Diantha had disappeared down, not daring to look at anyone, particularly men in trench coats.

She remembered she had some bills and change in her coat pocket from the five she had given Judy Blue, so she took a place in line for the token booth, fidgeting. Maybe she should take the pins out of her hair. They'd surely spot her in her raccoon coat . . . She slipped off her left glove and pulled the pins from her hair, letting it loosen around the band into a ponytail, shaking her head back and forth. She put the hairpins in her pocket with the spare change.

As she slipped two dollar bills under the window grate, she heard a man shout, "There she is!" She grabbed the two tokens, terrified, sank into a half crouch, prepared to run, expecting to be pounced on. People crowded around her but almost at once she realized they were not looking at her; they were watching a man in a tan trench coat elbow his way through the sea of people pouring down the escalator to the platform, following a woman in a purple beret and a raccoon coat.

That did it. She didn't pause now. She went back through the tunnel with the relentless rush hour throng, blended into the group heading for the Shuttle, pushed her way on with the same fervor as the rest, and breathed a sign of relief as the Shuttle train jerked out of Grand Central, moments later sliding into the Times Square station. There was no sign of men in trench coats.

She steered around the thick crowd listening to the thunderous music of a jazz combo, thinking that the music was nice but it caused a traffic jam of people. Torn newspapers, half-eaten hot dogs, pizza slices, crumpled soda cans, candy wrappers lay scattered on the stone passageways everywhere you looked. People just dropped things where they stood, never bothering to look for a trash basket, and when one did find a trash basket, it was usually filled to overflowing. Graffiti marked the scarred walls. The pungent combination of greasy and sweet smells came from the hot dog and caramel popcorn stand in the underground passageway to the BMT subway.

What the hell was that address Diantha had given her? Blast all of this to hell. She had told Silvestri she'd be home after seven. She'd never make it now. What would he think? He'd likely just be disgusted with her and think she was too unreliable for him to bother with.

Hold on one minute there, she thought. *Why are you putting yourself down? If he thought that, he wasn't worth bothering with.* "Sure, you keep telling yourself that, old girl." She had spoken out loud, but no one ever paid any attention to people who talked to themselves in New York, especially on the subway. She laughed. Even chic young women in expensive raccoon coats talked to themselves.

Her mind was a blank. She would have to trust the address would come back to her. East Sixteenth Street, Diantha had said. Something East Sixteenth Street.

She let her eyes roam slowly back and forth over the crowd, young, old, in overcoats, down, fur, leather, shivering in denim, wearing hats, bareheaded, baldheaded, carrying briefcases, newspapers, books, dark-skinned, light-skinned, Asians, men, women, children sleeping in strollers, infants in carrying sacks.

No FBI types though, no clones of clones, tall in tan trench coats and short tan hair. She shivered in the depths of her raccoon coat, but not because she was cold. What had they wanted of her? And were they really FBI?

Down the stone steps, strewn with garbage, that led to the BMT lines, she was thinking less about where she was going than about what she had become involved in. She automatically walked in a broken field around the standees, a few yards down to the middle of the platform, passing another staircase down which people continued to stream. A young man with waist-length hair was playing a Mozart violin concerto near a big trash container. People were listening and putting money into his violin case, and impulsively Wetzon gave him what she had in her pockets, all except for the hairpins.

Two trains pulled into the station almost at the same time, an N and an R. The N was crowded with people, while the R was fairly empty with plenty of seats and everyone visible. Ordinarily, she would have taken the R so she could sit to Fourteenth Street, but this was not an ordinary situation. Just in case they were still looking for her . . . She hovered by the door of the R and then as the doors were about to close, moved as if to get on, turned, and scooted across the platform to the N and pushed her way unceremoniously into the people-as-sardines pressed into one another. The doors closed on the half-empty R as she watched.

"Push, lady, push." A cheerful tub of a man with a Spanish accent got on behind her and, holding onto the sides of the open doors for leverage, belly-pushed her and himself into the jammed car. She was squeezed into a rigid position, held up by other bodies similarly squeezed. The conductor's voice came crackling over the PA system, warning everyone to clear the doors, and then the doors of the N bumped shut. Her face rested against someone's canvas backpack.

Her heart sank when she heard yelling on the platform and someone pounded on the side of the train. But the conductor announced implacably, "Please step back. There is another train just behind this one."

She was wedged between two taller women and a man in work clothes stained with paint, who needed a bath. The man behind her actually opened a newspaper and read it over her, the work clothes stained with paint, who needed a bath. The man behind her actually opened a newspaper and read it over her, the pages flapping on the side of her face not pressed against the backpack. God, she hated being short. What she wouldn't give for three or four or five more inches. That wasn't asking for much.

People screamed at each other in Spanish, but they were just having a conversation. The two women, young and intense looking, were talking about the mathematical philosophy of a point. A point? A dot? The train jerked, throwing everyone wedged together off-balance. The women talking about the point were interrupted by the man in the paint-stained clothes. "I think I might be able to help on this," he said. The three began to argue abstractions and Wetzon tuned out. 619 East Sixteenth Street. That was the address Diantha had given her.

The next stop was Fourteenth Street, Union Square.

When the doors opened, people burst forth, carrying Wetzon with them, pushing and shoving their way from the train, across the platform. She climbed the first flight of stairs, went through the turnstile past the token booth, where there was the usual line, and headed for the staircase to the street.

"Oh!" The frightened cry came from a woman in front of her on the staircase. Wetzon, holding up her new coat to keep it from sweeping the stairs, looked up, ready to run.

A tiny mouse was scampering around, terrorized, desperately looking for a way out. Behind Wetzon another woman let out a soft cry. The mouse saw an opening and darted up the stairs and into the night, where she, too, wanted to run.

She came out at Union Square, a dilapidated area of the City now undergoing a great resurgence. Part of the square was paved over like a parking lot and the best farmers' market in Manhattan was here two or three times a week all year round, with fresh fruits and vegetables as well as flowers, plants, meats, fish, and baked goods from farms in New York State, New Jersey, and Pennsylvania.

The builder William Zeckendorf had built a towering condominium on the east side of the square, and the community which was gentrifying as fast as her Upper West Side. But it would never have the elegance of its neighbor Gramercy Park, two or three blocks to the north.

"Six nineteen," she murmured over and over to herself, "six nineteen . . ." The wind swept across the empty square with a wicked bite. She fished into her carryall and put her beret back on, adjusting it down over her eyebrows.

The building was one of four almost identical brownstones obviously built by the same builder, probably in the late nineteenth century. Each had about twelve narrow stone steps leading to an ornate black iron grate door in front of a heavy wooden door. Six nineteen's door was a light-colored oak with a gleaming brass doorplate.

To the left of the door were two small highly polished brass plates. The lower one said #1 Trapunto, and the upper said #2 Anderson. There was a bell next to each number. She opened the iron grate door and tried the knob of the oak door. It was locked.

Now what was that dumb signal Diantha had given her? It was so stupid, all of this. She felt as if she were in a cloak-and-dagger film, and a B one at that.

Two short rings, one long, count ten, do it again. She made a refrain out of it, counting under her breath, "And one and two, and one . . ." She did it. A buzzer sounded, so Diantha must have made it home safely. She pushed the oak door open and found herself in a small vestibule, facing two doors. To her immediate right was a tall, mission-style combination umbrella stand-coatrack. A bright brass lantern hung from the ceiling, lighting the area. On the walls was beautiful William Morris wallpaper with a design of arches within arches in mauves and purples.

The door on the left had a brass "1," the door on the right "2."

She closed the oak door behind her, listening for the snap which indicated the door was locked. Then she removed her glove from her right hand and took out the key which had grown warm in the palm of her hand.

Suddenly uncertain, she stopped. What the hell was she doing here? It was preposterous. Still, she *was* here. She might

as well find out what Diantha thought was so urgent. She unlocked the door and it opened inward. A staircase began just a
few steps in front of her, going up, under a dim, hanging fixture
of a brass chain with a Tiffany globe.

Again she closed the door behind her and listened. Silence.
The floor creaked from somewhere above her, as if from a foot-
step.

"Diantha?" Her voice came out husky. She cleared her
throat. There was no welcoming response. Ah well. She picked
up the front of her coat and climbed the narrow, steep staircase.
There were prints on the right-hand wall of Victorian women in
bright dresses. It appeared Diantha lived in the upper half of a
brownstone, a duplex all her own.

When Wetzon got to the top of the stairs, she paused. There
was that same creaking noise again, and then a faint rustle.
Someone was here. "Diantha? Are you here?"

No answer.

She moved forward, drawn by something—she didn't know
what—the sound, perhaps, the subdued light, a fuzzy sepia mist,
in the large front room at the top of the stairs, as if she'd entered
an old movie. The windows facing the street had their blinds
drawn. She took in the paintings on the walls, the mauve velvet
upholstery on a long traditional sofa, two wing chairs in wide-
and-narrow-striped fabric, their backs to her, facing the fireplace
in which dying embers glowed and snapped. The walls were a
deeper mauve-brown.

Her eyes focused on a book that lay open on the floor next
to one of the wing chairs. A half-filled glass of dark liquid was on
the small round table that was placed between the two chairs.

"Is anyone here?" she asked, perplexed, afraid, not afraid,
growing angry, knowing that someone was there.

A figure rose tall from one of the chairs and turned to her. An
apparition.

She staggered backward, as if hit by a tremendous weight,
breathless. "No!" she cried.

"Wetzi," the figure said. "It's okay. Don't be afraid. I'm real."

Her knees buckled under her and she felt herself slumping

forward to the floor. Her mind told her no—she had to be dreaming—but her eyes betrayed her.

The figure standing near the chair was Teddy Lanzman.

42

THE SLAM OF A DOOR somewhere in the distance woke her. It reassured her. Of course, she'd been dreaming again. Teddy was not alive. What a cruel joke. She rolled over and pressed her face into the pillow. The velvet of the pillowcase caressed her cheek. Wait. What velvet pillow?

She opened her eyes. Oh God. Teddy was looking down at her. She was lying on Diantha Anderson's velvet sofa. And Diantha Anderson herself, still wearing the brown fur-lined storm coat, came up behind him.

Wetzon sat up and the room spun and dipped like a runaway merry-go-round, making a fun house image of Teddy and Diantha.

"You jerk," she heard Diantha say. "What did you do? Jump out at her and yell boo?"

"Shit, lady, I've been through hell and back and you're yelling at *me*? Why the fuck didn't *you* tell her?"

"There wasn't time, and where we were was hardly the place." Diantha smiled down at Wetzon. There were little tense lines around her mouth and eyes. "How're you doing?"

"Okay, I think. I can't believe this." Wetzon stared at Teddy's familiar face. Short sprouts of beard decorated his cheeks and chin. She put her hand out and touched him; he was warm and splendidly alive.

Diantha gave Teddy a poke with her elegant knee. "And what do you think the last two days have been for me, you ungrateful bastard?" Her eyes blazed and she shook a fist at him. She was beautiful. Her short Afro was one shade darker than her skin.

Teddy smiled and put his arm around Diantha. "Come on, who're you kidding? You're my girl, aren't you? It comes with the territory."

"I'm my own girl," she said affectionately. They stood separate but together as Wetzon watched. Very much together. They made a stunning couple, two tall, beautiful people.

"Would you two mind telling me what's going on?" Wetzon demanded.

"I'll make some coffee," Diantha said. She took off her coat and picked up Wetzon's raccoon, which was lying on the floor where Teddy must have left it after she fainted, and hung both in a closet near the middle of the floor-through space.

The section of the apartment Wetzon was in had a long row of windows that overlooked the street. Beyond the closet were rolling doors which Diantha opened, revealing a formal dining room. Its long far wall of windows faced the rear of the house, possibly looking down on gardens and backyards. Diantha disappeared to the right into what must have been the kitchen.

Wetzon's attention returned to Teddy. "Well, you look a little better than the last time I saw you."

He sat down next to her. "I am not dead. I was never dead. I don't know who that poor bugger was who is dead. When I got back to my office I heard someone rattling drawers, going through my files. I ducked into the next office—which has a connecting door to mine. I figured I'd catch the guy when he came out. Then the lights started going crazy and I heard someone come through the stairwell doors." Teddy's jaw tightened, and she saw that his eyes were red-rimmed and sunken, lids heavy with exhaustion or worry, face tired, drawn. "Whoever it was had a flashlight. I could see the fucking thing bobbing on the floor. I couldn't see who it was, and I was trying to figure out what was coming down when the lights came on again and this guy disappears into my office. I hear someone yell, then pop, pop, pop and the lights go out for good. And that's it."

"Jesus, Teddy, then you were in the hallway with me and—"

"And the killer, Wetzi. That's why I couldn't let you know I was all right. I know what a silencer sounds like . . . I went down the stairs right behind him."

"You had to have seen him. Is that why you're hiding? God, Teddy, everyone thinks you're dead. The station even offered a reward."

He snorted. "Listen, by the time the lights came up, I was out of the building and so was the killer. I never saw him."

"Then who was murdered?" She touched the sleeve of his sweater. It was the cream-colored Aran one he had worn the night they'd met for dinner. He was really alive.

Shrugging, he said, "You've got me. I don't know. What I do know is whoever got the poor bugger was after me . . ." His laugh was cynical. "And we know that all black men look alike."

She ignored his last remark. "No, Ted. The police are not that stupid. The guy didn't have his hands blown off. So they might take prints. They have to know by this time it wasn't you. They're not telling because they don't want the killer to know. And they must be hoping you'll come forward with information that'll clinch who did it."

Diantha returned with a tray holding a china pot and three cups. She set it down on the red-lacquered trunk that doubled as a coffee table and laid out buff linen napkins, spoons, and a plate of Stella D'oro rusks.

"I'm not about to turn myself in. I'd be a dead man. Let them do their job and find out who killed me, then I'll come out."

"Well, thanks anyway for letting me know."

Diantha smiled at Wetzon's sarcasm, but the smile faded rapidly. "Well, we needed another head—" Then, hearing what she'd said, "I'm sorry. That's awful. I didn't mean it that way."

"Wetzi—" Teddy held her shoulders and looked into her eyes. "You can't tell anyone. As soon as they find out I'm still alive, I'm dead. I don't trust anyone."

"Teddy, I've got someone you can tell. You can trust him. Remember when we talked about having someone special? You told me you had someone and I told you I did too? But neither of us wanted to share at the time." He took his hands from her shoulders and shook his head no before she could go on. Wetzon looked at Diantha, who was putting a log on the fire and stoking it. "You said your someone special had something in common with me." Diantha straightened up and carefully replaced the fire screen. She pulled up a footstool and sat opposite them. Wetzon smiled at her. "I now know what we have in common. But did you know we'd already met—accidentally?"

"Had no idea, at least not then." He and Diantha exchanged that look again. "No one knows about Diantha, not at the studio, or anywhere. We were keeping ourselves private."

"I wasn't ready to make a real commitment," Diantha said, "at least not yet. So my office knows nothing about Ted. I figured there was time enough for that."

"So this became my safe house—"

The fire welled up, glowing, warming. "But why would someone try to kill you?" With shaking hands, Wetzon brushed the strands of hair out of her face and rebanded her ponytail. "Do you know Peter Tormenkov was murdered? Does it have anything to do with him? What was that scam he was going to tell you about?"

"He told me about it. Yeah, I read in the *Times* that he was killed." He picked at a small wool ball on his sweater. "Listen to me, Wetzi—he spilled his guts to me. I've got him on tape. And the tapes are somewhere in my office. At least they were. I've got to get them—"

"Teddy." Wetzon turned from him to Diantha. "I'm very confused. The FBI was trying to take me in when Diantha caused a riot and saved me. At least, they said they were FBI."

Teddy's mouth dropped open. "No! Why? Why would they be after you?"

"Maybe because they know you're not dead and they think I know where you are. Was Peter Tormenkov really working for them?"

"Not according to him. But they were trying to get him to testify against his firm. He was involved in it up to his earlobes. He knew if he flipped, he might not live too long. He thought he'd do better with me. If he got a lot of TV coverage, he might be so visible they wouldn't risk killing him."

"Teddy, investment bankers don't kill each other. They just rat on each other. It's a different kind of death."

"No, there's more to it than that, Wetzi. It's a major scam—"

"Okay, look." Everyone had forgotten the coffee. She was getting tired and needed something, food or coffee. She sat on the edge of the sofa and poured the hot liquid into each cup. "I told you I have someone I care about and trust. Now let me tell you that he's a detective with NYPD."

Diantha made an odd noise.

"Oh, Wetzi, I don't believe it. Not you."

"Why not me? His name is Silvestri and I want you to talk to him. I would trust him with my life." She suddenly realized that no matter what happened between her and Silvestri, she meant that.

"But what about mine?"

"Yours, too."

"Easy for you to say, Wetzi." Teddy ran his fingers through his hair. "I don't know. Diantha?"

"I don't trust anyone," Diantha said. She sipped her coffee and watched Wetzon over the rim of her cup with narrowed eyes.

Wetzon wondered if *anyone* was a euphemism for *cop*. "He's not just a cop. I can't explain it. You'll have to trust me. He's different."

A horn honked on the street. Diantha's body jerked. She put her cup on the trunk and stepped to the side of the window. Parting the blinds a fraction, she looked down at the street. Weary, she let the blinds go and turned back to them. "I'm not for it."

"I don't think you guys have a choice." Wetzon was surprised about how severe she sounded. "You've got to trust someone, besides me. What about someone at Channel Eight?"

They both shook their heads.

"Then let me call Silvestri. I'll ask him to meet me here. I won't tell him what it's about."

Teddy looked at Diantha, who was staring into the fire. He got up and began pacing, the floor creaking under his feet. Finally he said, "Okay. But, Wetzi, know this. We're dealing with people who think nothing of zapping helpless old people for their stocks and bonds, and other people who know exactly what's going on and don't give a damn, who go along because it comes down to percentages, dollars. Millions. It's a major fraud, and it involves at least one home care service, and lawyers, brokers, accountants, and brokerage firms. It's endless." He stopped pacing and stabbed his finger at her. "If they think nothing of killing harmless old people and each other, there's nothing to stop them if they decide to kill me—again—or you—or even this noble Silvestri of yours."

43

THE INTERCOM BUZZED with the signal—two short, one long. They, all three, jumped at the first sound and fell silent, counting mentally to ten between signals. Then two short and one long came again.

Wetzon stood up. She felt wired; nervous energy flowed through her limbs. She looked down at her hands, two claws, tensed. "I'd better let him in."

Diantha slithered on tiptoes, silent as a cat, to the side of the window, barely separated the blinds, checked the street. "Black Toyota?"

Wetzon nodded, her hand on the banister. "Yes." Her voice sounded gravelly. She started down the stairs.

"Wait! Remember, not a word about me from either of you until I say okay." Teddy walked swiftly toward the second set of stairs and ran up, surefooted, disappearing into the darkness of the upper floor. The floor creaked, then all was silent.

The women looked at each other, and Diantha nodded. Wetzon crept down the stairs, listening; she opened the door slowly inward, staying behind it. No one entered. Hand on the door, she peered around it into the small vestibule. "Silvestri?" No one was there.

Perplexed, she edged out the door into the lantern-lit space. Silvestri's left arm came around her shoulders from the back. "For chrissakes, Les. You have no respect for danger." He sounded exasperated.

She didn't care. She held onto his arm because it felt so good having him there, being able to touch him. He let go of her, almost shaking her off, and she turned. He had a gun in his right hand. "Are you alone?" he asked.

"There's someone upstairs. It's okay. Really." She smiled at him tentatively. "You don't need that."

He put his gun back in the shoulder holster under his coat. "What's going on here?" He had shaved since she'd last seen him, but his beard was a dark shadow on his jaw.

"Come upstairs." She pushed the door and went through. He followed her, closing the door behind them, mounting the stairs, alert and taut. She felt, rather than saw, that he kept his hand inside his jacket, on his gun.

As they reached the top of the stairs, Diantha came forward, her midcalf gray cashmere skirt flowing around her long slim legs. If Silvestri was surprised, he gave no indication.

"This is Diantha Anderson," Wetzon said.

Diantha extended her hand and gave Silvestri's face a finite examination. He did the same with her, meeting her eye to eye, for they were about the same height. "Can I take your coat?" Diantha asked.

Silvestri shrugged out of his jacket. "Nah. I'll just leave it here." He folded it over the railing of the staircase, his eyes moving upward toward the darkness of the second floor as if he knew someone was up there, listening and waiting. After a brief moment, he left his coat and came back to where Diantha and Wetzon waited. He was wearing his navy blue turtleneck sweater and the brown tweed jacket with the suede elbow patches and blue jeans. "Someone want to tell me what this is all about?" His eyes inventoried the room.

"Making a list, checking it twice, gonna find out who's

naughty or nice . . ." came skimming across Wetzon's mind. She drowned a giggle in a cough. *Just plain silliness,* she thought. *This is serious.* "Silvestri—"

"Let's sit down, please," Diantha said, drawing them to the sofa. Silvestri kept his eyes on her, not giving much.

Wetzon sank into the sofa again. Her nerve ends were raw, her hands and knees shook. Silvestri sat on the arm of the sofa, near enough to Wetzon for her to detect any seams in his flat professional façade. Diantha took the stool, watching Silvestri watching her.

"Silvestri—" Wetzon tried again. His eyes met hers fleetingly, the coldest, toughest slate. They turned back to Diantha. He was on duty all the way. "Silvestri, Diantha . . ." She picked over her words, feeling for the right ones. ". . . Diantha was a close friend of Teddy Lanzman's."

"Oh?" Silvestri crossed one foot over the other at the knee. He was wearing soft black leather loafers and white socks.

Diantha said nothing. In the sepia shadows of the room, one was left with an impression of high molded cheekbones and dark flinty eyes.

"We have something we want to tell you about Teddy," Wetzon said, looking up at him.

"Les, if you're holding out information about a murder, you're in trouble."

"I'm not, Silvestri. Honest. I just found out."

"Ms. Anderson?"

Wetzon leaned forward. "Diantha, I'm begging you," she pleaded, "you've got to trust him."

"Wait a minute, Les. Ms. Anderson, technically, if this is information about the Lanzman murder, you should be talking to Bernstein at Manhattan North." He got to his feet.

"Bullshit, Silvestri!" Wetzon's fist hit her thigh. She was fuming. She felt he was playacting for some reason known only to him.

"Okay, let's cut through this," Silvestri said, talking to Diantha, ignoring Wetzon. "What do you have?"

"I know someone," Diantha began slowly, "who may have

some information about this, but he feels his life is in danger and he wants protection before he comes forward."

"Shove over, Les." Silvestri settled on the sofa next to Wetzon. He sat back, totally relaxed, as if what Diantha had just said was something he had been waiting to hear. "Is there more coffee in the pot?" he asked casually.

Diantha gave him a questioning look. "Wetzon, I wonder if you'd be good enough to bring us another cup and the rest of the coffee."

Wetzon stared down at the tray on the antique Chinese trunk. It held three cups with coffee in each at various levels. Three. Silvestri knew. She looked quickly at Diantha.

Diantha smiled a cautious smile at Silvestri. "Touché," she said. Her fingers worried the gold stud in her earlobe.

As Wetzon creaked across the long expanse of floor into the dining room, she heard Silvestri ask, "What do you do, Ms. Anderson?" Ha! That was good for a small laugh. Last year when he and Wetzon had first met, she had to explain what a headhunter was. Now he knew three headhunters.

There was a fine Oriental carpet in mellow roses, browns, and greens under the cherry French country dining table. To her right was an arched doorway that led, as she had thought earlier, to a small but immaculate kitchen, very efficiently laid out. All white, cabinets and countertops, with black trim, *Eurostyle* was the word for it.

The Braun coffee maker was also white and black. She opened and closed two of the tall cabinets before she found the cups and saucers. Everything was so neat and orderly, she summoned up guilty thoughts about her own messy cabinets. She had let things go because Carlos wasn't housekeeping for her anymore.

She detached the coffeepot, carried it and a cup and saucer back into the living room, where she found Silvestri leaning across the trunk talking intently to Diantha, gesturing with a half-eaten rusk.

"I give you my word," he was saying, "that if need be I'll go directly to the commissioner—"

"If need be? Who will decide that?" Diantha asked tersely.

"I will. You'll have to trust me."

Wetzon silently set the cup and saucer down and poured coffee for Silvestri, placing the coffeepot on a folded napkin to protect the old trunk from the heat.

"Ah," Silvestri said, but he wasn't looking at her or the coffee. He was looking over Wetzon's shoulder. She and Diantha turned. Teddy had come down the stairs and was walking slowly toward them.

Silvestri went to meet him, extending his hand, his smile broader than Wetzon had ever seen. "Dr. Livingstone? Or should I say, Ted Lanzman?"

"I have no one else to trust, Silvestri," Teddy said, taking his hand. "This better be good."

Wetzon felt a tiny surge of pride as she watched Silvestri. He was the director of the play, without any doubt. There he was, slightly shorter, stockier, not nearly as handsome as Teddy, but he was very much in charge. "You knew, Silvestri," she said. "You knew all along."

Teddy sat on the floor next to Diantha. He rested his hand on her thigh. She touched his hand, his face, his neck, his hand again.

"I didn't know anything," Silvestri said, pleased. "But the dead man was carrying someone else's ID, and then the M.E. report came through. That did it." He sat down again next to Wetzon. "Man, I thought you'd never come out."

"Who was it?" Teddy asked.

"An FBI agent, name of Lawrence King."

"Dear God," Diantha murmured.

"FBI again," Wetzon said. "Maybe that's why they were trying to pick me up." She described what had happened at the Hyatt.

"Yeah," Silvestri said. "But they get a little too pushy. This is our case and one of their guys stuck his nose in. They're looking for you, Lanzman. They think you did it."

"Me! But I didn't even know who this King was. He was going through my desk. That's not exactly legal, is it?"

"Will you go to the commissioner now?" Diantha demanded.

"Yes. But I want the whole story. Beginning to end. I knew if you hadn't done it, you would have to surface at some point, and there was a good chance you would get in touch with my friend here." His hand fell lightly on Wetzon's knee and then left.

Teddy asked, "How do you want to do this?"

Silvestri's notepad and pen came out from his inside pocket. The movement revealed his gun in the shoulder holster. Diantha's eyes met Wetzon's across the trunk.

"I've got Tormenkov on tape. He spilled the whole scam." Teddy bit nervously on his knuckles. "They killed him—"

"Yeah. Where is it? Do you have it?"

"It's in the office."

Silvestri's face fell. "It's probably gone. Either the killer has it or the FBI does."

"Nah," Teddy said lazily. "I guarantee it's still on the shelf with the others." He licked his thumb and wiped it on the front of his sweater.

"How could you know that, Teddy?" Wetzon grumbled. Teddy had switched from earnest and sincere to egotistical and obnoxious again.

"Oh, I know, Wetzi-Petzi. I marked it 'Interview with Dan Quayle.'"

Diantha let out a shriek of near-hysterical laughter, shocking them, and Wetzon followed. Even Silvestri laughed.

"Look, Silvestri," Teddy said, "I want a promise from you. You give me that and I'll cooperate all the way."

"I'll see the commissioner, Lanzman. We'll give you protection until we get the killer, and then some."

"Nah, man, I have to go with that. That's understood. But what I want is an exclusive. I want this story, it's mine. It'll get me to *Sixty Minutes*. That's what I want, man."

"Ted, for godsake," Diantha said.

Wetzon stared at the handsome, arrogant face. Teddy knew what he was doing.

"I can't promise you anything, but I'll talk to the commissioner." Silvestri didn't seem a bit put off, but then Silvestri hardly ever reacted to anything.

"You do that," Teddy said.

"I could really use a beer," Wetzon said, trying to keep her sentiments about Teddy out of her voice.

Diantha got up. "Anyone else?"

"Yeah," Teddy said. "Silvestri?"

Silvestri nodded.

"I'll help you." Wetzon stood and stretched her arms high, lowering them slowly.

They settled in with Millers, which was not Wetzon's choice but all Diantha had, drinking from the cans.

"The lawyer," Teddy explained, "feeds the old folks to this home care service, Tender Care. Tender Care sends an attendant into the home and practically takes over the old person's life. That's how it starts. They're looking for stock certificates and bonds. Lots of these elderly don't trust brokerage houses. They like to have the certificates at hand or in safe-deposit boxes. The bare bones is, they rip these old people off of everything they own that's negotiable, and if an old guy or gal gets suspicious, accidents happen. A peaceful death in sleep, by asphyxiation with a pillow, a fall."

"Oh God, Peepsie Cunningham."

"You got it, Wetzi. Tender Care deals with some guy in management, who has to okay transactions, and at least one broker at L. L. Rosenkind. The broker asks no questions and cashes in the certificate or the bond when some old lady comes in with identification. Then they split it three ways: the lawyer, Tender Care, the manager at L. L. Tender Care pays off the attendant and the manager takes care of the broker."

"Did it hit other brokerage houses?" Wetzon asked. She put the can to her lips and took a swallow, then described the incident at Bradley, Elsworth and the old man named Mitosky with the Russian accent. "His obituary, if it was his, said he'd been born in England."

"Could be. Tormenkov thought maybe. Tender Care employs a lot of Russian immigrants. These people usually don't talk. Remember, Wetzi, how we ran into a stone wall in Little Odessa?"

Silvestri looked down at his notes, folded the pad, and slipped it back in his pocket. "I'll deal with the tape."

"You and only you, Silvestri. It's hot. And so am I."

"Okay, Les, let's go."

"Where?"

"I'm taking you home and then I have work to do."

She didn't even protest. It would have done no good. Besides, she was exhausted. The shock of seeing Teddy suddenly alive, the escape from the FBI . . . She listened as he curtly instructed Diantha and Teddy not to leave the apartment for any reason, not to make any phone calls out or let anyone else know where Teddy was until he got in touch with them.

"So, coach," she said, as Silvestri put on his seat belt and started the car. "How'd I do this time?"

Silvestri didn't respond. He pulled out of the parking place, made a right, and drove over to Third Avenue, where he made another right. Wetzon looked out the window. Maybe he was still mad at her. She thought about Teddy. *So we all have our buttons, don't we,* she thought. Teddy's was fame. She looked at Silvestri's hard profile, the set of his jaw. *What's yours, Silvestri?* She looked down at her hands in her lap and sighed. *What's mine?*

As if in response, not taking his eyes from the road, Silvestri reached over and covered her hands with his, giving them a gentle, lingering squeeze.

44

"LISTEN, WETZON," Joe Flanagan said. "I don't care how you do it, but I want you to deliver De Haven."

"I'll do my best, Joe." Whatever Joe Flanagan wanted, Joe Flanagan got. He was head of the region in retail sales for Loeb Dawkins.

"No, Wetzon, that's not good enough. I want this guy. He's supposed to be here at twelve today. I don't want him to slip away. You get him here, and I'll have a contract ready. I don't want to hear Shearson got him. They're all after him, but I want him. You get him for me."

"Okay, Joe." *Seig heil*, she thought as she hung up the phone. "Jesus. How the hell am I going to do that?"

Smith opened the door and poked her dark tousled head in, catching Wetzon's last words. She grinned impishly. "Good morning, good morning, darling Wetzon. What's up? Do what? Here, B.B., hang up my coat, will you, there's a dear." She came in and closed the door behind her. She was wearing a taupe silk outfit with a wide brown alligator belt and high-heeled brown leather boots. Her olive skin had a ruddy sheen from the cold and her dark-lashed oval eyes glowed with goodwill.

"My, you look terrific, partner," Wetzon said. It was amazing how Smith's moods careered from highs to lows. It was also nice that she was now on a high. Or was it?

"Oh Lord, I feel terrific," Smith said, raising her arms to the ceiling and opening them wide, heaving a great, satisfied sigh. She flipped through her stack of pink message slips and then tossed them all into the wastebasket under her desk.

"Oh, Smith."

"Oh, Wetzon," Smith mocked. "How the hell are you going to do what?" Her attention switched to her fingernails. "I need a manicure."

"Get Kevin De Haven for Joe Flanagan. Deliver him gift wrapped, for godsake. Joe ordered him."

"Does De Haven want to be delivered?"

"I don't know."

"Well, come on now, Wetzon, call him and find out."

Wetzon punched up De Haven's number.

"De Haven."

"Kevin. Wetzon. How did your meeting go with Joe Flanagan yesterday?"

"Wetzon, pal, don't get me wrong. He's a terrific guy. I really like him. All these guys you've introduced me to are swell guys. But I'm thinking right now I'll stay with Merrill."

"Stay at Merrill? And take a payout cut that steep?"

"Tell you the truth, Wetzon. My manager and Dan Tompkins, the head of our region, took me to Lutèce last night for dinner. They really went all out. Jesus, we cracked a bottle of wine a hundred years old. It was something. And you know this guy has been like a father to me—"

Wetzon's heart sank. "Kevin, how much did they offer you to stay?"

"They said they wouldn't take all of the institutional accounts away from me, just some—"

"Just the biggest ones."

"Aw, Wetzon."

"And what about the payout? Can you keep the twenty-eight percent?"

"They said instead of reducing me to eleven percent, they would give me eighteen."

"And you're going to accept that?" *You schmuck*, she thought.

"They've been so decent to me, Wetzon."

"They're screwing you, Kevin. What's Flanagan offering you?"

"Well, a quarter of a mil up front and other stuff."

"Did you tell your manager that?"

"Oh yeah, listen, I've been absolutely honest with them. I wouldn't not tell them. I'm that kinda guy. You know me, Wetzon."

"What did they say to that?" *They probably said, drink up, schmuck.*

"They said I shouldn't take it. I'd be throwing my career away here. Wetzon, honest, he's like a father to—"

"Kevin, I just want to ask you one thing and then we'll let it go. If you had a son and he was offered a quarter of a million dollars to move to another major firm where he could continue to do his kind of business without interference from the firm, and at a higher payout, would you tell him not to take it?"

De Haven groaned. "Don't do that to me, Wetzon."

"I just ask you to consider clearly what your choices are, what they are offering you and what Joe is offering you. Joe tells me you're coming back to see him at twelve today."

"I don't know, Wetzon. I just don't know."

"Kevin, I'll pick you up in a cab and take you to Joe's, then wait for you and take you back to the office. How's that?"

"Aw, Wetzon."

"I'll be downstairs in front of your building at quarter to twelve. Don't think about it, just do it. It'll all work out, I promise you. I'll call you just before I leave my office." She hung up the phone, tingling with a kind of triumph, as if she'd won a race. She had, temporarily at least, outsold a great salesman. A wave of euphoria hit her like a sudden madness, and she turned her face to Smith, who let out a loud whoop.

"Delicious," Smith said, applauding. "Oh God, what a fee that will be."

"Let's not count it until it's ours."

Then they both recited their litany, "It's not over till it's over. And even when it's over, it's not over."

"I love the way that looks on you," Wetzon said. Wetzon had the same outfit in black. They'd bought it at Loehmann's last fall.

"You've never even worn yours. Don't you like it?"

"It's down to the floor on me. Karan cuts for people like you . . . and her. I need about six or seven inches taken off and I haven't had time to take it to Sebastian."

"You haven't even noticed something else about me today," Smith accused, hands on hips, smiling.

She'd noticed that Smith was in a great mood, but how to say it? "I don't know, Smith." She studied Smith with narrowed eyes. "There's something about you today."

Smith thrust her left hand under Wetzon's nose. She was wearing a monumental diamond on her finger. "Leon and I are engaged!"

Wetzon took Smith's long thin hand. The ring was made up of baguettes of diamonds and emeralds arranged in a circle, coming to a raised peak with a huge diamond in the center. She felt sick. The ring looked exactly like the one Arleen had worn at dinner. God, Leon was a shit. She covered her feelings with enthusiasm. "What a magnificent ring! Congratulations! I'm so happy for you." Wetzon put her arms around Smith, who turned sweet and girlish on her.

"It *is* beautiful and it *is* wonderful."

"And you deserve the very best of everything."

The telephone, which had been silent, rang. They both looked at their phones. Two calls had come in at once.

"I certainly do. Did you see how it's set? It's an antique. It's been in Leon's family for—"

B.B. opened the door. "Leon for you, Smith."

"Let me talk to him for a minute," Wetzon said. "I want to congratulate him." She reached for the phone.

"No!" Smith said sharply, then softened. "Not yet. I'll tell you when it's okay." She picked up the phone. "Leon, sweetie pie." She sat down at her desk and hunched over the phone, closing Wetzon out.

Wetzon returned to her own work. What a strange and secretive person her partner was. She wondered again about the advisability of having their lawyer be one of their husbands. Maybe she should talk it over with Arthur Margolies.

Her thoughts swerved to Teddy. Another week had gone by and no word from Silvestri on what was happening, and there'd been no news in the papers about Teddy. In fact, his murder seemed no longer newsworthy. It was almost as if the whole experience of finding him alive had been a dream. "You've got a great imagination, kid," she murmured, imitating Silvestri.

Smith made kissing noises and replaced the receiver on the phone. She took up their earlier conversation. "After you deliver De Whoozis, let's go get a facial."

"But I have so much work to do. Besides, we'll never get a last-minute appointment at Georgette Klinger's."

"Come on, Wetzon, what's really hot on the fire? And don't tell me that decrepit old charity case you're peddling all over the Street in our name. I have this wonderful new place for us to go for a facial. Katerina opened her own salon. Katerina of Hungary. Sounds nice, doesn't it?"

"Katerrina of Hungarry," Wetzon said. "Drrinks yourr blood while she worrks on yourr skin."

"Be serious, Wetzon. She's taken a few of Klinger's ladies with her. Let's do it. I'll call." Smith smiled at her. "Just us girls."

Wetzon thought briefly about the pampered luxury of having a facial. "You're absolutely right. I should be clear after two-thirty, I would think. Make us appointments for after that. It'll be nice." They smiled fondly at each other.

"Oh, by the way, I almost forgot," Smith said. "What was the name of that crazy old lady who jumped out of the window?"

"Peepsie. No, I mean, Evelyn Cunningham. And she wasn't crazy and she didn't jump. Someone pushed her."

"Whatever." Smith dismissed her correction with an impatient wave of her hand.

Wetzon was thinking that maybe after her facial she would look in on Hazel.

"I thought you said Cunningham. I heard two women in my elevator discussing the Cunningham collection that's going to be auctioned off at Yorkeby's next week."

"Cunningham collection? I suppose that's possible. They're an old New York family. Could be a relative."

"Didn't you tell me the place was full of antiques?"

"It was. A lot of Oriental stuff. Big vases, porcelains, carved screens, bronze pieces. You know."

"Do you have the *Times?*"

Wetzon pulled the half-read *Times* from her carryall and thumbed through it looking for the auction announcements, with Smith hovering over her shoulder.

"There it is." Smith pointed to a headline "Cunningham Collection at Yorkeby's" in Rita Reif's "Auctions" column. It was just a brief mention of the eclecticism of the collection that was to be auctioned with several other small collections at Yorkeby's the following week.

"I guess Marion's taken charge."

"Who's Marion?"

"Peepsie's niece, the one who's been living in Europe. Hazel told me she was coming in to settle the estate."

"Now why couldn't I have a long-lost Aunt Peepsie," Smith said enviously. "Let's go to the exhibition. Look, it says the viewing goes on until five. We can go after our facial. Wouldn't it be fun to see what it looks like? Maybe we can even buy a piece."

Wetzon's eyes rested on the ad for Yorkeby's next to the article mentioning the collection. Pictured in the ad was one of the two huge vases that had stood on either side of the archway before the entrance to Peepsie's living room.

She closed her eyes, and the room manifested itself on her eyelids. She saw Ida, felt Peepsie's fear. A fragment of an idea sparked like the last tiny light on the tip of a candle that remains for a moment after you blow out the flame.

"Yes, let's," she said to Smith.

45

DE HAVEN WAS NOT STANDING in front of the Pan Am Building as they had arranged, which didn't surprise her. So here she was waiting again. In her previous life, performers often sat around waiting for directors and choreographers to work their magic. "'They also serve who only stand and wait,'" she said out loud. "So what do you think, Michael Stewart?"

Michael Stewart grunted at her. He'd been double-parked across the street when she came out of her office and she readily admitted to herself and to him, she was glad to see him.

She addressed the back of Stewart's neck where his hair bunched at the collar of his red flannel shirt. "I'm going to find a phone and call him."

Her watch read twelve o'clock. Damn him. She found a pay phone in the lobby and took the scrap of paper on which she'd scrawled De Haven's phone number out of her coat pocket.

"Mr. De Haven's office." The voice on the line was young and crisp.

Blast. He usually answered his own phone. "Mr. De Haven, please."

"Who's calling?"

"Mrs. Goldstein."

"Hold on, Mrs. Goldstein."

"De Haven."

"Where are you, De Haven? I'm waiting downstairs."

"Mrs. Goldstein! How nice of you to call." De Haven had a thundering laugh. "I was just on my way out to lunch. Can we talk in a little while?"

"A very little while." She hung up the phone grumbling and went back out to Forty-fifth Street. The cool wind swooped across the open plaza but didn't seem to bother anyone. Workers were going out to buy lunch from the food carts lined up on

Forty-fifth Street that sold everything from falafel and hot dogs to burritos and egg rolls. Some people were already carrying paper packages back from one of the multitude of salad bars in the area. Snow still lay in dirty frozen piles here and there, but most of the physical evidence of blizzard had disappeared, eroded by the grime and perpetual motion of New York City.

She opened the rear door of the cab and looked back. De Haven was coming toward her, coatless, looking like a celebrity in a gray pin-striped suit. She watched women's heads turn as he passed them.

"Wetzon, old pal," he said, clapping her on the shoulder.

They settled back and she repeated Joe Flanagan's address on Fifty-first Street and Sixth Avenue to Michael Stewart.

"You know, Wetzon, you really did it to me."

"Did what?"

"You know. Put the knife in." He grinned at her, salesman to salesman. "By asking me would I tell my son to give up a quarter of a mil."

They went up to Flanagan's office together.

"He's in your good hands now," Wetzon said to Lauren, Flanagan's assistant, after Lauren, a thin young woman in a softly tailored black suit, ushered De Haven into Flanagan's office.

"Jay Campo's in there with him," Lauren said. "Joe says you don't have to wait." Her phone jangled and she went to answer it.

Dis—missed, Wetzon said to herself. It was all right with her. She found a pay phone in the lobby and called the office. "Hi, Harold. Any calls for me?"

"I'll ask Smith. Hold on."

"Wait!" Damn. He was gone. Why the hell would he have to ask Smith? It was really irritating.

"Hi, sweetie pie. How did it go?"

"Fine, I guess. Joe's smooth. I think we'll have a done deal. He had Jay Campo here to clinch it. Are you taking my calls?"

"No, sugar, do you want me to?"

"No, that's all right. I don't understand why Harold couldn't just read me my messages."

"Because you don't have any, sweetie, and he knew I wanted to talk to you the minute you called in."

"Oh. Okay. What time is our facial?"

"Two-thirty. I have Katerina and you have Saskia. Aren't you coming back?"

"I thought I'd grab a sandwich and see what bargains I can find at Saks."

"Oh no fair. I want to go with you."

"Then meet me there. I'll be wandering around the second floor about one o'clock or so."

"I can't, sweetie." She was suddenly mysterious. Her voice dropped as if she didn't want anyone else to hear, which was ridiculous because no one else was there. "I'm having lunch with—"

"Excuse me," B.B. interrupted. "I have a message for Wetzon."

"Really, B.B., this is most unprofessional," Smith snapped angrily.

"It's okay, Smith. What's the message, B.B.?"

"Hazel Osborn called. She'd like you to call her."

"Okay. Anything else?"

"No."

"Then you may hang up, B.B.," Smith said. The chill in her voice was powerful. There was an immediate click.

"Smith, really. He didn't do anything wrong."

"He should have given me the message to give to you, Wetzon. What if I was on an important call and he interrupted like that? You're much too easygoing. That's why everyone always takes advantage of you."

"What—" Oh, forget it, she told herself. "Smith, do me one favor."

"Anything, sugar." Sweetness dribbled across the telephone lines.

Wetzon switched the receiver to her other ear. "If Silvestri calls, tell him where we'll be—Katerina's and then Yorkeby's. Okay?"

"Well, of course, I will. You can count on me."

She hung up the phone, put another quarter in the slot and punched out Hazel's number. The line was busy.

She went out onto Sixth Avenue. Michael Stewart wasn't around, so she crossed the street, heading for Fifth Avenue. The backstage entrance to Radio City Music Hall was about a quarter of the way down the block and the door was open. The dancers were taking a break, eating, gossiping.

Wetzon stopped for a minute and watched the group of girls in dance work clothes, high-cut leotards, shiny tights, leg warmers, plastic sweatpants, T-shirts and sweatshirts, towels rolled around long thin necks. She closed her eyes for a minute, breathing in the nostalgic smell of perfume, sweat, and makeup, and felt a tiny tug of yearning which drew her closer to the door, like a voyeur.

"Wetzon! Is that you?" She opened her eyes. One of the dancers pulled away from a group.

"Margie." Wetzon went right through the open door and hugged the lithe creature, a flashier double of herself, with a reddish Clairol'd topknot. Margie's breastbone and collarbones were particularly pronounced. There wasn't a drop of extra flesh on her.

They stood holding each other, arms on arms.

"You look wonderful—"

"So do you."

"Not since *Chorus Line*—"

"Remember—"

"How are you?"

"What've you been doing?"

"Headhunting? My God, how about Carlos?"

"You ought to call him."

"I've meant to. I will. I've been here for the last six months. I'm lucky to have it—steady work, I mean."

"Your little girl—"

"Eight now. Do you believe it? Darren's on the Coast. He got married again, you know."

"I didn't know." Makeup could not cover the age lines around her eyes and mouth.

"Break's over." The dancers began moving into the depths of the Music Hall's backstage area.

"Time to go back, I guess."

"I guess." Wetzon felt wistful.

"Take care, Wetzon."

"You, too, Margie. Call Carlos."

"I will."

The meeting with Margie Lewis depressed Wetzon. Old dancers. What did they do? They were lucky to get jobs like Radio City. What could they do? She no longer felt like shopping. When she got to Saks, she went to the phone booths on the street floor and tried Hazel again.

A heavily accented woman's voice answered after four rings. For a moment Wetzon had *déjà vu.* The woman sounded like Ida.

"I'm very sorry. I must have the wrong number. I was calling Ms. Hazel Osborn."

"You haff correct number," the voice said. "Ms. Osborn iz resting."

"Who is this?"

"I am Basha. Home attendant."

46

WETZON WANDERED THROUGH THE designer boutiques on the second floor of Saks, unable to focus on the clothes. She had left a message with Hazel's home attendant that she would call again; so taken aback was she by the home attendant that she hadn't even left her name.

"Is there something in particular you're looking for?" The sleek young saleswoman with the Caribbean tan and sun-streaked hair was an unwitting intruder. Chunky gold bracelets clunked as the woman straightened the clothes on the sale rack. "We don't have too much left in your size."

Wetzon stared blankly at her. "Thank you. I was just thinking—I'm sorry—looking."

But she *was* just thinking. Was this home attendant part of Hazel's mysterious plan or was Hazel now so sick she couldn't fend for herself anymore?

"No," she said under her breath. It couldn't have happened that fast. Worried now, she went down the crowded escalator to the street floor and waited impatiently for a man in a shearling coat, a notepad and a beeper resting on the ledge, to relinquish the phone.

She called Hazel's number.

"Hello." Good. It was Hazel. Wetzon was so relieved she swallowed a lump in her throat which kept her from responding immediately. "Hello?"

"Oh, Hazel, it's you." She sat down on the tiny corner seat in the phone booth, shaky.

"Hello, dear, how are you?" Was Hazel's voice a little strange, a little more formal than usual?

"It's you I'm worried about. I'm fine."

"I'm really doing quite well. Basha is just wonderful. She is taking such good care of me, aren't you, Basha? I would really love a cup of hot tea, Basha, please."

"I take it she's standing right there?"

"Of course, I would just love it if you and your nice young man want to come by tonight."

Wetzon heard a faint click as if someone had picked up the phone and was listening. Wetzon responded, "We thought we'd stop by for a bit after dinner. How's that?"

"Lovely, dear."

"Do you need anything?"

"No, no. I am being wonderfully cared for." There was another click now as if someone had hung up. Then Hazel whispered, excitement like a fever in her voice, "Call me later." The connection was broken.

Wetzon put another quarter in the phone, ignoring the growing line of impatient people. She called the Seventeenth Precinct for Silvestri. She got Metzger.

"He's still downtown," Metzger droned.

"Ask him, when he calls in, or gets uptown, if he can meet me at Hazel Osborn's about seven o'clock. It's important. I'll call back later." Wetzon yielded the booth to an effete man in an ankle-length black mink coat and a pale blue Tiffany's shopping bag. She buttoned her coat, turned up the collar, and walked up Madison Avenue to the Burger Heaven on Fifty-fourth Street. There was time to stop for a burger before she met Smith.

The restaurant was crowded. She ordered her favorite, a Roquefort burger, rare, and brewed decaf, then slipped her coat off and draped it over the back of the chair. Dishes clattered, voices—loud and modulated—with Asian, Indian, Brooklyn, and New York accents, blended.

Why did Hazel want to see Silvestri? Did that mean she was onto something? All the same, when she called her again, Wetzon was determined to ask Hazel the name of the home care service she was using. The one Teddy had mentioned had the unforgettable, creepy name Tender Care.

The burger oozed meat juices and melted Roquefort cheese. She stared at the bloody mess on her fingers and her plate and gagged, setting the half-eaten remnants down. She put her napkin over the plate so she wouldn't have to look at it, covering the body. It was like a flashback. She found a Wash 'n Dri in her carryall and wiped her hands and mouth.

"Here's your coffee, dearie." The waitress set the cup down in front of her. "Are you finished with that burger?"

Wetzon nodded. Efficiently, the woman cleared the plates from the next table as well, stacking them on her arm as she worked, wiping down the table for the next customers. She was a pleasure to watch—a real professional—well over fifty, Wetzon guessed, lined, heavily made-up face, yellow-pink-dyed hair, strong, very pronounced muscles in her arms and shoulders. This was her career and it was obvious; she was not just another performer waiting for a big break as so many waiters and waitresses in Manhattan were.

Smith was getting out of a cab in front of the Galleria on Fifty-seventh Street as Wetzon approached the building, and they went up in the elevator together.

"Any calls for me?" An unshaven man in a soiled trench coat stared at them openly. Wetzon studied him out of the corner of her eye. He was wearing corduroys that hung too far over his worn blue Adidas with knotted laces.

"Nothing important. Laura Lee Day. Howie Minton. The usual psychic vampires." Smith stuffed her gloves into the inside pocket of her mink coat.

"Smith, you are so uncharitable."

"I am not a charity." She played with the diamond-and-emerald ring, rolling it around and around on her finger.

"Anything with De Haven?"

"Yes."

"Well, tell, for godsakes." Wetzon edged away from the man in the trench coat. Was he FBI? No, he couldn't be. He was too messy. The belt of the trench coat had slipped from one loop and dragged on the floor.

Smith's laugh bubbled. "It's a done deal. He signed a contract!"

The elevator stopped at the eighteenth floor, and the man in the trench coat picked up his canvas briefcase and got off. Wetzon's relief was extreme; she was getting decidedly obsessive.

"How long were you going to let me wait?" she grumbled at Smith.

"Oh come on, Wetzon." Smith shook her arm. "Lighten up. Count the gorgeous dollars, you dummy. Money, God, how I love it." She hugged herself and closed her eyes.

Jesus, Smith was having a goddam orgasm about the fee. "When does he start?"

"Monday!"

"That's quick. Why is he going so fast? Do you think he has a problem?"

"Oh, Wetzon, you are so suspicious. The only problem is they want to cap the fee."

"What? How much?"

"At fifty thou."

"Oh no! They want to cheat us out of thirty thousand dollars. What did you say?"

The elevator opened on the fortieth floor. "Here we are," Smith said.

The women stepped into a large white-and-silver salon with pale gray upholstered sofas and chairs in the waiting area. A dark-haired woman wearing an open pale gray lab coat sat at a clear Lucite desk. She wore gray hose on her long slim legs, and high-heeled, open-toed gray shoes. On the desk in front of her were a phone and an appointment book. A Lucite nameplate said gold. She pressed a small white button on the desk and moments later a svelte woman with a long thick fringe of straight blonde hair appeared. She, too, wore a long crisp pale gray lab coat over a charcoal-gray cashmere sweater and skirt and had clear, beautiful skin.

"Ms. Smith, Ms. Wetzon. Please come with me," the blonde said. She had a slight accent and a Lucite name tag on her lab coat that said Margot.

They were led up a broad curved staircase, carpeted in pale gray plush; the walls were papered in gray-and-pink peppermint stripes.

"Katerina and Saskia will be with you shortly," Margot said, opening the doors to two side-by-side rooms. "There are hangers for your clothes. You may put on the robes and sit comfortably. Enjoy your facials, please." She smiled a cool, reserved smile without opening her lips.

Wetzon waved to Smith and entered a white-on-white room, empty except for a large white Naugahyde extension chair that was made to tilt back and become a massage table. A pink-and-gray quilted throw lay over the footrest part of the chair. On one wall were glass-enclosed shelves containing row upon row of jars and bottles. A small pink-tinted globe hung from the ceiling.

Stripping down to her camisole and half-slip, Wetzon hung her coat and clothes neatly on the hangers and wrapped herself in the pink-and-gray robe. The room was cool. She pulled off her boots and sat back in the Naugahyde chair, covering herself with the pink-and-gray quilted throw.

"Hello, hello!" The door opened. "I see you make comfortable. Good. Good. I am Saskia. I take good care of you." Saskia, a woman of indeterminate age, small, with curls of unnatural auburn pinned back under a gaudy floral and rhinestone hair clip, spoke with a Slavic accent. She smiled at Wetzon through glossy pink lips, showing crooked, yellow teeth. "Sit back. Rest." She pressed her hands solidly on Wetzon's shoulders, then covered Wetzon's hair in a tight paper turban. "First I clean face." She wet a wad of Kleenex and twisted it expertly into a cool cover for Wetzon's eyes, tilting the chair back into a reclining position.

Wetzon could hear bottles opening and closing. Saskia's hands flew over Wetzon's face with a soft cream cover, a wipe-off, an astringent, another layer of cream, and finally a slow, gentle massage of the cream into the skin. With her eyes per force closed under the cool cover and the warm cream being massaged into her face with fairy fingertips, Wetzon felt her body releasing, ping, ping, ping into deep relaxation. "Enjoy, enjoy." Saskia's soft voice was soothing, hypnotic. "Now ve clean pores." The voice came from a great distance. A door closed. A door opened. "I have hot, very hot herb pot. I put towel here." She covered Wetzon's head with a bath towel. The heat was wonderful. She smelled lavender and chamomile essences. "You rest now," Saskia said. "I come back ten minutes. Sleep."

Wetzon lay in the chair and the herbal heat, almost dozing under the towel. She could hear her own breathing magnified, and she could hear the faint murmur of Smith's voice from the room next door. What did Smith have to talk about? Who wanted to talk during a facial?

A woman sobbed softly. "I beg you."

A voice whispered, "No . . . dangerous . . ." and then lapsed into what sounded like Russian.

"They send me back." Crying again.

"Sheheh. My clients . . ." Russian in harsh whispers.

turban, grease on her face. Well, everyone looked like that here.

The plump woman took her arm firmly and steered Wetzon back to the room, waiting until she sat back in the chair and then covered her with the quilted throw. "I send Saskia. Must be more patient." The woman smiled a decidedly unfriendly smile and left, closing the door behind her.

Wetzon lay uneasy in the chair until she was sure the woman had gone. Could she have dreamed the fragment of conversation? Throwing off the quilt again, she rose and shook some change from her wallet. She was sure she had recognized the voice of one of the women who may have been in the kitchen area, the one who was crying. It was Ida.

47

WETZON STOOD AT THE END of the peppermint-striped hallway at a white pay phone mounted in the open on the wall and punched out Silvestri's direct number at the Seventeenth Precinct. The phone rang about twenty times. A click finally intercepted the ring, and the ringing continued as a buzz. A woman's voice answered, "Rodriguez." The sound was garbled; Rodriguez was eating her lunch.

Wetzon could hear laughter in the background. "I'm looking for Sergeant Silvestri."

"Not here."

"How about Metzger?"

"Not here."

Damn. "Did they say when they'd be back?"

"No," Rodriguez said through swallowing noises. "Anything I can do?" She sounded bored.

"I don't think so. Tell them Ms. Wetzon called." She started to hang up and had a thought. "Hello?"

"Yeah?" Rodriguez's voice was muffled again. She had gone back to eating.

"Can you give me the number of the Detective Squad at the Nineteenth Precinct?"

Wetzon hung up quickly, repeating the number over and over in her head, put a quarter in the slot, and punched out the numbers, jiggling from one foot to the other, listening to the ringing.

"Galvin."

"Sergeant O'Melvany, please." Over her shoulder, she saw Saskia round the corner down the hall and stop short when she caught sight of Wetzon on the telephone. "I'll be right with you, Saskia," she called hurriedly, putting her hand up to keep her away.

"O'Melvany."

Bless him. "Sergeant, this is Leslie Wetzon. Do you remember me?"

"Oh yeah. Well, I don't have anything to tell you—it's gone downtown."

"I know. I have something to tell you."

"Yeah?" He was polite but doubtful. *Probably a dyed-in-the-wool chauvinist*, she thought.

"I'm at a salon called Katerina of Hungary in the Galleria on East Fifty-seventh. I think Ida Tormenkov is here, or may have just been here. I heard her. Can you come and meet me here now?"

"I'm busy now, Miss Wetzon." She could hear in his voice that he thought she was a pain in the ass.

"Please, Sergeant. Just check it out."

"Lady, you want me to stop everything and come there because you *think*?"

"Humor me. I'm not a crank. Silvestri—"

"How long will you be there?" He was grudging.

"I'm in the middle of a facial, so at least another forty-five minutes."

Saskia was smiling with surface concern, but tapping her foot nervously as Wetzon retied the belt of her robe, which had come loose, and trundled down the hall toward her. "Tch, tch, tch, all good vork of heat vasted." She helped Wetzon back into the chair. "But I see vhat I can do." She wet and reapplied the eye compress and went to work on Wetzon's skin. "Beautiful skin. So lucky. No blackheads. Very sensitive, no?" She smeared Wetzon's face with a thick sticky mixture and then swathed her with an ice-cold mask of wet Kleenex. "Rest now." Saskia turned off the lights and left the room.

Wetzon was impatient, turning back and forth, trying to find a comfortable place on the chair. She could not lie still. Her back complained. Her thoughts roiled.

There was a knock on the door. "Wetzon?" The door opened.

"Smith?"

"I'm finished. I'm going to be made up. Meet me there." Smith closed the door without waiting for Wetzon to respond.

Wetzon had no intention of having someone else do her makeup and certainly not with mascara and materials that had been used on other people's eyes. She wondered how long it would take O'Melvany to get there, how much time had passed since she had spoken to him.

Saskia entered, switching on the light, and Wetzon lay back while Saskia removed the final mask and cleansed her face again. After the final step, the moisturizer, Saskia untied and discarded the turban and handed Wetzon a large mirror. "Beautiful, no?"

"Yes, thank you." Beautiful, yes. She always felt beautiful after a facial. It was the pampering.

"I leave this." Saskia handed Wetzon a bill and left the room, closing the door discreetly.

Wetzon threw her clothes on, took her hair down, combed it, and rolled it back up into its neat knot. She looked at herself closely in the mirror and reddened her mouth with lipstick. Gathering up her coat and carryall, she stepped out into the corridor, passing an elderly woman in one of the pink robes, her hands held out in front of her, fingers stiffly separated to keep a manicure from smearing, being led to Smith's vacated room. Wetzon strolled casually, eyes and ears alert, in the opposite direction of the pay phone, looking for Smith.

Smith's laugh rang out and Wetzon followed it until she came to another open space similar to the kitchen. This one had half a dozen high stools in front of a broad expanse of makeup mirrors and tables. The light was soft and diffused. A slim young man, his left earlobe sporting a ruby stud and a tiny hoop, was highlighting Smith's eyes. She seemed to be enjoying herself. Could this be a new, less judgmental Smith?

"You look absolutely stunning, Ms. Smith," he gushed, giving Wetzon a flirtatious wink.

Smith smiled at herself seductively in the mirror. "I do, don't I, Jeffrey?"

"Not that you didn't before, but you should really use emerald-gold on your lids. What an impact. With those fabulous eyes—"

Oh yuk, Wetzon thought. All this self-love was more than she could tolerate right now, and she certainly was not going to hang around and listen to all that. "I'll meet you in front, Smith." She saw Smith's eyes meet Jeffrey's in the mirror. Some private joke, a shared secret, a didn't-I-tell-you look?

A gaunt Chinese woman in a red Adolfo suit trimmed with black braid sat at the cashier's desk. "Is this your first visit, Ms. Wetzon?"

"Yes." Wetzon put the bill and her American Express Card on the pink counter.

"Well, we do hope you are pleased and will be back to see us again soon." A dark line outlined the crease in her eyelids. She handed Wetzon a small pink-and-gray shopping bag and gave her the charge slip to sign. "Some complimentary samples of our treatment products."

Wetzon returned to the reception room and sat down on the gray sofa next to a small round-faced woman with short white hair who looked somewhat familiar. She was thumbing through a copy of *Town & Country.* In the little shopping bag were tissue-wrapped small tubes and jars, a lipstick, and an eyeshadow. Wetzon was delighted. She loved samples of cosmetics. She rolled the bag of samples up and slipped it into her carryall. Lois-

Jane Lane was on the telephone switching someone's appointment.

"Did you buy those here?" The woman next to Wetzon asked in a warm, scratchy voice. She looked a little like Maureen Stapleton.

"They were complimentary samples."

"Oh goodie, I love all those things."

Wetzon didn't notice Margot until she stood in front of them. "Ms. Stapleton?"

"Oh yes. Thank you. It was so nice meeting you."

The white-haired woman followed Margot up the stairs as the elevator doors opened and O'Melvany stepped out. He flipped a lighted cigarette out of the palm of his hand and put it in his lips, inhaling. He was wearing the same dark brown suit and sweater he'd had on the first time Wetzon had seen him. And he was not wearing an overcoat.

Wetzon got to her feet and went to meet him. "How is your back?"

"Better." He rubbed his back and then his orange-yellow mustache. He added grudgingly, "Your friend has been effective." He strode across the entrance room to the Lucite desk and showed Lois-Jane Lane his ID. "I'd like to see the owner, please."

The woman stared at O'Melvany's ID; her face turned pasty. She rose. "Please wait here." She disappeared up the stairs, in a big hurry.

"This better not be a waste of my time, Miss Wetzon. I'm sticking my neck out here," O'Melvany said, glowering at her. He looked at the nameplate on the desk. "Do you believe it? Lois Lane." He walked around the desk and looked through the appointment book, unconcerned, humming faintly, "Doo, doo, da, doo, doo." Ashes from his cigarette fell on the gray carpet.

A woman in her forties with beautiful, clear skin and shoulder-length chestnut hair, wearing a pink lab coat over a wool challis print skirt, came down the stairs, followed by an agitated Lois Lane.

"I am Katerina Sakar. I own this salon. You want to see me?"

"Sergeant O'Melvany. Nineteenth Precinct." He showed his ID, then put it back in his inside pocket.

"I would appreciate your not smoking here." Katerina took a paper cup from the rolling Lucite table, partially filled it with water, and held it out to him. O'Melvany dropped the stub of his cigarette into the cup, and she delivered it to Lois-Jane, who took the offensive cup up the stairs and returned moments later empty-handed. "Now, what can I do for you, Sergeant?" Katerina's smile infused her face with tiny lines. She was older than she had initially appeared.

"We're looking for a woman. Ida Tormenkov. She was seen here a short time ago."

Katerina's smile froze. Her voice, however, did not change. "I do not know an Ida Tormenkov," she said flatly.

"Perhaps yes, perhaps no. But if you do, and she's here, I suggest you ask her to give herself up."

"Why? What did she do?"

"She is wanted for questioning in a murder—"

Inadvertently, Wetzon gasped. Katerina's eyes followed her gasp and they locked into hers for a brief instant. So they were finally calling Peepsie's death murder.

Smith chose that moment to come flamboyantly down the stairs, mink coat flying. "Dear Katerina," she cooed, barging right in. She batted her eyelids at O'Melvany. "And who is this lovely man?"

O'Melvany looked confused, then beamed, and Wetzon groaned inwardly. No one was safe from Smith's seductive charm.

"I do not know an Ida Tormenkov, Sergeant," Katerina repeated, ignoring Smith.

"Sergeant what? Ida who?" Smith looked puzzled.

"I can get a search warrant, Miss Sakar," O'Melvany said, turning his attention back to Katerina.

"What's going on here?" Smith whispered loudly, sidling over to Wetzon.

"You must do what you have to do, but you will not find the woman here."

O'Melvany nodded at Wetzon. "This lady says otherwise."

Katerina's cold and furious eyes found Wetzon, as did Smith's. "Wetzon," Smith snapped, "why do you always humiliate me? After this, how can I ever come back here?"

Wetzon felt her face flush. Had she been wrong? Had she simply fallen asleep and dreamed it? Had the Russian accents just triggered a memory?

"I cannot help you, Officer." Katerina did not move.

"I suggest you tell Ms. Tormenkov to come forward. If she's innocent, her life is in danger." O'Melvany thrust his card at Katerina, who refused to take it. He shrugged and dropped it on the Lucite desk in front of Lois-Jane Lane. "She can call me in confidence at that number."

"I'm sorry, Sergeant," Wetzon said when she and Smith and O'Melvany stepped out of the elevator and into the street lobby of the Galleria. Smith was fuming. Wetzon could almost imagine steam coming out of her ears.

O'Melvany touched his forehead to each of them and strode out to the curb. Wetzon followed him to where a police car was parked at a fire hydrant, a uniformed cop at the wheel. O'Melvany bent awkwardly and spoke to the cop through the rolled-down window. The cop picked up his transmitter and talked into it, then he nodded to O'Melvany.

"I guess Katerina stopped us cold, didn't she?" Wetzon said.

O'Melvany turned to her with his hand on the door. "We'll see about that."

48

THE LAID-BACK ENTRANCE to the Galleria encouraged unpredictable air currents that billowed scarves and coats and lifted
hats unceremoniously. The wind worked pathways through
Wetzon's raccoon coat and froze her freshly processed cheeks,
swirling dirt and grit that had lodged in previously frozen snow-
drifts into tiny vortexes. She took the lavender beret from her
carryall and put it on, pulling it down over her ears.

Smith, who had followed her to O'Melvany's car, was standing nearby, silent for once, possibly trying to figure out what was
happening before forging forward again.

"Sergeant." Wetzon's words whipped around her almost lost
in the wind. "You said Ida was wanted for questioning in a
murder . . . does that mean Peepsie—I mean, Evelyn Cunningham's death is now officially considered murder?"

O'Melvany rested his elbow on the roof of the car. The cold
didn't seem to bother him. "I have nothing official to say about
it. They're calling the shots from the commissioner's office.
There's a special squad on it—your friend Silvestri has the assignment." Wetzon shaded her eyes from the wind and looked up
at O'Melvany. He sounded envious. He opened the door and got
into the car. She tapped on the window and he rolled it down.
The younger man at the wheel eyed her with interest. "Sergeant,
I think I know where that other shoe may be. You know, the
mate of the one I found on the street after Mrs. Cunningham was
pushed off the terrace."

Smith had evidently had enough, grown bored with not
knowing what was going on. "Let's go, Wetzon." She tugged at
Wetzon's coat.

O'Melvany rubbed his wiry mustache and frowned. "Now
how would you know that? We went over that place with a fine-
tooth comb."

"Did you look inside the big urn that was at the entrance to the living room?"

O'Melvany's wiry orange eyebrows rolled over each other.

Wetzon put her hands up on the edge of the open window and leaned toward him, raising her voice over the wind. "They're auctioning off her furniture at Yorkeby's. We were on our way over to the exhibition now."

"Oh, for pitysake," Smith said.

O'Melvany stared straight ahead out his front window, then with one long arm, reached behind him and opened the back door. "Get in, Ms. Wetzon. Let's take a ride."

"Come on, Smith." Wetzon got into the backseat of the car and slid over, making room for Smith.

"This was going to be a fun afternoon, Wetzon, just us girls," Smith grumbled, but she got into the car, as Wetzon knew she would. One thing Smith hated was being left out. She settled in behind O'Melvany and gave him a lovely smile.

Grunting, he rolled up the window and took a cigarette out of a pack of Marlboro's on the dashboard and lit it. The carbon smell of the match filled the air, giving way to the sharp smell of the cigarette. "Yorkeby's," he said to the other detective.

"This is my partner—"

"Xenia Smith," Smith interrupted in a throaty voice. "So pleased to meet you . . . ah, Lieutenant . . ."

Wetzon elbowed Smith, who shifted out of the way, smiling a contented smile. *Why did she have to ply her charms on everyone?*

"Sergeant," O'Melvany corrected. "Sergeant E. D. O'Melvany." He spoke over his shoulder. "This is Detective Galvin."

Galvin negotiated a U-turn expertly in the midst of the rush hour traffic on Fifty-seventh Street, and they headed east toward First Avenue, reaching Yorkeby's about twenty minutes before the exhibition closed.

O'Melvany, all long and lanky arms and legs, ducked his head and unfurled himself from the car. He reached down to open the rear door, giving first Smith and then Wetzon his hand. The icy wind coming from the East River was unrelenting. They hurried to the entrance of the modern box of a building where the internationally renowned auction house held the auctions of much of the world's antiques and artwork.

"We're closing in fifteen minutes," a haughty black man in a dark blue guard's uniform announced. O'Melvany flashed his ID. "Yes, sir, what can we do for you?"

O'Melvany looked at Wetzon. "The Cunningham collection," Wetzon said.

"Second floor exhibition room. Take the escalator."

O'Melvany moved forward quickly and Wetzon, scooting after him, missed Smith. Smith was at the information desk talking to a woman in a severe black suit, with gold-rimmed glasses resting on the tip of her long thin nose. The gray, jewel-neck sweater was a close match to her hair. She was smiling warmly at Smith, who reached into her pocket and handed the woman her business card. Smith fluffed her curls and laughed affectedly. She caught up with Wetzon on the escalator.

"What was that about?" Wetzon didn't bother trying to keep annoyance out of her voice. O'Melvany was using the escalator as a staircase, going up two steps at a time.

"She's going to call me whenever there's a consignment of—"

"What's this we're looking for, Ms. Wetzon? Some kind of jar?" O'Melvany suddenly seemed annoyed.

Another uniformed guard stood at the entrance to the exhibition room, to the right of which was a small table with catalogues for sale at two dollars each. A similar catalogue, very well thumbed, hung from a cord attached to a hook in the wide doorframe.

"You can't smoke here," the guard said, pointing to the No Smoking sign.

O'Melvany took a long last inhale and put his cigarette out in a tall deco ashtray, where a dead cigar butt stood upended in the sand.

"I don't exactly know what they're called—see—" Wetzon pointed to a copy of the ad on the table. "This is it. I think it's some kind of temple urn."

Smith wandered ahead of them into the exhibition room,

which was arranged somewhat like a grand living room. Oriental rugs were on the floor, furniture was arranged along the walls and in conversation groupings. Lamps and accessories were decorously placed on the end tables and coffee tables. Paintings and tapestries hung from wires on the walls.

A few stragglers were still examining items in the exhibition even though it was so near to closing. A slovenly old man in work clothes, in need of a shave, was studying the underside of an old trestle table. A thickset man with a loupe in one eye was holding a piece of jewelry while a woman in a red sports jacket and pleated skirt watched him, hand on an open glass exhibition case. Smith drifted over to him and looked over his shoulder. The man handed the piece of jewelry back to the woman in red, who replaced it on the glass shelf and locked the cabinet. He ran his hand over his bald spot, put the loupe back in his pocket, and took a turn around the room. Smith followed the man, a seductive smile on her face, as he walked toward the escalator.

"There it is!" Wetzon saw the huge urn with its vivid blues and reds on the far side of the exhibition room. It seemed even larger than she remembered.

"May I help you? We're about to close." The woman in red stood next to them, looking from O'Melvany to Wetzon, a question on her face.

O'Melvany flipped his ID at her and put it back in his inside pocket. "Sergeant O'Melvany, NYPD. We're looking for something that may be inside that urn."

Wetzon was already standing next to the urn on tiptoes, trying to see into it, but the urn was almost as tall as she was.

"I'd like to upend it," O'Melvany said.

The woman looked pained. "Morris," she called in a thin voice to the guard near the entrance. "Would you bring us a flashlight and call Mr. Falkland, please." To O'Melvany she said, "I don't think we have to move it." The guard returned with a long stainless steel flashlight and handed it to O'Melvany. "I'll be right back," the woman said. "Morris, please see if you can help Sergeant O'Melvany without disturbing the exhibition." Her tone implied, *See to it that these boors don't do any damage.*

O'Melvany shone the flashlight into the urn and peered inside. "Nothing here." He said it as if he hadn't expected otherwise.

"Are you sure?" Wetzon had been so certain.

"Give me a break, lady." He handed the flashlight back to the guard as the woman in the red jacket returned, followed by a pale, elegant man.

"I'm Gerard Falkland, the managing director." The man ignored Wetzon, speaking directly to O'Melvany. "How may I help you?"

"We're finished here," O'Melvany said, dusting off his hands.

"No, wait!" Wetzon said. "Where's the other one?"

"Other what?" O'Melvany shoved his hands in his pockets and headed back toward the escalator.

"The other temple urn." Wetzon looked around urgently. Smith was engrossed in something in a flat-topped case. Jewelry, of course.

"What other urn?" O'Melvany paused, rubbing his mustache.

"Was there another urn?" The woman turned to Gerard Falkland.

"As a matter of fact, there was. It had a hairline crack near the base. I think we may have returned it." He ran his forefinger along his aristocratic nose. "Wait—let's have a look. Follow me."

He led them to the fifth floor, by an elevator decorated with exhibition notices, and unlocked a double door of staggering proportions with a key from a large ring of keys. They entered a massive storage room, windowless and musty with the smell of old wood and aging upholstery. It was pitch-black. Falkland reached out and pulled a large lever, bathing the room in brilliant light.

"Oh my God," Wetzon gasped. Furniture was piled many feet high from one end to the other, almost to the ceiling. Shades of *Citizen Kane*.

"It may still be here . . . somewhere," Falkland murmured, motionless, eyes searching.

Wetzon walked slowly into the ordered disorder. The sheer abundance was mind-boggling.

"Please, do be careful." Falkland's calm demeanor had begun to fray.

"I don't see it," O'Melvany said, moving cautiously into another aisle.

"I'm afraid it's just not here anymore," Falkland said. "Shall we go?"

"Ms. Wetzon?"

"Please, wait." Wetzon darted into an area she had not checked and caught her boot on the edge of a worn tapestry. A cloud of dust flew in her face as she clutched at the tapestry to keep from falling.

"Good heavens! I asked you to be careful." Falkland came down the aisle toward her in high dudgeon.

"I'm sorry. All right . . . let's go," she said, defeated. She tried to prop up the bulky tapestry to put it back where it had been, when it slipped from her hands and slid to the floor, revealing the urn, gleaming and majestic, next to a large carved open armchair with a damaged seat. Cracked or whatever, it was beautiful. "Eureka!" Wetzon cried.

"May I?" O'Melvany strode over and moved the chair.

"Go right ahead." Falkland watched dispassionately as O'Melvany rolled the urn to the small clearing near the entrance to the storage room. "There's only a hairline crack, but of course you understand we cannot sell anything that's damaged—"

O'Melvany tilted the urn and Falkland grasped the bowl and together they turned it gently on its rim. Wetzon held her breath as they picked it up and righted it.

On the floor where the mouth of the urn had been was a small, dusty blue Gucci shoe.

49

"ALL THAT FUSS over a dirty old shoe!" Smith frowned. She spread the tarot cards out on the marble top of her coffee table. Hyper, hands shaking, she was sitting on the edge of her off-white sectional. Her mink coat had slipped from the arm of the sofa, where she had thrown it when she came into the room, and lay crumpled on the floor.

Wetzon came out of the bathroom in time to hear Smith's gripe about the Gucci shoe and decided to be smart for once and let it go. Smith wasn't paying attention to Wetzon anyway. She seemed totally wrapped up in the cards, almost as if she were on a mission. Hiking her skirt up, Wetzon did a *grand plié* and scooped Smith's coat up from the floor, shook it straight, and laid

"Here!" She thrust the cards at Wetzon. "Hold them and concentrate." She left the room.

"Concentrate? On what?" Wetzon looked at her watch. It was six o'clock. She wanted to call Silvestri, make sure he was going to meet her at Hazel's. She wanted to call Hazel . . .

Smith returned holding a squat vase of very thick glass in which rested a small white candle. She sat down again and lit the candle with a match from a book of matches near the chrome ashtray on the coffee table. The flame expanded. Smith sighed deeply. "Shuffle the cards," she said.

Wetzon shuffled.

"Okay. Stop. Give them back to me." Smith plucked a single card from the deck and put it faceup in the center of the table between her and Wetzon. "The queen of swords," she said. "Cut the cards to your left—left hand, please."

"Smith—" Smith was acting crazy. Really crazy.

"Please, Wetzon. It's important. Humor me." In fact, as nervous as she was, Smith seemed to have pulled herself together. There were no seductive "sweetie pie" and "sugar" words. She was direct, if obtuse, and full of a kind of reeling urgency.

Wetzon obediently cut the cards to the left with her left hand and gave them back to Smith, who laid them out one by one into a Celtic cross. Wetzon's stomach growled audibly. Smith looked daggers at her.

"Sorry." Shit. Smith was making her nervous.

Smith wrapped the remainder of the deck in a silk square, putting the package aside. She began to turn the cards faceup. "No! No . . ." She mumbled something else which Wetzon didn't catch and then once more, "No!"

"Do you want to tell me what's going on, Smith?"

Smith turned up the card above the queen of swords. It had a skeleton riding a horse. The card said *Death*. "The queen of cups, the queen of wands covering, the queen of pentacles crossing, and upheaval—death—in the near future. I don't like it one bit." Smith gathered up the cards abruptly. "You'll stay with me tonight."

"Oh come on, Smith." Wetzon stood up, cross. "Let's have a

cup of tea and forget about this. I feel funny about making Mark hide out in his room." All at once she felt chilled, weary. The only thing she had left on her agenda was Hazel. But no doubt about it, Smith had spooked her. "I want to make a couple of calls, okay?"

Smith shrugged. She pulled off her high-heeled boots and left them on the floor near a stack of magazines and newspapers, which were part of the scenery in Smith's apartment. "I'll make coffee, if you want. It's decaf." She left the room and came back a minute later carrying a white cordless phone, which she handed Wetzon.

"You're on." Wetzon sat down on the sofa and pulled up the aerial. She dialed Silvestri's number at the Seventeenth Precinct.

"Metzger." Artie Metzger's resonant monotone suited his basset hound appearance.

"Hi, Artie."

"He said if you called, to tell you he'll meet you at seven."

"Good. You told him where?"

"Yeah."

She disconnected and dialed Hazel's number. She could hear Mark's and Smith's voices humming in the kitchen. The kettle began to whistle. She got a busy signal and disconnected, pushing the aerial back in place with the palm of her hand.

"Come on into the dining room, sweetie pie," Smith called, sounding like herself again. That was a relief. "Mark is making omelets."

Wetzon crossed the living room toward the sensual odor of melted butter and eggs frying. Her stomach growled again. "I'm probably having dinner with Silvestri later," she said. The dining room table was laid out for three. On the sideboard next to a stack of legal documents the coffee machine chugged.

"Well, you can have a bitty snack with us, sugar. I can hear your tummy all the way over here."

"I just have to confirm with Hazel that I'll be there at seven." She watched Mark put a small omelet on each dinner plate. "This looks great, Mark."

"Sit down, honey bunny, and eat," Smith said, kissing the top of Mark's dark curly head. "You need a haircut, baby."

"Aw, Mom." He rolled his eyes at her. His voice cracked, going from high tenor to manly croak in two words.

Smith would soon have an adolescent boy in her midst. Wetzon wondered how she would handle it.

Smith yawned. "By the way, First Westchester is hiring that old geezer of yours."

"Oh, Smith, that's lovely news. Doesn't that make you feel good?"

"Hardly."

"Well, it makes me feel good." Pulling out the aerial on the phone, Wetzon dialed Hazel again.

"I forgot the fries." Mark started to get up.

"Sit, baby. Eat. I'll get them."

"No potatoes for me." The phone rang three times. Wetzon cut into her omelet and pale melted Swiss cheese oozed out. "This looks delicious, Mark." It *was* delicious.

"Hello." The voice was barely audible.

"Hazel?"

"Leslie . . ."

"Hazel, I can hardly hear you. We'll be over at seven."

"Lovely. I have to go now, dear." Hazel raised her voice to normal.

"Wait! Your home care service—is it Tender Care?"

Smith came back into the dining room with a serving plate of French fries. "Mark, honey, why don't you serve everyone?"

"Yes." Hazel's line disconnected.

"Damn!" Wetzon swallowed what was in her mouth without chewing and choked.

"Tender Care? Did I hear you say Tender Care?" Smith poured coffee for Wetzon, who began coughing, and patted her on the back gently.

"Yes." Wetzon shrugged off Smith's arm and stood up, rushing into the foyer to get her coat. Tender Care was the company Peter Tormenkov had told Teddy about. He had specifically mentioned Tender Care. Which meant Hazel was in danger.

"Where are you going in such a rush, Wetzon?"

"Dammit, Smith, I'm afraid for Hazel. That's the company involved in some kind of stock fraud and Peepsie Cunningham's murder."

"Oh, but that can't be, sugar." Smith beamed. "That's Arleen Grossman's company."

Wetzon clutched the frame of the archway of Smith's dining room. "What?" Her head began to spin. "What did you say?"

"I mean, it *was* Arleen's company." Smith looked like the cat who swallowed the canary.

"Was? What are you talking about, Smith? This means Arleen Grossman is a thief and maybe a murderer." Wetzon's hand was on the door.

"Wetzon, you have to be mistaken." Smith's features began to swim together, breaking up under her makeup. She followed Wetzon into the foyer. "Wait, please."

"What's the matter, Smith? I have to go. I'm really worried about Hazel."

"I wasn't going to tell you about this, Wetzon. I tried to get you involved—we are partners—but you are so overly cautious—" Smith's mouth was stiff and wooden. "Arleen—oh dear God, I bought the company last summer. I'm the owner of Tender Care."

50

WETZON HAD HOPED TO FIND the ubiquitous Michael Stewart downstairs waiting for her, but she was disappointed. She stood under the canopy in front of Smith's building, looking up the street for a cab, holding the collar of her coat closed at the throat.

"Cab, miss?" Smith's doorman came out and stood beside her. "Cold night, isn't it?"

"Yes, a cab, please, and, yes, it's a cold night."

"There'll be one along soon, I'm sure." He turned a switch that lit a cab light on the front of the awning. "There always is at this time." He slapped his hands together in his leather gloves and turned up his coat collar.

But he was wrong. She waited impatiently, hunching her shoulders against the cold, then gave up. "I'm going out on Third Avenue. Thanks anyway." She moved off in almost a trot, veering around a fur-wrapped woman in dark glasses carrying a heavy briefcase in one hand and a Chinese take-out bag from Pig Heaven in the other.

At the curb on Third Avenue an old woman was being helped out of a cab by an old man, and from the corner of her eye, Wetzon saw a well-dressed young couple across the avenue dart in front of traffic toward the cab, waving and screaming. Wetzon put on a burst of speed and got there first in a flurry of raccoon. The old man, dignified in a cloth overcoat and English tweed cap, smiled at Wetzon and held the door open for her after depositing his wife on the sidewalk.

She settled into the cab and he slammed the door closed. The disappointed couple shouted at her angrily and cursed out the driver, who shrugged. "Where to?"

"Ninety-second, between Park and Madison, as fast as you can."

She sat back. Smith was the owner of Tender Care, and

Arleen Grossman was running it for her. What a mess. How could Leon have possibly let Smith get into it? What kind of lawyer . . . ? No . . . wait . . . how could she blame Leon? It was, after all, a profitable company. Oh my, was it ever profitable. She wondered how the money from the sale of the stock certificates was fed into the company. Or was it? Maybe it just went into Arleen's and her partners' pockets. Arleen had certainly manipulated both Smith and Leon.

But now what? Arleen had said she might have to take an extended trip. She would try to leave the country to avoid being arrested.

Why had she worked so hard to befriend Wetzon? Because Smith had probably told her about Peepsie Cunningham's death. Arleen had wanted to confuse Wetzon, make her doubt Smith, perhaps even make Smith look guilty.

Damn, what was taking so long? The red light seemed endless. "Please, please hurry."

Smith had bought a company whose purpose was to defraud. Did that make Smith responsible, liable? What were the legal ramifications of all this? Poor Smith.

For once, Wetzon's caution had worked to her benefit. How much money had Smith paid for the company? The cab stopped and didn't continue. "What's holding us up?" She crossed and uncrossed her legs.

"There's some problem up ahead," the driver said. He rolled down his window and stuck his head out. "Traffic's backed up on Ninety-second Street. Street's blocked."

"Problem?" She rolled down her window and peered out. What was happening up ahead? She saw rolling red-and-blue lights of police cars. It was Hazel's block. What if it was Hazel? Her hands began to tremble. "I have to get out here." She paid the driver and got out.

As all the residential streets in upper Manhattan were, Ninety-second Street was narrow. There were frozen banks of snow, cars parked on both sides of the street, and also police cars, an emergency van, lights, people. Curious bystanders clustered on the street or leaned out of apartment house and brownstone windows. Tragedy, even in New York, was an event.

The activity was concentrated in front of Hazel's building. A fat woman in a purple all-weather coat, with a child in a stroller, blocked the sidewalk. What the hell was she doing out in this cold at this time of the evening? The child was bundled in a bright red-and-blue snowsuit and hat, its face pale in the streetlights, its eyes round and frightened. The woman, whose mittened hands rested on the curved handle of the stroller, was dark-skinned and appeared too old to be the mother. She was probably a nursemaid or baby-sitter, drawn outside by the noise.

Wetzon pushed by the woman, angry that she had to run an obstacle course to get to Hazel's building. She dodged two boys in torn jeans and Jets jackets, one holding a skateboard, and was stopped by a policewoman. "You can't go any farther," the woman said, blocking her.

"Please, Officer—" Something caught in her throat. "Please. My friend is in that building."

She saw O'Melvany first. You couldn't miss him—he was that tall. Men in street clothes, probably detectives, were milling all over the area. Police in uniform were stopping foot traffic. An EMS van was parked on a slant near the front of the building, its lights flashing.

"Please, please, let me through. I have to get through." She felt herself panicking. "Sergeant O'Melvany!"

Two blue-coated EMS men wheeled someone out of the building on a stretcher. A man in a red down jacket was with them, bent over, talking to the person on the stretcher. It took her several seconds to process Silvestri.

In the eerie-colored lights, the raised voices, police car radios squawking, it seemed a scene from *Walpurgisnacht*. Silvestri was scrunched down over the figure on the stretcher. A scream rose up from the cold pit of her stomach and filled her, spilling out, "Silvestri," in a wail of pain. She was oblivious to the people around.

Detectives, police, onlookers, heads swiveled in her direction. Silvestri straightened, looking for the source, and she saw him as another pale face above the red down jacket. Round-eyed and pale like the child. He was holding someone's hand. Someone on the stretcher. His eyes swept the crowd.

She saw the IV then and another EMS attendant. Silvestri spotted her, waved, and pointed, and they were escorting her through the throng, and she was rushing, stumbling toward them—toward Silvestri, toward the figure on the stretcher, about to be moved into the van.

Silvestri's arm came around her shoulders like a vise, fiercely protective, holding her, but moving her forward. He was saying something but her heartbeat was exploding in her ears, drowning out every sound but its own thumping.

Hazel lay wrapped in gray blankets. The right side of her face was swollen and discolored, her head was covered by a gauze bandage.

Wetzon clutched the hard edge of the stretcher. "Hazel." Her voice came out thin, trailing. Hazel's good eye found her. "Leslie . . . dear . . ." The good side of her face tilted into a grotesque smile. "I did it . . . didn't I?" Hazel's eye went to Silvestri, with a bit of the old sparkle. "Got the goods on them, didn't I?"

Wetzon took off her glove and touched the lined cheek, lines like railroad tracks, deep creases. She felt Silvestri's warm breath on her face, his arm tight around her. "You let her be a decoy, Silvestri." She pulled away from him, accusing.

"Sergeant, we've got to get going," one of the EMS men interrupted.

"She set herself up, Les."

"I did." Hazel's voice was weak but sure.

They folded up the wheels and moved the stretcher into the van. Hazel's body rolled helplessly from the action. "Where are you taking her? I'm going along."

"Leslie . . . dear . . ."

"Yes?" She leaned into the van, bending to catch the failing voice.

"My purse . . . it's upstairs. Lock up for me, please."

"But I want to go with you."

"Please . . . I'll feel better if I know you're doing it."

"I'll go with her," Silvestri said. "I want to get a statement any-way." He left them and went to speak to a policeman near the entrance to the building, returned quickly, and got into the van behind the first paramedic.

"Silvestri! Don't let anything happen to her." Wetzon stood there, letting the unspoken words hang between them. His turquoise eyes made her a promise they both knew he might not be able to keep. She watched as the second paramedic slammed the doors of the van and climbed into the front. The whining siren cut through the protective shell she'd put between her and the people on the street, leaving her alone. She saw faces staring at her from across police lines, curious faces, hungry for information.

The policeman on the door let her through into the lobby. O'Melvany and another detective were talking to a small, muscular woman in a white uniform. Reddish scratches covered one cheek, and her bleached platinum hair was in wild disarray. The woman's hands were cuffed behind her. She looked terrified.

"Basha," Wetzon said out loud as she pressed the elevator button. She would have thought the elevator and the elevator man would be in the lobby.

The woman jerked her head up. O'Melvany nodded to Wetzon, his hands resting on lean hips.

She was thinking that Basha would be sent back to Russia, or wherever she had come from, and this was good. The elevator door opened, and she got on.

"Oh, Ms. Wilson," the elevator man said. "Awful about Ms. Osborn, isn't it? It's a terrible world we're living in now. You just can't trust anyone anymore." He took her up to the fifth floor without saying anything else.

Hazel's door was wide open and all the lights were on in the apartment. A strange man in a white jogging suit stood in the middle of Hazel's living room holding one of her large Staffordshire dogs upside down, looking at the markings on the base.

"Who are you? What are you doing here?"

The man looked up without embarrassment. He had a salt-and-pepper-close-cropped beard. He set the Staffordshire piece beside it. Saul Bellow's *More Die of Heartbreak* was lying next to it, half open. The receiver of the telephone dangled loose, off the hook, down the side of the night table. She put the receiver back on the phone and, kneeling, gathered up the scattered contents of Hazel's purse, putting everything back as neatly as she could, holding onto the house keys in their little leather pouch.

On the floor, almost hidden under the night table, was a small notepad. She picked it up to place it back on the table near the telephone. There were some numbers on the pad. She stood up and put the Bellow book into Hazel's purse. Hazel could read it while she was getting better.

Enough of this. She would come back later and straighten out the apartment. She turned out the lights in the doorway and started down the short hall to the door, stopped, came back, and turned the lights on in the bedroom again. She went over to the

Puzzled, she sat down on the tilted mattress, picked up the phone, and punched out the numbers.

One ring . . . two . . . three . . . four . . .

"Hello? Hello?"

Wetzon hung up the phone quietly.

The voice was Arleen Grossman's.

51

"SILVESTRI." HIS VOICE, CRISP no-nonsense professionalism, shocked her out of the mental maze she'd slipped into.

"Silvestri—listen—I mean, how's Hazel?" Her words popped out confused and erratic.

"The doctor's with her. Where are you?" He sounded impatient, as if he'd been expecting another call.

"At Hazel's—this is important, Silvestri—" She was gasping for breath. "This woman, Arleen Grossman—"

"Slow down, Les—"

"Please, Silvestri, time means everything. She'll get away."

"What the hell are you talking about?" Now he seemed angry.

"This woman, Arleen Grossman, I guess you know all about her. She runs Tender Care—"

"Does she indeed?" She could almost hear the iron gate clang shut between them. His tone was frigid.

"What kind of thing is that to say, Silvestri? Are you being sarcastic? What do you mean, 'Does she indeed?'" A large moth flew in her face suddenly, flapping its powdery wings, and she cried out, brushing it away.

"What's going on there?" Silvestri was alert now and listening.

"I'm okay. It's nothing, it's stupid. A moth flew at me. Please tell me what you mean."

"Look, Les, we both know your partner is the owner of record on Tender Care, so you can stop all this—"

"No, Silvestri. No, it's a frame." The moth made sweeping runs around the bare bulb of the lamp, bouncing off the warm surface. "This Arleen Grossman is the one. She sold it to Smith. Smith is a dupe. You've got to believe me."

"You don't know what you're talking about, Les." She had his full attention now, but she didn't like what he was saying to her or how he was saying it. "I shouldn't even be talking to you about confidential information in an investigation. Get your ass over here and stay out of this."

"Silvestri! Listen to me. Arleen Grossman is still around. She hasn't left town. We can stop her. My theory is—"

"Cops don't work with theories, Les, they work with facts." Fatigue diffused his voice. "You stay out of this. I can't keep protecting you. It's an FBI case. Let the cards fall—"

"You're wrong, Silvestri. I can't stay out of it. I'm involved—and I don't need you to protect me."

"Les—" There was a warning in his voice.

She hung up on him. And to think, he called *her* a hardhead. He wouldn't even hear her out. She slipped off the mattress and turned out the lamp. The moth was plastered against the bulb, burning to death.

As she moved around the apartment, turning off lights, the phone began to ring. She picked up her carryall and Hazel's black leather bag. The phone continued to ring. She walked out into the hallway, jaw squared, closing the door firmly behind her, locking it.

"I can't keep protecting you," he'd said. It was a rotten thing for him to say.

Arleen Grossman had not left the country yet. Wetzon closed her eyes as she waited for the elevator. Where did Arleen live? East Seventy-second Street. She remembered Smith—or maybe it was Arleen—had told her that Arleen had a second-floor apartment in the old Wharton mansion between Fifth and Madison.

Wetzon was determined to stop her from leaving town and

sticking Smith with the mess. She didn't know how, but she would come up with something on the way. She had to.

The elevator man was blessedly silent. On the fourth floor an old man with thick glasses and gnarled hands got on, leading an ancient shelty on a worn brown leather leash. The old dog moved as slowly as the old man. The milky veil of cataracts covered its eyes, and its brown-and-white coat was thin and lank, with sharp bones showing through.

They left the elevator ahead of her at an arthritic pace. She shuffled with impatience behind them. The lobby was empty; everyone was gone. She bolted around the old man, almost brushing into him and his dog and then, ashamed, felt obligated to hold the door open for them.

The sidewalks were wet.

How was it possible Arleen did not know they were onto her?

A young Chinese man in a thin canvas jacket and jeans was locking a delivery bike to a No Parking sign in front of Hazel's building. He opened an umbrella and came toward her carrying a large brown paper bag. She caught a strong whiff of fried rice as he passed her, and she realized that except for the bit of omelet at Smith's, she had not had anything to eat since the half hamburger at lunch. She was hungry now, but food was not first priority.

Sleet and wet snow dribbled unevenly from the heavens, reflecting diamonds in the streetlights.

Hazel's battered face materialized like a distorted balloon. *Hold on*, she thought. *Hold on*.

On Park Avenue a cab stopped to her wave, and she asked the driver to drop her off on the corner of Madison and Seventy-second. The fur on her coat was wetter than she'd thought possible from her brief walk.

The white stone mansion with the expansive entrance stood out even among the other elegant town house mansions on the block. It had the same kind of iron grillwork outside door that Diantha Anderson's brownstone had, but this was more ornate, and interspersed with polished brass balls.

Sweat came then, cold and icy, on the back of her neck under her sweater, dripping under her arms, bathing her in dampness. She stood where the cab had left her, staring at the mansion across the street with its lights on behind iron and brass window gates, like a fortress. The snow fell wetly on her face, coat, and hat, forcing her to move.

A black limousine was parked just in front of the mansion. Wetzon could see the silhouette of a man's head in the driver's seat, leaning forward over the wheel. Arleen's limousine? Waiting to take her to the airport?

Traffic was exceptionally light coming out of Central Park to her right. A car drove by toward the Park, window open, its radio playing rock, piercing the tranquillity.

Down the block to the right of the mansion a cab was double-parked, its call light on, waiting for someone to come out of the apartment building on the corner.

Wetzon jaywalked across the street and strolled past the limousine. Out of the corner of her eye she saw Arleen's brother sleeping, his head on the wheel. He must have gotten tired of waiting for her and was catching a few zzz's before she came down. She passed the limousine and went on to the corner of Madison, turned casually and came back, faster. She hoped he wouldn't wake up and see her. But there was something odd, which she hadn't noticed earlier. The limousine window was down on his side. Snow was coming in and he was getting wet. He couldn't be sleeping that deeply.

Brazen, she passed the limousine and ducked around the back of the car, hugging the rear and side. She came up slowly behind the open window. Suitcases were piled up on the backseat. John Grossman didn't move and wasn't going to. Blood was seeping from a small hole in the side of his head. Arleen would have to find another way to get to the airport.

Wetzon came back on the sidewalk and closed her eyes, taking a deep breath. Wet snow and cold filled her nostrils. Don't get distracted, she told herself. She should have been terrified by the danger around her, but she wasn't. Her adrenaline was pumping, and she felt warm, slightly high, but very calm.

The iron door opened easily, as did the etched glass and wood double doors. She was in a narrow marble-floored vestibule. On the right wall was an opening, fluted like a shell, cut out of marble. Its purpose was decorative, but someone had recently put a cigarette out in it. According to the mailbox, which was inset on the left wall, A. Grossman was in 2F. She pressed the buzzer for R. Argentuille in 3R and waited with her hand on the brass doorknob of the large, leaded glass and iron door. Sure enough, the fool in 3R buzzed her in without even checking whether she was legitimate.

She entered a sweeping lobby, the floor inlaid with stars and circles in black-and-cream marble. A curved staircase on the left was marble as far as she could see. On the right, a carved Gothic refectory table stood between two tall Gothic armchairs. A brass pot filled with white-and-yellow mums was on the table.

In front of her was an elevator. Scratch that. She would go for the stairs and not chance announcing her presence. Holding the front of her wet coat, her carryall, Hazel's handbag, and trying to make as little noise as possible on the carpetless marble, she heard the sound of someone in the small vestibule, the rattle of keys. She'd made it to the second-floor hallway when she heard the downstairs door open. Except for that, the building was strangely quiet.

The second-floor walls were papered in an Oriental design with a lot of standing cranes and palms. The woodwork was cream. The door of 2F had black enamel on it, particularly striking because the layers of paint were few, unlike many in New York where a door might have up to eighty years' worth of coats of paint. This door had been efficiently stripped before being repainted.

Ear to the door of 2F, she listened. The wood was so thick it was impossible to hear anything going on in there. She put her hand on the knob, then pulled back. What the hell was she doing here? She could get killed, couldn't she? But surely Arleen had not shot her own brother. Perhaps she, Wetzon, could persuade Arleen that she couldn't get away with it. That Wetzon was her friend and had come to warn her that— Without conference with her head, her hand turned the knob and the door opened.

A black-and-brown Fendi overnight bag was right in the door-way next to a leather makeup case. She stepped into a small foyer. A straight chair with an upholstered seat, a Regency side table, an oil painting of a bowl of flowers; overhead, a small brass chandelier. A small Oriental carpet on the dark parquet floor. The foyer led straight into a large living room, which was dimly lit by porcelain lamps scattered about the room.

No sound came from the living room. Behind her Wetzon heard the elevator drone downward. She closed the door behind her and moved farther into the apartment. The decoration in the living room was antique. An Aubusson carpet, plush sofas, drap-eries, the works. Very expensive stuff. A marble table held an ar-ray of liquor bottles and a large crystal ice bucket. The ceilings were at least fifteen feet high, maybe more, and had sculpted plasterwork that had to have been commissioned by the original Wharton, because no one did that kind of work anymore, and if someone did, no one could afford to pay for it, except maybe a Japanese businessman living in the United States and getting paid with yen.

On the floor near a French ormolu table desk was a heap of fur—it looked like Arleen's coat—just dropped there. Where was Arleen?

"Arleen?" She set the carryall and Hazel's purse down on the overstuffed sofa and walked around the room with more assur-ance than she felt. To the right was another room, perhaps the bedroom, but it was dark.

When she turned back to the living room, she was closer to Arleen's fallen coat. She moved a chair out of the way, came close, bent over, and lifted the coat off the floor.

Arleen lay on her side, a swollen, grotesque fetus in a coral silk dress. Her bosom was deeper coral, growing deeper yet as Wetzon stared. In her right hand, almost hidden, was a gun.

52

"OH MY GOD," WETZON BREATHED, hand over mouth. She straightened, knees quivering, and sat down hard on the side chair. Arleen had killed herself. She must have realized that she couldn't get away. How horrible. Wetzon covered her face with her hands. She'd had enough of killing. But where did this leave Smith? If Arleen was dead, who would save Smith?

Leon, of course. Leon had to have handled the arrangements for Smith. He could testify for Smith, explain she didn't know.

She forced herself to look at Arleen's face. The pallor seemed altered somewhat. In death, her eyelids twitched. Wetzon shuddered. It was over. She would find a phone and call Silvestri, or O'Melvany, or 911 . . .

"Wezz—" Someone spoke faintly and very close to her.

Wetzon shot out of the chair. The sound had come from Arleen's body.

"Wezz—" It came again. Arleen's lips trembled. The body didn't move. "Help me . . ."

Wetzon knelt, forgetting the gun. "Arleen? It's all right. I'm going to call an ambulance."

"No." Arleen's eyes were black slashes, half-open, staring. Wetzon bent closer. The mixture of blood and Giorgio perfume gagged her. "Go away . . . murder . . ." Her lips opened again and a pink blood bubble oozed out. She was dead.

What did she mean, "murder"? Wetzon got to her feet. What had Arleen been trying to say? That Arleen had been murdered like her brother? Was the murderer still here? Ice, like a serpent, began to crawl up her spine.

"Hello, Wetzon."

Wetzon spun around. Leon Ostrow, wearing a crisp clean Burberry, was standing a few feet from her near the door to the bedroom.

"Leon! Fantastic. How did you get in without my seeing you?"

"You were rather involved, my dear. After Xenia reached me, I came right over to talk to Arleen. I saw you enter the building and just followed." He had both hands in his raincoat pockets. He walked across the room and stood next to Wetzon, looking down at Arleen's body. He prodded it with the toe of his gleaming black wing tip shoes. The body rolled over. "Well, now she's really dead." He sounded almost pleased. He had to be thinking about Smith, too.

Wetzon took his arm at the elbow. "What are you doing, Leon? Shouldn't we call an ambulance, the police?"

"Of course, my dear." He shook her off; her hand fell to her side, brushing against the wet fur of her coat. "And we will. We will. After all, I am an officer of the court." Leon smiled. He walked over to the desk and opened the side drawers, one at a time, removing papers, rifling through them. He was taking his time.

Wetzon was bewildered. He was behaving so strangely. "What are you doing, Leon? Come on—" She stopped. Leon's raincoat was crisp . . . his shoes were shiny . . . nothing was wet. "Leon—" She began slowly thinking. Tender Care had used a lawyer for referrals, Peepsie Cunningham had had a lawyer. . . . No, it couldn't be.

"Ah, Wetzon my dear." Leon's eyes blinked at her from behind his glasses. He straightened. "I'm really sorry about this." He sighed and came around the desk. "I've always been quite fond of you personally."

She drew back from him cautiously. Perhaps she was missing something. "Leon—I don't believe this—not you."

"Stay where you are, Wetzon." He took a small gun from his coat pocket and looked at it. "You know what they say, after the first it gets easier. I made a spectacular debut with the newsman."

"Newsman? You mean Teddy Lanzman? No, I don't believe it."

"He called my office after Tormenkov talked to him. He left me little alternative."

"Why? Leon, just tell me why?" She'd had a shock, but her mind was working with precision. She was standing between him and the door. Maybe she could make a run for it. If she could keep him talking, she would buy time for herself.

"Suffice it to say, my dear Wetzon, I had certain monetary obligations, trading losses. Trust funds I had borrowed money from which had to be replaced. When Arleen came to me with her idea, it seemed so simple." He stood over Arleen's body now; Wetzon stepped backward. Leon pushed his glasses back up the narrow bridge of his nose with his forefinger and cocked his gun at her. "I have no qualms about shooting you now. Your problem has always been, Wetzon, you don't know when to keep your nose out of what doesn't concern you." He looked at Arleen again. "I'd rather it was with Arleen's gun, but if I have to, I'll do it with mine."

"But old people, Leon. How could you?"

"We do what we must."

She spoke through clenched teeth. "Please, Leon. Think this through. Killing me is ridiculous. Don't you know the police are looking for her, and probably you, too?"

"Now, Wetzon, it's you who are being ridiculous. How would they be looking for me?"

"Because you didn't kill Teddy. You killed an FBI agent who was sitting at his desk."

Leon's head snapped back. His thin face took on a tinge of green.

"Ahhh. So I have nothing whatever to lose then."

"What about Smith? I thought you loved Smith."

"Smith . . . yes." He seemed to be thinking, calculating. "Well, you and I both know that Xenia, bless her heart, will take care of herself. I would have been on my way to Brazil already, Wetzon, if that bitch hadn't gotten so greedy." He looked down at Arleen. "It was always one last transaction with her. She was going to meet me at the airport with the rest of the money, she said. She thought she could out-think me, take a later plane, to Morocco." He spoke deliberately, logically, as if he were arguing a case. "No one out-thinks me." He knelt and reached for the gun in Arleen's hand.

My God, Wetzon thought. *He was going to shoot her with Arleen's gun.* She took a few rapid steps backward. *They would say Arleen killed her.*

Her sudden movement stopped Leon. He whipped his gun around in her direction. There was a tiny, muffled explosion. Leon stood up and stared at her. Somehow, he'd lost his glasses. He had a surprised, almost comical, look on his face. He pointed the gun at her. Wetzon dropped to the floor. The gun wobbled in his hand.

A third eye opened, ruby-red, between his eyebrows, and Leon pitched forward over Arleen's body.

53

"FBI!" THE DOOR BURST OPEN behind Wetzon. "Stay where you are!" a woman's voice shouted. Wetzon huddled on the floor, out of the line of fire, and stared at the empty space where Leon had stood.

Line of fire? What would they be shooting at? Oh my God! "Don't shoot!" Wetzon cried. "They're all dead." *Everyone is dead.*

As through the bottom of a Coke bottle, she saw Judy Blue slip around the open door, back hugging the frame, Mets cap on her head, jeans showing lumps and bumps of belly and thigh, navy windbreaker above them. Both hands held her gun. She thought, *Oh yes, Judy Blue, why not, of course.* There wasn't even the smallest sensation of surprise. She sank against the wall.

Behind Judy Blue were two men. One long-haired and scruffy, in gray sweatpants and a New York Rangers sweatshirt, walkie-talkie in hand. The other in a trench coat, slick and clean-cut as one imagined an FBI agent to be.

"Hand over your gun." Waving the other two past her into the room, Judy Blue stood over Wetzon, gun pointing.

Wetzon craned her neck and watched Judy Blue's round black face and Mets cap come into sharp focus. "Are you crazy?" Wetzon said. Her voice to her own ear was ragged. "I don't have a gun."

"Get up." Judy Blue watched as Wetzon struggled to her feet, trying not to step on her coat.

"They're both dead," the man in the Rangers sweatshirt said. "Grossman's gun is still warm." He spoke into the walkie-talkie. "Get an ambulance."

Judy Blue nodded. "Take off your coat," she said to Wetzon.

"This is stupid," Wetzon muttered, but she took off her coat and placed it on the arm of the sofa. "I was trying to stop Arleen Grossman from leaving the country, but she was lying on the floor like that when I got here. I thought she was dead, but she wasn't. Leon must have been in the bedroom all along." Sweat trickled down her sides under the sweater. "Oh shit, Judy Blue. I am not a murderer. That much you should know."

"I don't know anything. You led us on one dandy chase these last weeks." Judy Blue wedged her gun into the area behind her thick waist, under her open jacket. "Cover her." The trench coat held his gun on Wetzon while Judy Blue frisked her expertly.

"See, I told you."

"I always err on the side of caution."

"No one else here," the Rangers sweatshirt said, coming out of the bedroom. He spoke into the walkie-talkie again. "All clear here—come on in."

Moments later, Wetzon heard pounding footsteps up the marble stairs, down the hall. Three more men. And Silvestri— grim-faced, dark-rimmed eyes, a flash of something—*it couldn't be joy,* she thought—when he saw her.

Judy Blue shrugged. "For chrissakes, Silvestri, I thought this was supposed to be our turf. Whassamatter," she drawled, "don't you trust us?" A smile flicked quickly across her chunky face and was gone. She left them, disappearing into the antiques and agents, out of Wetzon's view.

against the wall and watched two FBI men dusting for prints. Everyone was talking loudly. Wetzon turned her attention back to Silvestri, who was making emphatic arm motions. Judy Blue kept shaking her head. Finally, Judy Blue threw up her hands. "Okay, okay," she said. "But two hours is all you get. It's your ass, Silvestri."

"Come on, Les." Silvestri took Wetzon's arm. "This your coat?" He picked up her coat and helped her into it. He was distracted. "Let's get out of here."

"What did she mean, two hours?" Wetzon asked. He was almost dragging her along. The hallway was blocked by an FBI man and some of the tenants in the building were clustered around the elevator at the end of the hallway, whispering.

"Go back to your apartments, please. This is official government business." An older man in a business suit under the ubiquitous trench coat was hustling the tenants onto the elevator.

Silvestri rushed her down the stairs, past a man with a medical bag going up. Outside, a siren wailed.

"I've got you a reprieve for two hours to see Hazel, then you have to be downtown."

"What for? I don't know anything else." She stopped on the

"Oh God, what about Smith. This is so awful. Who's going to break the news to her? She'll fall apart when she hears about Leon."

Silvestri raised an eyebrow at her. "I think she'll be able to handle it, Les. Right now she's not my priority. We'll see her downtown later."

An ambulance pulled up and double-parked, lights flashing.

"Who is your priority?"

Silvestri didn't answer. He ran out into the street and flagged down a cab. "Come on, Les," he called to her, holding the door open.

"Tell me—" she insisted, coming to him.

Silvestri pushed her into the cab and climbed in after her. "It's not good. She's not responding—"

54

WHITE PILLOWCASE, WHITE SHEETS, nurses in white uniforms, coming in and out of the white room. Doors closing, opening, closing. White light. Hazel's white face, lined, dear. The IV dripping into her frail arm, the machine monsters, beeping and slurping. Tubes in her nose. The room of the dying.

Wetzon took Hazel's thin hand in hers and pressed it gently. "Hazel . . ." Silvestri brought a chair and she sat down near the bed. He stood behind her, close.

Hazel's eyelids fluttered and opened. Their normal sharp blue looked faded, somehow. "Leslie dear," she murmured. Her hand squeezed Wetzon's.

Wetzon's eyes filled. She had a huge lump in her throat. "Hazel—hold on, please. Don't let go." She choked.

"Leslie . . ." Hazel's eyes rose over Wetzon's head to Silvestri. She smiled slightly, sighed, and closed them as if it were an effort to keep them open. "I like your young man," she said. She seemed to slip away, and the sound of her breathing grew ragged.

"Hazel—" Wetzon said urgently. "You can't do this. You have to finish telling the story of the Peepsies."

A faint noise like a small rumble rose from Hazel's chest and pushed through her parted lips. A weak giggle. "Peepsie . . . Peepsie . . . Peepsie . . ." she whispered. Her eyelids twitched several times, but didn't open. "We were in chapel." She spoke so faintly that Wetzon had to put her head next to Hazel's to hear. "Dr. Pennybaker was talking about the Israelites in the desert . . ." Hazel smiled, and the wrinkles in her face and the bedclothes blended, became part of the smile. "He said the Israelites called up to God, 'Peepsie, Peepsie, Peepsie . . .'" Her voice was thin and high. Another giggle rumbled slowly up her body, shaking her. Hazel squeezed Wetzon's fingers hard, then released them.

The machine made a straight humming noise.

"No!" Wetzon cried. "Hazel! No! You can't die." She stood and touched Hazel's white face.

"Please step outside," a nurse said. Wetzon hadn't even seen her come in. A small, dark-skinned man in a white coat pushed the door open, followed by another nurse.

Silvestri pulled Wetzon away from the bed. Tears ran unheeded down her cheeks. Her nose dribbled.

"Outside, please," someone said again.

Leaning forward, elbows on knees, she hid her face in her hands. Deep, devastating sorrow gripped her.

Silvestri crouched in front of her and took her hands away from her face. She looked down, away, not willing to share her grief.

He held her face in his hands. "Why do you act as if you're alone? You are not alone, Les. Do you hear me? You are not alone. Les?"

Slowly, her eyes rose to meet his. She touched his face, leaned her head against his chin. His beard was rough. "I hear you," she said.

BANTAM MYSTERY COLLECTION

- 28479 **THE ART OF SURVIVAL** Maxwell $4.50
- 24958 **DEATH OF A GHOST** Allingham $3.95
- 28506 **POLICE AT FUNERAL** Allingham $3.95
- 28073 **JEMIMA SHORE'S FIRST CASE** Fraser $3.95
- 28071 **A SPLASH OF RED** Fraser $3.95
- 27723 **MURDER MYSTERY TOUR** Babson $3.50
- 28096 **MURDER SAILS AT MIDNIGHT** Babson $3.50
- 28061 **MANHATTAN IS MY BEAT** Deaver $3.95
- 28070 **OXFORD BLOOD** Fraser $3.95
- 28547 **DEATH OF A BLUE MOVIE STAR** Deaver $3.95
- 27663 **THE RAIN** Peterson $3.95
- 28297 **ROUGH JUSTICE** Peterson $3.95
- 28019 **YOUR ROYAL HOSTAGE** Fraser $3.95
- 28590 **MURDER AT THE CAT SHOW** Babson $3.95
- 28495 **THE DA VINCI DECEPTION** Swan $4.95
- 27860 **THE SCARRED MAN** Peterson $4.50
- 28824 **CUPID** Reid $3.95
- 28044 **SAN FRANCISCO KILLS** Flinn $3.95

Bantam Books, Dept. MC, 414 East Golf Road, Des Plaines, IL 60016

Please send me the items I have checked above. I am enclosing $_____
(please add $2.50 to cover postage and handling). Send check or money
order, no cash or C.O.D.s please.

Mr/Ms _____

Address _____

City/State_____Zip_____

MC–2/91

Please allow four to six weeks for delivery.
Prices and availability subject to change without notice.